THE SEAL

Chloe Garner

A Horse Called Alpha

Copyright © 2022 Chloe Garner

All rights reserved.

No portion of this book may be reproduced in any form without written permission from the publisher or author, except as permitted by U.S. copyright law.

ISBN: 9798370624032

THE QUEEN'S SEAL

Stasia walked along the southern castle wall, watching the crowds go past on the other side of the river. In a little way, she would get to the part of the castle market where all of the stalls were up as close to the river as they could get, facing away from the castle and forming a solid line of backs where she wouldn't be able to see anyone inside the market, from here at street level.

It hadn't occurred to her until last week that that arrangement had probably been on purpose.

She should have seen it sooner.

There was a stretch of road, here, that was not used as much, despite how close it was to everything, because there really wasn't all that much here but blank castle wall.

The people going to the market would take either the bridge ahead of her or the bridge behind her. The ones going to shop in the artisan quarter behind the castle were either coming from north or south - by the Veridan's ever dubious cardinal directions - and almost never from the craftsman's district to the east. And the only people going to the castle itself along this road were a small population of people who lived in the artisan quarter closer to the south end of the castle than the north end.

And few of them had routine business, there.

It was an ingenious place to put a secret door, and that was exactly what one of the Veridan queens had done.

Stasia couldn't see the stonework well enough, but she thought it was a part of the original design.

She leaned into the thick vines growing there, sliding through them and disappearing into the dark, overgrown path through the wall, going to the nearly-unused gate on the inside of the castle wall and putting her head against it to try to see the guard standing there.

"Stanley," she said.

"Seal," he answered.

She put her hand through the bars, opening her fingers to reveal Melody's ring, then closing her hand again and stepping back enough for him to unlock and open the gate. He closed it and locked it swiftly behind her and went back to looking boring.

Stasia adjusted her hood and walked across the open lawn to the side door of the castle that she was now accustomed to using.

She ended up in the dank sub-basement of the castle, a level with no light to speak of and a smell of disuse. She took off the cloak and put it on a hook, lighting a torch and carrying it the length of the hallway, then extinguishing it and going up a set of round stairs for four levels.

From here, it was all by memory.

She had no idea where she was, but this was the path that Melody herself had shown her, and this was the path that she followed when Melody summoned her.

She ended up in Melody's quarters. It was the room that she had met with Constance in, the day that she'd been summoned here to take care of Farang, a room with many doors and many secrets.

Today, Melody was sitting on a couch with a cup of tea, having a very pleasant and very staged conversation with Lady Westhauser.

Ella, for her part, was dressed to make a point.

That point was almost always lost on Stasia, but she

knew that the white velvet shrug and sweeping white velvet train made Ella stand out in the castle in a specific way, and that the noblewoman's seamstress had gone to great lengths to do it on purpose.

Stasia closed the door to the stairwell behind her and went to the doors on the opposite side of the room, stooping to look through the keyhole and finding a vivid blue eye peering back at her in surprise.

Stasia blinked at her, then sighed.

"Charisma, I swear you're worse than the court ladies."

"She's so pretty," Charisma complained, but Stasia heard soft footsteps as Amber's oldest younger sister left.

"She's keeping watch," Melody murmured. "She means well."

"But I have to keep busting her," Stasia answered. "And she's giving them the impression that you tolerate being spied on."

"Come sit," Melody said, shifting.

"Not yet," Stasia muttered, going and checking the closet where Constance had hidden Faris.

Melody sighed, her put-upon noise, not her annoyed noise, as Stasia checked the three closets and the trunk that were all big enough for someone to hide in. She'd caught Gina, the youngest daughter, in the trunk once and a closet once.

From here, she went to the washroom, finding a maid working there.

The woman startled as Stasia came in.

"Miss Fielding," she said. "I didn't hear you."

"You weren't intended to," Stasia answered. "You can finish here later, please."

"Yes, miss," the woman said, gathering her things quickly. Stasia followed her to the pair of doors that she had just rousted Charisma from, taking the opportunity to peer up and down the hallway as menacingly as she knew how, then she closed the doors and went to go sit at the other armchair next to Ella.

"You're very impressive," Ella said demurely into her tea. "At some point, I'm sure they're all just going to give up."

Stasia looked sideways at her as she picked up her tea, and Ella struggled to suppress her smile.

Sitting back with her tea and glancing at the door that led to the main hallway, Stasia turned her attention to Melody.

"How are they doing?" Melody asked, and Stasia shook her head.

"Jasper is about ready to just start going through buildings one at a time and see who runs," she said. "They can't get any leads on any of the warlocks since they got the sighting of Sanma at the port, back three weeks ago."

"Skite is strange," Ella said. "There's too much going on in the Black Docks and Highrock, and he's focusing on everything but the warlocks. I ask him about them, and he says that they're the guards' problem, now. He killed his one and he's not going to spend the rest of his life worrying about them."

Melody sighed.

"I suspect he's fishing for additional accommodation from Finwalk, which he won't give. The stone elves retreating has given the king a sense of confidence, and he's started looking at the future."

"There's no future unless he can get the city settled," Ella said. "Highrock is a mess. I went through Lesser Highrock for the first time since the siege, and I don't even recognize it."

"I agree with you," Melody said. "But he says that the way to get things back to normal is to act like they're normal."

Stasia sighed, and both women looked at her.

"What?" Stasia asked.

"This is the point where you say something tangential and insightful that completely ignores any relevant knowledge of Verida or how things work here," Melody said.

"Do I?" Stasia asked, and Ella nodded energetically.

"It's my favorite part," she said.

Stasia frowned at her and Ella grinned wider, then Stasia turned her face to Melody.

"You were attacked in the street," she said. "They all know that. That would have never happened with Constance."

"My mother would have never walked on foot through the streets, either," Melody said.

"Something is different," Stasia said. "And everyone knows it. It doesn't feel safe, even if the stone elves aren't attacking the estates anymore. How many people even remember before your mother was queen?"

"Few were old enough to clearly remember the continuity of what life was like," Melody agreed. "Many of whom are here within the castle."

Stasia nodded.

There were certainly a disproportionate number of old ladies and old men running around, telling people how things ought to be done.

"What's the thing with the buttons?" Stasia asked.

Ella laughed.

"There it is," Melody agreed, sitting back and enjoying her tea for a moment, then turning her face toward the doors behind her.

Stasia went up to check them again, but the hallway was still empty.

"Lady Ulmar," Melody said as Stasia sat down again. "All of the seamstresses were prepared for a rapid transition of fashion patterns, but apparently Lord and Lady Ulmar are setting the pattern for it, rather than me."

Stasia wrinkled her nose.

"And that matters, doesn't it?" she asked.

Melody nodded.

"No one is that particularly inspired by my dress, to begin with, so I missed it in its infancy, but at this point, I don't know how to rein it in without seeming petty."

Stasia looked from one to another of them, then shook her head.

Stasia was in peasant clothes today, the durable nature of the better stuff appealing to Stasia both as a function and as a textile, but there was nothing colorful or fashionable about it. Melody was in a dark-hued, severe gown with high collars and puffed sleeves. And Ella. Lady Westhauser was unlike anything Stasia had seen before anywhere.

"Should we be doing something different?" Stasia asked, and Melody waved her off.

"No," she said. "No. That isn't the problem. Neither of you are members of court. The issue is that the court is rebelling from under my authority, and... the buttons."

They didn't just wear buttons in a line. The ladies all over the courtyard and the court room were in diagonal, diamond-pattern buttons, in serpentine buttons and starburst patterned buttons. It was like the their garments were now intended to be rather more like puzzles than straightforward pieces of fabric, and the buttons were just barely keeping up.

"If you want me to go through and just randomly cut buttons off of people as I go, I'm happy to," Stasia said, and Melody smiled.

"I'm certain you would make excellent work of it, too," she said. "But it would look petty and everyone would guess that it was from me."

"I could speak with Sandra," Ella said. "It's a hideous affectation, but I'm sure she could make something of it."

Melody shook her head again.

"No. They're both very well-received offers, but the truth of it is that it's a symptom. The problem is that the court has not accepted me, and this is my problem to solve."

"Excuse my impertinence and my utter disregard for how things are done in Verida, but you're absolutely wrong," Stasia said. "If we are the queen's guard, then this is the kind of thing that we're here to help solve. The king's guard can deal with making sure that the warlocks don't make it onto the grounds. I'm here to make sure that Melody is a success."

Ella nodded and Melody sighed again.

She was such a stern woman. Strong. Constance had had a different air to her, one of unquestionable confidence. And Stasia couldn't put her finger on what was different about it, but it was important.

"Can you just kick them out?" Stasia asked.

"Could," Melody said. "But I need liaisons to the various groups around the city that they represent. I knew that this was going to be a challenge, but I find myself unexpectedly tired by all of it. I'm due to speak with Lord Palora this afternoon about access rights to the Wolfram north of the city and I know that he is going to bring Lady Palora. She and Lady Ulmar..." She shook her head.

"Old Lady Palora," Ella said with a shudder. "We've declined every invitation from them. I can't imagine if Lord Westhauser expected me to socialize on demand."

"She doesn't approve of Lady Ulmar's flamboyance, but she goes out of her way to reprimand me in each way she can think of," Melody said.

"You're the queen," Stasia said. "I mean... If I told the men down at the fish market that there was an old bat who was openly disrespectful to you every time she saw you, they'd gladly haul her out to the middle of the harbor and teach her to swim. The entire city would be outraged if they knew that something like that was even possible. You are the spirit of Verida, and to let them act like that around you..."

"Is how it has always been," Melody said wanly. "The queen is the breath and spirit of Verida, you are right, but within the castle, she has all of the normal politics of any woman of power. Lady Westhauser, I'm sure, understands."

"My first year was really hard," Ella agreed. "And that was just with staff pushing back against me. I just ignored the noblewomen, mostly."

Melody nodded, then straightened herself and lifted her chin.

"This is the burden of the queens," she said. "Among all the others, this will not be the one that overcomes me."

"I think you should ban buttons," Ella said, setting down her tea.

"Can you do that?" Stasia asked.

"I can do as I please," Melody answered. "Queen Viktra banned shoes for a time, though that was as a punishment because the court had taken to abusing her servants. The question is, do I look petty and out of control if I do so."

"So what?" Ella asked. "Ban any woman from court who wears more than a single button at her throat. Be petty. You won't be out of control for long."

"Unless they try to organize without her," Stasia said. Both women looked at her again with humor and Stasia stretched her eyes and shrugged. "So what? It's what I do. It's what the merchants would do, anyway. If my father suddenly got impossible to work with, they'd all just cut him out, and then it doesn't matter how rich and powerful he was, he wouldn't be anymore. Well. He would still have a lot of money, but... You get my point. They can choose not engage her as queen, if they're willing to just go for it."

"It would be just as bad for them as for her," Ella argued. "The women of Verida have power because the queen has power. If they all abandoned her, yeah, she would become... forgive me, your majesty, she would be nothing more than a figurehead, but they would just be housewives."

"Why?" Stasia asked. "Why would any of them be any less just because no one is speaking to the queen?"

"They wouldn't," Melody said. "Not in the context of their homes, as you're observing. But here. The power over how the city runs. We use a much more... delicate form of power than the men have, and for the women of the court, Lady Westhauser is entirely right that it is sourced directly through my person. If they terminate access to that, none of them are able to bear influence over anything but perhaps their own husbands and sons."

"Which isn't nothing," Ella said, "but can you imagine Lady Ulmar or Lady Palora sitting at a shop like Quinnia with their tea cups and their lace fans with nothing to do but complain to each other?"

"I need women within the castle who are on my side," Melody said. "Who are concerned for my interests because my interests are theirs, and who are willing to take risks on my behalf because those risks have rewards that they are interested in."

"Then bring in a bunch of teenagers who are ready to drip off your every word," Stasia said. "If that's all you're looking for."

"That won't work," Ella said.

"Why wouldn't it?" Melody answered, and Ella sat straighter.

"Because you need women with connections," Ella said.

"Give them power, they'll make connections," Stasia said passively. "If she's the source of the power, and disconnecting the court means that they lose it? That's different than just needing to exist within a network. Right?"

Melody looked at her thoughtfully, then nodded.

"I wouldn't burn the bridges," she said. "I would certainly prefer the women who already know how the game is played to come back to me. Even the ones I find personally distasteful. But I wouldn't mind driving them away for a time while I reorganize the court into something that looks less like my mother and more like me. And younger women... is a very insightful ploy, I think."

Ella frowned, then nodded.

"I can see how that would work, I suppose. Do you know how to find such women?"

"At the university," Stasia said, feeling as though that was patently obvious.

Once more, both heads swung to look at her, and Ella grinned.

"I would go teach a course, if it were me," Stasia said. "Actually get to know people and find the ones who are smart enough and interested in the right things and choose them by hand. But if you wanted to do it faster than that, I bet just asking for recruits would work."

"Good," Melody said. "Very good. Yes. I will look into taking on a class at the university, splitting my time between campus and here at the castle."

"Are you sure you have the time and energy for that?" Ella asked. "I think it's a really good idea, but... I know I would have signed up in a heartbeat if I'd heard that Queen Constance was going to teach, when I was at the university, but I know that my professors were often very busy with all of their responsibilities. And you're already... the queen."

"Are you volunteering to help me?" Melody asked.

Ella went stiff, like she hadn't seen that one coming at all. Now Stasia grinned, reaching for her tea innocently and watching to see what Ella would do next.

"Mum," Ella said. "I'm unqualified. I would... I wouldn't know..."

"You graduated," Melody said. "Did you not?"

"I did, Mum," Ella admitted.

"And you've kept up classes since then, because you love them," Melody said.

Stasia knew that, but she didn't know how many other people did.

"Yes, Mum," Ella answered.

"You're qualified to teach on your own, in your various fields of experience," Melody said. "I'm not even asking that. I'm asking for someone who can do some of the grunt work of administering a class so that I can make sure Finwalk doesn't push me out of any more of the advising meetings than he already is."

"I would be honored," Ella said. "I need to talk to Lord Westhauser and..." She paused. "No. I don't. I will, but... yes. I will do it. Thank you."

Melody dipped her head, as though she had actually just done Ella a favor rather than put a huge load of repetitive and thankless work on her, but Stasia was skeptical of formalized education to begin with, so maybe she didn't know.

"Is this what you summoned us here to discuss?" Stasia asked, and Melody drew a sharp breath and shook her head, standing.

"No, it is indeed not," she said. "I actually require the two of you to adorn battlement, if you will, and accompany me into conflict this afternoon."

"Battlement," Stasia said. "If you'd wanted me in my dragonskins, you should have said."

"Not at all," Melody said, going over to a cabinet that Stasia had been in only a few moments before. "I do apologize, Miss Fielding, but in my line of work, battlements may be a bit different than you're used to."

Melody raised an eyebrow and turned back around with a dress draped across her arm.

Stasia blinked at it.

"You mean that for me," she said.

"I do," Melody answered. "And I know that you aren't going to like it, but Lady Westhauser did help me with this, and I hope that you will find it less objectionable than you might have."

Ella shot Stasia a look that might have been an apology, and Stasia sighed.

"If I can get kidnapped by an evil magic man and not complain about anything that happened that night, I can wear a dress without whining," she said. "Give it here."

Melody gave her a flat smile.

"You can change in the washroom," she said. "We are already fashionably late."

Stasia pulled the sword belt tight around her waist as she came out of the washroom, lifting her face to find Melody with her hands on her hips and Ella with her fingers on her cheeks.

"That will do," Melody said, "though the sword is entirely unnecessary."

"If I'm going to battle, I'm wearing it," Stasia answered. "It isn't the purple one."

"How many swords do you have, now?" Ella asked, falling into step next to Stasia as Melody went ahead of them, opening the doors to the main hallway and looking over her shoulder at them.

"I open doors, now," she said, and Stasia nodded.

"As you should."

They followed Melody down the wider hallway and Ella looked Stasia up and down.

"It's good work," she said. "Sandra had your measurements. I hope you don't mind."

It was good work. Stasia hadn't worn an expensive

gown in more than a year, now, and she didn't much like being in one, now, but she had to admit that Ella and Sandra had done their best to keep the worst of it off of her.

"Seriously, though, how many swords do you have?" Ella asked.

"Three," Stasia whispered back. "This is the one that I stole from the guard house before I disappeared this spring."

"And you have a purple one?"

"Of course I do," Stasia answered. "My father ordered it for me for my birthday and I got it two weeks ago and I sleep with it now because it's so amazing."

"You do not," Ella scolded, and Stasia grinned.

"I don't, but I threatened to. It's so beautiful. He found a tanner who managed to match the color and the patterning of my dragonskins just exactly, and the swordmaker did something magic with the grip so the metal is actually this darker purple color..."

"Ladies, decorum if you please," Melody said, turning to face another pair of wide doors. "They will not be merciful on you, or me either. Hold your ground at all costs."

Stasia looked at Ella and squinted a question.

How difficult could this possibly be?

Ella shrugged.

They went in.

"Oh, my gosh, I never ever want to be in the court," Stasia said as they followed Melody back down the hall almost four hours later. "Never."

"Do any of them have friends?" Ella asked. "Or is it all just politics?"

"I like to imagine that they go home at night and change completely," Melody said. "Or else I wouldn't be able to look at them as human, much less worthy of my time and attention."

"I can't believe Constance put up with them," Stasia said. "She was so no-nonsense. For that matter, so are you."

"Some of them are key to the success of Verida," Melody said, letting Ella close the doors behind them as she went to pour hot water over tea out of a kettle. Stasia was shocked to see steam come up from it; someone had known that they were on their way back and left it ready for them.

"I felt like going around the room there at the end and just poking every single one of them in the eye," Stasia said, throwing herself onto her arm chair and tipping her head back to look at the ceiling.

Oh, look. The ceiling was beautiful, too. She hadn't noticed, before.

"Thank you for being there," Melody said.

"Is this what you need the unspoiled teenage girls to fix?" Stasia asked, hearing Ella settled into a chair nearby.

"No, unfortunately," Melody said. "These are not contacts that are voluntary to me. These are women who are important, politically and economically, and so I must maintain lines of communication with them. The ones who are active on my behalf are an entirely different network with no crossover at all."

"I went to school with the young lady Hulland," Ella said. "I had no idea her mother was so..."

"Yes," Melody said as Stasia finally lifted her head and accepted her tea. "She has always been thus. She approached my mother about arranging a suitable marriage for young lady Hulland, but my mother was unable to do so before she passed, so that will now fall to me."

"I'm not entirely certain I understand why we were there," Stasia said.

"For one," Melody said as Ella tried to take over making the tea. She moved Ella's hands away and shook her head. "It calms me, if you don't mind. There's a ritual to it. For one, the two of you represent rather important focal points of both power and money within the city over which no one has had any influence or control for many years. Even the old Lord Westhauser was independent of the castle. And the Gormand family has played it close to the vest, on account of Minstrel Fielding's unwillingness to involve himself in Veridan politics at all. He just... likes putting goods on boats, it seems, and has no care for the men who oversee such things."

"That's my father," Stasia agreed.

"Are we betraying the men in our lives, being here?" Ella wondered aloud.

"You know that I don't represent my father at all, right?" Stasia said.

"I'd heard," Melody said. "I'm intrigued, but I had heard."

Stasia nodded, then looked over at Ella.

"We don't represent the men in our lives. We represent ourselves and our own power. You run the entire Westhauser estate by yourself. That's huge. The wealth that represents."

"I do, Stasia," Ella said. "I represent Skite and he represents me. It's not like with your father. We're a team, and I don't want to work against him. Not at all."

"I thought that he'd already agreed that you being here was a good idea, or else... you wouldn't be here," Stasia said. "Is it all that different?"

Ella pressed her lips, glancing at Melody, but the queen was pouring a third cup of tea and kept her eyes down as though to force Ella to work this through on her own.

"Everything is political," Ella said. "I'm used to that. Family politics always came first, and who was allowed to do what where when was... I grew up with that. Being somewhere that you weren't supposed to be was a political statement. Doing something without permission was a political statement. Who you walked with down the street was a political statement. The only thing about all of this that's surprising to me is that it's still every bit that political. And that, I guess, everybody is so emotional about it. Like, they're shocked when we walk in the room standing next to each other, because how dare we. The family would just get on with beating us to pulp for standing with the wrong person, but they're offended."

"Don't take that part too seriously," Melody said. "Part of it is a social-sanctioning maneuver to make you obey without even being told. If they can make you start guessing what they want from you, you're they're performing dog for forever."

"Oh, I see it," Ella murmured.

"I'd rather a guy take a swing at me with a sword, personally," Stasia said.

"Another reason you are so valuable to me," Melody said. "You remind me that there are much greater things at stake than the discomfort and insult of that room of women. While we must endure them, because they will be critical to moving the war back up into the mountains where it belongs and returning Verida to the occasionally-unpredictable machine that it prefers to be, I will not submit my own concerns to them. And now we will discuss men with swords."

"What?" Ella asked. "Which?"

"What else is there for news on the warlocks?" Melody asked. "I fear that Finwalk is going to attempt to keep me from tracking it. He means well, but we haven't yet worked out that I am not an icon for people to look at and feel nice about. If he isn't going to tell me what I want to know, I'll get my information elsewhere."

"I told you, the guard haven't found any sign of them," Stasia said.

"I mean have they done anything to draw attention?" Melody asked. "Any rumors of where they may be?"

"Babe thinks that they may try to go back around," Stasia said. "If they don't have a leader, it's possible they'll retreat to get new orders."

Ella shook her head.

"I think that it misunderstands assassins," she said quietly. "They don't work well in teams to begin with. Skite thinks they've splintered and that they're all pursuing their own interests, now."

"And what would those be?" Melody asked.

Ella shook her head.

"We talk about it at dinner, sometimes," she said. "Maybe they're trying to put together their own plan to kill you. Maybe they'll try to destabilize Verida another way. Or maybe they end up like the stone elves who take refuge here, and they'll just... start living a life as best as they can figure out, given who they are now. It depends on how... broken they are, and how attached they are to being alive, I think."

"I hear rumors of how the stone elves in the city are treated," Melody said. "I expect you know better than that."

"They aren't bad people," Ella said. "Weird, yeah, but they aren't bad. A few of them have been caught out as stone elves, and... well, the Black Docks are a bit more willing to look the other way when someone goes running past with a mob on their heels. A few of them are taking refuge around where Skite knows where they are, but a few of them died before they could disappear. Some of them weren't even stone elves. They were just... weird humans."

"Babe told me that stone elves from the mountains don't speak any language that we would recognize," Stasia said. "Is it really so hard to make sure that they speak Veridan?"

"Veridans don't know that the stone elves have their own language," Ella said, twisting her mouth. "I hate to say it out loud, but the average Veridan thinks there's only one language in the whole world."

"I wouldn't accuse the average Veridan of believing such a thing," Melody asked. "But certainly a great number do."

"Skite is trying to keep them in cover," Ella said. "But it isn't easy. They don't like being told what to do, and they don't like hiding in a strange place. Plus they don't like each other."

"Why not?" Stasia asked.

"I don't know," Ella told her. "Skite just says that they don't."

There was a rapid, soft knock on the door and Melody lifted her head.

"Enter," she said, and a girl of perhaps sixteen came in, looking quickly at Stasia and Ella to acknowledge them, then she looked at Melody.

"There are two king's guards downstairs asking for you," she said. "They wouldn't... I'm very sorry, mum. They wouldn't come back another time."

Melody rose quickly, Stasia and Ella falling into step behind her once more as she started for the door.

"No one should attempt to send away members of the king's guard who come to me with news," Melody said. "Ever."

The girl gave her a deep bow, trying not to make eye contact, and they were past, moving quickly with the sound of fabric as the three women went down the hallway in formation.

Babe and Sterling were standing in the main court room, hands clasped behind their backs, waiting.

They both immediately registered Ella - she was

hard to miss - and gave Stasia polite nods as they turned their attention to Melody.

It was Babe who first saw her as he started to tell her that they needed a private word with the queen, and would she mind...?

Both his eyebrows reached for his hairline, and Stasia lifted a brow of her own.

"Am I so different?" she asked.

He looked her up and down.

"Just ain't never seen you done up like that," he said.

"You look lovely, Miss Fielding," Sterling said, giving her a belated but sweeping bow of greeting.

Babe gawped at her a bit longer, then Melody cleared her throat and he straightened to look at the queen.

"Mum," he said.

"I assume you are here with news of some kind," Melody said. "Not just interested in seeing to the type of company I keep?"

"You ain't supposed to be here," Babe said, a new realization coming to him. "Guard would've told me you'd come through."

Stasia lifted a shoulder and he frowned, then turned his attention to Melody once more, formal now.

"Yes, mum," he said. "Jasper sent me to tell you that we found evidence that one of the warlocks was holed up in an apartment south of the castle market. Family is dead, room full of stuff you aren't supposed to be able to get, here in Verida, according to a pixie who brought us information. We've taken the stuff and Jasper and Matthias are watching the apartment, in case the warlock comes back."

"Do you think he will?" Melody asked, and Babe worked his jaw for a moment, then shook his head.

"No, mum. But... Jasper wants to know if... where we should take the magic implements, ma'am."

"Bring them to me, here," Melody said. "This

afternoon, yet, if possible."

"We have folk who can look through them, mum," Babe said. "You oughtn't trouble yourself..."

"Your commanding officer knows me and my interests better than you do," Melody said. "I want it in my own possession as quickly as possible. Thank you."

Babe gave her a little bow and Sterling made a better show of grace, then the two men turned and left.

"Jasper knew I would want it," Melody muttered. "Why didn't he just send it?"

"Because he doesn't think you should have it," Stasia answered. "But he knew that you would want it. He's giving you a chance to think about it. What business do you have, taking all of that stuff? What if someone finds out about it?"

Melody gave her a subtle look - Ella didn't know enough to work out what was going on, but Stasia was hinting dangerously close, at this point - then nodded.

"I have experts on my staff," she said. "Ones who will go through these things and see if there is anything useful to glean."

"And Jasper has experts, too," Stasia said.

"Jasper has Skite's expert," Ella said, not enjoying being left out of the conversation.

"Yes," Stasia said. "And a few pixies who have had a positive history with him. Bringing all of that stuff here brings up questions, Melody. He gave you a moment to reconsider. You should, even if you don't change your mind."

Melody sighed, then nodded.

"Very well," she said. "You will bring it to me."

Stasia bit her lip, then nodded.

She'd walked right into that one.

"Go," Melody said, motioning. "Set it up before they're too far gone."

Stasia nodded again, dashing after Babe and Sterling

and catching them just outside the doors.

"Guys," she hissed, stepping to the far side of the steps where they were out of the way. The two palace guards stationed at the bottom of the steps looked up at her with curiosity, but she could keep her voice down enough to make this work.

"You really do look nice," Babe said. "I was just surprised."

She closed her eyes, fighting back the need to mock him.

"I'm supposed to bring it," she whispered. "Where can I find you?"

"We're having a lovely late lunch at an excellent restaurant just on the far side of the castle market," Sterling said easily. "It would be wonderful if you could join us."

Stasia nodded.

"I've got... steps between here and there, but I'll be there soon."

Babe gave her one more bewildered look - not recognizing her in the dress really had shaken him - then the two men set off again and Stasia went back into the castle, having to find her way back up to Melody's quarters on her own. She got lost a couple times and had to ask for help once. That didn't go well; a strange woman wandering the castle and asking where to find the queen was suspicious at best, and Stasia got herself reported to the head of the household staff. The maid that Stasia had asked for help was about to go find Petrault - disaster - when the head of the staff had abruptly recognized Stasia and hissed an order for the poor young woman to take Stasia up to the queen's quarters immediately.

"I feared you'd gotten lost," Melody said as the maid closed the door behind Stasia. Stasia pursed her lips, annoyed, and made for the washroom.

"I did," she said. "We need to figure out some way

for people to know that I belong here without everyone knowing I'm here. Or something. None of this makes any sense."

"You'll get used to it," Melody said. "Did you arrange it?"

"I'm going to meet them for lunch," Stasia said. "I just need to keep going, or else they're going to give up on me."

"That's not true," Melody said. "They're watching the apartment."

"I know that," Stasia said. "But I'm hungry."

She changed quickly, coming out to look at Ella and Melody as they sipped their tea.

"You were very helpful today," Melody said. "Thank you."

Stasia shook her head, annoyed and flummoxed.

"We need to figure out what this thing is," she said. "Because having it be everything and nothing means that I don't do anything well."

"You're just annoyed that you got lost," Ella said.

"What is it with this place?" Stasia asked.

"It's designed that way on purpose," Melody said. "I'd say you'll get used to it, but that actually probably wouldn't be true. Make sure no one sees you leave."

Stasia paused.

"Why?" she asked. "I mean, I'll admit I kind of like this cloak-and-dagger thing, but... why?"

"Because I don't want anyone to ever know if you're here or not," Melody said. "I want you to have a reputation of appearing and disappearing at need. It gives me an aura of invulnerability, because there's no telling if my mysterious guard is here or not. Everyone has to be extra careful."

Stasia considered that, then pointed.

"That's a good answer," she said, and Melody raised an eyebrow.

"I'm so glad you approve," she said, and Stasia ducked her head.

"I'm going now," she said. "I'll be back soon."

"Do you want to get dinner with me tonight?" Ella asked. "Skite is busy, so I'm planning on staying in town and riding home with him tomorrow night."

Stasia frowned, then nodded.

"Meet you at Felligan's?"

Ella grinned.

It meant that the evening would have a decidedly non-serious bent to it, if they were starting out at a goofy college bar, but sometimes the world merited a silly night.

"I'll see you there around dark."

Stasia nodded and went to the door that took her to the spiral stairs. She hesitated, but there wasn't anything else to say.

Back downstairs.

More hallways.

More stairs.

More doors.

At least this time she knew which way she was going.

She found the guards, all five of them, lounging around a table at an outdoor restaurant that Stasia had never patronized at before.

It was hardly a surprise; even more than a year on into her time in Verida, she could basically eat at a new restaurant every day of the week and never run out of places to try.

Now, they weren't all good. Many of them traded incredibly cheap fare for very low prices, and Stasia - even disinherited Stasia - thought that her food was worth spending better money on than that, but it kept soul in body, and that was something.

This was a nicer place for outdoor-only food, and the woman running it appeared to be the cook and the server, which meant slow service but usually pretty good food.

Matthias got up to get her a chair and Stasia sat down next to Babe and Colin.

"What have you been up to, today?" she asked.

"Wedding plans," Colin muttered. "It's like she's importing family she's never heard of before for this thing."

"She's excited," Sterling said with an easy grin. "As mystified as the rest of us are, it appears she's actually looking forward to being married to you."

"Sterling said you pulled some kind of magic trick at the castle this morning," Jasper said, his eyes obscured under his hat as he sat slouched low in his chair. He was watching the building across the street.

"Not my trick to talk about," Stasia answered.

"Everything under control, there?" Jasper asked. "She's still getting her feet under her, for figuring out how much risk she's asking people to take."

"We're all taking extra risk, just now," Stasia answered. "Speaking of?"

Matthias took a leather satchel off the back of his chair and handed it to her.

It was heavy, a satchel that a messenger might have worn on two shoulders rather than one, or hung over a donkey's back.

Stasia glanced at Babe, who pressed his mouth.

"Careful with that," he said. "We done what we could, to keep things from mixing that oughtn't, but you still don't want to jostle it about overmuch."

Stasia nodded, hanging it off of the back of her chair.

She made eye contact with Babe, who was avoiding looking at her, now.

They'd talked about this last night.

He was working, tonight, so they'd gone walking down at the docks the night before, her hand in his, just taking in the air and the dark, talking or not as they felt like it. She did more of the talking than he did, but not by so much as she might have once guessed.

They'd talked about this.

He looked at her to see if she was still looking at him, and she busted him, raising both eyebrows.

He sighed.

That was going to be as close to a yes as she was going to get.

"So," Stasia said.

Sterling and Matthias looked at her. Colin got out a deck of cards and shuffled it.

"I wanted..." Stasia started, waiting for Babe to lift his head, but he didn't. "We decided..."

Matthias was watching her with polite focus. Sterling waited a moment, then turned his attention to Colin, watching to see what he was going to deal.

"It's been..." Stasia tried again. "Sometimes..."

Why was this hard?

"Babe and I are seeing each other," Stasia said quickly.

"You see all of us," Colin commented.

"Romantically, I mean," Stasia said, glaring at him.

"Was I not supposed to already know that?" Matthias asked.

"I knew before they did," Jasper muttered without shifting.

"I was beginning to fear that it was one of those weird, sexless things," Colin said, shaking his head and dealing cards to Sterling. "We're in love, but we don't actually like touching each other. Glad to see I'm wrong."

Stasia blinked.

Sterling shot her a sideways look and winked.

"We're all very happy for you," he said, picking up his hand.

"Told you," Babe muttered.

"We have to announce it," Stasia complained. "It's rude for them to all just assume."

"Have you spoken to your father?" Jasper asked.

"No," Stasia said sullenly. "I wanted you guys to be the first ones to know."

"We were," Colin said cheerfully. "I expect your father just wonders which of us it is."

Stasia turned her head to give him a very dark look, which he delighted under.

"You fitting for purple ribbon?" Sterling asked.

"What?" Stasia asked.

"Means are we getting married," Babe said. It was the same tone he'd used for 'told you'.

"No," Stasia said, outraged at how poorly this was going. "We're seeing each other. Why...?"

Sterling grinned, and Jasper chuckled.

"Seriously, was it a secret, before?" Matthias asked. "I thought we all just... knew."

"I mean, the decision between spinstress and that guy... I could understand taking your time," Colin said.

"Babe on the other hand," Sterling said. "Gonna be a rich man, now, aren't you?"

Babe shifted to look at her, and Jasper lifted his hat with his thumb.

"Actually... that's not true, either," Stasia said.

Colin looked over at her and Sterling set his hand face-down on the table.

"Papers are finalized," Stasia said. "My father disinherited me."

"Over Babe?" Colin asked. "Even I think that's an overreaction."

Jasper let his hat fall again and he settled lower in his chair.

"Not because of him, idiot," Stasia said.

"Because you asked him to," Matthias said, and Stasia looked over at the young man, nodding.

"I did."

"Because you want to make your own path in the world," Matthias said. "Are you afraid?"

The table went still.

It was such an earnestly-asked question.

"I am, a little," Stasia told him. "But I'm also really excited."

"You have any marketable skills?" Colin asked.

"She works for the queen, idiot," Jasper murmured, teasing at Stasia's words.

"I have lots of ideas," Stasia said. "I actually don't even have time for everything I want to do. I'm really excited to finally be able to... do whatever I want."

Colin grinned.

"I can't think of a time that I've seen you constrained," he said. "You always do whatever you want."

She shook her head.

"It didn't matter, before. Now I'm making decisions that actually matter, and..."

"Everything's new," Matthias said, and she turned to look at him again, nodding slowly.

"Yes."

He gave her a quiet little smile and nodded.

"Congratulations," he said. He gave Babe a furtive look and dipped his head. "I think that the two of you are an... unusual match, but you both needed someone unusual, if it was ever going to work."

"That's a curse," Jasper muttered. "Concluding success at the announcement of a new relationship."

"But it will work," Matthias said. "You... see that,

don't you?"

"Not like you do, buddy," Sterling answered, picking up his cards again.

"Thank you, Matthias," Babe said, shifting. "Means a lot."

Matthias nodded quickly, looking around the group in his insecure way, then Jasper lifted his hat with his thumb again to look at Stasia.

"You got that out of your system?" he asked. She pursed her lips at him.

"Fine," she said. "Yes. Back to business."

He grinned.

"How is Melody?" he asked.

"You once told me that I'm not allowed to ask that," Stasia answered.

"That's when the queen is old," Colin said. "Not when she's young like she is."

"True always," Babe said. "Casting doubt on her fitness is always wrong."

"Unless you're me," Jasper said. "How is she?"

"I don't know," Stasia admitted. "She doesn't talk about any of it. I really don't have any idea."

Melody was moving pretty normally again, these days, but she always had this stiff, regal bearing to her that could have easily disguised ongoing issues with the wound she'd incurred weeks earlier. It was too soon for it to have completely healed, Stasia thought, though she did have a lot of people looking out for her.

Stasia hadn't told any of them about the high elves in the city being involved.

She didn't know much to tell, but she knew that it was a secret that the royal family had entrusted to her, and not even Babe knew about the visit from Melody's husband.

The elf.

Jasper nodded.

"Keep an eye on her," he said.

"To what end?" Colin asked.

"What do you mean?" Jasper asked. Colin shrugged.

"Just what I said. To what end? None of us can do anything to help her. Why would we keep tabs on something we can't do anything about?"

"Because I refuse to believe that there's nothing I can do," Jasper said. "Wyndham queens burn hot. I can't change that. But when it comes to our brand new queen, she's got time and power on her side, and I want to know if there's something going wrong, because there's a chance that one of us can step in to stop it. We all got bonuses to fight magic. Doesn't mean we have to stop short fighting exactly one kind, now does it?"

The men exchanged glances and nods, and Stasia reached over to take the leftovers off of Babe's plate, munching them while Sterling and Colin played cards for a few minutes.

"You gonna keep turnin' up at the castle unexpected?" Babe asked finally.

"Looks like," Stasia answered.

"That's a neat trick," Jasper said. "One I might be able to make use of."

"Can't tell you how I'm doing it," Stasia said.

"Oh, I'm just going to assume you're climbing the walls where no one's looking," Jasper said cheerfully. "They don't have Constance to spot you, anymore, now do they?"

"You didn't tell us Constance was the one who busted her," Sterling said, and Jasper nodded.

"The old queen herself," he said. "Got past every last blessed one of Petrault's men and was about to walk out the gate with Matthias when Constance called down the guards on her. That woman was incredible."

Sterling set the cards down on the table and crossed his arms.

"I want to hit something," he said. "All this running around looking for a guy who... I see everything, guys. I'm just waiting for the dagger in my back, and I want to hit something."

Jasper nodded.

"I know how you feel. We need to get some training in at the guard house. We've been on full alert for too long."

It had been weeks.

Stasia had the same feel off of Babe, though she was pretty sure that he wasn't just watching his own back; he was watching hers, too. After Tillith had taken her, he'd never really gone away again. If he wasn't on duty, he was watching over her. In the first few days, it had been making sure she was eating and drinking and taking care of herself, with as sore as her feet were, but even once she was back in her boots and wandering the city as she saw fit, he set appointments with her - they might have been dates, but for the fact that he never asked - and he had this habit of looking over his shoulder every time they turned a corner.

There were still warlocks on the loose, and one of them had gotten her once.

It had impacted him more than it had her, at the end of the day.

"It's not just us," Matthias said, and Jasper grunted.

"What do you see, Matthias?" Sterling asked.

Matthias wiped his mouth with the back of his wrist, coming to sit next to Sterling with his back to the street.

"I see people fighting over the price of stuff rather than just talking about it. I see... boys throwing each other into the river, but it isn't each other, it's the littlest ones they can put their hands on. I see women... chasing their kids with wooden spoons or brooms... I hear people screaming in their homes, women with bruises, kids with welts, kids that are sleeping on the street rather than going home."

"Always been like that in Verida," Babe said, and

Matthias shook his head.

"It's like a contagion," he said. "You used to see it in Lower Highrock, yeah, but now it's Upper Highrock and the working district by the meat markets, and even the crafting district across from the castle. I saw a pair of women, merchants' wives, shopping in the artisan quarter, one of them had a black eye and the other one wouldn't let anything touch her arm. She was holding it up against her chest like it was probably broken."

"Verida has lost her mind," Jasper murmured.

"I talked to my ma and my nan," Colin said. "They both remember when Constance first came to the throne, and she said that everyone was anxious and upset and they grieved, and that the stone elves tried to attack the city a couple of years later, but they said that it's nothing like now. That neither of them have ever seen the city like it is now."

"The stone elves used to make a run on the city every four or five years, anyway, back then," Jasper said. "Not likely that it was even directly tied to the changeover."

"How old was Constance when she took the throne?" Stasia asked.

"It was only about twenty years ago," Babe said. "Her ma lived a good, long life, for a Wyndham."

"Ebenezer's victory was six years after she took the throne," Jasper said.

So Jasper remembered, too.

He looked at her from under his hat, his expression confirming that he remembered things just the way Colin's grandmother did.

"Is it because they're afraid for the queen?" Stasia asked.

"They're soft," Babe said. "Don't any of them remember a time when the attacks were regular the way they haven't been, these last fifteen years?"

"It's everyone, Babe," Jasper said. "Not just the

younger generation. Everyone is afraid because the queen is vulnerable. Too early in her reign, too. They're afraid that the king isn't going to hold power long enough to actually get good at it, and that the stone elves are going to resupply up in the mountains and come pouring back down here and finish the job."

"Reds won't let it happen," Babe grunted.

"Army's not what you remember of it," Sterling said. "If you'll forgive me saying it. I went up with my parents to do training with young soldiers, once a year, when we still had the school, and the fort was... it was always packed with men doing stuff. Working and training and shipping in and shipping out. It's not like that, now. It feels empty. They took heavy casualties up in the mountains from the supply snarls at the handoff to Finwalk, and he's..."

"He's not prioritizing recruiting because he never served," Jasper said. "He is my king and I will lay down my life for him, but I never pledged to agree with him."

"The populace doesn't see the fort," Colin said. "And they've always pretended that the soldiers up in the mountains were immortal and infinite. That's not it."

They looked at Matthias, who licked his lips.

"It's complicated," he said. "I think it's nearest that... they're afraid that the queen isn't strong enough. But that's not the whole of it. Babe isn't completely wrong. They didn't like being reminded that the stone elves can just walk down here and try to kill us. But I think it's still more than any of that, even combined."

"Is it something the warlocks are doing?" Stasia asked.

Matthias looked at her sharply.

"Making people afraid with magic?" he asked.

"Would work," Jasper muttered.

Stasia shrugged.

"I'm not suggesting I think it's possible, but we know

that they were casting specifically on Melody, trying to make her do what they wanted her to. Maybe, is it possible, to cast on everyone at once, just gradually over time...?"

The men looked at each other once more.

"Casting despair?" Sterling asked. "Would seem to fit what's going on."

"I don't think it's necessary," Matthias said. "I think that the queen's injury on its own is enough to start what we're seeing."

They all looked at Jasper, who rose.

"I think that you guys let your eyes wander," he said. "Stacy, you should walk. You aren't going to want to be here when he figures out that we stole all his stuff."

The men were moving.

Babe squeezed Stasia's elbow.

"See you at the entrance to the market in two hours?" he asked.

She shook her head.

"I'm getting dinner with Ella," she said. "If I have time in between, I'll see you at the guard house."

He nodded and followed Colin and Sterling across the street. Jasper was already through the front door.

Stasia hadn't seen anyone go through the door, and she was pretty sure she'd been watching close enough that she would have noticed it, but she also knew that the door was only one way into a place.

She picked up the satchel and put it across her shoulders, setting off toward the nearest main intersection.

She'd wanted to get down to the port today, but it didn't look like that was going to happen.

No wonder Minstrel took a carriage everywhere. Walking took up the entire day.

She'd wanted to stay and watch the fight.

She always wanted to stay.

The problem was that Jasper had been right about her having the casting materials, and the last thing she wanted was to turn herself into a hostage in the middle of all that.

With just any other guy? She was getting to be confident enough over her own feet that she might have risked it, but when it came to the warlocks, she was still scared witless of them when she thought about it too hard, and carrying around his stash of goodies?

No, she walked fast.

She hoped nothing bad happened to the guys, but she walked fast.

If anyone could survive it, it was the five of them, and she just couldn't think about it any more than that. This was their job.

Would she have preferred Babe be a merchant, wake up in the morning and take an innocuous trip down to the port, spend the day changing goods for money and back?

She'd had a thousand opportunities at that, over the years. More. Clearly she wouldn't have preferred it.

She loved Babe for how strong and how fearless he was, how he went charging in, where people needed him, and she wouldn't have asked him to change, no matter how ill she felt in the pit of her stomach when she remembered him lying on the table in Melody's sitting room with a dagger sticking out of his chest.

She made her way past the castle market and crossed the river, taking the long path along the side of the castle to the secret entrance and going through again, once more going secretly through the castle up to Melody's personal sitting room.

"Do you have protection on this door, in case it's ever not me?" Stasia asked as Melody looked up from a heavy paper she was reading.

"More than you will ever know," Melody answered. "And none you will ever see."

Stasia nodded, satisfied.

"I brought everything," she said, going to put the satchel on the table and sitting. "Are you sure this is safe?"

"Very little of value is safe," Melody answered. "Particularly at this level. Would you sit with me while I go through it, in case I react to any of it?"

That was not the answer Stasia had anticipated, but she nodded quickly, settling in her chair as Melody carefully unpacked everything one piece at a time and laid it out on the table.

"Are they going to get him today?" Melody asked as she worked.

"I don't know," Stasia admitted. "I hope so, but they've been really elusive, up to now."

"They have been," Melody agreed. "Hate to miss an opportunity, though."

"Do you think it's possible that they're casting on the whole city, making people feel hopeless?" Stasia asked, and Melody lifted her eyes.

"Yes, I think that's possible. Do you think it's happening?"

Stasia was a bit stunned.

"Maybe," she said. She'd expected a lecture about how magic was unknowable and how long was it going to take her to stop asking silly questions about it? It took her a moment to recover from Melody acting like something was actually... tangible and knowable. "The city is in a bad way, mum."

"I would go out and see it for myself, but we all saw what happened last time," Melody said with dark humor.

"Do you know what those things are?" Stasia asked, uncomfortable.

"Some of them," Melody said. "Though they're variants I've never seen or used before."

"Will you use them?" Stasia asked.

"I will consult with others who may know better than I do what these differences mean," Melody said. "You do not play with such things when you do not understand them. Do you think that someone is casting on the city at large?"

"Matthias doesn't," Stasia said.

Melody raised her eyes again, lifting an eyebrow, and Stasia sighed.

"I don't know," she said. "I wouldn't know how to recognize it, if it was happening."

"Does it feel unnatural?" Melody asked. "Or simply like things have conspired in a way that men are struggling to feel optimism?"

Stasia listened to Matthias' words in her head again, the families struggling, the children living outside to avoid having to go home again.

"I can't know," Stasia said. "It's bad, where we are right now, but... would it be this bad all by itself? I don't understand why it's so bad. We won. We should be celebrating. I get that everyone is upset and disappointed that Constance is gone..." She hesitated, wondering if that was insulting to Melody.

"Me above all else," Melody said. "Of course."

"Of course," Stasia said. "So... sad I might understand, but it's more than sad. Everybody kept telling me all summer how tough Veridans were. How, if the stone elves came into the city, the citizens would take up arms and drive them back. And then I come home to a city that's slowly tearing itself apart, and it's not even getting any better, even after the worst threats are gone."

"Certainly not the most auspicious beginning to a reign," Melody said. "Finwalk is organizing his advisors and his court, but I had expected to see an improvement in his effectiveness, before now. He has a sense that someone specific is working against him, keeping him from making progress on his chosen initiatives, but my instinct matches your own. It is the city itself working against him."

"It could be magic," Stasia said.

"Or it could not," Melody answered. "And if you had been any more certain about your opinion, I would have completely discounted it. If this is magic, it is well done. Again. It is thoughtful with an eye to the long-term, and it is completely invisible to me."

"Should I talk to Skite about it, again?" Stasia asked.

"No," Melody said. "But I have heard interesting reports out of the Black Docks. I would like you to put your own eyes on them and bring your observations back to me."

"The Black Docks?" Stasia asked.

"Yes," Melody answered evenly.

"Why not just ask Ella?" Stasia asked.

"Because you often can't see what lives around you for what it is," Melody said. "You spend very little time there, so I would like you to see what you notice that she might not."

"Yes, mum," Stasia said, nodding to her.

Melody finished emptying the bag - it had been packed completely full of many small things, it turned out, and she sat back on the couch, frowning at the collection.

"Your majesty," Stasia said slowly. Melody didn't look at her, but Stasia hadn't really expected her to. "If you... Everyone just wants to help, if they can."

"Miss Fielding," Melody said, her voice deep. "Certainly you can do better than that. Express yourself or do not speak. Vagaries do you no justice."

Stasia blinked.

"Okay," she said. "If you're still fighting an injury and no one knows what to do about it, you should tell us, because we have access to skills and knowledge that you don't."

Melody smiled, still not looking at her.

"There, now. Don't you feel better?"

She did.

But that wasn't the point.

"I'm serious," Stasia said. "And so are the guard. You know that you can trust us, and while I understand it's poor form to ask after the queen's health because it means... well, okay, I don't get it, but I do understand that it's true, anyway. But I want to be able to ask because it matters and because maybe we can help."

Melody looked at her evenly.

"You cannot."

"You don't know that."

"I do."

"How?"

"Because you have no magic, and neither does anyone you associate with. And the issues with which I struggle are magic in nature, which means that you have no means to address them. They would just cause you to question my soundness, in the same way that the city questions. Some days I wonder if they are not... a reflection of my own self, feeling unsound because I am unsound."

"But... are you?" Stasia asked.

"I carry on," Melody said. "It is my duty, and the city relies on me for exactly that. But I will not mislead you, since you show such courage in asking, and tell you that I am whole and well. It would not be true."

"We want to help," Stasia said.

"And that is a very positive and willing sentiment to hold," Melody said. "Unfortunately, it is also worthless. What I need is for you to spend a day at the Black Docks, observing, and to come back and tell me whether there is anything there that stands out to you. I need you to come next week and take a message to Lady Bentmoor. And I need you to find a life that you find satisfying and enjoyable.

Because that's what I need most from everyone. The city cannot return to its normal prosperity and happiness unless the individuals do. And I disrupted that, sending you as I did this summer, but I think that you would be at a time of transition, regardless. You must find a place for yourself, and then I will use that place. Do not permit the responsibilities I lay upon you to prevent you from flourishing in your own place, or I will have deprived myself of the most important of my resources: effective, connected friends."

Stasia nodded slowly.

"If there is a way to take load off of you..." she said, still wanting to argue her way into helping somehow. Melody laughed.

"No," she said. "The queen stands alone. Such has it always been and such may it ever be. No one, not you, not Finwalk, not my husband nor my daughters, no one can take that away from me, and I would not permit it, even if I were able. Verida needs a queen who stands up under her duty to her final breath, and I will not abandon that responsibility."

Stasia frowned, then nodded.

"Yes, mum."

"Very well," Melody said. "You have done everything I have asked of you today. You may go. I hope you have a very memorable evening with Lady Westhauser this evening."

Stasia rose, looking at the magic ingredients on the table, wondering that you might just... mix those together and get some kind of result that was nothing resembling the input properties of the parts. Magic.

There was magic in Verida.

"Is there anything you need from me, with those?" Stasia asked, and Melody shook her head.

"No. You may go. Please ensure that you are not observed, as always."

Stasia nodded and set off again.

To the guard house.

Hopefully to find all of the men still alive and one more warlock dead.

She could hope.

She sat up in the mess hall at the guard house for an hour before Colin showed up.

"Stacy," he crowed, waving as he went to get himself food and came to sit across from her. "What a great surprise."

"I assume that, since you're eating, everyone is okay," Stasia said.

"Oh, yeah," Colin said. "He put up a decent fight, then he ran. Everyone's feeling really down and defeated because we got that close and then he got away."

"Except you," Stasia said. "Because you're eating."

"You don't know that I'm not devastated," Colin said cheerfully, shoving a fork full of stewed vegetables in his mouth. "I just don't wear my emotions on my sleeve, like the rest of them."

Stasia laughed, then sighed.

"He got away."

"Jasper tagged him a good one, and Sterling just about ended him, but they're really hard to kill," Colin said. "I mean, I swear, this one has regrown limbs at this point."

Stasia nodded.

She didn't know if it was true or not, but it had the feel of truth to it.

"You're getting better at the truth and purity thing, aren't you?" she asked, and he took a half-glance behind him, then nodded.

"Turns out you can say a lot of true things sarcastically, and sound just the way I always have," he said with a grin. "Sarcasm makes the truth hurt less."

"If they believe you at all," Stasia said, and he shrugged.

"The guys do," he said. "And apparently you do, too."

She chewed her lip.

"It took weeks to find him," she said. "What are they even doing?"

"What we haven't found is more than one in a place," he said. "We don't know that they're even coordinating, anymore. They're still working magic, that's for sure from the amount of stuff they've got every time we track them down, but there's no sign that more than one of them is involved in anything they're up to."

"How are we supposed to stop them if we don't have the first clue what they're doing?" Stasia asked. Colin laughed again, shoveling more food into his mouth, then sitting up and weaving his fingers behind his head.

"You think it isn't always like this?" he asked. "Every guy who ever went against the king, he's got an idea what he wants to do, and we haven't got the first clue what that is until he shows up and actually does it."

"I talked to Melody about maybe them casting on the city," Stasia said. "I don't even know if it's possible, but..."

Colin shook his head, looking around the room for a moment, just up at the rafters and the walls, not looking any of the men just now.

"You're looking at it all wrong, Stacy," he said. "It isn't that they are doing this thing or that thing and that people are suffering and... whatever. We're going to win. It's just a matter of time and effort. In the meantime, we've got food and a roof over our heads and... I'm wearing the king's leathers. Gonna get married the week after the Water Lily Festival. Prove to me that anything is wrong. Because it isn't. This is just... normal. And everything is fine. You see it?"

"Is that really how you look at the world?" Stasia asked.

He looked up at the ceiling.

"I haven't spent much of my life thinking about how I look at the world," he said. "I just... do what I like doing and don't do what I don't like doing, and sometimes somebody says, 'hey, do you want to do this thing' and I jump and I'm lucky and I end up in a place like this one, where I'm good at what I do and I'm with people I like, and a pretty girl thinks that I'm a guy worth spending the rest of her life counting on, and... Bad stuff goes on, around on the edges, because that's what life is, but here in the middle of it? Why spend all of your time looking at it, even? You fight the stuff that's in your way and you enjoy the fact that life is good. And it is. Life is good."

She nodded, lifting her eyes as Matthias and Jasper came in.

"Should have known you'd come straight for food," Jasper said, coming to sit down at the end of the table and glancing at Stasia. "He gave you the update."

"He did. I'm sorry."

"Every time we get in his way, he has to be more careful next time," Jasper said. "We're slowing them down, even if we aren't stopping them, yet."

"Where are Sterling and Babe?" Stasia asked.

"Hitting each other," Matthias said, leaning against the wall with his arms crossed and watching the room.

He looked like Jasper, like that.

And then what he'd said registered, and Stasia bolted out of her chair, heading for the door.

She heard Colin laugh, behind her.

She made it to the rail, where half a dozen other young men were standing, watching, and she leaned over it, looking down at Babe and Sterling circling each other.

She'd watched the two of them fight, before, but she

hadn't seen it since they'd come back from the mountains, since Sterling had gotten fast and Babe had... become even more like himself.

Sterling was working a fast-footed circle around Babe, who simply stood, watching with his eyes half-closed, shuffling his feet now and again when Sterling got too far to one side or the other.

Sterling came at Babe with a flurry of attacks, Babe blocking almost all of them with a sense of inevitability. He was so slow compared to Sterling, but Sterling looked like a bird attacking a housing timber. Stasia realized with a start that the blows that Babe didn't block with a sword, he was actually blocking with his own body. It wasn't that he was too slow to get a sword in the way; it was that he chose to use his arm or his back to stop the strike.

The men yelled down encouragement or good-natured abuse, and Sterling worked faster and faster, scoring more hits against leather and fewer against metal, but Babe still looked entirely in control of the entire event.

Powerful.

He was so powerful.

Finally, Sterling stepped back, signaling the end of the exchange, and Babe lifted his face to find Stasia. He waved her down and she came down the stairs.

"You feel better?" she asked Sterling, and he wiped sweat off of his forehead with an easy grin.

"I do," he said. "Makes you remember what you're good at."

"You're the best," Stasia said, and he shook his head with a wider grin.

"No. But I hang out with them," he said.

"Sterling," Stasia said, lowering her voice. "You are the best. You know that, right?"

He frowned, looking over at Babe.

"I can't beat him," he said. "Not anymore. I could,

once in a while, before, but not anymore."

"But he can't beat you," Stasia said.

"He doesn't have to," Sterling said, stepping closer to her so that he was certain no one else could hear. "That's the genius of it. He never has to win. He just doesn't lose."

Stasia looked up at him, and he nodded.

"Not that I don't appreciate the vote of confidence," he said with a wink. "I'm going to go wash up. That was exactly what I needed today."

She nodded and let him past, turning her attention to Babe again.

"You keeping up your practice?" he asked, unbothered that she'd been telling secrets with Sterling.

"Not like you have," Stasia answered, drawing her sword and a dagger. "You have to go easy on me. I'm in a dress, today."

"Don't have to do nothin' of the sort," he said with a grin. "You gonna wear those kinds of things, you gotta be ready to take care of yourself. 'Specially since you can't scale a building like that, to get away, now can you?"

She shrugged, pulling out a cloth from her pocket to tie her hair up higher on top of her head, swishing it back and forth to make sure it was going to stay, then picking up her sword again from where she'd propped it against her hip and turning her full attention to him.

He nodded.

"Show me what you've got," he said.

She nodded, attacking him.

It didn't feel like she had to prove anything, anymore. She'd survived all of the stuff up in the mountains, she'd survived warlocks. She wasn't trying to show everyone that she wasn't a soft, unpredictable spare daughter. She wasn't just here on a whim. So she could focus on working on her steps and her motions with the pair of blades, Babe letting her work stuff out as she did it, punishing her from time to time where she made a mistake that she hadn't seen, but otherwise just kind of working with her on sorting out her balance and her strengths and her weaknesses.

She needed to spend some time out climbing; her arms weren't as reliable as she liked them to be, because she'd spent so much of the last weeks doing the queen's bidding. It was something she needed to do two or three nights a week, if she was going to stay in top shape, and sword-fighting helped highlight where she was losing it, but it wasn't the same strengthening activity that actually climbing was.

They might have worked for half an hour, or perhaps a bit longer, when Babe put his arms out and took a step back, looking over at something Stasia had missed.

She knew that she needed to eventually pull her awareness back and be able to see everything going on around her when she was fighting, but right now she needed all of her focus on her opponent, and it hardly surprised her that she'd missed that Matthias had come down and was waiting at the bottom of the stairs.

Oh.

She was out of breath and tired, but she was still sharp with her motions. She wouldn't be for much longer, but she was still sharp now.

And that was why Babe had quit when he had.

That was why Matthias was here.

"Only if you want," Matthias said, drawing a pair of shorter swords and holding them out to the front and down, crossed just above his feet.

She nodded, wiping her face and taking a big step back to catch her breath.

"Water?" Babe asked, and she nodded.

Sterling tossed a leather bag down and Babe came over to stand next to Stasia, offering it to her.

She put away her blocking dagger and took the

water, drinking it slowly in big gulps until she knew that she shouldn't take anymore.

"Quit before you get sloppy," Babe said. "He's better than he was when you fought him that night by the fort. A lot better. But you still shouldn't go so far that you're making mistakes."

Stasia nodded, handing the water back over and taking out her dagger again.

"Did he fight with two swords before?" Stasia asked, and Babe shook his head.

"Picked it up from Colin," Babe said. "Suits him. Give him a few minutes to show you how he works before you go hard."

Stasia nodded, stepping up to engage Matthias. He put the two swords out and they circled, working at their feet and watching each other.

He did feel more confident, easier.

It was comfortable, being there, rather than the way it had been before, where she'd been nervous and he'd felt pushed into something that he wasn't sure if he could do it.

He was still growing. It shocked her, seeing how much he was still growing. He was taller than Sterling and gaining more on him. Probably most of an inch since they'd gotten back to the city.

He had to stop sometime.

It was just going to be... shocking when he finally did figure out how big he was going to be.

Regardless of how fast he was getting taller, his arms moved like he actually knew how long they were, which was new, too.

She touched blade to blade, feeling out his balance through the connection. He didn't push back against her hard, but it was enough to feel all the way to his feet.

Remarkable, that connection of metal to metal. Like a conversation in an entirely new language.

She'd never noticed it, before, but with a sword and a sense of pause, of being able to take her time, she was discovering all kinds of things that were... really satisfying.

He attacked, just going through mechanical motions that were familiar to both of them, but it inspired further confidence, and Stasia went after him energetically for a quick exchange.

Two swords was a different problem.

He had reach on her with both arms, which was something she had to be careful of - particularly with nothing but some pretty durable material for defense - but it also made him slow with both hands. If she could get inside of him, he had nothing that would move fast or intercept.

It was costly, carrying two swords, and it made it so that he had to win quickly. In a longer, technical fight, he was probably at a disadvantage.

She knew that Colin carried two swords and two daggers, and she had actually seen him fight with a sword in his left and a dagger in his right, to put his opponent off balance, but she had always thought that it was just Colin showing off. Or seeing if he could win a bet with a beltmaker somewhere. One of those.

But to see Matthias make it work, using the length of his own limbs combined with the two swords... She could see how this would be the right decision.

He held the pair out to either side, breathing slow and evenly, watching her.

And then she wondered just how much of what she was thinking she was telegraphing to him.

He was reading her.

He met her eye and nodded.

Yes. He'd seen her realize it, and he wasn't hiding it from her.

Stasia frowned, trying to figure out if she wanted to adapt to that or just keep working at the mechanical nature of what she was doing.

She found herself off-balance and self-aware again, and the look on his face was nothing short of pity as she tried to work it out.

"Just..." he said. "Just go with it. You can worry about it later."

She nodded, going through four more intense exchanges and then backing up, calling it. Someone else shouted that they were up next, and Matthias turned his attention to the next man as Stasia went and leaned heavily against a post next to Babe. He offered her the rest of the water and she took it, letting her head hang for a moment as she breathed, and then drinking more of the water.

"You do your squad proud," Babe said evenly.

"I'm an embarrassment to everyone here," she said. "I'm just better than just about anyone out there."

He grinned.

"But we all know the kind of work it takes to get to here," he said. "What happened with the two of you, there at the end?"

She closed her eyes, thinking about leaning against him and rejecting it. She didn't want Babe to get a reputation for coddling her or treating her special until the idea that they were together got to be more normal.

"He can read everything I'm about to do," she said. "I didn't realize that, before."

Babe laughed quietly.

"We all can, darlin'," he said, and she shook her head.

"No, not like this. I don't think. Maybe. I don't know. I think it's different."

Babe looked over at her and she handed the empty water skin back, tipping her head back against the post and looking up at the gray sky.

"He's reading it off my face," she said. "Watching me think about stuff."

"Mmm," Babe said. "I know what you're talking about. Had that sense myself, a few times. Didn't... put my finger on it like that. He's discovering who he is, as a guard and as a man, and he's realizing..." Babe paused, then nodded. "It would be easy to blame all of it on what happened with us, say that everything that's changing is on account of that stuff, but it ain't. That stuff... it was fitted for us. This is who he's always been. He's just workin' it out."

"I can't beat him," Stasia said, and Babe laughed.

"You're not meant to. You're meant to challenge him, and to work up your own skill where you'd beat anybody who ain't so good as he is. Which is, as you say it, most of 'em."

"Are you staying close because you're trying to keep me safe?" Stasia asked.

"You don't like me bein' around?" Babe asked.

"Answer the question," Stasia said.

He sighed, looking around.

"You've got dinner plans tonight," he said, and she nodded.

"With Lady Westhauser."

"Can you get a drink, before?" he asked, and she nodded easily.

She wouldn't mind sitting. No. Not at all.

"Geez, I'm tired," she muttered, looking over at Matthias again as he dispatched the first challenger and went on to the next one. "He was being nice to me."

"He cares more about you gettin' stronger than he does them," Babe said. "Ain't nice. It's bein' part of the same team."

She nodded and Babe went to the pole that crossed the entry gate to the guard house, lifting it for her and letting her out past him.

They walked in silence for a time, just watching the things they were passing.

Stasia missed Schotzli. The city looked different from horseback, but she had no place to keep the mare, so it took her a special trip down to the Sapphire to retrieve her from her father's house.

"Never have liked you puttin' yourself in danger," Babe said after a time. "Gettin' used to the idea of it, but never did like it. Runnin' around the city, takin' rooms, lookin' after strays as you needed to, that was one thing. Goin' out with Jasper to have your back is another. Even knowin' that your pa and the guards at his house would be there if you needed 'em... You bein' all on your own like you are now makes me unsettled in a way much foreign to me, and I'm still workin' out what it means."

"Many women live on their own in Verida," Stasia said. "And most of them don't carry a sword."

He grinned and nodded.

"Now that's true enough. I'll give you that. But they also..." He swallowed. "Don't want you to hear it that I don't believe in you, or that I've got some idea of how things should be..."

"Is it different because we're... officially together now?" Stasia asked, and he nodded.

"Before, was just a friend, a dear friend, out on her own," Babe said. "Now it's my girl, and I got a need to know that I'm doin' what I can to keep you safe."

"I don't need it," Stasia said, knowing even as she said it that it was disingenuous. Skite had killed a man to save her, not that many weeks before, and that only because Babe hadn't been there first to do it.

"Maybe it'll change, once we've got rid of all the warlocks," Babe said. "Maybe it won't change 'till I see that... see what things are gonna look like, with us. That you really do see to yourself like you always done and..." He looked over at her, some mix of confusion and guilt. "I don't mean to talk you down to less than you are."

"I worry about you more, now," she said. Shrugged. "I don't mind that you feel protective, but you've got to be able to do your job, and I need to be able to do my stuff, and... right now I'm really not getting to any of it, because I'm so busy, and..."

"Do you not think of the warlocks at all?" he asked.

"Try not to," she said. "What can I do about it?"

He nodded.

"That's what bothers me most," he said. "Anybody else, you'd stick 'em and they'd run off yelping, but the warlocks, if one of them comes for you, it's gonna be because you're valuable to 'em and they got a specific use in mind. And... It's takin' us this long to find 'em, when they aren't actively avoidin' us. What's it gonna be like when they know we're tearin' apart the city, lookin' for you?"

"I'm going to be hard to hold on to," Stasia said. "I can climb and I can run and I can hide... I'm not going to just let it be easy. I know that last time I needed saving, but..."

He grinned.

"Can't imagine trying to hold you when you ain't of a mind to let it happen," he said. "Honest truth. It's just... Neither one of us know what we're doin' here. Keep sayin' it and keep meanin' it, and if I'm botherin' you, you ought say it and we'll talk it out. I don't want to crowd you. Just don't like you bein' alone like you are."

She wasn't going to try to convince him that the first few nights after he'd stopped sleeping on the floor in her room hadn't been hard. She'd slept in thick socks for a week, and kept checking the window last thing before she lay down to make sure that it was good and out of the way, if she needed to go through it.

She'd slept with the lamp burning the first two nights, even knowing that that was one of the stupid things that burned down buildings.

Babe turned aside, going down a narrow alley and

opening a small door that he had to turn sideways to fit through after her. They went up a small set of stairs and through a shredded curtain into a dim bar that overlooked the street. It appeared that they just pulled heavy canvas across the space that would have been the street facing wall of the room to keep the rain from coming in. There were no doors or windows on that wall, just an open space covered with curtaining.

At night, it might be pleasant, but during the day it was sweltering. They went through the curtains and sat out on the roof of the floor below, leaning against a wrought-iron rail and watching the day wrap up below.

"I want you to be happy," he said as they sat.

"I don't think that's your problem," Stasia answered. "I'm working on that for my own self."

He narrowed his eyes and she shrugged.

"Look, I look at it from how my father would have thought about my mother, and I have no doubt he would have put her happiness first all the time. So I see that. But at the same time, I'm a spinstress. A disinherited one, no less. I'm on my own and... I don't want you to act like it's your problem, whether I'm happy or not. I just want to enjoy being around you. I want us to have fun. And then there's the whole staying-alive part, and we've got to work that out separately, but I swear, it can't be that hard, in the long term, right? Most people generally survive?"

"Point of fact, nobody does," Babe answered with a half a smile. "And the guard especially are prone to just not turnin' up one day."

She shuddered.

"Don't say that," she said. He shook his head.

"If they ain't got rid of me, passin' a sword clean through my chest, it ain't like to happen on just any ordinary Tuesday, either. I'm sound. I just can't let it go past, thinkin' that what I do for a livin' has got no risk to it. It does."

She nodded and looked over at the silhouette of the castle. At this distance, the humidity made it kind of blurry, an idea rather than a building.

"I'm sitting down and having secret conferences with the queen," Stasia said. "I never expected that. I never expected any of this."

He grinned.

"Would expect to hear that you're thrilled to be doin' the unexpected, like that," he said, and she nodded.

"Oh, I am," she said. "And I'm doing it on my own for the first time."

Was that it? She frowned, looking at the table as he ordered two beers from the server.

"I just got myself disowned by my father," she said. "Disinherited completely. Is it that I don't like you stepping in and now I have to report to you on what I'm doing, instead?"

"You don't owe me anything," he said. "I don't want to put a leash on you, and if you'll excuse me sayin' it, neither did your pa."

"No, he didn't mean it," Stasia agreed. "But I still couldn't do anything without everyone assuming that he was... accountable for it, you know?" she asked. "I spoke to the queen and apparently everyone started telling him about it. Even now, Melody wants me on her side because I represent one of the richest merchants in the city, but I don't. And... I'm not saying you're trying to control me. You're not. He wasn't. He was, is, the best father anywhere. And you're..." His eyes came around to meet hers, and her voice caught. He was right there, across the table from her, just the two of them, and... "You're unbelievable. I still... keep expecting everything to just go back the way it was, because this isn't even supposed to be possible. I like that you're around all the time and that... we seem to belong together..." She laughed. "Jasper said he knew it before we did."

"Reckon he probably did," Babe said. "Wish I could say what it was he saw, but..." He shrugged. Stasia nodded.

"I just never believed that anything like this could ever happen. If I was going to marry, it would be for strategic reasons, and..." She shook her head. "You're incredible to me. But... I need to figure out what part of all of this is my life, and that doesn't mean I want you out of it. I just... I need some time to figure out what it means for me to be on my own like I am and for me to... support myself and... everything."

Babe frowned.

"You ain't going short, are you?" he asked. "For money?"

She laughed.

"No. No, that's actually not even what I'm thinking about. The queen pays me and I've got a lot of other stuff going on, and..." She looked out at the castle again. "It's all new. Do you see it? I came to Verida not that much more than a year ago, not more than a year and a half, at least, and everything is new. Even the queen is new. And I can do anything and I can be anything, and I can be with someone... someone that I chose..." She looked at him, then grinned helplessly. She really was giddy with all of the possibilities. Yeah, the city was in a bad way, but... "I have a place here. And I'm going to find it. All of the pieces of it. And I need you to be..." His eyebrows went up. "I have no idea. I have no idea what I need from you, because I've never had anyone like you before in my life. Maybe we're doing it exactly right and I just don't even know, yet. You know?"

He smiled, looking at his hands, then taking the two glasses from the server and giving one of them to Stasia.

"Don't let me off the hook too easy," he said. "You're more right than you're wrong. I'm treatin' you like a charge, and that's not how it ought to be. Not forever. With the warlocks out there, I can't tell you I'm gonna change, but when this part is done, you hold me to it. You're a full-grown woman on your own in a city that's gonna eat out of the palm of your hand, when you're done with it, and don't you go lettin' me get in the way of that."

She nodded.

"Deal."

"Deal," he agreed.

"So that it doesn't surprise you when it happens, Melody asked me to go to the Black Docks," Stasia said. He stiffened, but didn't object. "I'm going to go and I'm just going to... hang around and see what I see. But I need you to let me go without you, because they react to you, and that's the opposite of what I'm looking for. And you get so angry, being there. I need to just... go see. It's not as dangerous as it was. I think... you know that? Don't you? It's okay for me to be there. I can take care of myself, with those guys, and with the rules that..."

"That the Rat King has made," Babe said. She nodded.

"With Skite's rules, I'm actually safer there than basically anywhere in Highrock," she said.

"Just don't go trustin' his word so far you get in over your head," he said. "It's nice for them to all say you're allowed to be there, right up until somethin' goes wrong and they just dump you in the river to get rid of the evidence. Nobody knows what goes on there, really, no convincin' me otherwise. Skite don't have eyes everywhere, and there's plenty of fellas willin' to do whatever it takes to stay in the shadows."

Stasia nodded.

"I said it's safer than Highrock," she said. "Not the market. I know that. There are men with knives in every corner of this city, and if I let myself get off alone, one of them may make a decision that that's their opportunity. And I will stick him through the ribs and he can run off, yelping.

I promise."

Babe laughed, then settled in his chair.

"We're gonna get this figured out so it works," he said. "And I know you're not helpless. It's just... that's what I'm built for. What I'm good at. Makin' sure you're okay. Makin' sure anybody's okay, but, you specific. Don't really know what to do with myself, these days, unless I'm on duty or with you."

"You let Sterling hit you a lot, apparently," Stasia said, and he grinned at this, drinking his beer.

"I'll admit, that's a fun new trick for how well it works," he said. "Still thinkin' on whether I'm gutsy enough to use it in a real fight, but don't see any reason it wouldn't go, just the same."

"Sterling is..." Stasia shook her head. "I don't know if I'm ever not going to be impressed at what he can do."

"You seen Jasper fight, since?" Babe asked and she looked into her beer, remembering.

"Just once," she said. "Right after. And it was... scary."

Babe nodded.

"I'll see your scary, for sure," he said. "Don't really recognize us, if I'm honest. It's strange, lookin' at four fellas I've known for years and seein' 'em... all new like that."

"Do you feel different?" Stasia asked. He grunted, clearing his throat and taking a drink, then shaking his head.

"I don't," he said. "Know I'm capable of more'n I'm used to, but I don't feel it. Not the way I think they do, either."

"I think Matthias is suffering," Stasia said, and he laughed.

"Matthias?" he asked. "Colin is dying."

"Colin has worked it out, here lately," Stasia said. "You've noticed, surely."

He nodded easily, then looked over at the castle.

"You may be right, about Matthias, though. He doesn't know what's him and what's it and what's just... fantasy, I reckon. When everything changes so fast, and you never have known whether you could trust your own eyes..."

Stasia nodded.

"It's... it's just all new. It's all of it new."

He nodded.

"It is. Scary, I guess. Never not gonna be scary, having everything change under you like that."

Stasia grinned.

Set her beer down on the table and crossed her arms, waiting for Babe to meet her eye.

It was the same feeling. He was there and it was incredible and unbelievable and he smiled like he couldn't help it.

"I'm not scared," she said. "I've never been more excited."

She got to Felligan's a bit late, finding Ella in a corner table with a pair of drinks already ordered.

Stasia waved and went over to sit across from her.

"Melody keeping you busy?" Ella asked quietly with an easy smile.

"Actually," Stasia said slowly. Once it was done, she may as well just do it. "I was out with Babe. We're... seeing each other... now. Officially."

Ella grinned and leaned across the table toward her.

"Remind me which one that is?" she said.

Stasia felt her face freeze, and Ella laughed.

"I'm kidding," she said. "Obviously I remember the man you kept disappearing with every afternoon while you were at the manor. I'm just maybe a little insulted that you thought you were keeping it a secret, all that time."

Stasia blinked.

"Did anybody not know?" she asked, and Ella tipped her head back and laughed.

"Skite did," she said, giggling behind her fingers. "He asked me once if you were ever going to tell me so that he could stop pretending not to know."

Stasia blushed, turning her face aside and Ella laughed again.

"We're happy for you, Anastasia. So happy. He's a good man. Strong. You deserve this."

Stasia put her fingers to her cheeks, feeling the heat there and Ella giggled again, then nudged her drink across.

"Drink. And tell me everything."

Stasia nodded, taking big drinks of her beer and raising her hand to order baskets of bar food to go with it. It was the kind of place where you yelled orders and you got what you got, and if you had a reputation for paying for it, you got your food faster. Both Ella and Stasia were known for paying for their meals - regardless of what showed up - and they soon had four baskets of fried munchables while Stasia found that the details just poured out of her with a truly astonishing rate. Things she didn't even remember seeing or thinking came back to her while Ella sat with her chin resting on the brim of her glass, enraptured.

How could she possibly care this much?

"And so we got drinks tonight and we talked, and I don't think anything is going to change, but... It just feels like it's so right, and it's working and..." Stasia shrugged, and Ella grinned.

"I'm glad he was the one who showed up that night, when Skite went to go get you," she said. "I know that it must have killed him, letting Skite go find you when you were missing, but... honestly, he was never going to find you, if it took Sly tracking you down, instead, for Skite."

"Babe wouldn't have given up," Stasia said. "But Sly

tracked me across a roof, so... Babe probably wouldn't have been able to do that."

Ella nodded, frowning.

"I don't like thinking about how... close that was."

"We got attacked at the manor house with an army of stone elves outside," Stasia said. "I don't have a corner on close scrapes, even hardly."

Ella twisted her mouth and nodded.

"It's easier when I'm there," she said. "Because I'm pretty certain nothing bad is going to happen to me."

"I know," Stasia said. "I feel the same way."

Ella grinned.

"So," Stasia said, munching happily. "You're not going home tonight, right?"

"I'm not going to the estate," Ella agreed.

"You're going back to the docks tonight?" Stasia asked.

"Yeah."

"Can I come with you?" Stasia asked. Ella grinned.

"Back to Skite's apartment? Well, I mean, we're frisky, but I'm not sure we're really that kind of friends..."

"Ella," Stasia said, shocked, and Ella giggled.

"I have no idea what you're asking me," she said.

"Melody asked me to go down to the Black Docks and just... see stuff. I was wondering if you could maybe show me around a little bit and let me wander, where I knew where I could go if something went bad..."

"Of course," Ella said. "I'd love that. It's growing on me, that place is, and if you're going to be there, I'd rather know it and be at Buddy's where you can come find me when you get bored."

"I'll take a cart home," Stasia said. "But it would be nice to have someone to walk down with."

Ella shook her head.

"No. The Westhauser carriage is down there. I'll

send notice to the carriage driver, and he'll be waiting for you to take you home. The carts don't run that late, and they mostly don't go to the Black Docks, yet. They have long memories of... the bad times."

"Were there any times but bad times, before recently?" Stasia asked, and Ella shook her head grimly.

"No. Skite has really changed everything for them, without a doubt. Do you know what Melody wants you to see? Because... it's not that big a place, but it's still a big place. Was she any more specific than just that?"

"Nope," Stasia fibbed. "I'm just supposed to go see. And I want to. I've wandered all over the city on my own, but Babe was such a... he has such a thing about the Black Docks, I wasn't supposed to go there by myself, and so I haven't been hardly at all. But everyone talks about them and how they've changed, and I want to go see it for myself."

"You've done the whole city?" Ella asked, smiling, and Stasia shrugged.

"Almost. I mean. Obviously I haven't done every street in Highrock, because that would be suicide, and there are too many of them. And Jasper, I think it was, warned me not to go to Cazia, so I haven't..."

"You haven't done Cazia yet?" Ella asked, and Stasia shook her head.

"I honestly don't know what to expect of an artists' colony that the king's guard are afraid of," Stasia said, and Ella beamed.

"I wasn't allowed to go, either, but I think it's because of the naked people."

"N..." Stasia started, then shut her mouth and frowned. "Really?"

Ella nodded.

"Oh, yeah. There are no rules in Cazia. The Cazians are crazy. They do whatever they want. We have to go. The two of us. Okay? Or are you still... ack, no, naked man, my eyes, my eyes?"

Stasia didn't know whether to burst out laughing or blush or something else.

"There are really naked men wandering around there?" she whispered.

Ella shrugged.

"Only one way to find out," she said.

Stasia bit both her lips and nodded quickly.

"I'm in. Sometime when stuff isn't so..."

"Like it is," Ella agreed. "Yeah."

"Yeah."

They ate the rest of their food, chatting about the castle and the markets and the estate, Babe coming up now and again as Ella did it on purpose just to see if she could make Stasia blush again, then they paid for their food and left, walking upriver to the main body of the Wolfram and crossing it north of the guard house. They went through the mostly-dark craftsmen's neighborhood, a few smiths and other workers still finishing orders, voices around them cheerful but quiet as they walked. The sun was down, by now, and the stars peeked through streaky cloud cover here and there.

"So do you know Sly?" Stasia asked as they walked.

"Yeah," Ella said slowly. "I know him pretty well."

"But he's not one of the men at the bar," Stasia said. "He asked when Skite was going to recruit me."

Ella laughed.

"He would. He's part of Skite's crew."

"He said that, but I don't know what it means," Stasia said.

"Oh," Ella said. "Oh, I guess I can see how you wouldn't. So... a crew is a group of thieves... or other criminals, I guess, but usually thieves who work together on bigger projects."

"He's a thief?" Stasia asked. She had a hard time

imagining that. He was so happy.

"Best in the city," Ella said. "The way Skite talks about him, he might be the best in the world."

"I liked him," Stasia said. "Wait, why would Skite recruit me?"

Ella grinned.

"Is that really so hard to imagine?" she asked.

"Um. Yes," Stasia said. "Why would I work with a crew to steal stuff?"

"Because it's hard to do and everybody likes a challenge," Ella said.

"No, seriously, wait, Skite steals stuff."

"Yup. I mean, he wouldn't admit to it in front of your guard friends, but... I mean, come on. We know this."

"Why?"

"Because... it's hard to do and... it's a challenge," Ella said, pointing as though her words were hanging in the air still.

"What does he do with the money?" Stasia asked.

"Divides it in equal parts. The Rats get one share, everybody else gets one."

"Do you do it?" Stasia asked. Ella grinned.

"You really want to know the answer to that?" she asked.

"You do," Stasia said, alarmed. "You do it, too."

Ella shrugged.

"Just this one time. No big deal, okay? I'm not very important."

Stasia boggled at her.

"But what would I do?"

"You can use a sword and climb a building," Ella said. "Do I really have to write instructions for you?"

"Skite isn't... he isn't, is he?" Stasia asked. Ella shook her head.

"No. He's not going to try to recruit you. And if you

told him you wanted to do it, he'd say no, anyway. You're in too tight with the guard, and... really, you'd be redundant with the other people in the group, anyway."

"There was a woman," Stasia said slowly. That day had been a bit crazy, words had been thrown about, and Stasia suddenly remembered the striking blond woman who had taken her to Sly in the first place.

"You met Brandyrose?" Ella asked, and Stasia nodded slowly.

"That sounds like the right name. She said some stuff and... I was really focused on something else. How am I just remembering her now?"

"Couldn't tell you," Ella said. "She made a pretty real impression on me."

"What does she do?" Stasia asked.

"She's the hawk," Ella said. "She watches everything from above."

"Above like..."

"Like up on top of a building, yeah," Ella said.

"I could do that," Stasia said.

Ella grinned.

"Do you want to? I told you, you're redundant."

"What do you do?" Stasia asked.

Ella scratched the back of her head.

"Do you really want to know that?" she asked. "I thought that you didn't like knowing stuff that you couldn't tell Jasper and Babe and them."

Stasia considered that as they went along for another few minutes.

She didn't like having secrets, it was true. Not ones from Babe. Though she did have them. A bunch, from the trip up into the mountains. And some other ones that were Jasper's and... like that. The idea of keeping Ella's and Skite's secrets from him, too...

"Don't tell me," Stasia finally said, and Ella nodded.

"Good choice," she said. "Keeping secrets is hard enough when you don't really have a relationship with someone. I wouldn't ever want to have to keep more secrets from Skite than I have to."

"You keep secrets from him?" Stasia asked.

"Stuff that's the queen's personal information," Ella said, nodding. "And a few other things like that. But not very much. We talk about everything."

"I know," Stasia said. "And I love that about you guys. I love how you know each other like you do. I wouldn't like him anywhere near as much as I do, if you two weren't... like you are."

Ella nodded.

"He's an honest thief," she said, grinning. "And I love him so much."

"I know," Stasia said. Ella nudged her with her elbow.

"But now it's not just me," she said. "Now it's you, too."

Stasia nodded, nervous.

"I know. And it's so exciting, but at the same time... what if it doesn't work? What if we aren't like you two? What if..."

Stasia made a vague motion with her hands, futility, and Ella shrugged.

"Could do what we did," she said.

"What's that?" Stasia asked.

"Get married first thing, so that you don't really have any option but to make it work."

Stasia shuddered.

The fact of Ella's marriage still terrified her. Sure, if Stasia had married, it would have been to a boy she had barely even met, same as Ella, but Ella had gone into it marrying a rival gang leader, and a man with a reputation of cruelty and violence.

Stasia couldn't even imagine.

"You have to fight for it," Ella said. "If you want it, you have to fight for it. Because otherwise, something else will be more important, and it will get away."

Stasia looked over at her, wondering what stories she might have told, if she'd been willing to, but instead she pointed.

"Jet," she said.

The bridge over the north branch of the Green River, where it forked to form the land known as the Black Docks.

Jet.

"All right," Stasia said. "Let's go see what there is to see."

Ella nodded.

"Let's go give you your first actual tour of the Black Docks."

They wandered for a time, just going up and down rows of tenement houses. In most of the city, the tenements were a portion of the buildings, and the rest of them were workshops and stores, larger apartments and free-standing homes, with bigger spaces allocated for markets and plazas, playgrounds and things like schools and theaters and things that people would gather to use. Stasia had observed that Verida was actually a collection of large neighborhoods that functioned like self-sustained towns, with local political leadership and a self-contained economy, as well as a local culture that they used to recognize each other. Even the heavily commercial districts, like the craftsmen's district to the north and the artisan's quarter to the west of the castle, were stuffed with people who lived there and the things that supported their lives.

The Black Docks were different. The cramped, low-cost housing was everywhere, and while there were streets where the first floors were workshops and stores and restaurants and bars, the way Stasia would have expected, the upper floors just dominated the space, all of the people crammed in to as little space as possible. There were no open spaces bigger than the intersections of streets or places where there were still signs that a building had collapsed. The markets were on little blind alleys where the stall-owners could force a cart to fit in against a wall, and everything was, as named, black.

"It's so dire here," Stasia said. She'd had that feel of the place every time she had come here, but as they went up and down street after street of it, she lost hope that she would discover another side to it.

"I know," Ella said. "But it's so much better than it was. The crime here is actually really low, when you compare it to the other poor districts in the city, and more of the kids are getting real educations. They're able to get teachers who will come and live here, because if you're a teacher in the Black Docks, you're untouchable. I mean, it's scary. I know a woman who got hustled on a corner because one of the boys thought she was pretty and then got offended when she turned him down, and five men - grown men, Stasia - came and beat him against a wall until he couldn't walk. They were the dads from the woman's class. Everyone wants the teachers to feel like... they're valued here, even men who never learned to read or write at all... It's amazing how much they value it. Because there's never been anything here. They can see it. They can taste it. Their kids aren't going to live the same lives they have, and they're fighting for it. It's so inspiring, to me."

Stasia nodded, still feeling the oppressive color and weight of the place in a real way.

"So," Ella said a while later. "It's still not perfect. Up

there, at the corner, you see it? That's Buddy's. Skite will be there tonight. Are you sure you want to go out on your own?"

Stasia nodded.

She owed it to Melody.

She didn't even feel unsafe so much as unhappy. She didn't want to be alone in this place because the malaise of the air itself might swallow her up.

"Okay," Ella said. "Well, we won't go home until you come tell us that you're done and I put you in the carriage, okay? Just make sure you can find it again."

"That road goes straight down to the docks, doesn't it?" Stasia asked.

Ella narrowed her eyes and tipped her head back and forth for a moment.

"I mean, it does, but it also goes a lot of other places, if you don't follow the right part of it."

"I'll figure it out," Stasia said. "And if I get lost, I'll just ask, right?"

She attempted a grin and Ella gave her a quiet, quick smile.

"You're actually fine, asking for directions from all but really the worst boys. Anyone selling anything will give you good directions."

"Smart," Stasia said, and Ella nodded.

"All right. Well, be safe. You'll be fine. You will. You'll be fine. Everyone can see that you're armed, and it's not that dangerous here. Not anymore. It's just... Be careful."

Stasia nodded and Ella went into the bar after another moment.

And Stasia was on her own.

She didn't know what it was that she was supposed to see about the place that Ella might have missed, but she was going to give it a good try.

She put her hands into her pockets and started

toward the sea.

The Black Docks faced a shallow section of the Sorbine Sea. She didn't know for sure how far out the shelf went, but she knew that the water was scarcely more than waist deep for at least a hundred yards, depending on the tide, and that it didn't get a lot deeper very fast for along way out, yet. They fished and they brought in flat boats full of goods, and that was about all the docks here were used for. Though Stasia had heard that you didn't buy fish off a Black Docks boat. It was one of those merchant things to say that translated into a warning that you never knew what you were getting, but it was almost certainly not any good.

She found the water easily enough, following the slope and the sound, and she went to lean against a post overlooking the black moonless water and the sound of the water.

Someone came up to stand next to her, looking out over the water with her. Stasia was about to move away when he spoke.

"It's a good effort, but the dress is from the neighborhood south of the meat markets and the shoes are from Greater Highrock. And no one has got time for hair like that. Besides, you shouldn't be trying to camouflage yourself. You stand out, and that's to your credit."

Stasia turned her head to look up at Sly. He grinned without looking at her.

"Evening," he said.

"Are you following me?" Stasia asked, and he shook his head, dipping his head forward and to the side.

"Nope, I was just sitting up there on my stool over there... you might remember from last time... and I saw some really familiar hair go by. Thought I'd come see how you managed to get this lost."

She laughed.

"Not lost," she said. "Exploring."

He nodded slowly.

"Oh. Okay. That makes no sense. Why would you explore the Black Docks?"

Because the queen told her to.

"Because I wasn't supposed to come here, before, and now I'm allowed, and I've been everywhere else."

He frowned.

"I see. Well, that's interesting. Except... it's still the Black Docks."

"You hang out here," Stasia said. He grinned.

"But this is home," he said. "And I don't explore."

"Call it what you like," Stasia said, and he laughed.

"You want to come meet the crew?" he asked. "I mean, if you're just... wandering around."

"You're serious?" Stasia asked.

He frowned playfully.

"I think it's inevitable," he said. "No way Skite's gonna keep you out forever."

Well.

That was one way to see a region.

"Okay," Stasia said, and he flashed a wide grin.

"Let me finish my drink, and we'll go track down Sam."

"Who is Sam?" Stasia asked, following him back to the little shed masquerading as a bar there by the docks.

"Big dude," Sly said, throwing himself back up on a stool and picking up a mug.

"Okay," Stasia said slowly, and he gave her a quick nod.

"That's who he is," he said. "He's the big dude."

"Okay," Stasia said.

"We ought to be able to find Ace, too," he said cheerfully. "Don't know where Brandyrose will be this time of night, probably not at the Black Docks at all. I mean, if you can get out, right? And Skite would kill me if I took you to see Tinman, so we won't do that, right? But we can get Sam and Ace, and if they like you... we're in business."

He tipped back his beer and wiped his hands off on his knees, standing.

"Ella says you're a thief," Stasia said.

"Ella," he said slowly. "Right. Hidalga. No one calls her 'Ella' here."

"Hidalga says you're a thief," Stasia said.

"That's true," he said. "Does that bother you?"

She considered.

"What does it mean?"

"I steal stuff," Sly said slowly, not following the question.

"I mean..." Stasia said, and he grinned, just... happy. "I mean, what do you do? What does it mean that you're the thief in the crew?"

He nodded slowly, the grin spreading again.

"What an excellent question," he said. "No one looks at thiefing as a set of skills, but that's what it is. It's a very evolved set of specific skills."

"Like... picking locks?" Stasia asked, and he nodded enthusiastically, setting off.

"Exactly," he said. "I specialize in entry and recovery. If it's in a place, I can get to it, I can get it out of wherever it's kept, and then I can get me and it out. As long as I can carry it. If I can't carry it, you need Sam."

"The big dude," Stasia said, and he laughed.

"You've got it."

"So how do you do those things?" Stasia asked. "Or is it a secret?"

"No secret," he said. "Lots of little secrets, but no big secrets. You learn to read a building to figure out where they're going to be keeping the various things you're interested in. You learn how to pick locks on doors and open safes by touch or by sound. You know how to look at a room and see where someone would keep the secret important thing that they don't want anyone to find. I can climb the side of a building without crushing a glass in my shirt."

"Well... I can do that," Stasia said, and he laughed.

"Well, you can sort of do that," he said. "I tracked you last time by the trail of blood you were leaving behind."

"I was barefoot," she said. "I do much better than that in boots."

"Do you now?" he asked, taking half a step away from her and grinning. "Show me."

"I'm in skirts," Stasia said.

He ran his tongue along his top teeth, then shrugged. "So?"

She narrowed her eyes.

Frowned.

He was so much fun.

"All right," she said. "Challenge me. Something you can do that you don't think I can."

His eyes gleamed.

He licked his lips and looked around, then nodded.

"I've got it," he said. "Come on."

She followed him through various curving turns and along merging and de-merging streets, finally pointing up the side of a five-story building. It wasn't that tall a building, but there were without a doubt five rooms stacked on top of each other, each more haphazardly than the last.

The hand-holds were thick and ready, but she was going to have to watch out for stones that were no longer interested in remaining a part of the wall.

Stasia looked down at her skirts, then nodded, rolling up the top layer of skirt and just tucking it in at the waist, and then pulling the underskirts through her legs and tucking that up into her belt as well. She shifted the sword further to the side, then tested everything to make sure it was going to stay.

She was ridiculously bulky, and if she were going

climbing all night, she would have worried about how much extra energy it was going to take her to get up at that distance off the wall, but for one climb, she was fine.

She looked over at Sly.

"I'm not racing you," she said, and he shook his head, mesmerized.

"Ladies first, of course," he said, winking.

She went and found the first set of fingergrips, getting her toes onto the wall easily enough and starting up.

She avoided the windows, which actually doubled the effort of the climb, because she had to duck back and forth a bunch rather than just going straight up, but she made it to the roof as systematically as she had expected she would, and she turned around to watch Sly through the last two-thirds of his climb.

He was very good.

He wasn't wearing a gigantic dress, but even then he was better than she was.

She watched his technique, enraptured, as he came up and over the edge of the roof, turning to sit with an easy, confident motion.

"You've actually got it," he said.

"Well, thank you," she said. "You're amazing."

He grinned.

"Thank you. Nice to be appreciated by someone who knows how hard that is. Brandyrose can get up just about anything, but she doesn't like to sacrifice her dignity by noticing that anyone else is good at anything."

"Well, I could learn a lot from you," Stasia said. "The way you look at a building... I can see it. You see things that I don't."

"You're a free-climber," he said. "Just do it, what, to get away? For something to do? You don't need to be able to climb a specific way, so long as you can get up, and there's nothing wrong with that. But if you need to be able to climb one-handed or with something delicate in your shirt or carrying a rope or, you know, a thousand other things that you might need to be able to do, to get into a building, you learn a lot of extra techniques."

"I've just never seen anyone do that," Stasia said. "Who's that good at it."

"Stop, stop," he laughed. "Now you're just flattering me. You do much roof-running?"

"My favorite part, actually," she said.

"You need to be careful, around here," he said. "There are places you can go through the roof, if you aren't quick, but..." He grinned. "Come on."

He stood again and set off.

"Try not to tear up your feet, right?" he teased over his shoulder as he started running.

Actually running.

Up here, it was pitch dark; Stasia was working off of starlight and the shape of shadows the edges of the buildings gave her from the streetlamps below.

She couldn't hit that pace.

But she was willing to see how fast she could go.

Was she doing what Melody had asked her to?

No.

Just flat no.

But boy was it fun.

They ran.

The moon finally rose above the horizon, just over half-full, casting the world in silver and shadow, and Sly went faster.

They came to a gap in the buildings where he leaped from the rooftop they were on up to a higher one fully a half-story up and far enough away that Stasia couldn't have touched both rooftops with her fingers and toes, stretched between them.

Sly made the jump like a cat, and Stasia came to look

at it, then backed up and took a full run at it.

Her foot arch hit the corner of the roof and she put both arms out forward. Sly wrapped his hand around her thumb and her wrist, pulling her up over her feet and turning to go on.

"You had it," he said over his shoulder. "Just faster this way."

He set off running again and Stasia put her hands up to her forehead, feeling overwhelmed and exhilarated and like she belonged in a way that she'd never done it, before, then she set off after him again.

They ran through the Black Docks as the moon continued to rise, coming to a solidly-built, slanting stone roof, where Sly stopped, leaning against a metal chimney and looking down at the world.

"Wait here," he said, and Stasia nodded as he hopped down out of sight. Stasia waited, and just a minute later, he reappeared with a pair of glass bottles of beer.

"You steal those?" Stasia asked as he handed her one. He grinned and shrugged.

"Thief."

He sat down with his knee hooked around the chimney, his other leg trailing down the rooftop. Stasia dropped a knee to either side of the peak of the roof and opened her beer.

"You go against everything I believe in," she said.

He laughed, still a bit out of breath and gleaming sweat in the moonlight.

"You're awfully good at it, for someone who doesn't believe in any of this," he said, tipping up his beer.

Stasia put back half of her own, genuinely thirsty for how hard she'd worked.

"We need to do this again," he said after another moment. "It's novel, having someone who can challenge me at it."

"Is that what I just did?" Stasia laughed. "I thought I was just trying to keep up."

"No one else can," he said cheerfully. "Tell me we can do this again."

Stasia frowned.

"Oh," she said. "I shouldn't... I don't want to mislead you. I'm seeing someone."

He laughed again, his face just easy and open.

"Of course. The guard from the night with Skite. I know that."

"That was before..." Stasia said. "Does everyone know?"

He laughed harder, leaning his forehead against the chimney.

"Drink up," he said. "This is Sam's building, and he's in."

"Why do you do it?" Stasia asked.

"Do what?" Sly asked.

"Steal," Stasia said.

He drank more of his beer and looked at her thoughtfully.

"You're fun," he said. "I've got everything I want, everything I need, and there's nothing I enjoy more than being good, really good at what I do. I'm not one of the kids down on the street, stealing from people who are going to go hungry if you lift the coin in their pocket. I do one, maybe two jobs a year that are really challenging, and I spend the rest of my time..." He shrugged and looked around. "Looking forward to the next one."

Stasia was still out of breath.

"You don't even try to justify it?" she asked. "You're taking things that other people earned. Making it less profitable to do productive things, maybe making people stop doing things that would have made the lives around them better."

He tipped his head, smiling thoughtfully as he looked at her.

"That's a lot to carry around all day," he said. "You worry about that stuff all the time?"

She nodded.

"All the time."

He frowned, playful, then sipped his beer.

"Come meet Sam," he said, pulling himself to his feet and coming to offer her a hand. He lifted her to her feet with one hand, like hanging from a metal bar, and Stasia followed him to the edge of the roof, where he reached down with one hand to grab the edge of the rooftop and started down the side of the building.

Stasia finished her beer and tucked it away, then followed, getting to a third-story window, where Sly put his feet through and disappeared.

Stasia climbed down to be level with the window, finding herself looking a broad-shouldered man full in the face.

He blinked at her, unsurprised.

"Well?" he asked. "Would you like to come in?"

He offered her a hand and she put a foot on the windowsill, levering herself up into the apartment where Sly was leaning against the wall looking very pleased with himself.

"Sam, this is Stasia. Stasia, this is Sam. Big dude."

Sam glanced over at him.

"Who is she?"

"Friend of Hidalga's," Sly said. "Pretty slick at a bunch of stuff. I think Skite's going to recruit her."

"To do what, replace Brandyrose?" Sam asked.

"First of all, don't even whisper those words," Sly said. "Brandyrose'd kill her just to make sure there wasn't any viable competition for her job. And second of all, of course not. No one can do what Brandyrose does. You know that, man."

"Then what would she do?" Sam asked. "What do we even need?"

"She's a merchant," Sly said.

There was a beat of silence, then Sam turned to look at her fully.

"Is that so?"

"I'm just wandering the Black Docks tonight," Stasia said. "And I ran into Sly on accident. I have no interest in Skite's crew."

"Nobody does until he recruits you for it," Sam said.

"That's not true," Sly murmured, teasing.

"Fine," Sam said. "Nobody who's worth having has any interest in it until he recruits you."

"I don't steal things," Stasia said, and Sam frowned.

"Neither do I. Is that... what did he tell you? You can't believe anything he says, right? He isn't all that preoccupied with what's true and what isn't, okay?"

"Isn't that what a crew is?" Stasia asked. "Thieves?"

"He's the thief," Sam said. "I'm just the heavy."

"Please, you walk off with more stuff than me every single time," Sly said and Sam glanced at him.

"He's not recruiting her, man," he said. "Who is this?"

"Doesn't the fact that you haven't got a clue who she is convince you that there's something important going on with her?" Sly asked.

"I don't even know what that means," Sam said. "Is she Highrock?"

"I have no idea," Sly said. "Skite just told me she was a merchant."

Sam turned once more.

"Who are you?" he asked.

Stasia should have felt endangered or out of place, but Sly was just so comfortable, and Sam wasn't actually aggressive. He was big, but he had the style of big to him that, much like Babe, was too comfortable within itself to need to threaten those around him. He asked. He expected an answer. But he wasn't angry about it.

Annoyed at Sly, but that was truly the full extent of it.

Stasia could have imagined herself sitting at the table in the corner with the two of them playing cards until the sun came up. It was a place that had a sense of fit to it.

"Do you know Minstrel Fielding?" she asked.

"Heard of him," Sam said, and Stasia nodded.

Was she supposed to admit this?

No telling.

But Ella had set her loose and... she didn't really care if she put a snarl in Lord Westhauser's social scheme down here. He deserved it for being too complicated.

As though she had room to talk.

"I'm his youngest daughter," Stasia said.

"Fielding," Sly said. "Down on the Sapphire?"

"Why do you know that?" Stasia asked.

"I know where all the money is," he said with a wink. "And you're dating a member of the king's guard?"

"She's with the guard and you brought her here?" Sam asked.

"She's out on her own," Sly said. "We came off the roof, man. How much more do you want from me?"

"You have anything illegal here?" Stasia asked.

"No, but you're going back out the window and not the door," Sam said.

"Minstrel Fielding," Sly said. "Really."

Stasia nodded.

"How are you not married to some kid with no jaw?" Sam asked.

"Wasn't interested," Stasia said.

He nodded.

"Fair enough. Why does he think Skite's recruiting you?"

"He's been kind of stuck on that every time I've seen him," Stasia answered. "I have no clue."

"How did you meet him?" Sam asked.

"Was looking for Skite one day, Brandyrose - right, that was her name? - kept me out of trouble at the bar, and she left me with him while she went to go find Skite for me."

"So I've got Brandyrose to thank for this," Sam said. "Now that's new."

"She likes trying to tie him down," Sly said. "She caught wind of him having an actual person in his life beyond Hidalga and she pounced."

"That does sound like her," Sam conceded. "But it doesn't explain why you think he's recruiting her."

"I'm not saying he knows it, either," Sly said. "Just... she's interesting and she keeps turning up, and we all know what that means, in the long run."

"Means she's already involved far enough that he's going to find use for her," Sam said chewing on the inside of his cheek for a moment and then nodding. "And you just thought you'd stop by to introduce her to the whole crew, get ahead of Skite himself?"

"He's not stopping me, is he?" Sly asked with a grin. "Makes it less likely she says no, if she meets a few of us first."

"How many of you are there?" Stasia asked.

"Counting Hidalga?" Sly asked.

"Shut up," Sam said. "She's dating one of the king's guard?"

"Seven, including Skite, too," Sly said. "Guard went to him to help save her life. They owe us now."

"They do not," Stasia said. "They can't. They... that's not how it works."

Sam looked at her with just a touch of pity, then he was fighting with Sly again.

"You think this is about the new job?" he asked.

"There's a new job?" Sly asked. "What did he tell you?"

"Nothing, man," Sam said. "Just, I heard Hidalga was here tonight and they're working on something that the Rats aren't in on. I figured... it must be us."

"I'm taking her to see Ace next," Sly said. "You want to be there for that?"

Sam grinned.

"I want to be there when you walk in to Yev's front parlor with a stranger wearing that," he said. "But I'm not actually going to be there."

"His beard is getting thick again," Sly said. "Gonna be itching bad, these days."

"It hasn't been that long," Sam said, and Sly shrugged.

"I'm taking her over there."

"You really think this has been a convincing sales pitch?" Sam asked. Sly grinned.

"Well, meeting you was just a bonus. What I actually need are your pants."

"Pants? My... what?"

"One second," Sly said, disappearing, with Sam charging after him into another room. Sly came back out with a pair of breeches and suspenders.

"That'll do," he said, holding it up in front of Stasia. "She's going to climb so much better in these."

"Those are mine," Sam protested, somehow missing having caught up with Sly. "What do you think you're doing?"

"Won't that be better?" Sly asked Stasia.

"Those are his pants," Stasia said slowly. "What are you talking about?"

"You've got... do you wear a shirt under there or something, or do you... you need a shirt, too."

He gave her an emphatic nod and managed to dodge

Sam again, going into the other room again with Sam on his heels. He came back with a linen shirt and held that up.

"He is a lot bigger than you, but I think we can make this work. I would have taken you to my place, but I didn't have any beer."

"Beer," Sam said. "What are you talking... you took my beer, too?"

Stasia took the bottle out of her dress and put it on the ledge, glancing sideways at him, then taking the clothes.

It didn't feel real.

Any more than the rooftops had.

But it felt like she could belong in the midst of this. Comfortably. Easily.

He was recruiting her and he knew exactly what he was doing, even if it looked insane.

Sam went still.

"What you mean climb?" he asked.

"You said we're going out the window," Sly said. "And we're going to Ace's by rooftop. It's hard in that much dress. She needs real pants to get across to that part of town."

"He's got you up on the rooftops like that?" Sam asked.

"I'm fine," Stasia said. "It's fine."

Sam blinked at her.

"You can... really?"

She nodded.

Easy.

"Yeah."

The corner of his mouth came up, and he glanced over at Sly.

"She is interesting."

Sly nodded quickly, giddy.

"Go change," he said. "Before Ace and Yev turn in for the night. We do not want any part of that."

Stasia looked at Sam once more, who put out an arm

toward the other room with a sense of resignation that wasn't entirely truthful.

She heard the two men continue talking as she went into the second room and changed out of her dress quickly, rolling it up and putting it aside as she put on the pants and shirt.

They were both massively too big, but she tucked and tied and scrunched, and it came together where she would truthfully be a lot better going up and down like this than she had been in the dress.

She came back out of the room carrying her dress.

"I don't know what to do with this," Stasia said.

"Give me your address, and I'll send it to you by messenger tomorrow," Sam said with a shrug. "Once you figure out that we're all crazy and you just go with it, it gets a lot easier."

"I'll get these back to you," she said.

"Only because they do you absolutely no good," Sam said. "Don't worry about it too much."

"But don't let your lover on the guard find them, either," Sly cautioned cheekily. "Hard to explain."

She narrowed her eyes at him, and he grinned.

She re-situated everything once more, then shook her head.

"I've had weird nights," she said. "But this one is going to end up being one of the weirdest, I think."

"Doesn't hit my top twenty-five," Sam said.

"What is tonight?" Sly asked. "I don't even know."

Stasia shook her head and Sly went to the window, hopping up to stand on the sill and then disappearing upwards.

"Don't let him push you into anything you aren't actually fit to do," Sam said. "Sometimes the enthusiasm gets away from him when he has a new toy to play with."

"That toy being me?" Stasia asked.

"That toy being you," Sam agreed. "It was nice to meet you. I expect I'll be seeing you again soon."

"I don't know why you would," Stasia said, and he grinned.

"Neither do I, but it's still probably going to happen. Stay safe."

She nodded and climbed up into the window, following after Sly.

Oh, the relief of not having all of the fabric to deal with was immense.

Up on the roofs, Sly set off running again, and Stasia followed greedily.

It was like flying, and it made her laugh, and she pitied literally everyone else who couldn't do it.

Yev and Ace brought out a tea set and they talked about politics and trade and weather and festivals for hours.

Ace was a charming man with eyes that saw everything and a quick, easy smile. He did, indeed, have a thick, black beard, though Stasia wasn't sure what about it was important.

Yev wore a ruffled dress and had curly hair exploding at its restraints in a way that Stasia found familiar, and she heaped no end of abuse on either of the men in the sort of way that a woman who knew them both very well could do without hurt feelings.

They didn't ask Stasia about herself hardly at all, though Ace kept bringing up things that Stasia found oddly specific to her experiences, like they were old friends and he was remembering a story she had told him about the time that she went to Boton with her father to work out a contract amidst four different suppliers of lumber because they needed a partial shipment from all of them or else the contracts were pointless.

"Have you been involved in trade negotiations?" Stasia asked him.

"Oh, no, no," he said. "Just find the whole thing fascinating."

When they stood up to leave, Yev walked them to the door.

"You have a beautiful home," Stasia told her. "I hadn't realized that there were homes like this in the Black Docks."

"Most people leave, once they get money, but not Ace," Yev said. "So I've made it into what I wanted."

"It's beautiful," Stasia told her.

"Thank you."

"You never mentioned what you do," Stasia said to Ace.

"That's because I do everything," Ace answered. She frowned and he winked.

They left, walking down cobbled streets in the Black Docks, Stasia following Sly with a sense of complete overwhelm and bemusement.

This might have been one of the best nights of her life, actually. She'd had so much fun, and the men on Skite's crew were...

They were incredible. And fun. And... solid. It wasn't like the idiots in the bar who were always preparing to draw a weapon and threaten her with it. None of them were uncomfortable at all with who they were or who she was. It was similar to Jasper's squad, but... unburdened.

"I feel like I've known him my entire life," Stasia said. "What does he do?"

"Thing about Ace is that you don't start to get to know him until you realize that you don't know him at all. Which is something that most people never realize. They all spend all their time feeling like they've known him from childhood."

"What does that mean?" Stasia asked. Sly grinned.

"Means he's a con, and a pretty amazing one."

"A..." Stasia shook her head. "I don't know that word."

"Oh," Sly said. "Right. I didn't actually know it before Skite used it. Maybe he made it up. Short for confidence. I don't know if he means that Ace gets along by just being sure of himself, or if he makes other people confide in him, actually, but... he plays a role. Lies to people about who he is, convinces them that he's what he needs them to believe he is, then gets them to do something because they believe him."

"He's an actor," Stasia said, and Sly nodded.

"He is. He's a criminal actor. Why not?"

"You guys are just... happy," Stasia said. "How are you all so happy?"

He shook his head.

"What else would we be?" he asked. "We work with a great crew, none of us have anything we can't afford if we want it, and we're just hanging out waiting for the next thing to start up. I mean, Sam's a little grumpy, but you saw through that, right?"

Stasia nodded.

The whole city was bracing for the worst, and she'd just had a tea party with a man who had convinced her that he knew the ins and outs of trading at the port, like he'd been doing it his whole life. A tea party with the man.

"I've never known criminals like you," she said. "The men I've met are all grim and angry and... desperate."

"They do what they're doing because if they don't, they aren't going to eat," Sly said. "It'll make the best of us pretty grim, believe me."

"You don't..." Stasia paused, thinking about whether she was going to say it, but the thought had come to her and she was obviously going to say it. "You all live here, but none of you talk like you're from here."

"Can if you like," Sly said, switching to an entirely new dialect. "Black Docks runs in our veins, same as any of the rest of these lot. Grew up talkin' like this, wouldn't say nothin' to my ma any other way, you follow, but..." He shrugged. "It's a dead giveaway for a man to keep your eye on, isn't it?"

The switch was jarring and seamless at the same time.

"Are the rest of the men here... grim?" Stasia asked.

Sly frowned, lifting his head and looking around thoughtfully for a moment.

"Don't know," he said. "You know Hidalga."

"I do," Stasia said.

"So does that mean you've met the Rats?"

"The ones who sit at the bar and grunt at each other?" Stasia asked, and he laughed.

"Those'd be them," he said. "Would you call them grim?"

That actually was a hard question, as she reflected on it.

"Mostly just angry and aspirational, I think," she said.

"That's how I'd call it. They've got their eyes on the prize, those boys, and they mostly recognize that in a group like the Rats, most of them aren't going to be alive at the end of the game. They're determined to be the last man standing in the pack so that they get to be the Rat with the cheese, if you see my point."

"Would Skite approve of you saying that?" Stasia asked, and Sly laughed.

"I can't imagine him doing anything to stop me," he said. "But that's just how we are. Maybe he wouldn't like me saying it to you, what do I know?"

They passed a market that was still populated, even

at this time of night.

"You want anything?" he asked. "Lot of stuff you can't get anywhere else, up for sale in the Black Docks."

"I've heard that," Stasia said. "What would you get, if you were on your way out and never coming back?"

"Ooh, good question," he said. "Maddie's sweet loaf with the spices coming in from the pirate islands is a winner."

"Food?" Stasia asked, and he laughed.

"What else is there?" he asked. "I've got everything else. And so do you, don't you?"

She shook her head.

"I have, my entire life, but not now. My father disinherited me and I'm living on my own. That apartment where you tracked me from, that was mine because that's what I can afford."

He whistled, low, then nudged her.

"Then I'll get two of them, and they'll be my treat."

He handed a coin to a woman and took two buns off of a tray, handing one to Stasia and going on.

"This," Stasia said. "This is the first thing you thought of as illegal contraband available only in the Black Docks that you can never get again."

"It's the first thing I saw," he admitted. "I assume you're not in the market for powders."

"Powders?" Stasia asked.

"Pixie dust," he said. "Of the various flavors and colors it can be had in, at the low low price of your next two or three weeks."

"What?" Stasia asked, and he frowned.

"You don't know this?"

She shook her head.

"I got taken in by a man at the market who used pixie magic on me to take my stuff," she said. "Is that what you're talking about?"

"Wouldn't have pegged you for that sensitive," Sly

said. "Well, if they managed to go through your pockets on just a nudge of powder, you need to be careful with the fun stuff. But if you're going to buy the fun stuff, it's all here. Stuff you can't even imagine."

"You're talking about drugs," Stasia said, and he nodded.

"Verida specials," he said. "I've heard of the stuff they do on Altan, and that stuff just sounds... disgusting, compared to pixie dust. You get a powder from an honest pixie making a living selling illegal stuff, you've got a high coming at you that nothing else in the world is ever going to replicate."

"What's the catch?" Stasia asked.

"Yeah," he said. "It'll knock you through to next month with nothing to show for it but a constant reminder that you really need to do it again soon."

"You black out and you wake up addicted?" Stasia asked.

"Black out is such a... drab way to describe it," he said, and she looked over at him.

"You use this stuff," he said, and he grinned.

"I'm... perhaps more aware of it than the average Docker. I've been off it for years, but I know my way around the market, and, if Maggie's baking isn't the wow factor you're looking for, powders will kick it up quite a bit."

"It at least justifies being illegal," she admitted, and he laughed.

"Not that I'm regretting anything about having a wonderful diversion this evening, but what exactly is it you're doing here in the Black Docks, Miss Fielding?"

"I'm not entirely sure, actually," Stasia answered. "But..." She looked up. "I should probably go. Ella's... Hidalga's probably waiting up for me to make sure I get home safe."

"Glad someone is," Sly answered. "Where can I drop

you off?"

"If you could just show me back to the bar, to Buddy's, that would be... I would very much appreciate it."

"Gladly," he said, sweeping his arm forward.

"The buildings here," Stasia observed a short time later. "They're so badly-constructed. Do they not fall down constantly?"

"They manage to hold each other up better than you'd expect," Sly said. "But you see, here and there around the docks, that they're getting replaced as families make good and decide on moving up instead of moving out. Like Ace and Yev."

"And Sam's building was as solid as anything I've yet seen in Verida," Stasia said. Sly laughed.

"Going up the side of them does sort of acquaint you at a different level with construction quality, doesn't it?"

"It does," Stasia said. "There are lots of families here. Lots of children."

"There are," Sly said, not following.

"And they live in these tiny little apartments... just all of them."

"You here to save them?" Sly asked after a moment.

"Just... listening," Stasia said. "When I was walking with Hidalga earlier, when everyone was still out, there were kids playing..."

"Don't know what else they'd be doing with their time," Sly said. "Unless you're one of those frowny faces who say that they should be in school all hours to keep them out of the way."

"They sounded happy," Stasia said.

"They're kids," Sly said. "Again, don't know how else they ought to sound."

Even in one of the poorest regions of the city. Stasia couldn't work it out, but she was realizing what it was that Melody had sent her here to try to figure out, and she realized with a jolt that she'd mostly wasted her evening playing, instead.

With another jolt, she realized that that might be a part of the answer, if she could tease it all the way down to why she'd spent the night playing instead of working.

He turned a corner and put out an arm.

"That'll be your last stop," he said. "Thanks for the challenge, tonight. I'm serious about doing it again soon."

"I might just take you up on it," Stasia answered. "I'm out of practice, and you're a lot better than me."

He winked and waved, heading off in another direction through the dim lamplight.

Stasia shook her head, finding herself alone on a strange street once again, and she started down the slight hill toward the brightly-lit bar.

She pushed open the door and Ella lifted her head.

She was sitting at the table against the far wall with three other men, one of whom was Skite.

"Hadn't figured you on bein' out this late," she said, then frowned. "What happened to you?"

Her accent was so strange. Stasia blinked, then remembered her clothes.

"Oh," she said.

"Around with you," Skite said, nudging the man next to him out of the way and standing. He came over to her.

"You all right?" he asked, his voice familiar and personal. Ella was scrambling out of the booth, suddenly alarmed.

"I'm fine," Stasia said. He nodded.

"Don't care what they said, I'll kill them. My word."

"Nothing like that," Stasia said. She glanced at Ella as the woman came close, then she laughed quietly.

"I've been climbing buildings all night with Sly."

Skite's face changed entirely.

"You've been what? Those are Sam's clothes. I

should have..."

He looked at her with an increasing sense of bewilderment.

"How did that happen?" he finally asked.

"I went to the docks and he saw me," Stasia said. "So... now I've met Sam and Ace, too."

"But not Brandyrose or Tinman," Skite said. "He didn't take you to see Tinman, right?"

She shook her head.

"I met Brandyrose before, but that was... different."

"What was he doing?" Skite asked.

"Introductions to the crew," Ella said evenly, humor dawning over her early concern. "And an audition."

Skite looked at her sharply and Ella laughed.

"On whose authority?" Skite asked.

"His own," Ella said. "Why would it need to be anyone else's?"

"She couldn't tell me why you were here in the first place," Skite said.

"No," Stasia said. "I suppose not. Can I ask you a question?"

He looked back at the two other men, then nodded and followed her outside.

"We were about to send out Point to find you," Ella said once they were out in the humid darkness again.

"I'm sorry I let it get so late," Stasia answered. "It wasn't my intention, but I just had one of the best nights of my life. Your crew is... amazing."

"They are," Skite said. "Why are you here?"

Stasia licked her lips.

"Things are different here than in the rest of the city. Sly and the rest of them just drove it home for me, but I can see it in... everything. The rest of the city is falling into violence and despair, but here? The kids are playing and the people are doing their lives the way I think they probably always do, and your friends are genuinely happy, and... why? Why is everything here different?"

Skite frowned, glancing at Ella.

"I can't answer that, clearly," he said. "Not with authority. I don't spend a lot of time in the rest of the city, with all the time I spend going to and from the estate already, but if you want my opinion? It's because we're looking up. The rest of the city... they're seeing risk to their shiny futures and they're afraid of what they might lose. Here? Men think that their children are going to live better lives, that tomorrow can be better than today, and all they have to do is fight for it. So they are, and... fighting for a better tomorrow is satisfying work."

"You think that the hardest, most dangerous, poorest district in the city is different from the others because of their optimism?" Stasia asked, and Ella nodded.

"He's right. I wouldn't have put it that way, but he's exactly right. The people that I talk to... are enthusiastic."

"Huh," Stasia said.

"I might still kill Sly," Skite said. "It was absolutely unacceptable, what he's done. You know that I am absolutely not interested in you participating in my crew. I don't want you interacting with them outside of absolutely critical situations."

"I bet they're fun to work with," Stasia said, and Ella nodded enthusiastically.

"They're an ongoing pain," Skite said, but it didn't sound like he was arguing.

"Are you ready to go home, then?" Ella asked, and Stasia nodded.

"I can still just walk. It would be fine."

"Not on your life," Ella said, putting her arm through Stasia's.

"I'm going to close everything down with Veil," Skite said. "I'll meet you at the apartment."

"Okay," Ella called cheerfully, setting off with Stasia. She waited until Skite was out of earshot to speak again.

"So?" she asked.

"What?" Stasia asked.

"Do you want in?" Ella asked.

"No," Stasia said. "I'm not invited."

"Oh, you're invited," Ella said. "If the guys liked you, you're invited."

"I don't even know what I would do," Stasia said. "Sly made it sound like everything I can do, both he and Brandyrose can also do, and they're good at other things."

"Oh, the running around up on the roofs is nothing compared to what you're actually good at," Ella said.

"And what's that?" Stasia demanded. "No wait, I don't even want to talk about it. My life is trade and working with the king's guard. I can't be a part of a thievery ring. It goes against everything I believe. I don't care how fun they are. I can't do that."

Ella nodded sagely.

"You make an excellent point," she said. "Let me know when you change your mind."

"I'm not going to," Stasia said. "And Skite wasn't even inviting me."

Ella laughed.

"He isn't going to, either," she said. "But it doesn't mean you aren't."

Stasia narrowed her eyes at Ella, but the woman shrugged, inscrutable.

"You're serious," Stasia said, and Ella shrugged again.

"Skite likes to think that he runs that crew, but it's more like its own creature that he happened to assemble from very high-quality parts. It's got its own brain and its own stomach and its own legs."

"Would they go against him?" Stasia asked.

Ella snorted.

"Each and every time out," she said. "The question is would he go against them."

"I don't understand," Stasia said.

"Never mind," Ella said. "You want no part of it, and that's fine. You just keep telling yourself that and we won't even have to worry about it, will we?"

Stasia frowned at her, and Ella laughed.

"I'm glad you came tonight," she said. "I really was worried about you, but... I like you getting to know the Black Docks. This is really home to me, now, and I don't like that you just... you feel like you aren't allowed here. It isn't like that. Okay, I was a little nervous just leaving you, sure, but once you know how to be around here, it's a... This is my place, now. More and more every day. I love it here."

"It's a terrible place," Stasia said. "There are worse places in the world, maybe, but this is a terrible place. What's funny, though, is I see it. I can honestly see it."

Ella grinned.

"I'm so glad you came. This was a really good idea."

"I'm sorry I ducked out of our night," Stasia said. "But I needed to do this."

"You did," Ella agreed, stopping at a small livery stable that was brand-new construction compared to the buildings around it. Stasia had been here before.

"Venn," Ella called. "You in there?"

Her accent was back.

"Right and ready," the man called back. Strangely, that was a fake accent.

"He's from the estate," Ella told her softly, stepping back as the man climbed down from the loft overhead and disappeared into the shadows to go get the horses. "He's doing his best to fit in, here. Most of them don't."

Stasia nodded.

"Can I help?" she asked.

"Won't be a second," Venn called to her, the attempt at an accent gone. Stasia looked over at Ella.

"You should get back, then. I've kept you out too late, already."

Ella shrugged.

"We should do it again sometime. The Rats are mostly a waste of space, you can tell them I said that, but there are other people here who are worth meeting."

Stasia nodded.

"Soon, then. Send me a note when you're going to be in town again, if it's before we're summoned."

Ella sighed.

"The estate is doing well, again, too. Mostly. With the stone elves gone, everyone is just kind of going back to normal. I don't know what to make of everything, here. I didn't think it would be this hard."

Stasia nodded.

"I know. I didn't, either. Everyone makes all this big deal about the queen, you think that she's just all-powerful and everybody goes with it."

"Makes me angry that they don't," Ella agreed.

Stasia hugged her quickly.

"Go on," she said. "It's late and I'm fine."

Ella grinned at her.

"See you soon."

Stasia went to lean against the doorway to the livery stable, tipping her head back against the black-painted wood and looking up at the moon as it pierced the wispy clouds sharply now.

A few minutes later, the carriage pulled out of the barn, the matched black horses pawing at the cobbles and apparently eager to be out. Apparently the lateness of the hour wasn't strange to them at all.

The man called Venn came and got the door for her and Stasia climbed up, remembering once more the preposterous clothes she was wearing. Venn didn't bat an eye at them as he closed the door behind her and climbed up to the driver's step at the back of the carriage.

And they were off, rolling through the Black Docks in a Westhauser-emblemed carriage.

She put her hands behind her head and looked up at the ceiling of the carriage, astonished at the turn the night had taken.

She slept, she ate, she wandered.

The squad had started its shift at the castle, so Babe wasn't there when she came downstairs the next morning, and she actually made it to the port, finding a few men she had wanted to talk to, and then going all the way up to Fisharbor by cart to talk to some other men that she'd heard did some smaller-scale shipping during certain seasons of the year when the fish weren't to their liking.

She took the queen's letter to the Lady Bentmoor on time, and she stopped to speak with Melody for just a few minutes about what she had found in the Black Docks, but Melody had something else on her mind and hadn't had time to talk to her more than that.

Stasia went to see Schotzli, where Tesh caught her - the stableman had apparently been watching out for her - and summoned her into the house.

"You need to come for dinner," Tesh said. "Soon."

"Is something wrong?" Stasia asked, frowning, and Tesh nodded.

"Lady Alyssia is... changing things, now that you're gone," Tesh told her. "And Alice is threatening to find a new house. I don't think Mr. Fielding knows what's going on, either. He seems distracted, if you ask me, which you didn't, but if you ask me, he's got something weighing on him that he needs to talk out with someone he trusts and whose mind he respects, and I don't know anyone of that description outside yourself."

"Why is Alyssia still here?" Stasia asked. "She should have gone home by now."

"She doesn't tell me anything but when she wants new sheets," Tesh said. "I've served in fine homes most of my adult life, and I know my place, Miss, but I'm not going to lie to you and say I don't miss the way things were, when you were the lady of the house."

Stasia pursed her lips, feeling a bit grumpy, but she nodded.

"I may not be the lady of the house anymore, but Alyssia is going to have a hard time telling me that she's more of one than I am. She's a guest in this house and nothing more."

"You should come for dinner," Tesh said. "I'm sorry to ask it..."

Stasia shook her head.

"I'm tempted to go talk to Alyssia now, ask her why she's ignoring her own estate and instead trying to oversee my father's simple household. How is everything else, though? Other than my sister wanting everything her own way?"

Tesh gave her a tight little smile.

"We miss you," she said. "You set this house alight, and your father is... emptier, without you, but I can see that he's proud of you for what you're doing, and no one questions that you're right to... try. Whatever it is you're doing. I'll admit, you didn't ask me, but I'll admit I can't understand walking away from... all this... a father who loves you and can support you... I wouldn't go so far as to call it foolish, but I won't say I understand."

Stasia hugged her.

"I have to build my own life. I couldn't do that here,

but I'm doing it, now, and... I miss you guys, too, but I'm really glad I did what I did. I promise I'll come back more often. I was staying away to prove to everyone that my father isn't my backstop anymore, but once I get it solidified that I only come here for social reasons, I'll come more. I promise."

"Soon," Tesh said, giving her another quick hug. "The horse misses you, too."

"I know," Stasia said, looking over her shoulder out the window where Schotzli was pressed against the fence watching her. "I hate that I left her all summer and now I'm back and she's still stuck here. I need to figure out when I can take her up riding at the Westhauser estate. She'll be all out of shape, by now. I hope I can find a way to keep her, myself, soon, but..."

"It's not done, in Verida," Tesh said with a tight little smile. "It's just not done."

"I know," Stasia said, then smiled. "But I'm going to. I'll see you soon, but I have other things I need to do today."

"Very well," Tesh said. "We look forward to seeing you."

Stasia left, going out to give Schotzli one more big hug, then setting off to the port.

If she chose not to see it, she could ignore it.

Verida looked like Verida. She moved like Verida. The men and women were busy. The roads were full of carts and men and animals. The ports bustled with goods and ships and men, and the seagulls squawked and tussled for bits of scrap.

But it was there.

Stasia could feel it, especially after Matthias had pointed it out.

The city had suffered a mortal wound, and nothing was as it should have been.

There was anger where there should have been humor.

There was mistrust where there should have been agreement.

And there was pain. Everywhere. Hidden and covered over, but it was there, underneath of everything else, making men and women and even children lash out unexpectedly.

And it put her off balance.

She didn't know what to do with merchants who suddenly snapped at her over nothing, and if the price of everything was anything to go off of, no one else knew what to do about it, either. Things went back onto boats unsold, and at the same time the prices of everything at market went up and merchants and vendors alike complained about how they couldn't afford things that they had taken for granted, before.

Bakers had started charging for butter to go with their bread, in the mornings.

Stasia meant to talk to Ella about it, but she wasn't sure how much damage there had been to the Westhauser estate industries. The concern, the last time they'd discussed it, had been for men's lives, and it would have been callous to ask about herds of cattle and beehives and olive orchards.

But Stasia had noticed that the road along the coast, coming south to Port Verida, hadn't been lit the last two nights she had walked there, and she wondered where all of the oil was.

Finwalk cared about these things.

The soldiers up in the mountains, he wanted to just do what they did and for them to become invisible to him again the way they were to everyone else in the city, but he cared about the price and the availability of goods. He cared that merchants were deciding not to even put in at Verida, but rather go on to Boton or even Galadine.

Verida's potent prosperity was because all ships put in at Verida. They optimized their payloads with a liquid

Veridan market, and then they set off for new places. It made Verida an excellent place to set up a core of operations; many wealthy Botonese merchants were moving here, and Stasia had heard Galadine and Eladine accents on the streets even in just the last week.

If they couldn't keep the lamps lit and if the merchants were suddenly refusing to buy because they weren't sure they were going to be able to sell again in the next few days… Verida could fall apart completely.

They didn't produce enough food to feed themselves, in the best of times, and many of the estates were in a shambles, trying to sort out what crops were still coming in from devastated fields, what livestock belonged to who and what their numbers were, and what machines of various industries were in working order and which needed specialists to get involved in repairing or replacing them.

In the midst of all that, Stasia was making a killing, and she was certain that Minstrel was, as well. The lack of trust and the fear that the market was going to freeze up was keeping a lot of money from flowing the way it usually did, and Stasia was buying and moving stuff all over the city, hitting markets that she knew were emptied out for key goods and charging a hefty margin for the fact that she knew it.

The bigger merchants didn't have the capacity to react quickly like she did, and the smaller ones were giving up, blaming the intermediate markets and the ships' captains and the big merchants and… all manner of other things for why they didn't think that it was profitable to buy and sell, and they were leaving the market, either going to work in shops or start their own shops or leaving Verida entirely.

They just didn't have the geographic range to see where things were short, nor were they making the new economic contacts to figure out who was selling directly to customers who wanted that stuff.

Soon, Stasia was going to need to forge a relationship with a banking concern to hold her cash, because she didn't like leaving it in her apartment all day.

She needed to start investigating the rates the local bankers paid.

And how reliably they made loans. Her father ranted against bad bankers all the time, how they would just close up and take all of the deposits underwater with them, then start a new bank in another town or another part of a big city like Verida, and start all over again.

She got home from being out one day about a week and a half after she'd been down to the Black Docks and found a package wrapped in brown paper on her bed.

She put her hand on her sword and looked quickly around the room, but other than under the bed, there really wasn't anywhere to hide, and it was clearly empty.

She went to the package and pulled a note off of it, going to stand in front of the window to read it.

Sam said that since I stole his beer, I could be his courier. Didn't want to leave it outside where it might get nicked. See you again soon.

Sly

Stasia grinned, unwrapping her dress and going to hang it on the wall with her other dresses.

There was a quiet knock on the door and she turned to find Babe standing there.

She ran across the room to hug him, and he held her tight, sighing.

"Missed you more than I'd expected," he murmured. "You do okay, this week?"

"Wasn't abducted once," Stasia answered, stepping away. "You look tired."

He nodded.

"Finwalk had meetings all over the city this week," he said. "And then was up with his advisors most nights. I swear, that man is determined to not sleep until he's got everything under control."

"Then he's not going to sleep for a while," Stasia said. "I thought the point of having all of you on shift at the same time was so that you could take breaks and sleep and stuff."

He shrugged.

"It was a packed week," he said.

"Have you eaten?" Stasia asked, and he shook his head.

"Came straight here from the castle."

She frowned.

He really did look exhausted. Which he didn't do, normally.

"Are you okay?" she asked. He nodded, rubbing his thumb and forefinger over his eyes.

"Just a good sleep and I'll be right as ever," he said.

"If you wanted a good meal, we could go to my father's house," she said. "I saw Tesh this week, and she asked me to come soon, and... I still haven't spoken to my father, really, about... us."

He laughed and tipped his face toward the floor, then nodded.

"Let me put some water on my face. I'd imagined wearin' something other than my uniform for this, but... this is who I am, ain't it?"

"It can wait," Stasia said. "I just thought the food might be good."

He nodded.

"Kitchen rations ain't half bad, I'm not complainin', but a proper meal would be a delight. I'm just fit to collapse."

"Let's do it another night," Stasia said. "I can go down and buy dinner from one of the vendors on the street..."

He put up a hand.

"Don't you talk it back," he said. He lifted his eyes looking her in the face with a sense of surprise.

She took a quick step back, realizing how close she was standing to him.

"Does it occur to you that we might be doin' this all wrong?" Babe asked.

"In what way?" Stasia asked.

He leaned against the doorway, looking at her.

"Have I ever told you you're beautiful?" he asked.

Stasia looked down at her cheap dress, covered in dust and city grime from the distance she walked and rode every day, waiting for wash day.

"You're kidding," she said, and he shook his head.

"You are. And... I don't rightly know what to make of it, that you'd condescend to spend your time with a man like me. Humbled ain't the half of it. I keep waitin' for you to see the light of it, realize that this ain't doin' you no good at all and..."

She tipped her head.

"We're still here, aren't we?" she asked. "Do you know that every single person I've told that we're together... already knew that?"

He laughed quietly, looking over his shoulder into the hallway and stepping into her room and closing the door.

Being alone in her very own apartment with a man was still so shocking and forbidden. Something sizzled in the proximity of her stomach.

"I just don't have the way of it," he said. "Sterling and Colin, it seems they take to spending time with a woman like a fish to water, but... much as I like walkin' with you along the port road, I still feel like we're doin' all of it wrong."

"In what way?" Stasia asked again.

He swallowed.

And his eyes went to her throat. Her waist. Her mouth.

She took another step back.

It felt like being tipsy, just a bit off balance and like giggling might fix it.

Yes, she knew exactly what he was talking about. Had felt it.

This sense... his hands, his fingers against her skin... his mouth on hers...

They held hands when they went out walking.

Sometimes.

Sometimes they didn't.

She wanted him to have a sense that he couldn't keep his hands off of her, his eyes off of her, to be excited to see her, to push her around corners and into shadows...

Her breath caught at the thought she hadn't let herself have.

Her throat had gone dry.

She put her hand out to him, realizing just how far away he was, leaning against the wall, all the way as far as he could get, and he looked her in the eye, straightening his posture and taking a partial step forward to where he could take her fingers in his.

"Don't know how to ask permission," he finally said. "I'm distracted, at the castle. Can't keep my mind on the work. Jasper caught me at mistakes, this week, and I don't make mistakes. All I want to do is think about you, and then I'm here and I... can't even look at you. Feels like I got no right."

Stasia tried to swallow, but the attempt failed.

"I don't know how..." she started, struggling to find the words that she would actually say to him that captured it. "I don't know how to be, when we choose each other. I've... Everything is improper and unchaperoned and..." She laughed at a stray thought. "When I was coming back, with

Jasper, I told him that no one had worried about my honor, traveling alone with him, and he told me that I carried three daggers and a sword and no one needed to worry about my honor..." She covered her mouth with her hand, not sure where that had come from. "I don't know what the rules are."

"Do you want to marry?" he asked. "Is that... the rules?"

She blinked.

"I don't know."

He nodded, looking like he hadn't wanted to ask it because he'd been afraid of the answer.

He licked his lips and looked at her hand where he held her fingers pinched between his index finger and his thumb.

He took a slow breath.

"I've lived for seeing you tonight," he said. "I feel... silly... like a boy... and now I'm... here... and... It's like watchin' at a dance, one of the nobles' dances at the castle, with all the steps that I don't know..."

"Yes," Stasia said suddenly. "It's exactly like one of the formal dances. That's what we're doing wrong. I've been..." She covered her hand with her mouth, the absurd obviousness of it hitting her all at once. "I hate their dances. I don't... Why would I let this be like that? Why would I even... care about their rules? I'm a spare daughter. An independent spare daughter, no less." She looked at him, stunned as she worked it through. "We get to make up our own rules. You and me. How do we want to be?"

"I don't want to take advantage," Babe said. "You're... alone and vulnerable and you haven't got no one lookin' out for you. Ain't right, me just... There are rules for good reason."

She hadn't thought of it like that.

And then she laughed.

"You think I haven't got anyone looking out for me?" she asked. "If you screw this up, what do you think Jasper and the rest of them are going to do to you?"

He shook his head.

"I'm serious, Stasia," he said. "I don't ever want you to look at me and see a man who pressed an advantage, who took without askin', who... made you feel unsafe."

Stasia pulled her hand away from him, shaking her head hard.

"No," she said. "No, never. There is no one in the world that I feel safer with than you. You're the one who said it, that we're doing it wrong. And you're right. Formality like... like... You haven't kissed me. You don't touch me. And... it's a stupid dance that neither one of us even want to learn the steps. I promise, we don't. Neither of us. But I'm not a lady on the street that you're helping her up into a cart or getting a door for her. And that's all of us... ever thought to be, with anyone. We're doing this all wrong because we haven't thought about what we actually want."

"Maybe you haven't," he said with a kind of dry humor, and she saw herself, standing away like she was, distant and formal, if friendly and affectionate.

"You think I'm beautiful?" she asked, and he nodded.

"The strongest, most beautiful woman I've ever laid eyes on."

She could hug him.

Lifting up onto her toes and letting her weight rest against him, the rise and fall of his chest as he breathed, his arms holding her in snug and light against him.

But...

"I don't know how to do this," she said.

He nodded.

"I know. Neither do I."

She was frozen.

"Will you...?" she asked. It was all she had. He

dipped his head slightly, his eyes holding hers.

"You're sure?" he asked.

"Of course," she said, almost manic with a sense of giddiness and indecision. This, at least, she was absolutely certain about.

"I cross any lines..." he said.

"I promise," she said.

He crossed the distance between them slowly, his eyes on her mouth now.

She almost fell back another step, but managed not to as his hand found her waist. He dipped his face to hers, closing his eyes and just resting there for a moment. Stasia's body shook with the intensity of her heartbeat. He put his hand to her face, then his mouth to hers.

At the Westhauser estate, his lips had been gentle and polite and restrained.

In this very apartment, he'd kissed her with a depth and an intent that had shocked her.

But this was something different again.

Babe was big. She knew that. He was strong. She knew that. But she was completely washed away by how powerful he was.

Before, he had let her pick a pace and an intensity that suited her, she realized as they shifted back, step by step, to the wall. His weight leaned in on her as she put her arms up through his to put her hands into his hair. He kissed her harder, and she let go of everything but being there with him, his body against hers, safe and beautiful and together.

She didn't think she would ever tire of him kissing her, nor that he would tire of kissing her, but finally he turned his face down, pressing his forehead against her cheekbone and breathing hard.

"If we don't go now, we're going to come too late for dinner," he said.

She laughed.

"I told you it could wait."

He shook his head.

"We should go," he said. "We should go now."

"Are you okay?" Stasia asked.

He straightened, pulling away from her and letting go of her, looking at her face thoughtfully.

"I like who you are," he said. "Like that you ain't one of the girls who goes with her boyfriend down in an alley and lets 'im do as he pleases. Like that you still blush when Colin catches you by surprise with a joke. I like that about you."

"Do you think you're taking that away from me?" Stasia asked.

"Not if we go to dinner with your pa tonight," he said. "We stay here any longer, I'm not so sure."

She raised an eyebrow.

He was still breathless and she wasn't entirely certain her toes had found the floor again yet.

"I carry three daggers and a sword," Stasia said. "You let me worry about my honor."

He ran his palm over his forehead and through his hair, then he shook his head.

"No," he said. "I'm gonna worry about it, too. Because it ain't wrong. All this curtsyin' and how do you doin', we can drop that and I'm as happy as the next man. But you're a lady of quality and character and virtue, and I aim to be a gentleman about all of this. We just gotta figure out what that means. Just 'cause we ain't taken by the rules everybody else has don't mean we don't need any at all."

Stasia considered that for a moment, then nodded.

"Okay," she said. "Okay, that's fair. Let's go get dinner. I want to change, first. I'm not sure my father would even recognize me like this."

"I'll meet you downstairs," he said, looking around the room for just a moment, then going back out.

Stasia changed into her dragonskins and went down to find him on the street.

They walked alongside each other for a while before Stasia found something to say.

"Did everything go okay this week, at least?" she asked.

He nodded.

"Couldn't tell you if it hadn't, but the king is busy at work and we done a fine job watchin' over him while we were on shift. My mistakes and all."

She looked over at him.

"I really like it," she said. "You kissing me like that."

He kept his eyes forward.

"I ain't got anything to offer you," he said. "Nothin' but my loyalty and my heart and a great deal of heartache when the inevitable happens."

"I'll take it," Stasia said. "Because I don't need anything from you but your loyalty and your heart, and I don't have anything to offer you, either, but more of the same."

He let his hand fall away from his body, his fingers finding hers and weaving through them. He gave her a sideways smile and she leaned her head on his shoulder.

"I asked," he said. "But I'm still lookin' for an answer when you know it. Do you want to marry?"

"Do you?" she asked.

"I think I ain't too much a coward to tell you that it gives me a real fright, the idea of it. But if it's what you want, I'd also like to think I'm man enough to do right by you. And if you don't?" He paused and she felt him look over at the top of her head. "I'll own that I don't know what to make of it, then, either, what's to happen to us."

"Some just... go forward," Stasia said.

"Ain't given thought to children, either," he said.

"Babe," she said. "It's too soon. Everybody else may have already known that we were going this way, but I didn't. Can we just... deal with what is for a little bit before we have to worry about what comes next?"

"Reckon there's nothin' wrong with that," he said, kissing the top of her head. "I just had a long stretch of days to think about it, and while I got no answers for you, I kept findin' that my mind wanted to go to the future. I don't know how to be with a woman, to have someone who rightly expects somethin' from me."

"You did a lot of standing around, didn't you?" Stasia asked, and he laughed.

"That I did."

"I was busy all week," Stasia said. "I missed you, but I've been all over the city. I haven't really been thinking about things."

Well, she had. She'd been thinking about which weavers were still active, and where they were getting their wool and linen cord, and how much they were paying for it.

And whether the clay mines up at the estates were running loads of clay down to the potters in the crafting district yet, or if a load of clay from the Pirate Islands were a worthy investment. There were apparently settlements out there that dug it in quantities big enough to sell, and if Stasia swooped in with the right size ship at the right time, she could outbid what the Islands were likely going to be able to pay for it, and thus would Verida have dishes to replace the ones they were throwing at each other, just now.

When she'd thought of Babe it was with a sort of humor or a joke hoping that he would be waiting for her up around this next corner to surprise her, to lay hold of her and kiss her. Those ideas were going to keep coming to her, now, she knew, though the kisses would be different.

A shock went through her and she straightened to

keep from falling over.

"You went down to the Black Docks," he said. "I didn't get to see you after that."

"No," she said. "You were on shift the next day. It was... very useful and... I'm really glad I went. I saw a lot of things and I met some people that I think I really needed to meet."

"At the docks," he said, and she nodded.

"I don't think you'll ever see them like they are because you remember them as they were," she said. "And that's okay. But they aren't like that anymore. They're not beautiful and perfect, but they're changed and I don't... I really don't think they're that bad."

"You've been taken in by the Rat King and what he thinks he's doing," Babe said.

She waited to see if he would drop her hand, but he didn't. His fingers tightened around hers and she smiled.

"I'm friends with him," Stasia said. "And I like him and I admire him and..." She stopped herself from saying that she thought that he was smart and attractive, because that just felt intentionally antagonistic, and saying that about her best friend's husband probably crossed a line, too. "I think that he is not as casually dismissive of what the Black Docks are as you think he is."

He considered that for a while as they turned onto the road that ran along the Sapphire and the Fielding house came into view.

He let her hand drop, now, but she'd expected that and it made her smile. It didn't matter that he was the biggest, strongest man she knew, that he'd fought stone elves in the mountains and pirates on the sea, or that he protected the king professionally, now. He was afraid of her father.

"I'm willing to try," he said after a moment. "But the Black Docks are just... they can't protect themselves from a man like that."

"I think that's why they need a man like that," Stasia said. "Maybe."

He looked over at her and frowned, then shrugged.

"Maybe you're right."

She knocked on the front door, looking over at the sun to gage the hour, shrugging.

They probably wouldn't be done getting dinner ready yet.

They were early enough.

No.

Tesh wasn't going to kill her for this.

Yasmine might, but not Tesh.

The housekeeper opened the door and looked from Stasia to Babe and back.

"You might have sent word," she said, stepping aside to let them in. Her tone was hardly disappointed to see her. Stasia gave her an apologetic smile.

"He was on duty at the castle until this afternoon, and he hasn't had a quality meal the whole time."

"Now, I know for a fact that the castle kitchens are the best in the city," Tesh said, unexpectedly offended.

"Yes, ma'am, they are," Babe said smoothly. "But it ain't like they give the likes of us first pick at it, if you catch my meaning."

"Ah," Tesh said. "Staff eat last. I do know that rule well. Well, come in, come in. Minstrel isn't home yet, but we expect him any time."

"Never gets old, lookin' at the inside of this place," Babe said. "You do it a great service."

"It's a fine home, with or without me, and flattery will not get you a plate of food any faster in this place."

Babe winked.

"I find flattery is a grease most effective applied over time," he answered, and she laughed.

"Come sit," she said. "I'll bring in refreshments and

inform your sister that you're here."

Stasia looked up the stairs.

"She still hasn't left?"

"Not my place, miss, not my place," Tesh said, ushering them into the formal sitting room - Stasia would have preferred to wait in Minstrel's office, but she knew for a fact that Alyssia would never go in there - and then left.

"Your pa knows how to pick a place, doesn't he?" Babe asked. He had been in here, before, too, but he had a sense of awe that was just... charming.

"You've spent the last week at the castle," Stasia said. "This is just a show."

"It ain't even," Babe said, glancing at her with a cheerful grin. "Just less intimidatin' now that it ain't your house, too."

She tipped her head.

"Is that true?" she asked, but he rose as footsteps came around the corner and Tesh came in with Alyssia.

"What are you doing here?" Alyssia asked. "I didn't invite you."

"Do you think that I need an invitation to come to my father's house for dinner?" Stasia asked, wishing Babe would sit down.

He waited for Alyssia to take her seat on the other side of a marble table from them, then Tesh departed again and Babe re-situated himself on the couch.

"You do when I am the lady of the house," Alyssia said.

"You aren't," Stasia said. "You are a guest in this house, same as me. You are the lady of the Gormand household, which I understand you haven't seen the inside of since the stone elf threat started."

It was a guess, but she thought it was a pretty good one.

"It's being managed quite competently, thank you,"

Alyssia said. "But I am still father's daughter. He didn't disown me, so I am the lady of his house, too, so long as he isn't married and Meglyn isn't here. And I don't see Meglyn."

"You overstep," Stasia said darkly.

"You've made a terrible inconvenience for the kitchen staff," Alyssia answered. "I find that very rude, even for you, Anastasia."

"The king's guard work unpredictable schedules, and I wanted Babe to come tonight."

"Yes," Alyssia said, turning her attention to Babe. "He is here, though I fail to understand why."

"Your father asked for my professional evaluation of the property and setting a proper guard to it against thieves and villains," Babe answered. "I should like to see to the results as they are completed."

"Which is fine and well," Alyssia said. "But it is done. Do you think it necessary to intrude yourself into the household for a meal? It is unbecoming of the king's guard, participating in such improper social etiquette, even if it is encouraged by my insolent sister."

"I'm going to pause here at the doorway and pretend that I did not just listen to my beloved daughter treating honored guests with contempt," Minstrel said. Stasia jumped to her feet as Babe and Alyssia stood, and she ran to hug her father.

"You've been rather scarce," he said, and she shook her head.

"You know I've been around. Just busy, father. I think you'd be proud of me, though, all of the things that I'm doing."

"I know that you're ruffling feathers and agitating the established networks," he said confidentially. "I couldn't be prouder."

She beamed and he kissed her cheek then stepped away from her.

"Now," he said. "We are familiar, informally, but I expect one of my daughters to announce my guest, please."

"Sir..." Babe started, but Stasia put her hand up, interrupting him.

"Father," she said. "Please may I present Babe of the King's Guard. Babe, may I present Minstrel Fielding, my father."

Babe gave her a little look, as though he thought that this was unnecessary, but Stasia happened to know that Minstrel was insisting on formality as a discipline directed at Alyssia, and Stasia was well willing to go along with that.

Babe stepped forward.

"Sir," he said, offering a handshake. "It's good to see you in good health."

"And it's good to see you in the company of my daughter," Minstrel answered. "I feel better knowing that you and your brethren are helping to keep her out of the worst of trouble."

"Sir, I often feel that we cause her involvement in it, but we take it personal, seein' that she gets back out, too."

Minstrel gave him a genuine smile and nodded.

"You're right. That does sound more like her. Tesh told me that there were refreshments coming, but that we could seat ourselves at the table to take them, if we chose."

"Daddy, honestly," Alyssia said. "They show up at no notice this close to dinner and you expect the kitchen people to just adapt?"

"I defy you to go into that kitchen and tell Yasmine that you think she doesn't have the capability to add two plates to the table tonight," Minstrel said. "I dare say you'd eat with the horses tonight."

"Sir, if we are an inconvenience at all..." Babe started, and Minstrel held up a hand.

"Stop, stop, you offend me," he answered. "My daughter has come home for a meal. Nothing could possibly delight me more, and yet she manages it by bringing one of her friends that I so often hear of and so seldom hear about. Now I get to speak with you directly, at the leisure of a meal. I am beyond pleased that you are here tonight."

What Stasia loved about her father was that every word he said was true, and she knew it.

He put an arm out, inviting Babe to walk with him, and Stasia fell in behind them as Minstrel put an arm around Babe and escorted him through the main hall and into the dining room, pointing out things of note about the house and asking questions about how the work on the house had been done.

Babe seemed completely at ease, walking with Minstrel, and Stasia only narrowly avoided sticking her tongue out at her sister.

"You are absolutely unforgivable," Alyssia said.

"Why haven't you gone home yet?" Stasia answered. "You don't belong here."

Alyssia put her nose up and Stasia shrugged, going in to sit down next to Babe at the table.

He gave her a little smile, and her stomach fluttered, then he looked at the table and frowned.

"You're gonna help me, right?" he murmured to her, and Stasia nodded casually.

"Nothing to it," she answered in the same tone. "No one's watching that close, anyway."

A few minutes later, Tesh came in with coffee and thin-sliced fruit with crisped bread. It was a Botonese take on a Veridan appetizer, and Stasia appreciated her making the effort to understand how the Botonese took their meals.

Stasia stood to pour coffee, then pulled a plate of the little open sandwiches and put it in front of Babe, making one for herself and sitting again.

"So tell me, Babe, how is the king's business?" Minstrel asked.

"Transition is still happening," Babe said. "But he seems happy with how things are going, and the guard are happy to serve our purpose."

"Transitions are always hard," Minstrel said. "But for a man like Finwalk, he'll recognize that it's also a moment of great opportunity. I can't imagine that any of what's going on is easy, in light of all of the events up to this point, but I think that the merchant community rather unanimously believes that Queen Melody made an excellent decision in naming him."

Babe dipped his head.

"I understand that you may find the practice a bit odd..." Babe started, but Minstrel shook his head.

"Different from Boton, certainly, but the rule of law here is not held by the king, but rather the law, which means that operating under this king or that king is largely uneventful for most of the city. The work of administering such a complex city as this one is certainly not trivial, and it deserves a strong and invested hand to do so, and I actually admire the focus with which the king does these tasks. The administrative state of Boton is awfully concerned with self-preservation, and there is bountiful graft that comes of it. No. Odd is not the word. Imperfect, I will grant you, but what system created by men could be perfect? I find that there is wisdom here in the midst of a very difficult situation, and I am pleased to have had the honor of observing it as closely as I have."

"Daddy, do you spend time with King Finwalk?" Stasia asked.

"Of course, my dear," Minstrel said. "He even mentions you, from time to time. But he takes meetings with all of the important merchant guilds, and many of the important individuals, as well. It is impossible to know a king's mind; he keeps his counsel quiet and mostly just listens at this point, but I know that he has a vision of where he would like to go, and... spending time with him, I'm quite eager to see what that is."

"Merchants want a stable environment in which to do fair business," Stasia said. "Surely you aren't looking forward to him making changes."

Alyssia cleared her throat, but Stasia ignored it.

"You of all people should see the immense opportunities for reorganization, expansion, and increased efficiency that recent events have exposed," Minstrel said. "Just because the ingrained interests go against those new efficiencies doesn't mean that the king should, and I certainly hope that I always find myself on the side of efficiency, even when it goes against me in the short term, because an efficient market is a predictable market, and a predictable market is a good place to make money, in the long term."

"You know, sometimes I forget where Stasia gets her sharp mind," Babe said. "But the two of you are peas in a pod, no two ways about it."

"This is not appropriate dinner table conversation," Alyssia said.

Stasia drew a deep breath and looked at her sister.

"What would you care to discuss, then, dear Alyssia?" she asked.

"I've scheduled an appointment with a dressmaker to come to the house tomorrow for a fitting."

Stasia blinked at her.

"That's very nice," she said. "Is that all?"

"I've heard that the young Lady Pinnace is discussing engagement with one of the Blackmoor boys," she said.

"Can she not make her mind up, which one?" Stasia asked.

Alyssia gave her a dark look, and Stasia shrugged.

"Is that all, then?" Stasia asked.

"You're supposed to offer your own tidbits about things going on around the city," Alyssia said. "You're being very rude."

Stasia drew breath and turned to look at her father again.

"Do you know about thievery crews working in the city?" she asked. "I've just heard of this, and I thought that I would have heard about it before, if it were a common thing."

"Well, certainly you know about them," Minstrel said. "They're hardly rare. The pickpockets in the market are getting more aggressive and rampant, if nothing else."

"No, this is something different," Stasia said, mentally admitting that she'd been vague. "This is more organized and... bigger, I think, by a lot."

"Did you meet someone interesting?" Babe asked her passively but very pointedly if you listened carefully.

"Maybe more than one," Stasia said lightly. "And I'd never heard of anything like it."

"I haven't heard anything particular," Minstrel said. "Can you give me an example?"

Stasia frowned and shook her head.

"I would have imagined... very expensive things turning up missing and no one knowing what happened to them. Things that are very hard to steal, where it would have taken organization and planning to pull it off."

"Stasia," Alyssia hissed.

"How very interesting," Minstrel said. "No, I haven't heard of anything of the kind, actually."

"Crime in Verida happens on all levels," Babe said, his attention firmly on Stasia. "But we think that some of the highest crimes don't get reported or widely discussed because the victims either don't know it happened or go along with it as part of the take."

"Like, they're stealing from themselves intentionally?" Minstrel asked, and Babe shook his head, looking over at him now.

"No, sir," he said. "Like the plan involves makin' the

victim keep his trap shut because he's afraid or embarrassed."

"How awful," Alyssia said.

"How interesting," Minstrel said.

Babe finished his plate and glanced at Stasia, who nodded a very quick encouragement. He was welcome to help himself to more. He filled his plate and Stasia smiled, knowing that anyone else, she would have cautioned them to save their appetite for the actual meal, but not feeling concerned on Babe's behalf at all.

"So how is business, Daddy?" Stasia asked.

"Complex," he said thoughtfully. "I'll admit, I've missed having my greatest ally here to discuss the ins and outs of it with me each night. I think I'd never realized how clarifying it was to have your input routinely until you disappeared this summer."

"You were worried sick, Daddy," Alyssia said.

Stasia wondered if that was true.

"I'm here, now," Stasia said, thinking of what Tesh had told her.

"No, no, dear," Minstrel said. "Not on a night that we have guests. I wouldn't dream of boring the table with our conversations all night long."

Her moment of boldness hit her and Stasia sat forward.

"Actually, Daddy, one of the reasons we came here tonight is to tell you that Babe and I are... seeing each other, now, and... I wanted you to know."

"Excuse me?" Alyssia asked. "You're going to spend your entire life sticking your nose up at contributing to the family by marrying properly, and the minute he lets you off the leash, you run off with..."

She took a breath, looking for the appropriate level of insult.

"Careful, Alyssia," Minstrel murmured, folding his

fingers together under his chin and looking at Babe.

"Is this true?" he asked.

"Daddy..." Stasia said, but he flagged her with a hand, his eyes not moving.

"You have brought a young man to my home as more than a social companion. He will speak for himself, now."

"Yes, sir," Babe said. "I've respected and admired your daughter since I first met her, but I'm a soldier by trade and I never thought to find more with her than that. It has been... an awakening, sir, that I don't have words for, finding that she has feelings for me as well."

Minstrel's eyes flicked at Stasia, and she saw the play there. She suppressed a smile as he drew breath to speak to Babe again.

"I'm pregnant," Alyssia said.

His head jerked to look at her and Alyssia looked quickly at her hands.

"I'd been waiting for... the right time to announce it, and we are preparing the social announcements now, and I wanted... to be the one to tell you in person." She lifted her face and beamed. "I'm going to have a baby, Daddy."

"Well, my my," Minstrel said, standing. "Congratulations, my darling."

He went over and she stood, grabbing his elbows and putting her face out for him to kiss it. She never had known how to hug.

He took a half step back, looking her up and down.

"You look radiant, my dear. I assume that Gevalt is over the moon?"

"Yes, Daddy. I'm getting my maternity dresses made now, while there's still time to find someone and for them to get the right cloth, it's so hard just now, but... Yes."

Babe stood, giving Alyssia a little bow.

"Congratulations, Lady Gormand," he said. "I wish you all the best."

Alyssia nodded to him as though he had owed her that, then he sat and Minstrel once again attempted to hug Alyssia with the same awkward result.

Stasia had many questions, the foremost of which was: how? She'd been living here all summer and since. Was the child a Gormand at all?

More importantly, she wanted to know when Alyssia would take her pregnant self back up to the Gormand house to prepare for the arrival of the child.

She managed not to ask either as Minstrel came to sit down again.

"So, young man," he said, turning his attention back to Babe. "What are your intentions?"

Alyssia flustered, clearly not ready to return focus to Babe, but Stasia didn't have time to enjoy it.

"What?" Stasia asked, and Minstrel raised his eyebrows.

"You brought home a young man," he said. "I may have disinherited you, but I am certainly still your father, and it is a question I am perfectly within my rights to ask."

"It's a fine question, sir," said Babe. "And I sorely wish I had a fine answer for it, but I don't. Neither of us anticipated such a thing as ending up here, and my intention is to try to make your daughter happy, whatever road that might go down."

"Do you intend to marry her?" Minstrel asked.

"Daddy," Stasia said sharply, but he twitched an eyebrow and kept his eyes on Babe.

"Don't know that it's what she wants, sir," Babe said.

"Daddy, this will not do," Alyssia said. "People are going to talk, and it's no better if they marry than if they don't. You have to forbid it."

"Your sister is a legally-independent woman," Minstrel said, his eyes still resting gently on Babe. "I will do no such thing. I will ask questions of this young man, and I will give her my counsel as a father, but I will forbid her nothing."

Alyssia huffed again and Stasia frowned at her father. He was playing.

She knew he was playing. She just had no clue what the game was.

"She has a point, though," Minstrel said. "Have you considered my daughter's reputation, in this?"

"I'm not sure I follow, sir," Babe said. "Is it that you're concerned with what it looks like, her bein' with a member of the king's guard?"

"Oh, no, not at all," Minstrel said. "I had had genuine fears that she might be roving with a tribe of under-tasked dandies who kept her out to all hours. Finding that she had made the acquaintance of a man of your caliber in her adventures was quite reassuring. I hold the guard in the highest esteem, and there are few men who have more merit as honorable partners to a young woman such as Anastasia."

"Then what nature of her reputation ought I be concerned with?" Babe asked.

"She is commonly seen as a spinstress," Minstrel said. "And while it is hardly uncommon for a spinstress to have a gentleman companion later in her life, at this moment she will be seen as rejecting the traditions and stability of marriage in favor of the more superficial comforts of an informal relationship, should she remain entangled with you for the foreseeable future without any discussion of marriage."

"Daddy," Stasia said sharply. "I did not bring him here tonight for you to try to twist his arm and force him to marry me. I am a legally independent woman, and I won't stand for it."

"Easy, Stasia," Babe said, reaching over to touch her hand with the outside of his little finger. "I see what he's gettin' at."

Stasia wanted to argue that he didn't have to concede anything, as far as she was concerned, but there was something to this she hadn't figured out yet, and she pressed her lips firmly, instead, letting Babe play his role.

"Sir, you're right that my time with the army, and then further with the King's Guard, it's taught me a lot about the nature of honor, and the importance of it. And while I ain't got much for treasure, what I have I'm ready today to lay at her feet. My sword, where it ain't the King's first to lay claim to, is hers, and my heart is wholly mine to give, and I wholly give it. Don't know what comes to us in the future, and bein' a companion to this lady for the rest of her years, may they be many, is plenty for me, but I don't sit here today hopin' for the least of things."

Minstrel gave him a deep nod.

"That was very well said," he answered. "You're from the Black Docks?"

"Yes, sir," Babe said.

"You got out young?" Minstrel asked.

"First I was able to sign the papers to enlist," Babe said.

Minstrel nodded.

"Then you have my blessing, whatever the two of you choose for yourselves."

"Thank you, sir," Babe answered.

"What was that about?" Stasia hissed to him, and he smiled gently.

"You take me out of this chair and put Colin here, of last year, and you tell me you don't understand where your father is comin' from, testin' your judgment."

"But you're nothing like Colin," Stasia said.

"Your pa don't know that," Babe said, taking her hand and squeezing it.

When Stasia lifted her eyes again, she found Alyssia staring at Babe with such focus that she didn't even notice

Stasia.

The door to the kitchen opened and Tesh came in with a platter, Yasmine behind her with another.

They arranged the food on the table, then Yasmine left and Tesh went through the list of what was there.

"Where is Alice?" Stasia asked. It was a plant question, and she could tell that Tesh recognized it for what it was.

"In her quarters," Tesh said simply.

"Please set two additional places at the table, Tesh," Stasia said.

"You'll do no such thing," Alyssia said, missing a beat and then turning sharply to look at Tesh. "Thank you, that will be all."

Stasia looked at Minstrel.

"When Alyssia goes back up to the Gormand estate, will you sit alone at your table every night?" she asked. "Or will you keep the company that you have, appreciating it for the immense value it brings your life, regardless of its station?"

"They are servants," Alyssia said.

"Are you the reason they stopped eating with us?" Minstrel asked Alyssia.

"It is improper," Alyssia answered. "They have a table in the kitchen for them to use for meals."

"Do you think I have so little control over my household that that was not a decision I had made intentionally?" Minstrel asked. "You are out of line, daughter."

"I think that Stasia had run amok without proper oversight, and you had simply failed to notice the liberties she had taken with how she ran her household, so I set to putting them right, once she was no longer attached to the house."

At least she'd waited for Stasia to be out, from the

sound of it.

"You are a much beloved guest," Minstrel said. "And I will forgive you your oversight because I do know that you were acting with the best of intentions, but in this house, my staff are family. This is not a household of a size that requires I treat it like an industry. These women are paid for the time and energy they put into keeping the house, but Stasia is right: they are also members of the household, and you will not treat them as lesser."

"We do not wish to intrude into your time as a family," Tesh said, and Minstrel waved his hand at her.

"Please bring out two additional settings," he said. "And fetch Alice. We will wait for you."

Tesh gave him a little bow and disappeared into the kitchen. Stasia did her best not to look smug, but it wasn't a fantastic effort, really.

"You were with the army," Minstrel said, turning his attention back to Babe.

"Yes, sir," Babe said. "Both up in the mountains and at sea."

"Yes, those are both quite unforgiving," Minstrel said. "I've heard stories that the mountains are just as liable to kill you as the elves are, and I've experience the sea scarce little myself, but sufficient to respect how difficult an assignment it must be, if it doesn't suit you."

"It's just as you say, sir," Babe said cheerfully.

They spoke for several more minutes about Babe's experiences in the mountains and how they compared to being on a ship for months at a time, and then Tesh arrived with Alice and they quickly set the table for two more.

Stasia served Babe while he spoke to Minstrel, then gave him cues on the order of silverware, though she'd told him the truth: no one at the table save Alyssia cared at all which fork he used.

There were two more courses, then Yasmine came

out to sit with them for desserts and wine.

Stasia found herself enjoying the sound of Babe's laugh, the way it filled the house, as he and Minstrel filled the entire evening with stories. Alice was quite quiet, but that was just her way, and Tesh added a story here or there about working in noble houses and the way that nobles behaved when they weren't at court, but the stories of the court room were the funniest and the most commonly shared. Stasia suspect that, after Alice, she had spent less time around nobles than any of the people at the table, and once or twice she caught Alyssia laughing and sharing tidbits about hosting parties and how ludicrous it was that the nobles took themselves that seriously.

"Come," Minstrel said, pouring Babe another cup of coffee. "Stasia and I have a habit of going to play cards in my study after dinner. Come sit with us and play."

"Sir, I'm honored at the invitation, but I couldn't possibly," Babe answered. "I ought report to the guard house tonight, and make sure that my commander doesn't have orders for me for tomorrow."

"Of course, of course," Minstrel said. "I would never want to hold you when you have responsibilities to attend. Stasia, do you need anything from your belongings upstairs?"

"Just because I need to go don't mean the two of you can't sit and play cards," Babe said. "No call at all for her to leave with me."

"Oh," Minstrel said. "Oh, yes of course. And please don't let me rush you at all, either. You are a very welcome guest tonight and all nights."

Babe smiled and dipped his head.

"No, the hour is late enough for me. I'll be takin' my leave with gratitude, sir, and a real gladness for the idea that we can do this again soon."

He stood and reached over, taking Yasmine's hand.

"Lady, I don't have words for the meal tonight.

Thank you for your work. I won't soon forget it."

"Oh," Yasmine said. "It was... nothing. Thank you."

He dipped his head, then Minstrel stood and the two men shook hands.

"Don't be a stranger," Minstrel said. "You are always welcome here."

"Thank you, sir."

"Stasia, if you would like to walk your guest to the door...?" Minstrel said, sitting.

Stasia finished her coffee and stood, going out of the dining room and walking to the front door with Babe. He wrapped his hand around hers as they walked, and she couldn't imagine being happier.

"That went well," he said. "Though I feel like we stole your sister's thunder, her bein' pregnant and all."

Stasia had failed to even think about it again.

"You're too nice," Stasia answered, and he gave her a sideways grin.

"You ain't seen mean, darlin'," he said. "That's a good family you've got in there. Don't underestimate that."

She shrugged and looked over her shoulder, then stood up on her toes to kiss him.

Because she could do that.

He put his hands gently on her waist and kissed her once, then straightened.

"May I see you tomorrow?" he asked.

"I'll come by the guard house and we can get breakfast," she said. "I need to check in with Melody, and then I'm planning on going up to Fisharbor to talk to a man about letting a boat."

"A boat," he said. "Where are you goin'?"

"I'm not going anywhere," Stasia said. "It is."

He shook his head.

"Didn't take you long, did it?" he asked.

"What?"

"To head off and go be a captain of industry like your pa."

"It's what I know how to do," Stasia said. "And it's really fun, like a card game where everyone is playing who wants to, and you don't have to beat everybody else to win."

He narrowed his eyes at her playfully, then looked at the door.

"I need to see Jasper before he goes to bed tonight," he said. "He said somethin' to me today about work for me tomorrow."

"Okay," Stasia said. "Do you want to use my father's carriage? I'm sure he'd send it out for you."

"No," he said dismissively. "You walk home safe tonight, alright?"

"Same as every night," Stasia said with a grin. "I'll see you tomorrow."

He dipped his head again and kissed her cheek, just below her eye, then went and opened the door.

"Good night," he said.

Stasia smiled.

"Good night."

She turned to go back to the dining room, finding Alyssia standing at the base of the stairs, her entire body behind one of the curling rails that ended on the first step, only her shoulders and her face visible behind it.

Stasia went over to tell her off about spying, but Alyssia spoke first.

"Does he truly love you like he says?" she asked.

Stasia stopped, at a bit of a loss.

"Yes," she said finally. "I think he does."

Alyssia looked away.

"I knew my place," she said. "I knew that my role within the family was to marry a man who could take on Daddy's business, some day, and that I had a job that I needed to do, making the junction of families work. I've always envied you your freedom. But if that man truly loves you the way that he says that he does..." She turned her face back to Stasia, and Stasia was shocked to see tears on her sister's cheeks. "It's a gift that most of us will never know. And I think that I am happy for you. The one of us who could actually have it. Don't let it go for anything, Stasia. Not for anything."

Stasia nodded slowly, looking for the back of her sister's hand to come through in her words, but it didn't.

"Thank you," she finally whispered. "I don't... I don't even know what to do. I never thought..."

She shrugged, and Alyssia nodded.

"None of us did," she said. "And I will pay for it, in my circles, that you're seeing a man with no status at all. But you have to fight for it, if it's real and if it's true. Because a man like that... feeling like that for you..."

Stasia swallowed, finding a lump in her throat.

"Are you happy?" Stasia asked. "About the baby?"

Alyssia looked down at her stomach, where her hand was already pressed.

"It quickened six weeks ago. Back when I thought that everyone was going to die and the world was going to end around us. Gevalt wouldn't leave the estate. He says that it's his heritage from his father and that he would die with it. And I can't bear to look at him, that he would let the elves kill him and leave me alone in the world like that."

Stasia had never thought about it like that, and she felt a surge of pity.

"You have to go home, Alyssia," she said. "And I'm not even saying that because I don't like you being here. You can't hide here. You have to figure out how to make it work. You're going to have a baby. With him."

"I'm going to spend the rest of my life with him," Alyssia said. "And he is a kind man. He is good to me. He takes my side when his mother is intolerable to me, and he makes sure that the staff know that I am the lady of the house. But he refused... he refused, Stasia... to go to Boton with me, if the elves overran the city. And they were close. There were signs that they came to within eyeshot of the manor. Any one of them could have launched an arrow and struck him dead. And he wouldn't leave."

"He doesn't spend that much time at the estate, does he?" Stasia asked. "Doesn't he spend most of his time in town the way Daddy did, growing up?"

Alyssia raised a shoulder.

"He even comes here, sometimes, and will spend a night or two, but he always goes back, and... All he cares about is his legacy and living up to Daddy's expectations. He's going to be very successful, I know he is, but..."

She shook her head.

"You can't hide here forever," Stasia said. "I'm so sorry... but you have to figure out how to make it work. The elves are gone and..." She wanted to say that she didn't think they were going to come back, but the words caught in her throat as she realized that she wasn't that certain at all.

"I know," Alyssia said, looking down at her stomach again. "There's a child inside of me. It's so strange to think it. One who, with luck, will grow up to take on Daddy's legacy again. I pity her."

"You think it will be a girl?" Stasia asked.

"I hope it will be a girl," Alyssia said. "Because what's the use of a boy? Gevalt will just take him away from me and teach him to be a trader like everyone else in our family."

Stasia blinked at her.

She'd never had any idea her sister was in so much pain.

"So don't let him," Stasia said.

"What?" Alyssia said.

"Alyssia, I've never known anyone as strong-willed as you are. But all you do is try to enforce everyone else's rules. Make some of your own."

Alyssia pressed her mouth hard, looking like she was set to argue with Stasia.

And then.

"You're right," she said. "I am the head of the Gormand household, and I will be the mother of the Gormand heir."

"In a city literally ruled by a queen," Stasia said. "What you say matters. I mean, obviously I don't think that you should go to war with Gevalt, but... Things don't always have to be the way that they say. Sometimes they get to be the way that you say, and you just... have to say it."

Alyssia sniffed and rubbed her cheeks with the heels of her hands, then she nodded.

"You're right," she said. "This is... this is my only life, Stasia. It's the only one I get."

Stasia nodded, feeling sad for her, but watching something important happening all the same.

"Don't let them steal it from you with all their rules," Stasia said. "I may be the spare daughter, but you don't have to follow all of the rules, either."

Alyssia nodded.

"Thank you," she said. "And I am. I really am happy for you. He seems... Well, he seems perfect for you."

There. Those were the words that would have been backhanded, if Stasia had been listening for it like she usually did. The thing was, she didn't think that that was how they were intended, tonight.

"If you need to get out of the house and be around someone who doesn't think that the rules are the definition of life, send me a note and we can meet somewhere in town. For food, please, not for dress fittings. But... any time. I'm doing a lot of stuff, right now, but I can almost always... We can get a lunch together any time you like. Maybe... actually get to know each other."

Alyssia sniffed again and nodded.

"Do you have my address?" Stasia asked. "Here, let me get..."

She went to the door and took one of the calling cards from the stack there, flipping it over and getting a pen out of the small entryway desk and writing down the address of her new apartment. She went and gave it to Alyssia, who shook her head.

"I still can't believe you're living someplace like this," she said.

"It's mine," Stasia said, unbothered, now. "I'm not defined by the room where I keep my bed, and now I'm not defined by someone else owning that room, either."

Alyssia looked at the card again, then shook her head.

"Meglyn would die," she said. "Do you know if Daddy has told her yet?"

Stasia shrugged.

"Don't much care, either way," she said. "I expect if he just managed to shove Babe into thinking that he actually has to marry me, she'll be invited to the wedding, but other than that... I never think of her."

Alyssia shook her head, tucking the card away.

"This is the only life you're going to get," she said. "I'm... proud of you, that you aren't letting it slip away from you."

Stasia went to hug her sister, and Alyssia grabbed at her elbows. Stasia dodged, putting her arms around her sister.

"I'm happy for you," Stasia said. "You're starting a new adventure, and you've got a chance to decide for yourself how you want it to go. I hope that it makes you very happy."

Alyssia had to work at it for a moment, but she did eventually figure out how to return Stasia's hug. Stasia let her go and stepped away.

Alyssia brushed at her eyes again.

"I'm going up to bed, now," she said. "I'm so tired all the time. I don't know how other women do this."

Stasia nodded, and Alyssia brushed past her to go up the stairs. Stasia watched after her for a few moments, then went to find her father, where he was talking to Tesh about routine house issues at the dining room table.

He raised his eyebrows at her.

"Well," he said. "That was an eventful evening."

"What's going on at the port, Daddy?" Stasia asked, sitting down next to him. He frowned.

"What have you heard?" he asked her.

She shook her head.

"Very little, actually," she said. "But I'm watching the markets freeze up all over the city, the way we used to talk about happening in Boton, but I've never actually seen it happen before. I'm afraid that I'm missing something important, because the opportunities are just obvious everywhere, but if more experience merchants are afraid... clearly there's something going on that I should be taking into account."

Minstrel raised his eyes to look at Tesh.

"You're welcome to stay, Tesh, but I think things are going to get rather dry here for a while, and I don't want you to waste your evening feeling like you need to sit with us."

"I have other things I need to see to, tonight," Tesh answered, standing. "I liked your young man, Miss Fielding-Horne. I think he does you justice, and there are few I've ever laid eyes on that I would lavish with such praise."

Stasia gave her a genuine smile, then turned back to her father again as Tesh left.

"I find it difficult to believe that there are any merchants operating in this city with more experience than you," he said. "I'll see you that you haven't done a lot of in-person negotiating, but as far as seeing how markets behave and how to anticipate supply or demand, you've been sitting at my table discussing these things since before you knew your letters and your numbers. If you are confident and they are afraid, I would put my money with you over them every time. That said, these particular markets are new to both of us, and a measure of restraint and consideration is absolutely merited."

Stasia nodded.

"What's going on at the port?" she asked.

He shook his head.

"There's a lot of money moving around," he said. "Quietly, but with a sense that a lot of people are looking over their shoulders, expecting to be discovered. I haven't figured out more to it than that."

"Yes you have," Stasia said, and he grinned.

"My daughter," he said. "Yes I have. I have theories. I don't have a lot I can prove, but I think I'm beginning to get the shape of the men involved, though why eludes me entirely."

"Daddy, have you noticed that the city seems to be giving up?" Stasia asked, and he sat back in his chair, folding his hands across his stomach and frowning at them thoughtfully.

"I wouldn't have put it that way," he said after several moments. "But I can understand how you would. The merchants are... afraid. That is how I would have characterized it. But I would have said that it was because there is a lot of unknown right now, and there's something disrupting our markets that I can't see. Which is strange. I've loved the open-air auctions here, and how easy it is to track who is buying what and where it's ending up. The ships out at the port were the only real mysteries, and that's where we all compete. What's coming in, what's going out, which market are you buying from and what market are you selling into. Those are where the quick make their money. But here within the city... You've been popping up in a lot of the smaller markets."

Stasia grinned, flattered.

"You've noticed," she said, and he nodded.

"People tell me," he said, an admission. "But I think it's more than that. It's that the merchants there are coming to expect you. They don't know where to find things, but you turn up with exactly what they need and charge exactly what it's worth to them."

"I'm going to need to buy a cart," Stasia said. "Trying to figure out where to hire a stall is what's slowing me down, right now. But I could fill it and empty it eight times a day, if I wanted to. There's so much just sitting around waiting for someone to... do it."

He nodded.

"I understand. That moment when you realize you're doubling your money a couple times a day and start wondering what everyone knows that you don't, where you're going to lose the whole thing because your luck runs out."

Stasia stretched her eyes at him.

"Yes," she said. "Exactly. The port is just a disaster, right now. I literally watched a captain run down a pier and turn around an entire line of goods to send them all back onto the ship. I asked him why, and he wouldn't even tell me. He just said that they weren't going to sell at Verida and they were headed for another market."

"Not even the strangest thing I've seen," Minstrel agreed. "You do need a cart, but you should also be cautious. Markets like this, slushy ones, they have the propensity to suddenly freeze up entirely on you, and you can't offload whatever it is you just bought for any amount of money and you're stuck with it. Only thing you can do at that point is hope you can eat it all, literally, because it's of no value, otherwise."

"You send it somewhere else," Stasia said. "I'm hiring a boat out of Fisharbor for the week after next, at the end of their next big run. I'll just send anything I've got to Boton or the Pirate Islands or... whatever. Nothing is frozen solid. Ever. You taught me that."

"I did teach you that," he said. "But it's a high risk, high reward attitude. You're just starting out, and it may be wiser to be cautious."

Stasia grinned.

"You also taught me that, so long as goods got where they were going and everyone got what they were looking for, the worst that could happen is that you lost all your money," she said. "I've got a reserve for starting over, if I need to, but I'm taking stuff places that it needs to be. I don't feel like being careful, at that."

He scratched his chin, then smiled.

"That's definitely the girl I raised," he said. "You're playing a low, dirty game, right now. One that I don't have the capacity to run. But there's a lot of opportunity at that level, if it's just you and a mule to take care of. Be careful with renting a ship. I think you've got the right idea, hiring somebody off-season from other work, because that way when they get home, they aren't your problem anymore. That's very smart. But you front money for things to go over the water, you run the risk of nothing coming back."

She nodded.

She needed to keep that in mind. When it came to goods that she could put in a bag and carry from one part of the city to another, it was easy to assume they were going to get there. With a cart, the odds that she was going to dump it in the river were at least still very small. She would need to buy a mule, which meant hiring a place for it to stay and paying for its upkeep, which meant that if she was going to go bigger, she was committed to actually making money most days. It was just so easy, right now, with nothing but herself and whatever free time she happened to have.

"And how are things going for you?" she asked.

He shrugged, considering his fingers again.

"I've had some losses that were... unexpected. Guthrie thinks that we're just having a string of bad luck with ships, but I find it difficult to believe. I've done the math on it, and unless I'm missing something in my calculations, the odds of having this many ships fail to come in is... remote. There's something else going on."

"Pirates?" Stasia asked. "I've heard that they're getting more aggressive again, these days."

"Right on time, aren't they?" Minstrel asked. "No, that's not it, because the pirates aren't in the business of destroying my livelihood, actually. They let the ships go on, with the highest-quality stuff lifted off of them. This is whole ships and whole crews going missing. I can feel it, that there's a pattern to it, but I've looked at the charts and at the payrolls and I can't find it. It's breaking some of the other merchants who are over-extended to credit... you promise me that you won't take a loan from anyone but me, right?"

"I did promise that," Stasia said. "And I meant it. But I don't think that I want to play it that way. I'll use the cash that I have to finance my own purchases. I don't need leverage to make a good living at it, and I just don't want to take on the extra risk."

"Good girl," Minstrel said. "Everyone these days says that you need to leverage your cargoes, and I've just never seen the wisdom in that."

"I know, Daddy," Stasia said.

"I know you know," he said, smiling. "No, there's nothing wrong with where I sit. And I wasn't obfuscating when I said that there are immense opportunities out there, right now. I'm spoiled for choice, with everyone being so uncertain. Contracts are going unfilled all over the city, and if I had a warehouse of goods to sell, I would... well, I would compete with myself to be the largest merchant in the city again."

"Aren't there men in the city with warehouses full of goods?" Stasia asked.

"You would think, wouldn't you, my dear?" Minstrel asked. "But I can't find them. I'd be willing to take on the risk of finding markets for those goods, if they were just afraid to... I don't even know what they're afraid of. Loading them all up on carts and going to take people's money? None of it makes sense."

"Daddy, is someone manipulating the city in hopes of driving merchants out of business, to take over afterwards?" Stasia asked.

He frowned.

"It shouldn't be possible, here," he said. "The merchants are like cats. Forming a consortium to send a fleet to the dark side of Dernat is hard enough. Trying to make them act like a cabal and intentionally not sell into desperate markets? I can't imagine how they would enforce it."

"At the point of a sword, usually," Stasia muttered, and Minstrel frowned at her.

"Are your new friends making you jaded, my dear?" he asked.

She smiled.

"I used to wander Boton," she said. "Go to the little bars along the docks where the old men would drink, where I knew there would be fights, and I'd just watch. Got a man to teach me how to defend myself with a knife, got another one to teach me how to climb the side of a building to get myself out of harm's way. I've got all of these skills that I learned from hanging out with people that I thought were the most dangerous men around. And since I've come to Verida, I've been hanging out with much more reputable people, ones with money and with access to power and..."

"And you're discovering that the people that you thought were villains have no corner on villainy at all, do they?" Minstrel asked with a phantom of a smile.

"They really don't," Stasia said. "They fought because they were angry, but tomorrow they would forget it. I'm seeing people who can hold grudges through generations, right now, and..."

"There's a reason I never let you spend any time with the merchant community, when I wasn't hand-selecting the ones that I would invite home," Minstrel said. "Money makes people foolish, and it makes them confident, and confident foolishness is a dangerous, dangerous combination. Because when their foolishness loses that money, their confidence blames it on someone else, and it makes them volatile and sometimes even violent. If you're going to do this, you need to understand that. Don't do business with fools, because a fool will get you killed. Maybe not today, when times are good, though this is not that day, but tomorrow when they're bad or worse? It will be the fool that you regret."

Stasia thought about that for a moment, then nodded.

"I really like Babe, Daddy."

"I do, too, sweetheart," he answered with a real smile. "I hope that he is exactly what both of us think he is, because you deserve that in your life. I can tell you this, though. Whether or not he is authentic, that man is no fool."

Stasia nodded.

"I know. And he is authentic. I have seen him risk his life more than once, and... that's the only part in all of this that scares me. That I could lose him. But he is what he appears to be. I've never been more confident about anyone in my life."

He gave her a thoughtful look, then nodded.

"Would you like to play cards, then?" he asked. "I

have more conversation about the specifics of things going on at the port, but I always think better with a deck of cards in my hand."

"I would love that," Stasia said, and he pushed his chair back decisively.

"Then we shall do it."

She went home very late and very happy.

She'd won more games than she'd lost with her father, and she felt like a lot of the craziness around the city was something she could navigate, even if she couldn't understand it. Her father didn't see it as mass despair so much as a confused system of trade that was upsetting everything, and while she spent the walk home thinking about what Matthias was seeing, by contrast, it felt like it was something she could beat by going after the symptoms of trade. If everyone was anxious because their markets were barren, wouldn't that cause a lot of the behaviors Matthias was seeing?

And the Black Docks were normal because the trade there was always segmented away from the rest of the city, unmixed with the rest of the city's issues, and, as Skite had said, optimistic in its potential for the future.

She woke up the next morning feeling less confident that it was so simple as buying a cart and delivering things where they needed to go, and she got to the guard house feeling almost silly for how simple everything had felt in her mind the night before.

And then she saw Babe, and she was just... happy again.

He grinned when he saw her, and she smiled back because there was simply nothing else her body could do when he smiled at her, and now she was allowed because they had told Jasper and Colin, and now Jasper couldn't be upset that they were sneaking around and Colin was disarmed because he couldn't say something surprisingly insightful and crude that hinted at knowing something he shouldn't have.

She was glad that Sterling and Matthias knew, too, but Colin and Jasper had been the important ones, and now... now Babe could come walking down the steps and across the training yard to lift the barrier for her, and she could stand there grinning like a dummy at how happy it made her to see him.

Even if she saw him almost every day, anyway.

He put his arm around her waist and kissed her cheek and they set off. Stasia might have danced, but for the fact that it would have meant stepping away from him.

"You look tired," he said. "How late were you there?"

"I need to go more often," she answered. "My father isn't the only one who finds those conversations clarifying."

"So, late then," Babe said, and she grinned.

"I'm happy," she said. "And I feel like I can see what I need to do next."

"What's that, then?" Babe asked.

"I need to come by a cart and a mule," she said. "And increase my scale."

"Oh," Babe said. "You already got a horse, though, don't you? Or is she technically your pa's?"

"No, Schotzli is mine," Stasia said. "And someday I'm going to be able to keep her, again. But for now, my father is letting me leave her there, because I can't afford to stable her, and it costs him basically the hay she eats to keep her at the house. She isn't a pulling horse, though. She's never been trained in traces, and she wouldn't stand for it, I don't think. I just want a little mule, the size I could take up and down the stairs with me and keep in my apartment, if the world got that dear to me, who can pull around a little cart."

She had in mind a toy-sized animal, small enough that she could stand over top of it with her feet on either side and not put weight on its back. Just something that would stand at a cart and follow a lead. If she were a man, she might have pulled the cart herself and saved herself the cost of the animal, but she had an instinct that men would simultaneously patronize and exploit her, if they saw her pulling her own cart, and she didn't want to fight through those reactions.

"And that's how we fix the city is it?" Babe teased, and she grinned.

"It's strange," she said. "I've grown up on my father's stories about taking a full-sized cart all around the island, city to city and town to town, country to country, and how every time he rolled up to a town, everyone would come running to see what he had, and how it meant that there was need there - there was demand - and he was filling that need by being there. And it really was him fixing the world one leg of a trade loop at a time. He said that if they hadn't needed the things that he was selling, or if his prices were so high that his goods were no longer worth purchasing, they wouldn't have come pouring out of their homes to come look, and his journey would have been wasted. I really do think that a donkey and a cart can start putting things right. That's what I've always believed."

He smiled like he might have something to say to that, but then he shook his head.

"I like that that's how you see it," he said.

She tipped her head against his shoulder, then straightened and he let his arm drop.

"No, I know that that's a small piece of a very big problem," she said. "And I have other things that I can be doing that are going to help a lot more. I need to continue to be there when Queen Melody needs me and I need to keep working with you guys on finding the warlocks and getting rid of them..."

"Whoa," Babe said. "I want you nowhere near the warlocks, right? Not your problem at all. You get the feelin' it's somethin' we want you to be a part of, I'll ask the guys not to talk about them around you anymore, and I won't let them tell you where we are when we're huntin' 'em."

"I'm not saying that I'm going to go in there wielding daggers," Stasia teased. "It's just... I can be thinking about it and I can talk to you guys about it, and I can help figure out what it is they want and what that means they might be doing. It's the figuring-out part, not the stabby stabby part."

He snorted.

"Fair enough, then," he said.

They turned in to a bakery that they both liked and he ordered breakfast for the two of them, then they went back outside to sit at a little table to eat.

"You know, I know that everyone thinks that the city is wretched this time of year, because everything's just fallow and drab, but the weather is actually nice through the fallow season," she said.

"You mean you don't self-season the same way, stewin' in the hot?" he asked, and she grinned.

"Now there's an image," she said, and he laughed, grinning back easily.

"Jasper's sendin' me down to the merchant's row today," he said. "Got somethin' to keep my eye out for."

"Do you need help?" Stasia asked, and he shook his head.

"No. They're buyin' goods from somewhere, magic stuff that even the pixies don't know about, and Jasper reckons there's a merchant or a sailor down there bringin' it in as contraband. We've been trackin' a few men who might fit the bill, and I'm on to see if I can't spot 'em today. So I can't sit with you for long before I need to head down and take over for Colin."

Stasia nodded.

"I need to check in with Melody soon, too."

"And you're sure I'm not keepin' you from your trade empire?" he asked.

She grinned.

"It's... I want to say it's 'just fun', but that isn't it. This is what I'm good at, and I want to do it. But there's nothing that says I need to do work on it right this minute. I have time to do what I want to and what I need to, and there's nothing waiting on me, and I kind of love that."

He snorted gently.

"About yesterday," he said after a moment, and she tipped her head.

"Yeah?"

He frowned, and she held up a finger.

"If you try to take back anything about what happened yesterday, I will be sorely disappointed in you," she said. "Everything was perfect."

He nodded thoughtfully, taking another bite and chewing. It was like he had something he needed to say, but he hadn't figured out how yet, and so he had cued it to keep himself from bailing on even trying, but he still hadn't found words.

Stasia sat back in her seat, concerned and skeptical, but patient.

"Things between us..." he said slowly, and Stasia put her hand over her mouth.

"Please don't tell me that you've had a change of heart because my father got so intense," she said.

"No," Babe said, still not looking at her. He shook his head. "No, I ain't changed my mind or my heart none. But I did recognize that... just kind of makin' this whole thing up as we go along, seein' what comes... I done that my whole life and it's worked fine, but you and yours, you're planners and you're... careful... and it's made me see that you deserve to have a plan, settin' out, and to know what's aimed to come next."

Stasia wrinkled her nose.

"Did you just call me a planner?" she asked. "I've literally wandered around doing whatever struck my fancy my entire life. It is my fatal flaw."

He smiled gently, then lifted his face.

"You deserve a gentleman who's ready to devote the rest of his life to you, not just the week and the week after that. You really and truly do. And this idea that marriage was something we'd think about later, when we got the rest of the stuff sorted out and figured... I don't normally lie to myself, nor hide truths, but that's exactly what that was. Do you reckon on anything changing this season or next? Because I surely don't, and the only reason I'd put off such conversations, other than fear of where they lead, is if I'm not sure."

"Or because you're not a fool rushing in on a surge of emotion," Stasia said. "We have, neither of us, ever contemplated marriage as a viable option in our lives. We deserve more time to figure out what it is we actually want before rushing off to make commitments just because we're trying to prove we're brave to each other. Or worse, my father. What you said, last night, will stay with me for the rest of my life. And I believe that you meant every word of it and that it was true. But you need to know that you want what's at the end of that road, as you say, before you set off. And I sincerely hope it doesn't hurt you to hear it, but I'm not certain."

"I am," Babe said. "I seen men make mistakes all around me. Seen 'em fall prey to women who needed 'em for no other reason than that a woman needs a man, seen 'em fall prey to emotions, as you say, and overlook problems that were obvious to everyone from the start. Seen 'em commit to situations that were never gonna be happy because they felt that's what they had to do, to be a man. You look at me and tell me it's possible I'm makin' a mistake, I'll hear you out. You got good sense and a strong mind, and I'm happy to hear that I'm missin' something important. But I also know that what I feel about you ain't just emotion. I know when Jasper came down from that mountain by himself, I just about broke, and when I was layin' on a table, a dagger in my chest and no real prospect of goin' on once they figured out what had gone wrong with me dyin' like I was supposed to, I couldn't even look at you because I couldn't bear to see you hurt like that. I wasn't afraid, Anastasia. I wasn't afraid of nothin' but hurtin' you by dyin'. My squad needs me and I serve the King with undying loyalty, but none of that even feels like livin', next to sittin' here with you, eatin' bread. So you tell me. You tell me this is a mistake, and I'll listen hard and let you convince me. But if you can't? Then this is a conversation I'm ready to have when you are."

Stasia covered her mouth.

It was just too much.

"I don't deserve you," she whispered, and he snorted.

"Far as I can see it, that's my decision to make and not yours," he said. "Though you say it again, I'll be glad to explain to you just how wrong you got it." He brushed off his fingers and looked around, taking a breath that sounded like relief and pure joy. "Now. I'm not gonna put you in a spot to speak to that, as I had the whole night to sort through the words and find the ones I actually meant, true. But if it'd be okay with you, I'd like to stop by tonight on my way back to the guard house and finish this conversation when you're ready to have it."

She swallowed.

"Okay," she said, and he dipped his head.

"I'm serious, Stasia," he said. "I don't want to push

you into sayin' anything you don't mean. You need time, you take it."

"Tonight," she said. "My apartment."

He nodded, then reached across to cover her hand with his.

"Whatever it is you come to, it's okay," he said. "I mean that with my whole heart. Your pa ain't pushed me anywhere wasn't mine to end up already, and I don't aim to do it to you, neither. You want no part of it, you say so, and it's gone. Things as they are today are enough for forever. Told my mates, told your pa, not sneakin' and not lyin'. I'm happy. All right?"

She nodded again, still feeling like she didn't deserve him.

He winked, and smiled.

"I got a magic courier to track down. I'll see you tonight. Might be late."

She nodded and swallowed again as he stood and left.

She finished her breakfast quickly and left, making her way to the castle and the side door.

Melody wasn't in her chambers, so Stasia made herself comfortable, doing a loop of the room looking for unexpected staff or daughters, then laying across one of the couches with her feet up.

Melody arrived about an hour later, giving Stasia an odd look and then going to change.

She came back and sat, ringing a bell on the little table and waiting for a maid.

"Tea, please," she said.

The woman bowed and left and Melody turned her attention to Stasia.

"Do you have news?" she asked.

"Nothing specific," Stasia said. "I've been keeping my eyes open, all over the city, going to all of the markets and talking to people and trying to listen to things that are going on around me. I don't have anything new that I need to tell you, but I thought that today was a good day to at least see what's going on here and whether I can help make any new connections."

Melody nodded, turning her head as the maid returned with a tea set. Stasia hauled herself off the couch to prepare the tea - Melody had been prepared to do it, but Stasia cut her off instead.

Handing Melody her teacup, Stasia went to the doors, finding a dark eye looking through the lock.

It blinked and fled.

Stasia shook her head.

"I swear, you need to tan the lot of them every time you catch someone spying," Stasia said. "It's outrageous that the queen doesn't have reliable privacy in her own castle."

Stasia returned to the couch as Melody sighed.

"It's getting to the point that I fear you may actually be right," she said. "Fueling castle gossip is one thing, but there are things coming in from outside that should not have been out in the first place. I just sat through a tirade from Lord Palora..."

There was a thump on the doors to the main hallway, and the doors opened.

A man in a sheepskin cape came in, his arms up in the shape they'd taken as he'd pushed the doors open.

"Melody," he said as Melody's eyes turned stony without moving from Stasia.

Going with instinct, Stasia stood and drew her sword. The man laughed.

"Is this her? The queen's new pet? Isn't she a dream? What do they call you? The Phantom?"

Melody hadn't moved.

Stasia thought about calling for the guard, but she wasn't sure where they were. Around Finwalk, there would have been members of the King's Guard within vocal reach at all times, but Melody just didn't merit the same level of coverage.

Stasia was prepared to kill this man, if she had to.

He carried a sword, but it was a dainty one that looked like it was more designed to match his clothing than engage in a fight - thought the woman with a purple sword at home - but he was bigger than she was, and if he was trained, she shouldn't underestimate him.

But she was prepared, if that was what she needed to do.

"Who are you?" Stasia asked.

"Tell it that it doesn't get to talk to me," the man said.

"This is the head of the Queen's Guard," Melody said, still stone-still, facing the table. "You will do as she requires or she will deal with you as she sees fit."

Well, that was empowering.

"State your name and your business," Stasia said, trying to imagine what Jasper would say.

Babe wouldn't say anything. He would just stand there menacingly until the man guessed what he was supposed to do, but Stasia didn't have the aura to manage that, so she went with Jasper.

"I'm here to speak to the queen," he told her.

"Name," Stasia growled.

That actually sounded more like her than Jasper, but she was okay with it.

He sighed.

"I am Lord Palora, and you will stand aside. The queen has made some dramatic mistakes in her first decisions since she has come to the throne, and she clearly needs someone to point them out so that she can set things as they should be."

Stasia laughed.

"Oh, that's not how this works at all," she said. "You

may see yourself out, or I will do it for you."

He looked at Melody, outraged.

"You intend to let this mongrel speak to me like this?" he demanded.

"You miss the mark," Melody murmured.

"I could be the daughter of a coal-hauler and a bastard and I'd say the same," Stasia said. "You will leave this room."

"I was an advisor to Queen Constance and King Rupert. I am a senior member of the court in every sense. And I am watching a juvenile queen run the city into the ground. I will not stand by any longer. I will not be silent."

Juvenile.

He had just called the most powerful woman in the city, and a mother of teenage girls, juvenile.

Stasia was blown away.

Unfortunately, she also had the distinct impression that she was not going to be justified outright attacking him.

He was outrageous, but he wasn't dangerous.

"You do not belong in the Queen's chamber, sir," Stasia said. "I cannot yield on this. You must leave."

Palora was a man in his fifties, and he had a mane of yellow-orange hair that went to his shoulders and a stringy triangular goatee that went to his chest when he spoke. The way he stood, she was pretty sure he was proud of both of them. She couldn't imagine what manner of idiot would wear a sheepskin cloak in Verida, even in the cool season, but there he was.

"You are making compounding mistakes, Melody," he said. "Your mother would be ashamed of how things have gone since her death..."

"That is enough," Stasia said. "You will leave this room or I will be forced to make you."

"He will speak his mind and he will leave," Melody said, sounding tired. "Do you agree, Lord Palora?"

Palora stepped around Stasia.

"Your first mistake was naming a common trader king," he said. "He has no idea the immense needs of a kingdom the size of Verida, nor the complexities involved in making sure that goods get where they are needed. He thinks that the fact that he can run a middling-sized trade empire means that he is good at these things, but he clearly is not. He's never produced a good in his life, and he's never looked at the treasure it takes to support the army. If you had named someone with more experience, the stone elves would never have attacked the city. Now, you're seeing the consequences of a direct attack on the city. People are hoarding goods rather than selling them, because they fear what happens when the stone elves come back to finish us off. They are resupplying up there in the mountains, make no mistake, and we do not have the strength to hold them back again."

Stasia blinked at him, stunned.

"Furthermore," he went on, beginning to pace back and forth, "the port is not collecting the taxes that it ought to be. The merchants are freeloading on the rest of the city, making themselves rich on the backs of the men and women who actually produce goods, and while we pay our taxes, they do nothing to contribute to the welfare of the city and simply skim the cream from the top of the city's wealth. You need someone leading this city who understands where its goods come from is where its wealth comes from, and that merchants who are actively supporting the trade within the city are the ones who are facilitating the strength and power of Verida. The rest of them are parasites on our ports and our services, and they need to be reined in."

Stasia blinked with disbelief. Oh, boy, did she have arguments with that.

She saw a flicker of amusement on Melody's face that she didn't think Palora noticed, and Stasia attempted to control herself. Melody knew.

Melody knew.

"Crime is at an all-time high. The Rats are running amok through the whole city, inspiring entire new generations of crime in neighborhoods that used to be safe. We need to crack down on it everywhere it's found. Stop people from sleeping in public spaces. If they can't find themselves a place to stay overnight, we can certainly put them to work to earn their keep at city-provided hostels. Finwalk cares nothing for the quality of life in the city, so long as the wealthy merchant class stays sated. He is blind to all but the needs of his own breed, and the city is collapsing faster and faster under his mismanagement. Melody, if you continue to stand by and do nothing, you will be the queen who presides over the very end of Verida."

He straightened with the look of a man who was accustomed to being applauded, and Stasia twisted her face, astonished that he was proud of himself for his outburst.

"Is that all, Lord Palora?" Melody asked.

"Is that all?" he blustered. "How could there possibly be more?"

"Thank you for your input," Melody said. "I will remind you that for the common men and women of Verida, entering the queen's chambers uninvited and without appropriate chaperone would be a capital offense. You will not stretch my tolerance any further. Is that clear?"

She still sounded tired, but there was an edge to her words that was unmistakable.

"You made a critical error, Melody," Palora said. "You have to own that and fix it. Don't let the whole city go down under the weight of your own ego."

Stasia gawped at him.

"You've had your say, Palora," Melody said. "You will now excuse yourself and not return to this place without going through the proper channels. Good day."

Stasia moved between him and Melody, glaring at him. He scoffed at her and waved dismissively, heading for the door.

Stasia watched him all the way out the doors, then realized that he wasn't going to close them behind him.

She gave Melody a despairing look, and the woman shrugged.

"Had you not been properly introduced?" Melody asked calmly. "I'm very sorry that that was a surprise to you."

"Maybe next time, knowing who he is, I'll just stab him," Stasia said.

Melody laughed gently, then shook her head.

"He is a powerful man, in the city. He isn't like the Bentmoors or the Westhausers for estate strength, but he works hard to maintain political connections, both within the castle and without, and a great many people think that his ideas are... insightful."

Stasia went over to close the doors.

"Do you need me to say that I'm certain he's an idiot?" Stasia asked. "Because I can elaborate if you want me to."

Melody laughed, more honestly this time.

"While I'm certain I would find that entertaining, I assure you that it would not be enlightening."

"Is he seriously angling to get you to name him king?" Stasia asked. "Did I hear that right?"

Melody nodded.

"You have a good ear," she said. "He campaigned hard for it, even before my mother died, which is one of the strongest reasons I never considered him. Finwalk was actually surprised when I named him, which was one of his greatest selling points, as far as I was concerned."

"You jumped being king on him?" Stasia asked, and Melody laughed with real humor now.

"No, no, he knew that he was one of the men I was

considering, but he never expected that I would name him over the others. And Palora has a few valid points, that Finwalk is still expanding the scope of things that he takes into consideration when he makes rulings and judgments, and in whose input he takes when he holds council, and no one understands how expensive the war is until they've actually looked at the lists of costs with their own eyes. He made mistakes, at the beginning, trying to reduce those expenses, and men died because of it. But I hope that things are not so dire as Palora suggests."

"Oh, I know they aren't that dire," Stasia said. "I'm actually convinced that they're less dire than I thought they were ten minutes ago, because every other word out of his mouth was nonsense. Clearly if he's that wrong on everything I know about, he's that wrong on everything I don't know about, too."

Melody tipped her head back against her chair and sighed.

"He has many allies," she said. "Men and women who are perhaps not quite as... informed as you are, nor as confident in their own perspectives. They like the promises he makes about how life could be in Verida, if only we stopped responding to the interests of other cities and nations."

"Verida is filthy rich because we cater to the interests of other nations," Stasia said. "The port is..."

Melody held up a hand.

"You aren't going to change my mind at all, but know that I largely agree with you. He has been presenting his perspectives to the king vociferously all morning, and I would please prefer to not indulge his point of view with any further discussion."

Stasia nodded, coming to sit and check her tea.

It was most of the way to cold.

She poured another half-cup in and sipped at it,

finding it palatable enough, then heated up Melody's cup as well, sitting back in her chair and considering.

She frowned.

Looked at her tea.

Frowned harder.

Melody sighed.

"All right, what is it?" the queen asked.

"How far would he go?" Stasia asked.

"Be more specific," Melody said.

"Palora," Stasia said. "How far would he go to prove that he's right and you are inept? How far would he have to go, to put you in a position where you felt like you had to name him king?"

Melody sipped at her tea, then pursed her lips.

"Those are two distinctly different questions," she said. "One is about getting his way, with policy, whereas the other is about my independence and autonomy. I believe he would go to great lengths to reach new plateaus of stability wherein he has more access to power. Great lengths. But the Veridan queens are very, very independent by design. I cannot imagine a means by which he would be able to force me to do anything."

"You would stand up to the whole city?" Stasia asked. "If everyone demanded a new king and Finwalk was... completely unable to get anything done because no one will work with him?"

"For a newcomer to politics, you do come right to the point," Melody said thoughtfully. "I could envision a situation where I would be forced to name a new king. It has happened a few times in the past, and the records are always conflicted on what degree of sabotage and what degree of incapability led to it, but the situation is called a 'rootless' king, and a rootless king will inevitably need to be replaced. Finwalk is a long way away from that, but... yes, Palora certainly has the means to undercut him, so to speak. But I will not stand for a man that I have no faith in to take the throne, I do not care what the city or the court think of it. This is my one true job, and I will discharge it faithfully until my dying breath."

"Will Amber?" Stasia asked quietly.

Melody went still for a moment, then nodded.

"Two questions, again," she said. "One is whether my daughter will return to me with the strength required of her to take on this role as she must, when her duty is called upon, and I believe that she will. She will surprise even herself, I think, with the hidden strength that she has. The blood of the Veridan queens runs strong in her veins, and she simply cannot see that with her own eyes."

"I actually agree with you," Stasia said, and Melody nodded.

"The other question, though, concerns whether that is a known feature within my daughter, or if her perceived weakness is a literal threat to my safety, because she would be easier to manipulate or overpower than I will be, and there I think you may have struck on something important. As things stand today, if and when I die, my sister will take the throne, and one of the features of Veridan queens is that once they take the throne, they hold it until they die. Her daughters will remain low on the order of succession, and my youngest sister would be in line behind Beatrice, should Beatrice not survive to Amber's return. Once Amber returns, though, she will succeed me, and then Charisma, and then Gina, upon their subsequent returns from their pilgrimages."

That's right.

Stasia was basically committed to that same trip up into the mountains for the next four summers.

Or more? Would they wait for the younger daughters to get older, and Stasia would ultimately go eight times?

She was going to need to come up with something to

ask for from the elves that was worth more to her, if that was the case.

And if Melody died, her sister's daughters would go as well, wasn't that right? For another... Stasia had no idea how many daughters Beatrice had.

Melody was still thinking about something else.

"There will be those within the court who know the schedule, if not the meaning of it, to the pilgrimages. If they think that they can leverage against Amber's weaker nature, they'll be working toward her reappearance as though they could pick the date on the calendar today."

"Surely they wouldn't," Stasia said. "Not after everything with the stone elves when Constance died. They wouldn't."

"It depends on their intents," Melody said. "There are men in the world who care only for their own success, their own ability to control outcomes. When they are in power, they care only for maintaining that power, and when they are not in power, they care only for achieving it. Any means is acceptable for these men, but they cloak themselves in the appearance of good faith, of concern - if mistaken - for the welfare of the city and those around them. Even a queen cannot see into the hearts of men, and I do not know if Palora is a fool or a fiend, but I cannot rule out that he would be willing to cause my demise in time for Amber to take my crown, under the impression that she would be amenable to responding to pressure in naming the new king." Melody paused. "If that should happen, you must give me your word that you would stand by her and justify her confidence that she should trust her own wisdom and counsel. Do not let her be ruled by fear."

Stasia's heart broke.

"Yes, mum," she said.

Melody nodded, shifting.

"Let us not dwell on it," she said. "Playing kingmaker

in Verida is difficult when you aren't queen, a delicate affair that seldom works the way you expect it to. I will not be ruled by the fear for my own life. My kingdom requires more of me. Let us focus on what Palora, or another man, might do to undermine Finwalk in hopes of influencing the naming of his replacement. Or even to try to force Finwalk to govern in a way that is more in keeping with Palora's vision. This is where there are interesting things to be done about it."

"Okay," Stasia said slowly.

"Tell me what made you think of it," Melody said, and Stasia nodded.

"I had dinner with my father last night," she said. "And we had a long conversation about how the markets aren't working like they normally do. He said that with the way prices are going, he could double his wealth, if he were sitting on a warehouse full of goods, and... it made me wonder, what if there were warehouses full of goods, sitting and waiting for an opportune time to sell. My father and I were speculating that they were trying to drive smaller merchants out of the markets, but what if the point was simply to collapse the market and blame it... on you?"

"There is nothing illegal about declining to sell goods at market," Melody said. "And I will not make a precedent by interfering with the market in such a way as to compel men to either buy or sell. Verida's prosperity is too rooted in our markets and the freedom they have to make their best path forward."

Stasia had a fleeting thought of how the Black Docks were making a killing, buying and selling things that were illegal in the rest of Verida, but that was an argument for another day.

"See, the thing is, neither my father nor I could understand how you would get Veridan merchants to decline to trade when prices are good. It's hard enough putting together a consortium when everyone agrees they want to do it and that they're probably going to make money at it. Trying to keep everyone from doing something that would make them a bunch of money? How would you do it?"

"Promises of future profits, outright bribery, and when those don't work, threats," Melody said. "And bribery and threats are illegal. Proving bribery is hard, in Verida, because our laws are very loose toward business transactions, but the threats are actionable. If you can bring me witnesses - victims - of threats, I will absolutely act against them, and so will Finwalk. This is his passion."

Stasia nodded, finishing her tea and putting her cup on the table.

"There's more problem to it than that, though," she said.

"Go on," Melody said.

"If you hold on to a warehouse full of goods, yes, prices go up for a bit, but if you hold on to them long enough, higher prices will bring more goods to market and prices will come down and the market will normalize. You have to either keep buying more and more of it - bringing more and more goods to market in the meantime - or you have to freeze..." She paused, the pieces just sliding together like they'd been waiting for her to find them. "... freeze the markets so that no one will bring supply to demand." She blinked.

"All right, and how would one do that, Miss Anastasia Fielding-Horne?"

Stasia grinned.

"Oh, I'm going to empty their little piggy banks," she said. Melody raised an eyebrow.

"The honest merchants of Verida are fighting on your side," Stasia said. "Don't let anyone get in their way. The distortions in the market are going to be painfully expensive to maintain, and while you are going to lose some of the smaller merchants and the over-leveraged merchants to unexpected market behaviors... and if the whole thing collapses, a lot of people are going to get hurt, but if enough of us can work up the courage to go against them, I'm going to take all their profits. My profits will literally be their losses." Stasia nodded slowly, seeing it, delicate and intricate, the way the men who were trying to manipulate the market could be crushed by that market, so long as it remained healthy in the meantime.

"The fear," Stasia said after a moment. "I don't know if they're causing it or just capitalizing on it. We can't assume... I don't even know how he'd do it, but we can't assume that he's the one who's causing all of the..." Stasia shook her head. "It's all connected, though. The fear and the markets and the lack of stuff that people need... It's like if you could solve one, all three of them go away, but..." She paused. She wanted to say that you couldn't solve one without solving all three, but... "If the fear is unrelated, we still need to work it out. I'm not ready to say that the warlocks aren't involved. But... If you can just find a few truly fearless merchants who will go for it, really... dive into the frozen markets, break them up... It will be self-feeding. You'll pull the fearful ones off the sidelines when they see how much money the risk-takers are making, and it will build against the ones who are holding resources until they start to break ranks... You might even have price collapses when it all unwinds, and that's really just as bad..."

"How do I help you?" Melody asked.

Stasia frowned.

"I'm gonna need a warehouse," she said.

When she looked up, Melody was laughing.

"I've heard about this look, but I've never seen it before."

"What?" Stasia asked, a bit disconnected from the conversation.

"The world-conquering look of the high-end

merchant class," she said. "The thing that scares the nobles witless, because they can't compete with you, when you get that look."

"When does your class start?" Stasia asked.

"Pardon?" Melody asked.

"At the university? When do you start your class?"

"At Balewater," Melody said.

The lowest and the coldest that the river would run all winter. A specific date, unlike Highwater.

Stasia swallowed.

"Two weeks?" she asked, and Melody nodded, fascinated.

"Yes."

"Normally, I would say that you should restrain yourself from involvement in the markets, because someone of your stature can only artificially manipulate them. Everyone is going to try to follow your lead because they think that you have the force of the government of Verida behind you. And encouraging risk-taking among the poorer merchants is just ill-advised. But if you could find a group of people with a lot of energy and nothing to lose and give them seed money..."

"You're talking about the Queen of Verida teaching a class in applied economics," Melody said. Stasia bit her lips, attempting not to grin.

"With the second-richest noblewoman in the city as a TA," she said.

"She is, isn't she?" Melody asked, and Stasia shrugged.

"It's what I've been told."

"Is this what it looks like when merchants go to war?" Melody asked. Stasia shrugged.

"Do they really call me the Phantom?" she asked.

Melody nodded.

"There have been attempts made to call you the

Purple Phantom, but Phantom appears to be sticking. I need you to ask Jasper to teach you some of the other back routes around the castle, so that you can show up other places as you choose. I will inform Petrault that you are not to be interfered with unless you are directly impeding the King's business, but it will take the staff some time to begin recognizing you consistently. React with confidence, and I will intercede, should you find yourself in a situation."

Stasia smiled sideways.

"I'm gonna end up in one of the cells down in the basement," she said.

"And your squad will find you, if it comes to that," Melody said. "But you are the head of my personal guard, and I need you to be confident in that. Otherwise my power within the castle will be of no value at all."

Stasia nodded.

"I can do that."

"I will ask that Lady Westhauser continue to come and go through the front gate, with an escort as is normally expected, but you must be above the rules of the castle."

"Yes, mum," Stasia said. She looked over at the doors. "I don't like that you let him stay, after he shouldn't have been here in the first place and I told him to leave."

"I understand," Melody said. "I will not apologize."

"You should have a guard out in the hallway, in case you need him," Stasia said, and Melody shook her head.

"I will not act in fear of my life," she said. "This is my home, and I will live in it as any other person would their own home."

Stasia considered that, not liking it as an answer, but at least understanding it.

"All right," she said.

"Now, tell me about your plans to take over the world," Melody said, and Stasia shook her head, feeling the power of the idea again.

"I'm small and nimble," she said. "But the problem with that is that it isn't very powerful. I need to find a way to be nimble and powerful, but that's the trick, isn't it? My father can command a fleet of ships, but he can't find all of the markets that need flour to supply the bakers. The cloth that my sister wants for her new dress is impossible to get because the linen fiber from Boton got back onto the ship and headed for somewhere else, rather than going to the spinners here in Verida. Meanwhile, the spinners are buying bales of wool through the back door because the wholesale market has none."

"Have you considered hiring an assistant?" Melody asked.

"I'm hesitating to buy a mule," Stasia answered. "Feeding it is too big a commitment."

Melody laughed.

"You're going to have to start thinking much bigger, if you expect to change anything about the merchants of Verida."

Stasia nodded slowly.

"I can do this," she said.

"I believe you," Melody answered.

"I can do this," Stasia said again, and Melody smiled. "Show me."

She spent the rest of the day arranging for a stall at a local livery barn, a small cart that would quadruple - at least - her per-load capacity, and she took Schotzli up to the Westhauser estate to buy a mule because, in the end, she couldn't find anyone at the port who would sell her one, even though there was a small herd of them there, just standing around waiting for someone to make up their mind about unloading a ship.

She might have rented one, perhaps, but she was ready to commit to this, and she wanted to have an animal that would be her own.

If she was going to work him all day every day, it couldn't possibly be cheaper or easier to rent him.

That and rented mules were sad little animals, and if Stasia was going to be one of the people dragging a beast of burden up and down the roads all day, she wanted to know that hers, at least, was well cared for and healthy, doing its happy little job all day.

Ella walked out with her to talk to the shepherds, who also kept watch over the breeding herd of beasts of burden, and they gave her the pick of the young ones who hadn't yet been put to work on the estate.

Stasia was going to have to break him in to a cart, but he was the friendliest, gentlest little soul of an animal, and she was going to call him Marvin.

She took him back to the livery stable and paid the man to put him in with the other small animals - there was a pen for them, rather than individual stalls - and then she went back to her apartment.

It had been a very long day, but she was still in empire-building mode, and almost ran into Babe before she saw him there, outside of her door.

"Oh," she said. "Is it late, already?"

He laughed.

"Where have you been?" he asked.

"Where haven't I been," she answered, unlocking the door and letting him in. She took off her cloak and hung it on a peg, then looked around the room as Babe closed the door behind them.

"I should offer you something to eat or something to drink, but I have neither," she said. "But I do have a donkey."

"I... think I'm confused," he said. "But I don't need nothin' to eat and I'm fine for drink, as well."

She nodded, taking her shoes off and crossing her legs on the bed. He took a stool from the corner and came to sit in front of her, his knees almost touching hers.

"Oh," Stasia said. "Oh, I've been so busy today... I forgot to think."

He closed his eyes and smiled.

"Babe, no, I'm sorry," Stasia said. "I really am. I should have... You matter to me. So much. And... I love you." She paused, finding it kind of shocking how easy it was for her to say it. She meant it and it wasn't scary or awkward. It just, the words came and he lifted his eyes to look into her face with something like pain.

"But," he said.

"But I can't marry you right now," she said.

He frowned.

"Who said right now?" he asked.

She blinked.

"Is that not what we're talking about?" she asked. "You came here tonight to propose, but you want me to tell you what I'm going to say, first?"

He blinked quickly, doing math.

"No," he said slowly. "No, that's not it at all."

She licked her lips.

"I think that someone is trying to manipulate the Veridan market to drive small merchants out of it, either into other occupations or out of the city, and to collapse the commodities market to blame it on the king and force Queen Melody to name a new king."

He crossed his arms.

"Exactly what is it you been up to, today?" he asked, and she nodded quickly.

"Right. So, the thing is, manipulating an honest market, which is more or less what Verida has, is a really hard thing to do, and unless you win at it, you always lose really big. So... I'm going to go up against them and see if I can't make them... lose."

"Go up against them how, exactly?" he asked.

She was giddy with this, and she still felt bad because she still, not even with him sitting right here in front of her, couldn't think about her future with him because she was so excited with the immediate future, trading in Verida.

"I'm going to break their market resolve," she said. "They're trying to corner various commodities, keep them from making it to their demand pools, drive up prices, make people angry and... anxious about getting the things that they need, but it only works under very narrow circumstances, and since most of the stuff they're trying to manipulate, when I actually sat down and thought about it..." She'd had a lot of time to think, walking the tiny donkey back into the city. "... there aren't any of them that are really narrow supply. I can let them drive up the prices all they want to try to corner the supplies, I can go buy it somewhere else, take it to market, and make a killing because I'm the only one who's selling. Figuratively speaking. There will be a lot of other people doing the same thing, because that's how markets work, but... they're afraid that there's something wrong with the market, and it's making everyone really nervous, and so no one will sell, even when they have things to sell, because maybe the prices will go up some more and then they'll regret it? But I'm going to be the one actually making a profit on lots and lots of transactions, and I've just got to figure out how to get my volumes up..."

She paused, remembering herself again.

He shook his head.

"So you're not talkin' about fightin' some man who's got the stomach to go against the queen?" he asked, and she shook her head.

"Not like you do," she said. "Like I do."

He nodded.

"You thought about this might be dangerous?"

She hit a hard stop.

"Um."

He raised an eyebrow, and she twisted her mouth.

"No," she admitted. "I hadn't thought about that at all."

"All over this city, boys and young men, and even some men proper, are jumpin' carts and takin' their goods because everything comes at such a premium," Babe said. "I've heard of men comin' at goods carts and just burnin' 'em down for no reason, might be your bloke. They're stealin' anything they can get their dirty mitts on, and that's even before you account for a man who's got his eye on the queen findin' that some girl is out tryin' to undermine him, the minute you get successful."

She pinched her mouth thoughtfully, then nodded.

"I see your point," she said. "But I have to do it anyway."

"Oh, I'm not tryin' to talk you out of it," he said. "I can see it clear as day that you were born and bred for this. Watchin' you talk to your pa at dinner last night, I saw it, and I see it even more clear now. I just want you to come home every day, carryin' what's yours, and I want to know that you can see it from my side, that this ain't a safe city. Never has been, and gettin' worse."

She sighed.

"I have to do it, and I have to go to the little markets in the middle of the dangerous parts of the city, because they need all this stuff, too. I'll carry my weapons and I'll stick to hours that the sun is up, and maybe I'll learn when some of the police patrols are happening, so that I can kind of be around where they're going to be. Because they patrol everywhere but the Black Docks, don't they?"

"True enough," Babe said.

"And I'd be safe in the Black Docks, because they're not allowed to mess with merchants, so long as they're paid up with... Skite... right?" Stasia asked.

"Wouldn't know," Babe said, his voice slightly tighter, but not as much of a reaction as she'd had every right to expect.

"Okay," she said, nodding. "So I've got to make a plan and be careful. I hear that. But... this is what I'm going to do."

"I'm happy for you," Babe said. "I really am."

She blinked.

What had they been talking about?

Oh.

"But I can't marry you right now," she said. "I just got to be my own person, not my father's daughter, for the first time, and I'm doing this thing, and... I have to see what I can do on my own."

He looked at her thoughtfully, and for a long, painful moment she feared she'd hurt him.

"Course you do," he finally said. "I'm confused why you think this is an obstacle. We just got settled in to the idea that we ain't fated to be alone, the rest of our lives. I ain't runnin' off for purple ribbon any time in the immediate future. You tellin' me you don't want to see me, for now?"

"No," she said. "Not anything like that. Not even a little bit."

He nodded, then shrugged.

"So... do you want to just be, as we are now, for... come what may, or do you think there'll be a day, maybe next year or the year after that, where you might like to talk about us makin' this official and permanent?" he asked.

She hesitated.

He raised an eyebrow, and she shook her head.

"I'm not afraid of that," she said. "I just failed to think about it at all today, and I know it deserves it. I don't... want you to ask me, tonight. I don't want that hanging over the future with, like, a sense that all of this is just leading up to getting married, when... real life starts. I want this to be real and... mine. And I want to be with you and..." She bit her lip. "No one in my life has ever made me happy the way that you do. I never, ever want to let go of that. Ever. And if that's the answer you want... I guess that's the answer. But..."

"Nothin' formal for a bit," he said, and she nodded.

"Is that... okay?" she asked.

He grinned.

"We're both comin' at this wrong," he said. "Got nobody negotiatin' for us and got nothin' keepin' time. Neither of us need a commitment to keep ourselves goin' forward. Not surprisin' that it'd be hard to work out how things ought be. But..." He licked his lips and he nodded. "You tell me you're ready, and I'll go with you anywhere. Swear it to you on my own heart. I'll go with you. I'm pledged to the guard for another two years, and after that..."

She shook her head quickly.

"No," she said. "I wouldn't ask you to give it up for me. Not on my account. Promise."

He nodded.

"I reckon I'll end up in a trainin' role somewhere, at some point. Hate to think of it bein' up at the fort, because that's a lifestyle I ain't suited to, no more, but with the King's Guard, I'd be plenty happy. Maybe five years or so along the line, yet. That's what I see. But you tell me. And..."

She nodded, blinking at unanticipated tears.

"I'd like that," she said.

He paused, then he smiled, reaching over and pulling her across onto his knees. He pulled her face down to his and kissed her gently, then lifted her to her feet and stood.

For a moment, they stood chest to chest, just both of them kind of waiting to see what would happen next, then he reached up and put his thumb to her cheekbone, gentle.

"I'm gonna go," he said. "I'll be at the guard house tomorrow, if you want to stop by, then I'm workin' tomorrow night. After that, Jasper doesn't know how it's gonna go yet."

"I'll be by tomorrow at some point," she said. "Promise."

He shook his head.

"Doesn't have to be like that," he said. "You come if you want. I'll be trainin' and doin' normal work, stuff that needs to get done when I got the time to do it. But you stay safe, all right? Watch where you're goin' and make sure the lads know that you mean business, they try to stop you. At the end of the day, comin' home is more important than the stuff, too, right?"

She nodded.

"Okay. But I will stop by tomorrow. I... I don't want to get into the habit of not seeing you. That's... the last thing that this is about."

He smiled and put his fingers under her jaw, lifting her mouth to his once more, then he stepped away.

"Good night, Anastasia," he said.

"Good night, Babe."

The cart was a game-changer. She could carry stuff that she even knew she wasn't going to sell, just because she found it at a price that she liked.

She avoided the castle market, because it was crowded and had its own methods of procuring stuff. It was the shops and markets around the rest of the city that were struggling, and Stasia and Marvin cut a swath through them. She went to a bank at the end of the third day and converted coins into paper, then hid the paper bills up in a groove she cut in a ceiling joist, for a place to keep them.

Her father was right. If she pushed herself hard, she could double her money four or five times a day, like this.

Prices were all over the map, depending on who she

talked to and how they were feeling about the world when they talked to her. A lot of men were afraid of selling because they were afraid of missing out on better prices later, and it did make it harder and harder to find sources for things as the days went on, but she also found that the men she was talking to, these fearful creatures who had no idea how much their goods were worth, and therefore couldn't sell them, were also broke. They would sell her little parcels of goods, just to feed themselves and their livestock, which meant that they weren't buying anything.

She upgraded her cart after a week, buying a spirited young pulling horse from a merchant who was convinced that the goods he had stored in his house were worth more than the horse, and taking him up to the Bentmoor estate and presenting herself to Lady Bentmoor. The woman remembered her as the Queen's messenger from a few weeks back, and was glad to discuss with her the piling-up resources there at the estate that no one was willing to come buy.

Stasia asked if they didn't have some young men there on the estate who might cart everything down to Verida and find customers for themselves, but Lady Bentmoor insisted that the produce of the estate was much too much for her to attempt to sell it on her own. She needed the big merchants to come and take it away; just the issues of producing all of it were enough for her concerns.

And Stasia could see the truth in that.

The Bentmoor estate was the largest single estate in Verida, and while the Westhauser estate was highly-optimized for marketable goods, many of which they manufactured on site, the Bentmoor estate focused on producing the largest volume of raw goods of anyone in the city. Stasia could have made it her full-time job, just carting loads of olives down to the presses day in and day out.

The city was woefully short on lamp oil, and the fact

that two of the olive cartsmen had left the city during the stone elf threat, unwilling to come this far out of Verida's protective range to reach their suppliers, meant that there was a huge hole that no one had stepped into because they all had no free money to work with.

Stasia did it for three days, unable to resist the profit margins she could charge to the presses, and making a hard decision between supplying all of the presses and taking their top dollars or supplying the three that looked most likely to make it more than another few weeks on the supply of olives they were able to procure. The entire industry was wobbling and threatening to capsize.

After three days, she found a young man at the Bentmoor estate, a disorganized frenzy of a young man who had big dreams of going to live in the city and having an exciting life full of friends and nightlife, and she paid him to run the cart up and back all day long.

All day long.

She gave Lady Bentmoor an advance to pay for the olives that he could cart for two solid weeks, and she went to the olive presses each day to collect her money in payment for his deliveries, and she bought a second cart to replace the one she'd committed to the olive business, and she bought an older mare who would put up with the young man's hijinks better than the young pulling horse she'd bought already.

He took an apartment in the north end of the city and showed up to work reliably for all of two and a half weeks before she had to find a new young man to run the route for her.

When he came back four days later, she bought a third cart and sent him to Ella.

She had bales of wool stacking up in a barn that was now spilling out into a field as they got through the work of shearing sheep that had needed it all summer, but it hadn't been safe enough to go out and do it.

These, she sent directly to the artisan region of town west of the castle, setting up a booth there of her very own and hand-selling to spinners who returned the spun wool to the booth for her to sell it - herself - to the clothing makers up and down the street.

She hired a seamstress' daughter to occupy the booth, modeling after a group of artists Stasia had noticed who had just claimed an alleyway as a shopfront, and now she wasn't just a merchant. She was in industry.

Jasper verified with the queen that Melody did, indeed, want him to teach Stasia the secrets of the castle, and he took three days to show her around carefully, explaining how to use the secret passages to get almost anywhere in the castle.

Stasia was vividly aware of what a small fraction of the secret behind-the-scenes portions of the castle she was being introduced to, but it was an effective subset, and she rapidly formed the ability to pop up anywhere she wanted in the court-accessible regions of the castle.

She was walking down a hallway one afternoon, about a month into her attempt to trade the merchants of Verida blind, when a man called out to her.

She turned, expecting to be challenged that she wasn't supposed to be there, but the man seemed much more alert than alarmed.

"You're Stasia Fielding?" he asked. "The merchant who is taking all of the surplus inventory from the Bentmoor estate and selling it?"

Stasia considered that for a moment before she answered.

"I am," she said.

"I am Lord Marley, Quintin Marley, miss, very nice to finally make your acquaintance."

She shook hands with him, increasingly feeling like

this couldn't possibly be happening, and he looked around.

"My herd of cattle is in desperate need of reduction," he said softly. "We were unable to butcher anything while the stone elves were there. Every time we sent out men, they would end up getting ambushed, while the cattle, they only stole when they needed food, I believe. So they've been breeding unchecked all summer long, without the normal maintenance we do, and... now I can't find anyone to take the beef to market. We butcher it all on-site, because there's no way we could do a drive down to the meat markets, so I just... Miss, I desperately need someone who can buy eight to ten head of beef per day through to at least the Water Lily Festival. At least."

Stasia considered that for several moments, then nodded.

"Marley," she said, and he nodded.

"Yes, Miss."

"I will be checking your credentials with the queen, Lord Marley," Stasia said. "I prefer to work with her friends, you understand, because the queen's friends are much less likely to back out on a contract or tell unsavory friends where I am going to be with a load of goods. I am also currently running at my absolute capacity, so if she is willing to say that you are a friend to the crown, I will need at least a week to get to you."

"But you can," he said, and she nodded.

"I believe that I can," she said. "I will not commit to anything until I have come up to see your estate myself. I will bring papers for contracts, so please be prepared to sign. Prices are very, very good right now, and I will pass some of that on to you, I promise you, but the fields and pastures of Verida are packed with livestock right now. You aren't the only one who desperately needs to sell."

"I understand," he said. "Lady Bentmoor has spoken your praises loudly in certain ears, and someone mentioned that your father has a rather sterling reputation, as well, for dealing fairly with all of his suppliers. I'm not placing myself in your hands, Miss Fielding, but I am very, very motivated to work with you."

Stasia nodded.

"I will be in touch, sir."

He shook her hand once more, then skittered away like he wanted to make sure no one else got the idea to ask her for her services.

Stasia watched him with bemusement, then went about her business.

She would ask the queen about him, about whether he was supportive at court, though she knew that it wasn't a trick she could pull more than once or twice or she would create false allies for Melody, and that was worse than none at all.

The problem with beef was that it certainly wasn't what the merchants were hiding away and working at manipulating.

Flour? Yes. In the form of grain. She could see it clearly, and here there was actual underlying reason that it might be an issue: the stone elves had burnt crops up and down the estates, and the wheat had been hit the hardest, because it was dry and ripe. They'd largely left the herds alone, and the orchards and vineyards and big, green fruit-and-vegetable plots had been okay. They were too wet to burn reliably. But the wheat had blazed. Stasia had seen the giant black scars on the Westhauser property.

Ella said that they'd tried to get the winter wheat out on time, but there had been too much risk of the crop running into the summer crop and they'd only gotten a fraction of the land planted for the winter crop.

So the city was short grain already, which made it an excellent commodity to go after, except that Boton had had an excellent year, and was shipping grain over by the boatload at very decent prices.

Keeping those out of the Veridan market was a trick that Stasia hadn't figured out yet, but she was certain it was happening.

So she wasn't stealing profits from the merchants by shipping beef to market. She could set up just like she had with the wool, find a good nest of restaurants and make it known that she had butchered meat ready for them, support all three meals with fresh meat, and the attempt actually intrigued her.

The problem was that she already had two flaky boys taking her coin, and one highly self-motivated young woman, and she did not want to deal with paying more of them.

She was having a hard time figuring out where to stash all of her money, and she was going to have to start handing it over to bankers to invest on her behalf, even as she watched enterprises all around the city fail for lack of courage and lack of supplies.

Why would she trust her funds to that?

The only person making money, it seemed, was her, and she needed to invest all of it back into herself.

Which meant more livestock, more carts, more staff. She would have to hire an accountant before too long to make sure that she was taking in all of the money she expected and paying it out as she'd promised.

The whole thing was exploding out of control and beyond her wildest dreams, and she hadn't seen Babe in two weeks.

She kept meaning to go by the guard house, but the one time she'd done it, he'd been out. Jasper said they'd gotten a very solid lead on one of the warlocks, but they were taking their time about reeling him in, because they were sick of the men fighting their way out of one corner or another.

The time she'd seen him, two weeks back, he had

been at her apartment well after dark, just sitting there waiting for her when she'd finally gotten home from hiring out the entire livery barn for her personal use. There were businesses down at the port that specialized in this kind of transit support, but Stasia kind of liked the bewildered way the liveryman kept taking on her contracts, the way the boys had learned to dote on her animals because she gave them extra coins for it.

She was going to need another one, though, if she started taking on the estate work, and beef just wasn't a direct competitor.

Unless it replaced grain.

Melody was watching her as she walked, Stasia realized.

Stasia hadn't even seen her standing there.

"How is your world-conquering going, my dear?" Melody asked with humor.

"How do you feel about 'steak for breakfast'?" Stasia asked.

"I'm not sure I have the constitution for that," Melody said.

"No, as a slogan," Stasia said. "'Steak: the new Veridan breakfast'?"

"I'm not sure I follow," Melody said.

"Do you like Lord Marley?" Stasia asked.

"He's a fine man," Melody said, still bewildered, but looking quite amused by it.

"He's got a whole bunch of cattle he wants to slaughter, but no way to get them to market. I swear, these people and their unwillingness to conscript a kid to lead a horse and a cart into town... it's going to make me the richest woman in the city."

"I'm not sure what that has to do with how I feel about him," Melody said.

"Oh," Stasia said. "I told him that I only work for

friends of the queen."

Melody blinked. Once. Very slowly.

"Well, isn't that interesting?" she said.

"I won't do it again," Stasia said. "I don't want people to come put pressure on you to vouch for them to me. Last thing I want. Just seemed like a good tool for filtering down who I'm willing to work with and who I'm not, for the moment. I just don't know if I want to get into the beef business, unless I can make it compete with wheat."

"Hence steak for breakfast," Melody said, and Stasia nodded.

"I might be willing to have it be known that I have long thought that a thin cut of meat is an excellent way to start the day," Melody said thoughtfully. "And it might be, at that."

"They sell sandwiches all up and down the Port walk that are meat on bread," Stasia said. "It's what all the sailors eat for breakfast. It's just not common through the rest of the city."

Melody gave her a soft but amused smile.

"And how is the rest of empire-building?" she asked.

"Crazy," Stasia said. "I'm still a small fish, but I am earning all of this money that they're just leaving on the table. They're collapsing industries all over the city, though, and I need to figure out how to scale up faster without losing track of everything. I'm employing kids, and I'm trying to be really careful with where I send them and when, and it's leaving a lot of the city open, when I would prefer to be getting supplies to them. I'm not letting them go anywhere I know that there's a gang active, and that's..."

"Most of the city," Melody agreed. "Do you want police or guard escort?"

"No," Stasia said firmly. She knew that Babe wanted to offer, but that wasn't... the spirit of what she wanted to do, and it also didn't fit the image she wanted to project. "No, I don't want anyone to think that I'm successful because you're helping me. The point is for all of them to realize I'm making a profit hand over fist and decide that sitting back and waiting for a more favorable market is... the height of stupidity. I want them to come compete me out of business all over the city. And I can't do that if I'm getting special treatment."

"Tell me about grain," Melody said, and Stasia lifted her eyebrows.

"Oh," she said. "I'm pretty sure that they're buying up all of the grain coming in through the port and putting it in warehouses, somewhere on the south end of the city..." She paused. The 'south end' of the city was literally three quarters of it, by most definitions. "Due south," she corrected. "Between Cazia and the Black Docks."

"Lesser Highrock," Melody supplied, and Stasia shrugged.

That land was all Lesser Highrock, true enough.

"The parts without so many people in it," Stasia said.

"I know the region you're talking about," Melody said. "Do you think that Jasper and his men would be interested in investigating where all of the grain is going? Because I think that that would very much be in the king's interests to know."

Stasia paused.

Now that wasn't a half-bad idea.

"I could find out who owns the warehouses where they're keeping it," she said.

"Jasper is very good at that kind of thing," Melody said. "The work he's putting in to hunting the warlocks is nothing short of inspired."

"I'm sure it is," Stasia answered. "Let me think about it and talk to him?"

Melody nodded.

"Tell him that he may proceed on my authority as he

sees fit."

Stasia nodded.

"I haven't been around as much. Are you okay?"

"Not a question I'd care to discuss in an open hallway. Come for breakfast with me tomorrow?"

"Yes, mum," Stasia said.

"Good. I'll send word to Lady Westhauser and ask her to join us."

Stasia smiled.

Outside of buying things off of the estate, she had spent precious little time with Ella in the last few weeks.

"I would like that," she said.

"You're doing good work," Melody said. "I hear rumblings of it everywhere I go, people asking who you are and how it is you're doing what you're doing. I'm surprised it has taken the court this long to connect this person to my guard."

"I'm following it where it goes," Stasia said.

Melody looked like she might have had something else to say, but she shook her head.

"I will look forward to speaking with you in the morning," she said.

"Yes, mum," Stasia said, giving Melody a little bow and turning to go.

She had places to be today, and she was planning on taking Marvin down to the port after that to see what was going on there and if she could win a load of more unusual goods so long as she was there.

He was getting bored, these days, with all of the big-animal carts in use all the time, and Stasia missed the happy little animal.

She exited the secret gate and went to stand quietly on the road that ran along the castle wall, thinking about what order she wanted to do things in, but the thought of seeing the squad was more than she could resist, just now, and she found that that was where her feet immediately pointed her.

She went across the bridge and down the other side of the river, going to the bar at the gate to the guard house and waiting for one of the men to see her.

"Can I help you?" a young man asked, jogging over when he realized she wasn't going anywhere.

"Did you guys forget me that quickly?" Stasia asked.

"Excuse me?" the young man asked. "Is there something I can do for you?"

"Stacy," Colin crowed from the walkway on the second story. "Bart, let her in here. That's Stacy."

The young man gawked at her for a moment, then scrambled to raise the bar as Colin jogged down the stairs.

"Boy have you been a stranger," Colin said. "We've got new recruits. Aren't they adorable?"

"There's someone here who doesn't know me," Stasia said, still in shock. "I didn't realize that could happen."

"Well, you weren't wearing purple leathers, now were you?" Colin asked. "You can't expect the babies to recognize you out of uniform."

No, she wore merchant clothes, now, and ones suited for a woman. She had had two dresses made in the artisan district, signs of her new, personal wealth, and she was finding that it actually meant something to her, to pay for them.

"Guys," Colin yelled as they got into the mess room. "It's Stacy. She's come back to us."

She looked over at him, dour.

"How's the wedding planning going?" she asked.

He pursed his lips at her.

"Fair play, Fielding," he answered, his voice lower. She grinned.

"I really have missed you guys."

He nodded.

"We've missed you," he answered. "Some of us more than others."

"Where's Babe?" she asked, walking over to the back table with him.

"You only missed him by about an hour," Colin said. "He'll be really angry that he missed you."

It was just hard, with as long as the walk was from her apartment to the guard house. She could have written to him, but that would have frustrated both of them all the more. Since they'd stopped setting specific times and places for their next meetings, they'd just fallen out of touch.

"Everything okay?" Jasper asked as she went to sit with them.

She nodded.

"Yeah. I'm here to talk about a favor."

He raised an eyebrow.

"We were under the impression you were going to resist asking for help," he said.

"I'm available to moonlight, if you need armed guards," Colin said cheerfully.

"No, you're not," Jasper said flatly, turning his attention firmly to Stasia. "What do you need?"

"I think that there are men who are storing... what can only be a vast amount of wheat in warehouses somewhere in the city. My instinct is that they're using the ones at the very south end of Lesser Highrock, but I can't prove that to you."

Jasper folded his arms on the table and nodded slowly.

"Price of everything is through the roof right now," he said. "Why would they be doing that?"

"To try to collapse the economy and undermine the queen," Stasia said. She felt safe here, but she needed to be aware that there were always people listening. "I think that they're trying to force her to take specific actions, from a policy perspective."

Jasper watched her face carefully, then nodded.

"And what would you like us to do, to help you?"

"I just want to know where all of the wheat is and who owns it," she said.

He scratched his chin.

"Easier than anything we've been doing," he said. "Are you authorized?"

She nodded.

"I spoke to her today."

His face was very still for a moment, then he stood.

"Walk with me," he said, putting out a hand that left Sterling and Colin at the table.

Stasia rose and walked out of the room with him, down the stairs, and out onto the street.

"Nothing here," Jasper said, walking quickly.

She followed him, thinking about the things she wasn't going to get done because she was here instead, but at the same time relieved to be with him again.

It was like having the grown-up show up, when she was so exhausted with playing one, these past few weeks.

"How is Babe?" she asked, and he glanced over, nodding encouragement that that was an okay question.

"He misses you," he said. "Making mistakes now and again, but getting on with it. He's Babe."

"Things..." Stasia started, but she couldn't describe it. "I didn't mean for it to get like this. Things were just turning into... something... and then I kind of just... walked out on him. Is he upset at me? Do you know?"

"You would need to ask him, yourself, if you want to know his mind," Jasper said. "You know as well as I do how little he speaks it, in most company. But if you wanted my estimation as a friend and a brother, I think that Babe understands better than perhaps anyone the cost and the virtue of duty, and if what you're doing is because it's the right thing to do, and not because of a passing fancy because you've discovered you've got quite a talent for these things, he would not fail to forgive whatever personal grief it gives him."

Stasia tugged at her gloves.

Yes, she wore gloves now, with a dress.

Alyssia was going to die when she heard.

"That's what I was afraid of," she said, and Jasper glanced over at her, confused.

"I want him to be angry," Stasia said. "Not really angry, but... it's like there's a chance we're going to miss each other, because we're both always going to put the things that we need to do before each other."

"That sounds like a conversation you need to have with him," Jasper said. "I know nothing of it, and neither does anyone else within the squad. Colin's young lady expects him three nights a week unless he's on duty at the castle, and she is always there waiting for him."

"What a life," Stasia said with distaste. He laughed.

"Yes, I expect that you and Babe will likely never have it easy, making whatever it is between you work out, but I also know that neither of you are the type to let an obstacle stand, when it is between you and something important to you. He simply goes through such things as though he never noticed they existed, and you turn them all into staircases."

Stasia smiled, pleased with the image.

"I miss him," she said. "I really do. And when I see him, it's like... nothing else in the world ever existed. But when I'm out, arranging purchases and sales and listening to market news... I feel bad how little I think of him."

Jasper laughed quietly.

"Again, I know nothing of it," he said. "And while I am always willing to lend an ear, I doubt my ability to tell you anything useful. Perhaps Lady Westhauser might be able to offer better-quality advice?"

It was a good idea.

And Stasia didn't feel dismissed nor silenced by it. He wasn't trying to tell her that she was telling him things she shouldn't. He was just honest in the fact that he had nothing to say about it.

"Would it hurt you?" Stasia asked. "You probably understand him better than anyone."

He looked at the ground ahead of them as they walked, formulating his answer.

Finally he drew breath.

"I think that it would hurt Colin," he said. "And probably Sterling, as well. As much as they are invested in the present moment, the idea that someone they cared about as deeply as Babe cares about you being able to forget about them... I don't think that either of them would be able to overlook that. Maybe someday, when the relationship reached a point of maturity where the expectation of time and relationship is a given, but not when they're still..." He smiled quietly. "I've never seen his mind wander, before. I mean that fully and completely. Never. But I can see it happen, now. Something makes him think of you and it just takes him away from himself. I can't tell you what it would do to me, because I've never felt that way about someone, and I can't tell you how he feels, because I've never seen any of it before. I would tell you that nothing would surprise me, but what's closer to the truth is that everything surprises me."

"My father... we had dinner with my father, one night, weeks and weeks ago, and my father asked his intentions. And now he wants to talk about marriage."

Jasper opened a door for her and they went through, past a bored bartender and up a set of stairs into a room that she had been in once before.

"And how do you feel about that?" Jasper asked. "I assume you aren't delighted, given that you bring it up."

"I don't know what to do," Stasia said. "I mean, he wants to talk about... the rest of our lives, and then I turn around and just forget about him for weeks at a time, because I'm doing something that I'm so good at."

"You are good at it," Jasper said. "I hear it from all quarters, when I know how to listen. I swear, I am relearning this entire city by following you around in it. And I give you my word, he's proud of you for that. You just escaped your father. Would you feel like you were walking into a new cage, marrying Babe?"

"No," Stasia said. "It's just... what if this is all there is, for us? He has his work, I have mine, and... What if... I can't..."

"If you can't be a wife?" Jasper asked.

She went and sat down at the table.

Collapsed at it, more accurately.

"Yes."

"Do you know that the King pays a pension past the death of every soldier, regardless of whether they are in the service or not when they die?" Jasper asked her, coming to sit across from her.

"No," Stasia said, not seeing why that had any bearing on the conversation at all.

Jasper played his thumb along his lip for a moment, then nodded.

"For a soldier, coming back to the city and planning to live out their life here, finding a woman who will marry you and keep your house and bear your children is... to be efficient about saying it, it's trivial. A soldier is a strong man with the capacity to work at any number of industries. He has a bankroll of wages from his time in the mountains, and he has permanent wages coming to his family after he dies for twenty years after. These are the promises our King makes to us in exchange for our lives, up in the mountains. If Babe wanted a woman who was going to be at home with a hot meal each evening, he could have his pick of them."

"I don't see what you're saying," Stasia said, and Jasper smiled.

"I would think that you, of all people, would," he said. "Babe has shown no interest in doing things the way regular daughters would. I suspect that all that's missing for the two of you is understanding how a spare daughter does things."

Stasia stared at him for several moments, feeling like he had not only unlocked a door for her but thrown it wide open.

He smiled again and nodded.

"Now, tell me about the threat to the queen."

The summary poured out of her over the course of the next thirty minutes, explaining Lord Palora's appearance and her increasing conviction that someone was trying to force Melody to name a new king. Her suspicion that Palora was trying to get himself named king, and her fear that, if it didn't work now, that he would outright kill Melody after Amber got back in order to work on a weaker Amber instead.

Jasper mostly just listened, asking a question or two along the way where she wasn't clear on the finer details, and then he sat back in his chair and wove his fingers behind his head.

"You've been busier than I thought," he said. "And I don't think that Babe understands the exact scope of what you're trying to do, either."

"We talked about it, one night," Stasia said. "But... no, I hadn't really seen the scope of it until I really started getting involved in all of the different trade networks that are just limping along right now. I can't scale up fast enough, and everyone is just throwing money at me to get things where they need to be. It's... unbelievable. Labor is easy enough to come by, for what I'm able to pay, but I'm leaving huge swaths of the city untapped for their potential because the..." She looked at the table, feeling bad about how dismissive she was about all of it. "Everyone is hungry and angry and afraid, and it makes it too dangerous for me to be there with any quantity of resources. I swear to you, whoever is doing this to this city... there's no punishment low enough."

"And if there is no spider at the middle of the web?" Jasper asked. "If it's all a lot of different little things that add up to the situation where we are now?"

"What do you mean?"

"The warlocks are up to something," Jasper said. "I've now got hints from all three of them, and they're moving the same way. Even if they don't appear to be interacting, they're doing something, intentionally, and I can't believe that it isn't related to this fear that you have, where you're watching the city fall down around you in real time. Lord Palora is a disgrace to every group he hangs out with, and there are many, but I don't think he has the endurance nor the cunning to orchestrate what you're describing."

He put his hands up as Stasia started to protest.

"No," he said. "I think that it's possible that he would scheme such a thing, but Verida is resilient beyond my ability to characterize her, and for something to truly be weighing down on us like it is, and it is, it has to be something that is... more disbursed and perhaps entirely unintentional. Something that is inhibiting the men and women of Verida from making better decisions for themselves. Your idea of a generalized fear spell has sat with me for weeks now, and I can't help feeling like that's our real culprit. That Palora would be out of luck, if not for that."

Stasia twisted her mouth, then nodded.

"I can't do anything about a fear spell," she said. "But

I can run against Palora and make every bit of this too expensive for him to bear. I think. But I've got to keep scaling up, and... I'm so busy, Jasper. I miss Babe. I miss the squad. I miss..." Running around on rooftops and playing cards with the Westhausers and sitting at meals for way too long. "I miss having time."

He nodded.

"Do you know why the nobles always invite all of the wealthiest merchants to all of their parties, even though the merchants almost always say no?" he asked. Stasia frowned.

"Because power loves money?" she said, feeling like it was obvious.

He laughed.

"At the abstract, you've got it in one. But specifically, it's because the merchants are impossible to attract to smaller social gatherings. If you're going to get the important merchants to turn up, it's got to be because a lot of them are going to be there, and then all they'll do is talk about business all night, anyway. I can't count how many noblemen I've heard complain about it. They break into these conversations now and again and they make their social ties to the rich men of Verida, but in general, the rich men of Verida are simply too busy for the niceties of proper society. And I think that you understand why, now. There's always one more opportunity to pursue, isn't there?"

"There is," she said. "And... I'm missing out on them now. I really do need to go, while I've still got light. Will you tell Babe that I do miss him dearly?"

Jasper snorted.

"Tell him yourself," he said.

"I don't know when or where to find him," Stasia said.

"Tomorrow," Jasper said. "I'll order him to stay in all day, doing training with the new recruits, but when you get there, he's all yours for the rest of the day. I won't make space for you often, but you are about the king's business in a profound way, right now, and I've got to give you credit for it. I hope you break the lot of them."

She nodded, trying to figure out where in tomorrow's schedule she might find time to get to the guard house.

She hesitated, then nodded again.

"I'll make it work," she said. "Thank you."

He winked and stood.

"Right now, things are different, because you're fighting against a specific opponent, and it's a fight that you're going to lose if you don't win it fast enough. I can see that. But it's going to feel different every time, and when this is all done, you need to be sure that you don't miss out on life as you're too busy trying to support your life. Do you understand?"

Stasia considered that.

Her father had always held that the highest virtue was free trade between individuals resulting in a profit to both.

But he had always held that, sitting at the dinner table with Stasia.

Which meant that he had lied. Or at least been mistaken.

Stasia had always been his first priority, and tending his relationship with his daughter was his highest virtue.

Didn't it?

It did.

She'd never seen it before this moment, when she had thought that her father was so important that all of the schedules of the world would bend to his will.

And it wasn't that he wasn't.

It was that he had left a space in almost every single day for him to sit at the dining room table and talk to Stasia. Space that he could have filled up with more profit and more trade.

"You're completely right," she said, and he nodded.

"Go out and eat their lunch," he said. "You can leave me a note at the guard house if you need anything, and I'll look into the warehouses in Lesser Highrock to see if anyone is sitting on huge piles of grain. If you have anything else like that that you want me to track down, I'm happy to do it. The warlocks are a moving target. Stationary goods sound like a reprieve."

Stasia smiled.

"I have a list," she said. "But let's start with the grain."

"All right, then," he said. "Let's start with the grain."

She got up the next morning with a thought that she needed to let an apartment closer to the castle.

She didn't like the idea of trying to furnish and supply another place to live, just now, but the walking distance was just so significant.

She went to visit Marvin on the way, taking a route that wandered past a bakery she favored and giving the little donkey a pair of fresh carrots that had cost her ten times what they ought to have, but he deserved it.

He always came trotting over to her when he heard her footsteps out in the aisle, and if she opened the gate for him, he would go running to find his cart, standing in place while she secured it to him and then cheerfully following her around town wherever she might end up going.

He was a symbol of her entire business, that little animal was, and he was worth his weight in overpriced carrots at twice the price.

She got to the castle and took a wayward route to get to Melody's chamber, seeing a number of people who she was starting to be able to identify, if not by name, at least by role within the court, and arriving at the chamber through the main doors.

She could have made her entrance through any set of doors going into the room, save the washroom, but the main doors were fine today.

Did it matter?

She had no clue. She was just trying to be unpredictable.

She found Queen Melody and Lady Westhauser at tea, though there appeared to be a fine breakfast laid out for them that was waiting on their third guest.

"Good morning," Stasia said.

"Good morning," Melody answered. "I trust everything is well?"

"I found word waiting for me last night that my olive cart got a smashed wheel in an altercation with men who were hoping for goods that would be easier to carry and sell, but the young man who tends the cart promised a fair price to a potter nearby to keep an eye on it while he fetched a wheel and a repairman, and the olives made it to the press, albeit late. I think that the young man left out that he was injured in the attack, but for now I will leave that as his business. I must visit the potter and pay him his fee, today."

"How do you know he was injured?" Ella asked.

"There was a smear of blood on the back of the paper," Stasia said. Melody shook her head.

"It's always happened," she said. "There's no way to entirely prevent it. But the incidence of these things is unlike any other time I can remember."

Stasia nodded.

"Too many men without employment and without means to either use their time or support themselves and their families. There's no fixing it but forward, so there's no use fretting over it, for now."

"Easy for you to say," Ella said, not unkindly. "It

wasn't your blood on the paper."

"It has been before," Stasia said. "And it will be again. May I?"

"Please, help yourself," Melody nodded, and all three of them assembled plates of food, settling back into their chairs again.

"So I feel like I've been left completely behind, in your adventures," Ella said. "We haven't spoken since you started buying wool from me, when my wool merchant disappeared. Did I know that you were doing olives?"

"I started buying olives from the Bentmoors before I approached you," Stasia said. "I didn't want my first contact to be my friend."

Ella nodded.

"And now?"

"Well, I'm considering doing beef for Lord Marley, which means I'm going to have to start getting connections within the restaurant community, because I think most of the households buy from local butchers, rather than distributors."

Ella shook her head.

"They don't butcher in Highrock," she said. "They cart in beef. And I hear it's getting really hard to find."

Stasia sighed.

"Eight head isn't going to be enough," she muttered. "I can't get in to Highrock."

"You know my brother would help you, if you told him that that was your problem," Ella said, and Stasia froze with her hand halfway to her mouth.

Of course.

"How much would that cost me?" Stasia asked, and Ella shook her head.

"It's bad business for everyone, right now," she said. "I would make the butcher pay it. Just tell my brother... Give me a letter, and I'll find a messenger to carry it for you. Tell my brother that you are willing to bring in goods to Highrock markets, but that he has to supply you with a credible escort to get there, and that you won't pay for it. If he wants you to bring things in to sell, he'll cough up one of the boys to sit on your cart on the way in, and no one will touch it."

"Why didn't I think of that before?" Stasia asked.

"Because you're accustomed to using legal pathways to comport goods," Melody said dryly. "Unfortunately, in times of legal disarray, organized is better than legal."

Ella shrugged and nodded.

"I don't have introductions for you to the other gangs, and a lot of them aren't really community-oriented the way the Highrock family is, but you might be able to use them."

"Or you could leave it to the vendors to work out," Melody said. "They'll know their local powers. If you approached them and told them that you could source a supply of goods, if they could meet you at a safe location, like the castle market, to take possession of it, it would be up to them to figure out how to get it to their own store."

"They don't have transit," Stasia said. "Usually. But I'll think on it. I could have my carters go with them, and just come back with an empty cart, which is going to be much less appealing, especially if... How do I make it known that they don't carry any money?"

"Dress them like they don't have money," Ella said. "It's easy to see if a man is carrying enough weight to indicate coins. It won't save you all the time, but if he's going through every day like that?"

"I don't like putting my young men in danger if I don't have to," Stasia said slowly. "But... this could work."

"What else can we do to help you?" Melody asked.

"Can you recommend a good accountant?" Stasia asked. She was actually going to ask her father about his, but she was pretty sure that the man was absolutely full-time dedicated to the Fielding empire, and she was going to need to find someone who could do everything part-time for now. Paying the boys was one thing. Paying a professional a salary was... another level of commitment again.

"I'll see what I can do," Melody said. "I'll be at the university tomorrow. Would you like me to see if they have any students who would suit?"

"That would be perfect," Stasia said. "Yes. Please do."

"Which," Ella said slowly. "Speaking of..."

"Yes," Melody said. "If that is... all that you can think of that we can do to help you..."

"I'm supposed to be working for you," Stasia said skeptically.

"We need you to come to class tomorrow," Ella said.

Oh.

Yup.

That was right.

They'd started classes weeks ago.

"How is it going?" Stasia asked.

"They're adorable," Ella said. "I can't remember ever being like that."

"I very much doubt that you were," Melody said with humor. "The class enrolled out within a few hours, and we still have a full room each day that we are in session. We have gone through the basics of finding a legal, unmet demand and then finding a profitable way to supply it. We have discussed the tax implications of making a profit at the various markets around the city, the nature of standard contracts as they are used in the city, and the barriers to entry to buying and selling, from a legal perspective."

"Barriers to entry," Stasia said. "Anyone can buy a thing and then sell it for more."

Ella snorted.

"Do you carry it on your back?" Ella asked. "Do you

rent a cart or buy one? Do you move the goods yourself, or do you bring them to a centralized location and have buyers come to you? What about competitors who try to buy your supply or undersell to your customers? How much money does it take to stay in business? How much risk can you afford to take with your existing capital?"

Stasia chewed thoughtfully, then put her plate down on her ankle.

"You're making this sound a lot more complicated than it is," she said, and Melody shook her head.

"No, not for a great portion of our class," she said. "Even those who came from merchant families, if they've ended up at the university, it's because they weren't expected to follow in their family business, most of them. The things that you find obvious or overly-complex are entirely new to these students. We have started from the beginning and worked our way as quickly as possible through to the point of the class."

"Buying and selling stuff," Stasia said.

Ella laughed.

"We're providing seed money," she said. "The castle is. And we're going to send them out to start, and from here, there aren't going to be any more formal classes. Queen Melody and I will be in the classroom each week at the same time to answer questions and have discussions about how things are going, but she won't be lecturing and I won't be grading any more papers."

Stasia looked over at her.

"You graded papers?"

"So many," Ella said.

"The students will all be responsible for a complete accounting of each of their transactions, with signed receipts from any and all participants in a transaction with them, and at the end of the term, the week before Water Lily Festival, I will be awarding the top three most profitable students an opportunity to do simple work here at the castle, whether that be clerical or delivery or some other role. If one or more of the top three decline the role, it will cascade to the next students on the list."

"You need to tell them where they're safe and where they aren't," Stasia said.

"They know that," Ella said. "A lot of them come from wealthier families, but a lot of them, Stasia, they're looking at this as an opportunity to make a whole life for themselves. They've never even realized that this was a possibility for them, and right now, the opportunities are just endless and everyone sees it. We'll encourage them to go where they know, because that's where they're generally going to be the safest, but..."

Stasia nodded slowly.

"It's also going to be where they know that there are unmet needs. They could go sell door-to-door in certain neighborhoods and... if they know what they're doing..."

To start small like that again, doubling your money three, four times a day... Stasia felt a pang of nostalgia for it, and then laughed at herself quietly, realizing just how recently that was where she had been.

"Can you come?" Ella asked.

"Why?" Stasia asked. "You guys sound like you've got this under control."

"Because neither of us have ever done it," Melody said. "I have a certain amount of credibility because of who I am, and Lady Westhauser speaks as a major contributor to the industry of Verida, but the act of buying and selling goods... this is something that you are doing, and I want them to see what it looks like when it is done well."

Stasia licked her lips, then nodded.

"Yes. What time?"

Ella gave her the hour and the location on campus, and Stasia tucked it away in a pocket of her dragonskins, returning to her meal.

"Are they ready for this?" she asked.

"No," Melody said. "But they're hungry for it. I worry that I may cause a dent in university enrollment with this endeavor, as they may discover that they have either a skill for it or a passion for it. Verida is a rock that has dashed many hopes, over the generations, among those who thought that buying low and selling high was simple."

"Oh, it is simple," Stasia said. "It's just not easy."

Melody nodded.

"You've been raised on this," she said. "Any insights you can give them, any cautions or things to be aware of, these may be the tips that keep them going. As far as the class goes, I fully expect half of them to lose money in all, and consider it to have been an entertainment to have been in the Queen's own class for a term, but the top ten or twenty students... some of whom Ella and I have discussed in specific already, they may find that this is their new life's calling."

Stasia felt sorry for them, and then she reminded herself that this was the whole point.

These kids, young and enthusiastic and completely unaware that there was anything nefarious or politically complicated going on, were going to surge out into the markets of Verida and be the first wave of reinforcements to back Stasia's side of the war that she was fighting.

They were untrained and they were going to be unreliable, as a cohort, but Melody was right: a few of them were going to be very, very good at it, and when university students were putting seasoned merchants to shame... this was a very good first step.

"How long are you expecting me to talk?" Stasia asked.

"You'll have an hour," Melody said, and Stasia snorted.

"I can talk for ten minutes or I can talk for six hours. I don't know if I know how to talk for one hour."

Ella nodded.

"I can attest to that."

Stasia nudged her, and Ella grinned.

"If you were willing, I would love to tell them that they could find you at a consistent spot, perhaps a bar near the university, after you would normally have ceased your work for the day, if they wanted to discuss what they were doing," Melody said.

Stasia considered.

It was true that she mostly stopped work after dark. There were industries that would have loved to be able to unload goods during the dark hours, in order to be ready to use them at the earliest moment the next dawn, but she wasn't willing to have goods running around the city by unreliable lamplight or torchlight, so she just didn't.

Her days were starting at first light, on the other hand, and being out after dark for more than a handful of minutes was beginning to have an impact on her ability to focus during the day.

On the other hand, reinforcements were reinforcements.

"Okay," she said. "Felligan's. Warn them that I'm going to be there and that there might be a crowd."

"Felligan's has a back room, did you know?" Ella asked. Stasia frowned.

"Why?"

"They use it to store drinks and chairs and stuff," Ella said. "But if you ask, and if you have a drinks minimum for the room, they'll put everything outside for the night and let you use it."

"All right," Stasia said. "Thursday nights. I'll be there, and we'll ask for the back room, and..." She closed her eyes. "They're actually going to show up, aren't they?" she asked.

Ella bunched her face.

"I don't know," she said. "It depends. But they could. I think they really could."

Stasia nodded.

"All right. I think it's the right move. I'll be there."

"I'll talk to the bartender at Felligan's to set up the back room," Ella said.

Stasia finished her breakfast and set the plate back on the table.

"I know that I am neglecting the needs that you have for me here..." she said, and Melody shook her head.

"You are doing exactly what I need you to be doing. You have places to be, I understand, and I dismiss you with my gratitude."

Stasia went out through the door to the spiral staircase down to the basement, taking the shortest path out of the castle and through the secret gate, making her way once more to the guard house and standing with her elbows resting on the bar to watch as Babe fought two young men at once with training daggers.

She remembered those days.

He was in teaching mode, making mistakes that were obvious to her eyes, now, and letting the men fall for his feints as they tried to take advantage. The circle of very young men around him watched intently, and it wasn't until one of the older guards upstairs noticed her that anyone came to let her in.

"Morning, Miss Fielding," the man said, touching his hat.

She smiled.

"Good morning, Fenton," she answered.

Babe saw her and grinned, not missing a beat with the young guards.

"Bad timing," he called.

Stasia went to stand against the rail, crossing her arms to watch as the young men continued to attack. She wondered if Matthias had ever looked like that.

She knew she had, but she shuddered to think of it.

A few minutes later, Jasper appeared at the upper rail.

"Babe," he called. "You're dismissed for the rest of the day."

Babe finished off the two men he was training with, taking their daggers and looking up at Jasper.

"This a setup, boss?" he asked.

"Better believe it," Jasper answered with a grin. He held up his hand in greeting to Stasia, then went back into the mess hall.

Babe laughed, putting away the daggers and then coming to offer Stasia his elbow.

"It appears I have had my schedule cleared," he said, and she smiled.

"You may, but I don't," she answered. "You mind walking with me while I get some business done?"

"For you, I got nothin' but time," he said, lifting the bar for her and lowering it back behind them.

Stasia put her head on his shoulder for a moment, then straightened to walk alongside him.

"I've got to pay a potter for watching a broken-down cart for me," she said. "And then, if you don't mind being my escort, I've got payments to collect from the oil presses up here."

He looked over at her.

"This why you ain't been around so much?" he asked, and she nodded.

"You know that, right?" she asked. "That... I've got all this... stuff going on... and I really... Babe, I miss you so much."

He laughed quietly, putting his face forward again.

"I know it," he said. "Don't mind hearin' it, but I know it. Been busy, myself, and it sounds like you've got more work for us comin'."

"Yeah," Stasia said. "I've got theories on where to go next, but I need someone with better eyes than me and more time."

"Thought you weren't gonna take help from us," Babe said, his voice lower.

"This isn't for my business," Stasia said, and he nodded.

"Jasper came in last night, I hear, with a new energy. Matthias was a bit nervous about it, that maybe he'd lost focus or lost faith. That was you, wasn't it?"

"It was," Stasia said. "I'm making a lot of guesses, right now, but I think a lot of them are going to end up being right, and I really need to be ready to deal with it, if they are."

"Usually folk worry about bein' wrong," Babe observed, and she grinned.

"Oh, I hope I'm wrong on half of it. That all of this is just... people being people, and they'll come around when they're ready. Would mean that nothing I'm doing right now matters and... that would kind of be a relief, because that way I can't get it so wrong that the city never does bounce back."

Babe was quiet for a time, thinking about that, and then he nodded.

"There's a problem with that," he said, and she raised her eyebrows.

"Oh?"

He nodded.

"What you're doin' does matter, because you're bringin' stuff in that folk need. I hadn't realized you were workin' with the olive presses, but think on what this city would be like without light at night. So it matters. And then there's that you got this idea that the whole thing is on your shoulders, and that ain't the way of it at all. You got the rest of us, workin' right alongside you…"

She started to cut in, to say that she really did appreciate everything they did, but he held up a hand to dissuade her.

"… and there ain't a problem in the city that you're on your own for, that you got to try to solve on your own. The problems in this city are big enough, there's no way anyone expects you to solve 'em on your own, either." He looked over at her. "Right?"

She licked her lips, feeling a bit overwhelmed at all of it and at the same time, wanting to just lean against him and let him tell her that she didn't have to do any of it. That he had it under control and it was all going to be fine.

"Everything is so close to freezing up entirely," she said. "And people need so much stuff. The artisans and the craftsmen and the markets and the shops… they've all got an idea what they need, but they don't know where to get it, because they've never sourced their own materials before. The Veridan market has always had all of it, and they just go and order it or buy it when it goes by, and… He's destroying a work of art, Babe. And I can't recreate it. No matter how hard I work or how smart I am. He's destroying something that is… absolutely beautiful to me, and I can't reach him to take a swing at him. I'm doing my best, and… the money, Babe. I can't even describe to you the money I'm making. I need an accountant and a manager to deal with all of the people, and instead I've got a box outside of my apartment where everyone stuffs receipts so that I'll make sure they get paid. I mean, I know my father makes so much more than that, in any given deal he does, but I've got this torrent of money coming in and out, where he just gets one big wave that kind of floats in and then… he keeps it. It's… It's not chaos, but it is a storm. And… I'm not important enough that they would even notice, and even what I'm doing… it isn't going to save a single industry. The estates are starting to learn where to send their goods, but they're overwhelmed with just trying to bring them in, after they spent the entire summer trying to stay alive, first and foremost. The stuff that's rotting on the vine is profound, and it's all stuff that we can't get back, and some of it... not just the wine, obviously, some of it is really important to Verida."

"So we import it," Babe said.

"Easier said than done," Stasia said. "The courier merchants up here on the north end of the city are all just... missing. I don't even know where they went. But the ones down at the docks, they're doing... something... I can't even see it or name it, but they're doing something to keep the rest of the merchant fleet from trading here. They're all just sending ships elsewhere, completely full of goods, and they aren't unloading them here. And until I figure out why it's happening, I can't figure out a good way to get around it, other than working out of Fisharbor with a really small volume of goods."

He reached over to take her hand, putting his fingers through hers and keeping up a pace like he knew what it was to work hard.

"What did Jasper say?" he asked.

"He still thinks it's the warlocks doing it," Stasia said. "And that Palora is just making a scene and taking advantage of Queen Melody being in a difficult position. And he could be right. I can't prove that he's doing anything. It's just that... there are things going on that I can't explain. It all feels weird."

"Then that's a sign to me that Jasper ought take you serious," Babe said.

"He is," Stasia assured him. "Don't let me suggest that he isn't. He's just got his target in mind, and he thinks that it's the right one, and... we aren't working against each other. He's going to help me with trying to track down where all of the wheat is. He's taking it seriously."

"You do this run on your own?" Babe asked. "With money in tow?"

She nodded.

"At least once a week. I have receipts from the cart boys that are signed by the business owners that tell me how much product got delivered and what they know they're expected to pay for it, but if I leave them alone for too long, they don't have that much cash on hand, or they've spent it on something emergency. So I have to come up here a lot to get it, but it's... it's a long way, and I can't do it too often or I waste all my time."

"Why not have the boys collect it?" Babe asked.

"First, because I don't want them getting beat up," Stasia said. "Second, because I don't want them losing it and then having to decide if they're lying to me or not. It's just best if I handle all of the money on paper and then deal with the coins and the paper bills in person. Means I don't have trust issues."

"They could under-charge your olive presses and take a cut of it," Babe said.

"I have receipts from the estates for how much cargo they leave the estate with," Stasia said. "And you had better believe that the estates want credit for every ounce of it. So the quantity that leaves the estates needs to match the quantity that arrives at the businesses, though I'm going to have to try to hire away an apprentice from one of the butchers, I think. Up until now, I've been selling true commodities. The whole cart has a single value per pound, and that's that. If I'm going to get into butchered beef, I need someone who can assess the various values of the cuts, and..."

"And that means gettin' a man angry at you who uses a knife for a living," Babe said, and she shrugged.

"It's an easy market to hire in," Stasia said. "He'll find someone new who will run around cleaning up the floors and stuff without a problem."

She glanced at Babe, but she knew his concern was reasonable.

"I'm doing my best," she murmured. "But this isn't safe, and we both know it."

He sighed and shrugged, then grinned.

"You carry a sword like you know what it's there for," he said. "I wouldn't want to be the man who tried to separate you from your money."

She grinned.

"Thank you."

"I might know a fella," he said. "Just retired from the guard about a year ago, met him up at drinks last month. Sounds like he's havin' trouble fillin' the hours. Big guy, like me, I'd trust him with my life."

"That's not a bad thought," Stasia said. "Honestly, I'm not even that worried about people stealing from me, but that it gives them an idea that they don't want or need to respect me, and it sets me up for problems later. Can you tell me where to find him?"

Babe shook his head.

"No, but Colin'll know," he said. "I'll talk to him later."

Stasia blew air through her lips.

"That will save me a lot of walking," she said.

"Why ain't you ridin'?" Babe asked. Faster all the way around, and keeps you from bein' such an easy target."

"I should," Stasia admitted. "I tell myself that it's because I end up places that I don't expect, where I take an hour to get stuff sorted back out again, and what am I going to do with her in the meantime? Or when I go to the castle? If I was going through the front gate, I'd just ask them to stable her, but..."

He looked sideways at her.

"But you ain't goin' in through the front gate," he

said.

She considered.

"I think we both knew that," she said. "The palace guard aren't that inept, and it's hardly like I'd go along with being smuggled in on a hay wagon."

He grinned.

"We got a lot of theories, how you're doin' what you're doin'," he said. "Can't wait to see who's right about it."

She squeezed his hand.

"Prepare to be disappointed," she said. "Because it's not my secret to tell, and I don't know if you'll ever know."

He frowned.

"Just makes it that much more fun to guess," he said with a renewed grin. "Gonna drive Colin insane, which ain't a half-bad consolation prize."

She laughed.

They made it up to the olive presses, a huge region of the city where the vast quantity of olive oil was prepared in huge presses. Some of it would be used in food, and Stasia was beginning to get to the point where she felt okay routing some of the Bentmoor olives to the food presses, because food was important, too, but most of them were making burning oil. There were other things you could stick in a lamp and burn it; Boton used animal byproducts for their streetlamps, but the olive industry on the estates was designed to supply the street lamps of Verida, and the darkness was hard to substitute for, where olive oil could use butter or imported cooking oils instead, or different foods entirely.

She waved at men through the front office windows of the presses, going back to the three men she had sold to this week and leaving Babe outside while she went in to redeem her receipts.

She had a separate ledger that she filled in each

morning with her day's receipts, but the ones bearing the men's signatures, she returned for them to file or burn as they saw fit. It saved her from getting confused who she had charged and who she hadn't.

She came out with bags of coins from the first two men, and paper bills from the third. He was a younger man who was more influenced by university culture than the other two, and he maintained that paper money was the future of Verida. Stasia preferred it, certainly, from an ease of transit perspective; she knew that women commonly shoved such papers into their blouses for safe-keeping, where a pickpocket had the queen's own time trying to get them out surreptitiously. The problem was that many of the merchants around town, and even more of the regular populace were unwilling to tolerate it at all.

She had to go to a bank and change the bills out for coins, if she wanted to trade with anyone but the very high-volume merchants and the ones who had graduated from the university in the last five to ten years.

Fortunately for her, for now, she didn't need the bills for any upcoming reinvestments, and she could go just stuff them into another hidden cove in her apartment. If someone did break in there and ransack the place, it was going to explode with paper money.

She needed to get more of it back into play, but she was having a hard enough time supporting things as they were. She needed more high-level staff, people to do finances and to pay cart-runners.

She needed more carts.

Which was part of what she was doing today.

She set off walking with Babe again.

"Where to now?" he asked.

"Lumberyards," she said.

"Lumberyards?" he asked, and she nodded.

"I paid for a special consignment of lumber," she

said. "The trees coming down the river from the hill folk dried up for a few months, because they weren't willing to be stationary while the Stone Elves were down wandering around the hills, but recently they've started getting trees again and they don't have anyone to cart away the lumber after they cut it, so they're just piling up all of these felled trees and not paying the hill folk for them, and if they do it for much longer, the hill folk are going to stop sending them, and then..." She shook her head. "It's the same story over and over again. Something gets piled up somewhere, and then everything both upstream and downstream of it just dies. So I'm buying lumber for myself, today, and I'm going to steal the olive cart... it's in a livery stable not far from here, since he's finished his first run for the day and he won't go back up again until closer to the end of the day for the second. So I'm stealing that to go get lumber and hand-deliver it to a cartmaker in Highrock who is going to make me a whole fleet of carts, so long as I keep delivering lumber in sufficient quantities. This is the next step to scaling."

She would have thought that Verida would have had enough carts to go around, and it would simply be a question of finding the ones that weren't being used and buying them, but she hadn't had any luck at that, so now she was doing her own thing, and if she ended up with a dozen spare carts at the end of it... she'd have a nice bonfire on a beach somewhere.

She wanted to add two more olive runs per day, but the staff up at Bentmoor weren't able to support it until they finished the tomato harvest and the fig harvest.

Soon.

Soon, they would get caught back up enough to help her load the cart four times a day, and then she would pick up another estate for more olives and... maybe parts of the city would stop being dark at night.

Right now, the darkness was still spreading.

They harnessed the pulling mare on their own, then walked her to the sawmills along the river at the north end of the estates; they were rented from the estates, technically, but the men running them were independent professionals whose families lived there at the sawmills.

She handed over a stack of coins and talked to the sawmill owner while Babe and the mill owner's sons loaded the lumber into the cart. He was about ready to give up on the mill, let the estate reclaim it and go into the city looking for work.

"It isn't any better, there," Stasia told him.

"Can't make the rent, miss," he said. "Won't have a choice, if it doesn't pick up from here."

"You think about shipping your own goods?" Stasia asked. "Got a couple of strapping young men, there, who could do it."

"Wouldn't know the first thing about it," he answered. "Thought that the shipwright might want it, but when I went and talked to him, he'd switched over to all-imported lumber."

Stasia thought of a story she'd heard of a major shipment the previous week, and she nodded.

"It's a good thought," she said. "And he might have changed his mind, if you go talk to him again, but that's not even the front edge of what uses lumber here in the city."

"Time wasn't too long ago, the young man would show up here three times a day and just take it down to the castle market, sell it all," he said. "Don't know that I've got the time to go find all the people who need a board or two."

"Don't see that you've got much else to do with your time, anyway," Stasia answered.

He looked over at the graveyard of trees beyond the mill and shook his head.

"I've got a back-stock," he said. "But if it starts moving, I'm gonna be all-out just turning all of that into lumber again. I can't do both."

"Right now you're doing neither," Stasia said. "I'll be back again next week for another load like this one. If you want, I can talk to people while I'm out and get you a list of names of people who might be willing to buy from you. If nothing else, you've got a pulling mule and a cart, there. You've got an advantage over a lot of the people I talk to."

He scratched the back of his neck, then nodded.

"I see your point," he said, then nodded. "Yeah, I'll take that list, if you have a mind to make it."

She shook his hand, then went to get the horse ready to go. The mare was lipping at stray hay on the ground where a bale had landed before it was taken into the barn, and Stasia lifted her head, talking to the animal for a moment while Babe secured the lumber and shook hands with the owner's sons.

Stasia patted the mare's neck and put the lead over her shoulder, setting off again at the mare's natural, easy pace.

The high-strung gelding was a lot faster, she knew by the route efficiency of the two animals, and it probably should have been obvious to her, without needing to look at the data, but the mare wasn't nearly so likely to dump a cart and run off, and there was value in that.

Babe caught up to her gradually, taking her hand again as they walked.

"And this is how you're spendin' your time, these days," he said.

"Every day is different," she answered. "But this is the theme."

"Strange, you not bein' around more than you have been," he said. "It's not in the days, so much, but the lot of us are just used to you bein' around some."

Stasia nodded, then the realization hit her all at once.

"I'm lonely," she said. "I've got all these people I

work with all the time, and I'm just talking to everyone all the time. I'm never alone, not all day long, but I'm really... lonely."

She didn't have anyone that she was sitting down and actually talking things through with regularly, other than the queen. She could have gone home to talk to her father. He was always there to riddle through things with her, but she was seldom in that part of the city by dinner time, and she wasn't getting enough sleep as it was.

It occurred to her again that her father had done something really special, eating dinner with her every night, growing up.

Babe was watching her carefully, and she looked at her feet, smiling, then lifted her head and tossed her hair back.

"I am," she said. "But it doesn't mean I should be doing it differently."

"Fine enough," he said. "Not gonna get argument from me. I'm just wonderin' what's gonna change to make you set your mind different, another day."

"When Verida isn't under threat of a frozen market, with three-quarters of the city relying on street vendors for their next meal and everyone acting strange and afraid all the time," she said.

"And if that day don't come?" he asked. She looked over at him, wanting him to see it in her eyes.

"Then I'm going to keep fighting for it," she said.

He gave her a grim smile and nodded.

"I'll miss you," he said.

"It's what I can do," Stasia answered.

"I know. And I love you for it, make no mistake. But life is short, Stasia. People die every day, and much as we like to play at both of us bein' invincible, it's gonna be one of us, one of these days. I don't want to miss out on you, given how long it took me to figure out this was somethin' I wanted in the first."

"I don't want that, either," she said. "I'm hoping that it's only a few more weeks, really. That people... like the sawmill owner. Like him exactly. They'll see that not only is it their only choice, and it is, but that there's money to be made, forging new economic ties. That if they just hire a boy to run their cart around the city, rather than letting some merchant do it for them, they can take home more of the money and be better off."

It was tenuous, actually. The cost of running a cart wasn't nothing, and things got lost. When they got lost before you sold them, you never got paid for them. The merchants took on real risk, buying and moving stuff, and that would go back on the sawmill owners and the estates and the flour mill owners and the olive press owners... And a lot of them weren't equipped to manage that complexity on top of their existing businesses.

She knew that.

It was what merchants were. They were the ropes that tied together all of the free-floating pieces of an economy and made them react to each other, and it was an untidy and often thankless job, if you ignored the coins that accumulated in your pocket. Faster sometimes and not at all, others, but that was the thanks the merchants got, until they got big enough and important enough to start getting courted by people who curried power.

Stasia wanted to stay decidedly under that level, though she could feel it coming, and she knew there was no avoiding it.

If she was going to shake their little piggy banks empty, she was going to have to get bigger and bigger again, and somewhere up there, people were really going to start paying attention.

Merchants were going to start introducing their sons to her again and making proposals.

And she had just gotten loose of that.

She looked over at Babe again, feeling a quiet surge of humor at what he would think of that.

"I hope you're right," he said. "That all it's gonna take is inspiring them, and they'll all work it out for themselves. If I'm honest, I think the warlocks have got a hand in it, though, and it's gonna take breaking that loose, too, before folk are gonna start actin' like proper Veridans again."

"Are we racing, then?" Stasia asked with a smile, and he grinned.

"That's no fair," he said. "We're all helpin' you, too."

"But there are five of you," she said, and he rubbed his jaw.

"I'll see you, that's the truth. You're doin' all this on your own."

She looked over at the mare, not wanting Babe to see her feeling sorry for herself.

"I'm really good at it, though," she murmured, trying to be playful.

"One for the ages," he answered. "Hand to heart."

She swallowed, then leaned her head onto his shoulder.

"We should get lunch after this," she said. "Anywhere in the city you like. Maybe even somewhere I don't normally go."

"You sure you got time?" he asked.

"It's scouting," she said. "Looking for the easiest and the most obvious opportunities. I had to get this done first, and I need to go up to the estates and pay everyone, but you're right. I should take Schotzli more often. I'm just hiding from my father. Don't want to admit that I've gotten myself in over my head and need a horse when I have no place to keep her."

"You think he cares?" Babe asked.

"No, but then he'd know," Stasia said. "And I care. I made a big deal about not wanting his help, and he's keeping Schotzli as a personal favor. If he's stabling her when I use her every day for business, that's... different."

He nudged her with his shoulder, and she twisted her head to look up at him.

"Could you afford to put her in a barn like all the rest of these creatures?" he asked, using his chin to indicate the mare.

"I could," she said.

"Then pay your pa what it's worth to you and let the poor girl stay where you're both happy for her to be," he said. "And start usin' her instead of your own legs. I'd like to have dinner with you more'n twice a month, if it's all the same to you."

Stasia grinned.

"You're right," she said, a sense of relief hitting her as she realized it. "It's not a favor if I pay market value for it, and I can do that. I just can't keep her at my apartment."

She'd considered keeping Marvin there, more than once, because the little donkey made her so happy and he deserved to be kept well, but it was too small a space without enough fresh air, and it would have turned her apartment into a stall, dealing with the straw and hay needs of even the tidiest donkey.

"No, you can not," Babe agreed. "Glad that's settled. Now, I think I want to stop in at the guard house and get a pair of horses, because the sandwiches we got down at the port last time were the best I've had anywhere, and I like watchin' you watch the ships come in."

She smiled, closing her eyes as she walked and just enjoying the air and the smells of Verida outside of the main city, the sound of the mare's hooves on the cobbles and the presence of Babe walking alongside her.

"It won't be like this forever," she promised.

"No," he answered. "It won't."

She showed up at the classroom fifteen minutes ahead of time, finding students out in the hallway talking to each other and holding books against their chests. It was a festive and social place, and Stasia liked the feel of it immediately.

Rounding the corner to go through the door, though, she found that the hallway was filled with students because the classroom was packed.

Ella waved at her from the floor - the room was an amphitheater-styled construction with rows of tables leading down to a small teaching floor with two large chalk boards and a small lectern.

"What is all of this?" Stasia asked, getting down to Ella and looking back.

All of the chairs at the tables were full.

Most of them had an additional body crammed in between the chairs or behind them. The back wall was filled shoulder-to-shoulder, and everyone was settling over notebooks with pens and pots of ink, murmuring to each other in a roar of noise.

"I mentioned it to a few of the students this morning when I was at the library that you were coming, and apparently a few of them knew who you were and word got around, and..." She pointed. "The back row is all just... traders. They aren't even enrolled here. I'm going to have to ask Melody what to do about them, when she gets here."

"Why isn't she here?" Stasia asked.

"She comes at the last minute and leaves before anyone else," Ella said, as though that were obvious. "Her time is worth more than anyone else's."

"Oh," Stasia said. Sure. Okay. Wait. "Traders?"

Ella nodded.

"The castle market apparently emptied out certain quarters so that they could come hear you talk."

"Me?" Stasia asked. "Why? Do they think I'm giving away my father's secrets or something?"

Ella blinked.

"You really don't know?" she asked.

"Know what?" Stasia asked.

"They're here to see you," Ella said. "Everyone's talking about the woman in the purple leathers who shows up when you least expect her with what you need most, then charges you through the nose for it."

Stasia frowned, taking half a step back.

She should have been offended by it, but it kind of made her proud instead.

"Have you thought about what you're going to say?" Ella asked.

It sounded like it was supposed to be teasing, but Ella seemed nervous.

"No," Stasia said slowly.

It wasn't entirely true; she'd spent all of yesterday thinking about what she was going to do with this - apparently massive - group of potential merchants, but she hadn't thought about what she was going to say.

Melody arrived a few minutes later, coming down the stairs slowly while taking in the still-packing crowd.

"It appears something of significance is happening," she said evenly as she reached the floor.

"I told them she was going to be here," Ella said. "It's my fault."

Melody shook her head.

"No, it's an excellent development," she said. "The more people who gain faith in Miss Fielding, the better for all of us."

Stasia didn't like this plan, all of a sudden, but

Melody stepped forward and clapped her hands.

"Class is in session," she said. "Please find a place to be where you are out of the way and keep your conversations for after class."

The room took a moment to quiet, but everyone reacted to Melody's appearance with the same sense of awe that Ella had had around her, for the first several months.

"Very good," Melody said as they reached silence. "We have a surplus today because we are featuring a very special speaker. I want to remind you that only enrolled students are actually going to participate in the practicum that we are here to discuss. Also, we will restrict all comments and questions to enrolled students who have attended from the beginning of the semester." She went to stand at the lectern, folding her hands on it.

"Welcome to my special seminar on applied economics," she said. "For those of you who are... visiting this week, the intent of this class has been to discuss the way that the Veridan economy is integrated, both internally and externally, and how our prosperity as a city is related to those interconnections. Because this is applied economics, the second half of the semester is a practicum. There will be no classes in this room, though I will be here each week to meet with students who have questions or want to discuss particular issues they are facing. In this practicum, each student will be given one villing as seed money, and they will go out into the city to buy and sell goods and services in order to make a profit. At the end of the semester, they will present a ledger and all receipts proving their final total business worth, and they will return their seed money, if they made a profit. The top three students will be rewarded with a position at the castle, if they choose to take it. As we begin our practicum, I wanted to have one additional voice for you to consider, as Lady Westhauser has considerable experience with running an estate - a very large business -

and I have visibility to the affairs of the kingdom in a way that very few other individuals do, we have been able to lay a groundwork of knowledge that should serve our students well. But Miss Anastasia Fielding-Horne is out there, today, making money in actual trade, and I asked her to come today to give you an even closer perspective to the work that you will be doing in your challenge. Please join me in welcoming Miss Fielding-Horne."

She took a step away from the lectern and raised her hands to clap. The room joined in and Stasia thought briefly but very intensely about asking them not to do that.

Everyone who was acting like it was exciting that she was here was just... lying to her.

Surely.

And then she looked at the back row of men, not recognizing a soul but seeing men that she knew all the same. These were men looking for hope, the ones who had sold her animals and carts rather than let go of goods that they couldn't replace, because the cost of those goods had gone so high above anything they'd ever experienced before.

Stasia stepped forward to the lectern, then reconsidered and went to the chalkboards.

She felt safer here.

They were just really big books.

"All right," she said as the applause quieted and a hundred students hunched forward over their notebooks, pens ready.

Oh, now that was intense.

"What you're about to do is go find people who need stuff, people who have stuff, and you're going to connect them. If you're clever about it, when you're done you'll have more money than you started with. The only trick to it is to find people who don't have the stuff they need, and then go find the people who have that stuff and, for the right price, are ready to part with it. Right now, all over the city, the opportunities are oozing out of every single corner, but there are dangers, too, and you need to be aware of them if you're going to make it to the end of the term with money left in your pockets.

"So here we go. Let's start by talking about perishable versus non-perishable."

She did manage to talk for an hour.

She discouraged them from getting involved in food, because food spoiled so fast and it was easy to get stuck holding it after no one would eat it. She discouraged them from getting involved in anything elite, sophisticated, or cultural unless they were already an outside expert on those things, because evaluating the prices that they would fetch was too unpredictable.

She encouraged them to rent rather than buy, because it was likely that, in the timeframe they were working with, they would come out ahead, and she warned them that buying had hidden expenses that were borne by the owners when you rented, and that they shouldn't expect buying things like livestock, carts, and storage would bring immense efficiency. Don't plan on more than ten percent reduction in costs from buying unless you're an expert on that market and you know what you're doing.

She talked about staying in parts of the city where they were comfortable and familiar, because a man with merchandise going that way is going to be a man with coins coming back.

She talked about being fleet-footed and clever, and how the fact that they could come home and eat university food and sleep in a dorm meant that they had advantages that other merchants could only dream of. They weren't literally eating their profits every day. But she also warned them that it's impossible to come back from zero, if debt and wage-earning are out of bounds, so keep back seed money to restart in case of missteps or accidents. They probably wouldn't win the competition, but it didn't make the learning less useful.

Melody interjected here that their grades would be based on a combination of their decision-making and their raw profits, so zero would be very bad.

And then she got to the part that she had actually gotten really excited about, when she'd had the idea the night before.

"These markets," she said, taking a piece of paper out of a pocket and holding it up so that she could copy it onto the board. "Are special to me, and I am going to offer a bounty on each of them. The student who sells the most in any of these items, and yes I know I told you not to do perishable food, but wheat stores really well until you make it into flour, and the flour mills are actually really easy to sell to, right now... The student who sells the most of any one of these items, measured by gross receipts, so long as they make a profit on them..." She'd considered setting a twenty-percent floor on profits, and then changed her mind because... she didn't really care if they made a profit or not. She just wanted to blow the bad actors out of the water. "... will get twenty villing from me personally. I don't know how you guys are going to do, but I expect that is enough to take you from pretty competitive to very competitive. There is no limit on how many of these you can collect. If you corner all of these markets, I will hand you three hundred sixty villing. Lady Westhauser will ensure that you are not lying by going through your receipts extra closely, so if you're cutting any corners at all, you shouldn't go after these. She will find you, believe me. She's very suspicious and she knows all the tricks." She turned around, putting her list away.

The merchants in the back row were writing furiously.

She wondered what that meant.

"These are good markets right now," she said. "Just so you know. Like I said, there is opportunity oozing out of every corner of Verida right now for the quick and the clever. So be quick, be clever, and keep in mind that a disappointed customer will never buy from you again. Be honest. If they trust you, they'll buy from you every time they see you. Relationships win, even in a city as big as ours."

She looked over at Ella.

That was it.

She hadn't planned beyond here.

Ella stepped forward to the lectern.

"That will conclude our lecture for today. Registered students who have attended from the beginning of the semester can come down to get their seed money and their ledgers. I have them here."

Stasia figured out what the small wooden box at the side of the stage was - she'd had a phantom idea that it was a tips box for teachers, or something - as Ella went and opened it and brought a portion of the huge stack of books next to it to start handing out. One coin, one book.

Melody had left at some point while Stasia was talking; she hadn't noticed it.

"Where did Melody go?" Stasia asked Ella quietly as she brought her another stack of books.

"She left right at the end," Ella answered. "I think she knew it was going to be chaos in here and she didn't want to try to make everyone wait for her."

Stasia nodded, looking at the line of shining-faced students.

The city was going to eat them alive.

It was a sudden realization, and one that made her feel unwell for just a moment, and then she realized that the point wasn't for all of them to become successful merchants. The point was for them to move a bunch of goods around, and maybe even have a few of them discover that they were good at this, with some practice.

She waited until the last of the students in line left, feeling a protectiveness as Ella closed the box of coins and put it away again.

Dozens of merchants were still up in the back of the room, clustered and discussing what had happened.

For the first time, Stasia wondered if some of them weren't the men who were working against trade in the city; if some of these men weren't the adversaries she was fighting.

"Well, I think that went stormingly," Ella said, beaming. "You've got a gift."

"Don't say that," Stasia said. "This place is terrifying. It's like being a performing animal, but the exits go through the crowd."

Ella laughed.

"You really do need to come take classes here," she said. "You'd really like it, I think."

Stasia scrunched up her nose and looked around again.

It felt like a cage.

"I don't know," she said.

"You just need to meet the professors," Ella said. "They're fascinating." She put the box down on the floor next to the remaining ledgers, then sat down cross-legged next to it.

Outrageous.

"So what was the bounty thing about? You just put a huge distortion into our practicum."

Stasia made sure that the room really was empty enough to talk about it, then she sat down next to Ella.

"Those are the things that are most conspicuously

missing," she said. "The stuff that I still can't figure out where they're not coming from and where they're going. Markets that should be mostly self-healing because they have so much volume and the ability to buy from alternate sources elsewhere and import it cheaply enough to Verida. Why is it not getting imported? Where did the Veridan supply go?"

"Tallow?" Ella asked. Stasia nodded.

"No kidding. It's missing. And if one of these kids can dig up a source and go run it around to the candlemakers and the soapmakers and everyone else...? It's going to make a big difference to a lot of people."

"I prefer beeswax candles," Ella said, and Stasia raised an eyebrow as Ella slapped both hands over her mouth. "Did I just say that?"

Stasia grinned.

Beeswax candles were certainly nicer, but they were five times as expensive as tallow ones.

"Being Lady Westhauser has its perks, does it?" Stasia asked, and Ella giggled.

"So are you putting our students in danger?" she asked, rapidly turning serious again.

Stasia nodded.

"I thought about that a lot, last night, and I think..." She paused, breathing as she tried to find the words she needed. "Yes. I think there's every chance I am, but only if they're just extraordinarily successful. You know? If they can just run around doing little lots of... any of that stuff... no one is going to notice or care but the people making it and the people buying it. And they're going to make so much money, Ella.... I'm really teaching them the cheats, right up front, with these. There are other markets that are sorely distorted, but these ones are just money-making fountains. They'll probably pay a lot more for stuff than they should need to, but they'll be able to charge whatever they want, and people are going to pay it. There's no beeswax in the city, either."

"Because of the stone elves," Ella muttered. "My bee keeper is out doing hive maintenance full time right now and still way behind for the season."

Stasia nodded.

"I... My father taught me to never fall in love with a theory of how things work, because you start rejecting anything that goes against your theory, rather than adapting the theory. But I still have a story of what's going on, and it feels like... this was planned, even before Melody became queen, but when the stone elves came down from the mountains, there was this opportunity to go for it, and they did. So now it's really hard to tell what shortages are caused by the stone elves attacking the estates all summer and what's being caused by men who are trying to accomplish something nefarious."

"Nefarious," Ella mocked. "It's like a bedtime story."

Stasia laughed at herself and nodded.

"I know. And you're right. It's a sign that I'm falling in love with my theory, making out other men to be the bad guys, instead of just... men with their own ambitions and agendas, working against mine sometimes and with mine other times. Like is true all the time and everywhere."

Ella looked at the board.

"Stasia, if they're constricting the supply of wheat to Verida, I'm absolutely on board with calling them nefarious and every other bad name you can think of. Verida runs on bread. And the prices are just incredible, right now."

Stasia nodded.

"The wheat really is key," she said. "Because the wheat is most likely the only thing that's both a problem caused by the stone elves and being caused by outside forces."

"Why?" Ella asked.

"Because Boton had a once-in-a-century crop, and

their markets are swimming with it," Stasia said. "Prices are so low you wouldn't believe it, and for some reason, none of it is making it onto boats and across the Sorbine."

Ella gave her a strange look, and Stasia shifted.

"What?" she asked.

"So..." Ella said. "We have boats."

"What?" Stasia asked.

"The Westhausers," she said. "Lots of them. Big ones. They're made for going to the dark side of Dernat, but Skite didn't send them this year because of the stuff with the stone elves and the warlocks, and thinking that maybe we're playing nice with the bad guys... he's not afraid to call them bad guys, by the way. So... I'm sure the old Lord Westhauser is rolling over in his grave, but they're just sitting at the port, those ships are, waiting for orders. But Skite is kind of busy and frankly he just doesn't care. He's been running things the way his father did so that he doesn't have to make a new plan, which means when he canceled the trips to the dark side, this year... He's been getting really angry letters from the captain of the biggest of the ships, saying he's going to lose crew because they don't get paid a portion if they don't move anything..."

Stasia blinked at her.

"We can't land it at Port Verida," she said.

"Why not?" Ella asked. "Where else?"

Stasia shook her head.

"I don't know why not. I just know that no wheat comes in from Port Verida, which means that... I don't know how they're stopping it, but that's probably where they're stopping it."

"Well," Ella said thoughtfully. "I suppose Skite does own an alternate port. It's just going to involve the biggest chain of ferry boats ever seen. You can't get anywhere close to the Black Docks in one of those big ships."

Stasia nodded.

"I think it's worth it," she said. "The prices for grain right now? I... I really, really think it's worth it."

"Well, I can't agree to it," Ella said. "I can tell you that he will agree to it, but you have to talk to him."

Stasia nodded.

"I'll go with you, now, if you want. It's that important."

Ella put both hands on the cash box and shook her head.

"No, we'll do it today, but not right now. I don't want to burst in on anything going on with the Rats right now. I know that it's important to the city, but the Rats are in a weird spot right now, and... well, they're always in a weird spot, aren't they? That's just what the Rats are. Anyway. Meet us for dinner tonight. Do you know The Leaping Stag?"

Stasia nodded.

She went there sometimes with Jasper's squad. She liked it a lot, actually.

"Right," Ella said. "Is eight too late?"

Yes.

"No," Stasia said. "Not to get a big shipload of grain into the city."

"Four," Ella said, grinning as she stood. "Four big shiploads."

Stasia shook her head.

"Gamechanger," she whispered.

The day flew.

They all flew, but this one in particular flew, because she had lost the whole morning to being there at Ella's class, and she still had payments to make, money to collect, and young men and women to pay.

Plus she had a note from Queen Melody

recommending an accountant literally across the street from the castle, on the same road that the Gormands lived on, though actually in town.

She might have hidden in the doorway, once, with Jasper, when she was plotting to scale the castle wall, what, three lifetimes ago?

She spoke to the accountant, explaining her situation to him, and while he was attentive and very concerned with the details, she got the distinct impression that her sense of burden bored him. He dealt with bigger, more complicated problems every day of the week, and her intricate solutions with the signed receipts and all... they were an amateur flailing at making things work, as far as he was concerned. He wasn't dismissive, but she walked away with the distinct impression that he was going to be an amazing accountant, because he came with a built-in ability to scale up almost beyond her ability to consider.

He'd done it all before.

She took his rates and his quote for how many hours a week he was willing to devote to her, as well as what specific actions he was willing to oversee - which included taking custody of all of her receipts, transcribing them, and handing them off to either herself or a designated employee to collect and disburse funds.

It was like she had wings, coming out of that meeting.

She didn't hire him on the spot only because her father told her to never hire an important professional on the spot; to always speak to at least three or four before making a decision, because a man who made a good show of himself would be revealed as a charlatan in the context of three better-qualified peers.

So she was going to talk to a man down at the port that she knew took in piecemeal work, and she was going to ask her father's full-time accountant for referrals to get the last two.

But this time next week, no matter what, she was going to have a man who did these things, and she wasn't going to have to anymore.

Babe would find her a good, big man who would carry around bags of money for her - she planned on hiring a pair of them, both for accountability and safety, but that was tomorrow's problem - and then she would be able to focus on making connections and managing profit reinvestment.

Her first cart would be ready tomorrow.

She needed to go back for another load of lumber.

The second cart would take longer, because they didn't have the wheels premade, but once that got going, she would have another new cart every four days, so long as she kept showing up with the lumber to make them and paying the man the money he asked for having done it.

She made it to The Leaping Stag a bit early and sat in a corner, watching people come and go, drinking a glass of wine and breathing for what felt like the first time all day.

Ella came in a bit later, dressed in a leather dress with a linen shirt underneath it that looked like it belonged at the Black Docks more than anything else Stasia could imagine.

There was black velvet around the top edge of the leather, all the way around.

When Ella went for something, she went for it.

"Come on," Ella said. "We're upstairs."

"Oh?" Stasia asked, taking her wine and following Ella up the stairs and into a silent room where Skite was sitting with a nervous-looking man.

"That'll do for tonight, Veil," Skite said.

"I've got it," Veil answered. "Evening Hidalga. Miss Fielding."

Oh, now Stasia felt bad, not knowing who he was.

"Evening," Ella answered, going to sit down next to Skite.

Stasia waited until Veil left, then sat down across the table from him, setting the wine down in front of her.

Skite drew a breath that sounded put-upon, though his eyes sparkled at the joke.

"My wife informs me that you have a business proposition," he said. "I should warn you that those bore me."

"No one should know better than she," Stasia answered, and Ella snorted.

"Well, then," Skite said. "I am listening. Let us hope that you are able to entertain me enough to get through to the end."

Stasia twisted her mouth, struggling not to smile at the way he almost winked at her as he picked up his mug and held it in front of him with delicate fingers, waiting.

"Wheat," Stasia said. "It's not coming in through the port. I don't know why. I've been trying to figure out, but it's just... I can't find anyone talking about it, and if it's out on the ships, I don't know why they aren't unloading it. If it isn't on the ships, I don't know why not, because wheat in Boton is at an all-time low, for shipping pricing, and the price of wheat at the mills is... extraordinary. I do understand why it isn't available from the estates. That part at least makes sense. But the city is in a pincer, between the loss at the estates and the inexplicable lack of import, and it means that bread is now at a price that many families can't afford it. It's driving everyone to despair and violence, and it's... it's simply unthinkable that this is happening in a city like Verida."

"I could wholeheartedly agree or I could tell you that I simply don't care. Either way, I do not hear a proposition," Skite said.

"I think that something is keeping the wheat from coming in at port. I don't know what. I also happen to know that you didn't send out your biggest ocean-going ships this year after Highwater, and that they are presently resting at

Port Verida. I would like to propose that you send them across to Boton, fill them to brimming with wheat, and bring them back. To the Black Docks. And unload them by ferryboat."

His face changed.

It was subtle, but it went from teasing to deadly serious.

"I am very sad to inform you that I do not trade through the Black Docks. That overlap between my two professional lives would be inexcusable, not to mention very confusing for the Rats. I cannot have any part of bringing ships in to port." She was about to argue with him about how important this was, but he held up a hand. "That said, you are right that the ships are at rest, uncapitalized as it were, and if you were of a mind to rent them from me, for whatever reason you might have, I would be willing to consider it, at a one-hundred percent markup to crew salary costs. If you then chose to inform me, as the man who runs the Black Docks, that you intend to not-quite-dock four very large sailing vessels at the Black Docks and ask me to arrange for unloading and disembarkment, I would inform you that such services can be had at a price, and remind you that the Black Docks have a docking fee and a per-villing tax on any goods brought in through the docks. You would be expected to cover all of those at... whatever elevated value your goods might have."

Stasia scratched the back of her head.

"But you wouldn't unload it any further than the Black Docks," she said. He gave her a thin smile.

"I'm certain one of the Rats could help you locate a warehouse for temporary rental, and I would be happy to extend the unloading up to a Black Docks warehouse. After that point, I am afraid that you would be on your own for transit."

Ella was looking at her intently.

"So?" Ella asked.

It was crazy.

Stasia was too small-time to arrange for one full seafaring ship full of goods, much less four. Wheat wasn't expensive, the way a lot of the products crossing the Sorbine were, not on a per-ship basis, but Stasia had no idea how much the crew costs were going to be...

Just a minute," she said, pushing her wine out of the way and marking numbers on the table with her fingertips, trying to work it through.

She had the money.

She could run her business for the two weeks it would take the ships to go to Boton and return on what was left... she thought... it was snug, but she made profit every day, not losses...

It would change her plans for the next two weeks, expanding, because she wouldn't have the cash to burn on everything she'd been thinking about...

She looked up.

"You have a deal," she said. "Write up the contracts where there will be contracts and send them with Ella tomorrow to the guard house. I'll sign them and hand them back to her. The ships should be made ready to leave port as early as possible. As early as tomorrow."

Skite whistled, low.

"I'll send word to the ships' captains tonight to make ready," he said. "You will need to write out orders for them. Have you done that before?"

Stasia shook her head. Her father had done it all the time. She could ask him for help... if she could get south fast enough to get to him before he went to bed for the night, or maybe first thing in the morning if she could catch him before he left for the day...

"As you are a friend of my wife's," Skite said easily. "I would be glad to offer you a copy of orders that I have used with these ships in the past. It is not necessary to write unique orders unless you want distinctly different goods aboard each of them. I would advise you use duplicate orders, in this situation. Do you truly have the ability to amass the coins necessary to procure four ships' worth of products by tomorrow afternoon?"

Stasia considered.

It left enough time to get paper money converted over to coin, so long as she went fast and made good time at each of the banks.

She didn't want to wipe them out, but she couldn't afford to go to more than three.

"Melody, I'm sure, has a coin reserve that you could use to trade for paper, if you were up against a wall," Ella said gently.

Oh.

Well.

Was Stasia prepared to do it?

Babe would tell her that it was completely within the queen's interest, to have grain come into the city, and that she wasn't even asking her to cover any of the costs, simply the inconvenience of changing paper into coins.

She nodded.

"I can get it done," she said.

"There are pirates in those waters," Skite said. "You know it as well as anyone. It's a lot of risk, and you don't have to do it."

She nodded, resolute and finished with the decision.

"Write up the contracts, Westhauser. I will sign them and the ships will be on their way. I will meet with you next week to discuss the terms at the Black Docks. I assume they won't be committed to paper."

He shook his head.

"You are exactly right," he said with a phantom of a smile. "Well. You have managed to be profitable and entertaining at the same time. Very well done. I should have never doubted you."

Stasia was still doing math in her head.

Four big ships of wheat, though.

"I'm going to shake their little piggy banks empty," she murmured, and Ella beamed.

"Good. Let's eat."

She told Tesh that she was taking Schotzli, first thing the next morning. She rode up to the guard house and put Schotzli away herself so that she could stop by and say hello to Alfred and Olivet - Olivet attempted to unbuckle one of the straps on her arm; the poor horse was so bored - then she went to go watch the young men sparring.

Sterling came downstairs a few minutes later, leaning on the rail next to her.

"Jasper and Babe are out," he said. "Working on your lead, if I'm not mistaken."

"Glad to hear it," she said. She was sad that Babe wasn't here, but she hadn't expected him. "I'm meeting a friend."

"The lovely Lady Westhauser?" he asked.

"Yes," she said, glancing over at him. "Actually, I'm in need of a rather considerable amount of coins, changed from paper. Do the guard... have a stockpile that I could raid?"

"But of course," he answered. "How much are you looking for?"

She told him, and he whistled, but nodded.

"Ben's in," he said. "I can't see why he would say no, and Jasper would just do it, but I'm not the guy with the power, unless it's really an emergency and you're in dire straits."

"I'm fine to talk to Ben," Stasia said.

"Come on, then," he said, taking her up the stairs and through the mess hall, to a door that she had always presumed was a storage closet or connected to the kitchen.

"Ben?" Sterling asked. The man looked up from his desk.

"Yes, Sterling," he said.

"You know Stacy Fielding," Sterling said, shifting aside so that Stasia could go in ahead of him.

"Yes, we've met on a few occasions," Ben said, giving her a look that reminded her of Jasper. Like he didn't need to know that she was up to something to know what she was up to.

"Good morning," Stasia said, waiting for Sterling to close the door behind her. "I have a request."

"And it's coming to me," Ben said, folding his hands. "How interesting."

"I'm on my way to a financial commitment that will require I pay in coins rather than paper notes. And it occurred to me that the guard likely keeps a significant quantity of coins on hand. I am on a very tight schedule, and I believe that I can find enough bankers to change out the coins, but I need to get these coins into the hands of four ships' captains before this afternoon."

Sterling gave her a startled look, but Stasia kept her eyes on Ben.

"And you thought that the guard would happily aid you why?" he asked.

Stasia was surprised by this. She was searching for words when Sterling cut in.

"I'm very confident that Jasper would do it," Sterling said.

"Are you doing the King's work?" Ben asked.

"I certainly wouldn't be doing it if not for the queen," Stasia answered, having recollected herself. "And I work in the interests of strengthening Verida."

Why was she keeping it a secret?

Because she didn't want anyone knowing that there were four big loads of grain coming in. It was the kind of secret that if anyone breathed in range of the wrong set of ears, it might mean that her shipments would be met with the same fate that was already befalling the others that had to be trying to get in to Verida.

She didn't know Ben.

She knew that Jasper loved him, but Ben also trusted Jasper. Ben didn't know her.

"You have paper to cover all of the coins you need?" he asked after a moment.

"Yes, sir," she said.

"And you will explain yourself to Jasper once he is in again?" he asked.

"Without hesitation," Stasia said.

Ben glanced at Sterling.

"Do you trust her judgment?" he asked.

"You'll recall that she went with us, when Melody summoned us," Sterling said. "I think that it matters much less that I trust her than that Melody does."

"The Phantom," Ben said. "In my office."

"I can go to the banks," Stasia said. "But every day matters, and I want to hit the sail today, if I can."

He nodded.

"How much are you in search of?" he asked.

She told him, and he whistled.

"You won't get that from three banks," he said. "Not five. Bankers don't like being short coin like that, and they won't hand it to you casually in serious amounts. Have you spoken to the queen?"

"Getting it out of the castle unnoticed concerned me," Stasia said. "I don't anticipate being able to carry it. I'm planning on using a hay cart."

"Do you have strongboxes?" he asked.

She hadn't even thought of that. Of course she needed to procure strongboxes.

"No, sir," she said. "I will go from here to procure those, as well."

He gave her a slight smile.

"This has all come together at a moment," he said, and she nodded.

"Yes, sir."

"But you trust the parties involved? You aren't getting yourself into trouble?"

"Yes, sir," she said. "If I'm getting myself into trouble, it's because of honestly identified risks."

He nodded.

"All right. It's easy enough for me to send the recruits out to change back to coin over the next few days. Can even turn in some of the worn notes to destroy them and print new ones. I just don't like giving a man, or a young woman, for that matter, enough rope to do herself some serious damage. Nor do I like involving the King's Guard in merchants' affairs. I want no credit for facilitating this."

"It's my money, sir," she said, taking out the stacks of notes from her dragonskins and offering them to Sterling. "And it's the King's reputation on the line if the notes aren't good for coin. I could make a very strong case that presenting them to an agent of the king should result in changing them to coin without any questions asked at all."

She didn't offer it as a threat, and he didn't appear to take it as one. She was absolving him of being involved. He nodded.

"You go get your strongboxes," he said. "We'll get your coins counted out and ready for you. Bring the cart here when you're ready to load it. We'll keep it quiet that you're doing it."

Stasia nodded.

"I'm meeting Lady Westhauser here to sign some papers," she said. "And then I'll be ready to go."

He nodded and rose.

Sterling got the door for Stasia, leaving it open behind him as they went back through the mess hall and down the stairs. Lady Westhauser was standing at the gate, talking to one of the younger recruits.

"Let her in," Sterling called, going down the stairs with Stasia. Stasia took Ella back to the weapons room at the back of the yard and closed the door.

"Let me see," she said.

Ella got out a leather tube and poured the papers out of it, unrolling them and laying them out on a small table in front of Stasia.

She would have rather had a professional look at these, but they seemed simple enough.

"I have notes to cover the costs here," Stasia said, tapping the number with her little finger as she read.

"That's fine," Ella said. "Skite carries them."

She read quickly to the bottom of the page, then checked that the second contract was identical to the first, both with Lord Westhauser's name on them.

"I'm supposed to sign here to indicate that I got the money from you," Ella said, and Stasia nodded.

She took the pen that Ella offered her and signed both pages, then took out an additional stack of notes and counted them out.

The ships apparently had quite large and quite well-compensated crews.

It wasn't absurd, but Lord Westhauser was paying his men like professionals rather than laborers.

"The whole trip should be two weeks," Ella said, tucking away the notes. "But that's for four. We'll reimburse any quantities that are overpaid once the ships return to Port Verida, but Skite said to warn you that unloading was going to take longer than you think."

"Did he find a warehouse?" Stasia asked.

Ella shook her head.

"He'll do that today. Point will know who to talk to, and he will either buy it and rent it to you or secure a rental agreement and then let it to you at a profit. If he has to buy it, it may take him an extra day, but you should still go talk to him about the rest of it yet today."

She waved her hand over the ink until it was dry to the touch, then she tucked her copy away and indicated the next page.

"This is a generic order he wrote last night," she said. "Since you're only talking about one item, it's intentionally very simple. He said that, if you really want to keep the purpose of the expedition a secret, you can put a note in the order that says that it is a legal-to-trade commodity to be disclosed in a sealed letter not to be opened until they have left port. He's done that a bunch of times, and the captains are okay with it. You may get some pushback from them, because they don't know you, but if you're clear that you are very certain about the price, the legality, and the supply, the fact that you're trading at Boton makes it a much easier sell. This is going to be almost insultingly simple for these men. You might find that they're annoyed at you for asking them to do it, and you will get questions about how they're supposed to anchor off of the Black Docks. Just tell them to do the right thing, that they are responsibility for the safety of their ships, but the further they anchor from the Black Docks, the longer they're going to be stuck there at anchor while we unload. They can work it out."

Stasia committed all of that to memory, nodding quickly.

Ella grinned.

"I'm so proud of you," she said after another moment. "This is going to be a really big deal. To a lot of people. But you need to be careful. Once it gets here, there's going to be no keeping it secret. The Black Docks are full of people who talk, and those whispers are going to go everywhere, really fast. If this is actually dangerous, you need to have a plan."

"Maybe I'll just come stay with you," Stasia said, teasing.

"You are genuinely more than welcome," Ella said.

"Oh, come on, I've brought down enough trouble on your house," Stasia said, and Ella snorted.

"My husband is the Rat King," she answered. "You don't know the half of it."

Stasia nodded, reaching over to take Ella's hand.

"I'll figure something out," she said. "Hopefully it's all too surreptitious for anyone to come for me directly, and maybe Jasper's right and it's just the warlocks casting on the whole city that's doing it and there's no conspiracy running around down at the port."

"But you don't believe that," Ella said, and Stasia paused, then shook her head emphatically.

"No. The merchants of Verida are better than that. When prices go up, they go find supply. And there is supply. I can't even figure out how they've managed to keep it out, as it is..."

Ella grinned, and Stasia frowned at her.

"Why is that funny?"

"Because you cannot let a problem lay unsolved," Ella said. "The Black Docks are a fine place to be right now, mostly, but the flour shortage is hitting them, too. It just heartens me so that you're the one working on this, because it means that someone is fixing it."

"How does flour make it into the Black Docks?" Stasia asked on impulse.

"Haven't a clue," Ella answered.

"Have Skite look into it," Stasia said. "As a token

thank-you, I'll make sure that the mill that sells there is supplied first."

Ella gave her a little smile and nodded.

"After the ships come in," she said. "Until then, not a word. Not to a Rat or anyone else."

Stasia hugged her, then picked up the order template and folded it, putting it away.

"You have coins?" Ella asked, and Stasia nodded.

"The guard is going to change my notes," she said.

"Good," Ella said. "That's very good. It occurred to me that you can't exactly carry that quantity of coins out on your own. It would take me five or eight trips, with the right strongboxes."

"Strange problems," Stasia murmured, and Ella laughed.

"Merchant problems. You're officially one of them, you know."

"Never," Stasia said with a laugh. "Never did I think I would actually be doing this."

"You ought to ask your dad," Ella said thoughtfully. "Whether he knew."

Stasia frowned playfully, then Ella straightened.

"I'm going to go get these put away at home. I probably won't see you again until the ships have launched, so... smooth sailing? Is that what Skite told me to say?"

"Smooth sailing," Stasia agreed. "It's a good one."

Ella hugged her again, then opened the door and went out into the yard. She watched the young men training for a moment, then went on.

Stasia only paused a moment longer, letting Ella leave on her own, then went out as well.

She had a cart to abscond with and strongboxes to buy.

Merchant problems.

Around lunchtime, Stasia found herself standing next to the high-strung gelding in front of her second cart, watching Sterling and Ben load four strongboxes of coins into the bed of hay there and then cover them over again.

She had written her orders and her secret orders and she had sealed the secret orders with wax. Her father had a seal for wax, but Stasia didn't have one.

She needed her own.

Babe probably didn't have one.

What an odd thought, that she ought to discuss one with him, whether they wanted to share one in the future.

What a weird life.

She went and tied Schotzli to the back of the cart - she wasn't planning on returning here today - and she gave Alfred a carrot from the stash Jasper kept up out of reach by the door, kissing his nose. It had taken him some time, but he appeared to have put on all the weight he'd lost that summer.

She led the pulling horse out of the guard house and onto the road, plotting a course to the port. The main streets to either side of the river would be the safest, but they would take longer. No one knew exactly when ships were launching, right now, but if they had wind, they could probably get going yet this afternoon, so long as Skite's orders to prepare for launch last night had found everyone. It was possible they hadn't.

She was carrying a fortune, there behind her.

She wasn't one of the top merchants in the city, right now, but she would be if all four ships came in and she managed to sell all of the grain at market prices, even assuming the grain was a big enough quantity to start driving down those prices.

Which she thought it ought to be.

She'd done a bunch of estimates, trying to work out how much wheat the city of Verida would consume in a week, and she thought that she might drive the prices down as much as twenty-five percent, though that had an obscene number of assumptions in it, and she knew that her hope was to drive down bread prices, which meant that all of her assumptions were unwittingly leaning that way.

But it felt possible.

But even at a twenty-five percent discount, the wheat that she was going to buy into the city with that money, there behind her, was going to launch her into an entirely new peer group.

She wouldn't be up there with her father and his partner, nor even Gevalt Gormand, but there were thousands of men running around Verida, doing small-time trade, and she wouldn't be among them, anymore.

She would have the capital to make her own supply materialize, without needing to rent out fishing boats.

She wasn't sure what she was going to do with it, once she had it, and it kind of frightened her, the responsibility of caring for that amount of money, but...

Well, if it worked, she'd probably just turn Lord Westhauser's ships around and do it again.

Because being a grain merchant was respectable, and the city still needed grain.

She was going to have a warehouse full of grain, two or three or four weeks from now, if everything went to plan.

She, Isabella Gabriella Angelina Aurora Renata Anastasia Fielding-Horne.

The cart felt like it was on fire, behind her. Like everybody ought to have been staring at it, trying to figure out what was going on.

Where was she going?

What was she up to?

No one paid her any attention at all.

Even with the markets all but frozen, the streets were still packed with people going about their lives. It might have been less congested than it was, before Constance died, but Stasia could hardly remember.

She remembered how intense and crowded everything had felt, coming back down from the mountains. How much pressure there was on her ears from the noise of it all.

She couldn't remember what things felt like, before that.

She made it to the port, finally, and went out to the slip number of the first ship.

A man called out to the rest of the ship, and another man, the captain, by his clothes, came down the gangplank to her.

"Anastasia Fielding-Horne," he said. "He told me to look for purple."

"Captain Torte," she said. "I have orders and I need to speak with you, but for now I need to get strongboxes offloaded from my cart as quickly as possible. May I entrust it to your custody for now, and I will be back as soon as I can?"

"Give me the orders," he said, bored. "I'll review them while you finish your errands."

She went back to the back of the cart, elbowing Schotzli's nose out of the hay and pulling one of the strongboxes out of the hay.

"You know that normally they send guards to deliver order capital," the captain said, still bored.

"I'm a one-woman show, right now," Stasia answered. "Someday soon, I'm sure my guards will annoy you instead."

He raised an eyebrow, motioning another man forward to take the strong box from her - it wasn't quite so heavy that she couldn't carry it, but she preferred not to embarrass herself by walking with it if she could help it - and Stasia took out the first set of orders, handing it across to him.

He unrolled the paper, reading it quickly and then letting it fall back into its previous shape.

"I understand," he said, and Stasia frowned. She'd been expecting more from him than that. She looked him in the eye, and he raised an eyebrow again.

"Shall we be off?" he asked. "Or do you have additional orders that you haven't written down?"

"I expected a fight," she said. He shook his head.

"Port Verida is in an inexplicable state," he said. "We haven't been subject to it, but do not confuse that for unaware. These are good orders, if you're doing what I think you're doing, and I'll be glad to have this wretched port in my wake."

She took out the sealed orders and gave them to him. He tucked them away, entirely uncurious, and she wondered how much of what was going on he had actually determined.

"Is your crew all in?" she asked.

"Has been since dawn," he answered.

She nodded.

"If you are happy with the orders, that should be all you need from me," Stasia said, feeling awkward to just be handing him a box of money and walking away.

He'd known who she was, so clearly Lord Westhauser had spoken to him, or at least written to him, and this was the place that she had expected to find the ship, and the ship was... As she took it in, it was frankly gorgeous. It was one of the biggest ships sailing out of Port Verida, with heavy, rugged timbers made for transit through the nearly-frozen seas at the southern end of the continent. There weren't many ships like this one in the port.

And Lord Westhauser routinely handed more money than this to this man; the quantity of grain that would stuff the ship to the gills was a cheap commodity compared to what Lord Westhauser would have been using them for.

It wasn't that it was that much money.

It was.

It absolutely was.

But it was more that it was such a substantial hunk of her self.

She'd kept telling herself that she didn't care about the money, that she didn't need the money. That the money was just a mark of how much profit she was stripping off of the men who were distorting the markets in her favor. It was a score-keeping metric.

The problem, and it came to her all of a sudden, was that this was a win-or-lose moment.

If she handed the wrong man her hard-won profits and he disappeared with them, she couldn't do this.

She could start from nothing again, but the city was going to face starvation, in the meantime, and Queen Melody would be forced to make some very desperate decisions.

She'd grown to this point, where she could do this... and this was hers to do.

The ship's captain was still waiting.

"Then you should make way at your earliest opportunity," Stasia told him. "Fill your hold, fill your bunks, fill every space you've got and bring it all back to me. You don't have a months-long expedition in front of you, so I expect a full utilization of your space."

"Yes, ma'am," Captain Torte said, amused. "Will you be at port to greet us when we return?"

Oh, you'd better believe it.

"Yes, sir," she said. "I will be there."

He nodded, then gave her a begrudging smile and nodded again.

"Very well, then. I'll see you on the other side."

He gave her an informal little salute, then went back up the gangplank. As Stasia set off with the cart, the gangplank pulled up behind him, and there were shouts as men gave and received orders.

It was happening.

Stasia's throat caught.

It was happening.

She did three more stops and had three shockingly similar conversations with captains who were ready to be off.

They took her money, they took her orders, and they started untying the mooring lines. Simple as that.

Stasia had spent time around some of her father's captains, but they had always had either a ruthless disdain for her or a patronizing and false tone. The four captains, once they looked at her orders, had each treated her like an equal, and there was something unbidden and empowering to it that made her want to do it more.

She turned the cart, walking it back to the livery barn where she had liberated it from, then she took Schotzli and headed for the Black Docks.

It was late evening by the time she got to the bar.

Before she'd even dismounted, a man detached himself from the wall, holding up his hands.

"He ain't here, lass," Sly said. "Left me to watch. I'm to show you to 'im."

"You aren't a Rat," Stasia said.

"Ain't Rat business, now is it?" Sly asked with a grin, coming to pat Schotzli's neck. The mare danced sideways away from him, turning her nose to pick up the smells on his shirt, then nudging him. They eyed each other for a moment, then when he put his hand up again, she settled under it. Acquaintance made.

"You're using brackish," Stasia said.

"Good as any," he answered with a bemused smile. "You want a drink first, or are you ready?"

"I'm ready," she said, and he set off at a quick walk, his hands in his pockets. Stasia dismounted, leading Schotzli out of a sense of propriety.

It was saying something to ride a horse while someone else walked.

"What did he tell you?" Stasia asked after a few minutes.

"He said stand here, wait for the lady in purple, then go there."

"How did you know it wasn't Rat business, then?" Stasia asked, and he grinned.

"I ain't a Rat," he said playfully. "Now am I?"

"He trusts you," Stasia said, and Sly nodded.

"Might be the first he actually trusted, come to the Black Docks," Sly said. "Found me in a bad way and offered to make my troubles go away if I'd do some thievin' for him, so I signed my mark, and I been his creature ever since."

"Make your troubles go away?" Stasia asked, and Sly laughed.

"Mostly he beat 'em out of me," he said. "Good man."

She frowned, but Sly pointed.

"That's where you're goin'. I'll take the horse and leave her at the livery where the Westhauser animals are kept."

Stasia hesitated for a good long time at that, but Babe had trusted Skite and Sly with Peter, and she wanted even less to leave Schotzli standing outside.

"She goes missing, I will find you," she said, and he grinned.

"Promises, promises," he answered with a wink, taking Schotzli's reins and heading off in the opposite direction.

Stasia went to the door that Sly had pointed at and knocked.

A slider-bar opened at eye-level and a man peered out at her.

"Who're you?" he asked.

"Is she purple?" a voice called from inside.

"As a great bloody bruise," the eyes answered.

"Let 'er in."

The slider closed and the door opened. Stasia put her hand on one of her daggers, looking over at the man to evaluate him for menace as she went into the building.

"Miss Fielding, I assure you that you are here under my protection, not your own," Lord Westhauser said. She found him sitting at a table with a clear bottle in the middle of it and three shot glasses poured out. One in front of him, one in front of a grim-looking man with a shaved head and a waxed mustache, and one in front of an empty chair.

Stasia didn't like drinking goldbrew, but she was able.

She sat.

"Man at the door is Crescent," Lord Westhauser said. "He owns the building and it appears he will continue to own the building. We will be renting from him. The man here is Pekins, an old ally of mine when it comes to the trade wars."

"You know anything about trade wars?" Stasia asked, and Lord Westhauser gave her a thin smile.

"I've been in trade wars with an awful lot more blood than anything you've ever participated in," he said.

"Thought you didn't do that stuff," Stasia said, and Skite nodded. His expression changed. He was Skite now, accent or not.

He looked at Pekins.

"Are you enough convinced that she's got the wit and the constitution to see it through?" he asked.

Pekins worked at his mustache for a moment, then

nodded.

He was too thin for that look. The shaved-head thing was a look for a staunch man with meaty hands and sharp, angry eyes. Pekins had delicate hands, and it looked more like someone had held him down and shaved him as part of an awful joke.

Maybe it was the mustache throwing her off.

"I'm convinced," he said.

"Good," Skite said, picking up his glass and putting it back. Pekins did the same and then both men looked at her. Stasia sighed and drank the shot.

Just... swallow with your throat instead of your tongue. It was an acquired skill, and Stasia had it, but she didn't see the point. She was going to go home tipsy, at best, and unstable at worst, and she wouldn't have enjoyed anything she'd had to drink.

"Good," Skite said again as Pekins refilled the glasses. "Now, Pekins, here, has contacts in the underworld around the city, because where else would he have contacts, now would he?"

"Rats live in cages, and they only talk to other Rats," Pekins said.

"Are you a Rat?" Stasia asked, surprised.

"I'm the biggest Rat there is," Pekins said.

Clearly Stasia was missing something.

"I'll send Ace down to talk to you like in the old days," Skite said. "If it will make you less grumpy."

"See through it now, don't I?" Pekins asked. Skite snorted at him with a dismissive, wrinkled nose, then he turned his attention back to Stasia.

"So, having a man who has to use underworld channels to distribute goods has its advantages, as you might immediately discern."

"You're going to have him help me move the wheat," Stasia said. "I thought we agreed we weren't going to tell anyone until it got here."

Skite closed his eyes with an approximation of humor.

"I never said wheat," he said. "I was going to give him a week to work without any context at all before I even told him it was a food commodity."

"You've got wheat coming in?" Pekins asked.

"Maybe," Stasia said. "Why? Why is it so hard? I can't find anyone who will tell me."

Pekins looked from Stasia to Skite and back.

"You don't know?" he asked.

Stasia crossed her arms.

"I found it quite easy, actually," she said.

He fidgeted with his mustache for a moment, then looked at Skite.

"If they find out where this stuff is coming from..." he said. Skite raised an eyebrow.

"What?" he asked. "What, exactly, is going to happen?"

Pekins sighed.

"I'm a Rat in a cage," he said. "What do I know? Only what I see with my beady little eyes."

"Well, what a fortunate coincidence for you that you have some of the best eyes in the market," Skite said. "And you're sitting at a table with one of the smartest women I know."

Pekins sniffed.

"You know a lot of women, Skite?"

Skite gave him a smile that looked like a threat, then lifted a finger to point at Stasia.

"Tell her."

Pekins sighed again.

He didn't want to be here.

"Boats come in. Got stuff on board. Everybody wants to sell when they got a hot hand, right? Watch the crew pull the loads off, walk 'em down the boardwalks toward the shore, and then something happens. Wind changes. They all turn right round and go back to the ship, put the sails back up, keep on going."

Stasia nodded.

"I've seen that, too," she said. Though the description of the wind changing was oddly precise and accurate. It was like they got hit with a headwind and blew away with it.

"You figure out why?" Pekins asked.

She shook her head.

"I've been trying for weeks... months now, to work that out, but I can't."

He sniffed, giving Skite a very dark look.

"It's because their ships' masters are standin' on the edge of the docks, wavin' 'em off. Sailors know. They can feel it when they put in to the port. Air isn't right. They know, and when they see the men who are supposed to be waiting there for them, eager, and instead he looks like he's been bled dry, they know, and they go back. They say it's the mark of a plague, and I think maybe they're right, and we just don't know we've got it, but the sailors do, and they go load up all the goods again and the captains take new orders when they come, and they get out. No one wants to be here. Verida is sick."

Skite shoved the table at him a fraction, a jarring motion that startled both Stasia and Pekins.

"Speak plain," Skite said. "I'm in no mood for your riddles, tonight."

"I am, as much as I know how," Pekins said. "It's been a long time, hasn't it, since I've been allowed to actually talk to them. You fill in the blanks the best you can figure them out. But I don't think anyone who's actually been outside of the Black Docks recently would argue that the whole city is sick."

"The whole city is starving," Stasia said. "Whether or not there's anything else going on, people need food, and without it, they start behaving differently."

Pekins looked sideways at her.

"You think you can get around the monster at the gate by going through the side door," he said.

"I think until I figure who and what the monster is, I'm best trying to go around him, yes," she said.

"And you expect me to participate," he said to Skite, an accusation.

"I do," Skite said. "If you want another one of your ships to unload at the Black Docks."

Pekins wrinkled his nose.

"You've been holding that over my head for years, now," he said. Skite sighed.

"You haven't even been here that long. If you want out, go kill your father. What do I care?"

Stasia looked hard at Pekins, but he didn't react to this.

Instead, he looked at Stasia.

"I want thirty percent," he said.

"No," Stasia said, insulted. "I can get everything out of here on my own. I don't need you and if that's the price you're going to charge me, I don't want you."

"Oh, you can't do anything, without his say-so," Pekins said. "You're in it now, and if he's sitting you down with me, you shouldn't look at this as voluntary."

Stasia didn't let her eyes budge.

Relax.

Don't check your cards. You know what they are.

He's bluffing or he isn't.

The game is between the two of you, now.

"I think you misunderstand me," Stasia said. "Skite is a businessman with whom I have a very limited contract. It involves this building, if I'm not mistaken, and a substantial quantity of labor. Rats, I assume, and I also assume that they are not technically slave labor, because I think he knows I wouldn't approve of that."

"Rats are compensated in unusual ways," Skite said. "It doesn't make them unpaid."

Stasia still didn't look at him.

Pekins was positively vibrating.

"Now," Stasia said. "He brought you here tonight, which means that he trusts you. Why, I couldn't possibly say at this moment, but he trusts you with my life and with the lives of thousands of Veridans who are living on the edge of starvation. Those lives may not matter much to him, but he wouldn't risk them for no gain. He isn't empty inside, much as it may look like it. So I am free to come and go as I please. I am free to negotiate as I please. And I am free to tell you that I would never pay you more than ten percent of my gross to move product, and I would prefer a per-service upfront payment that is agnostic of the value of goods I may end up moving around the city."

The man went very still.

"What does she know?" he asked.

"Blessedly little," Skite answered.

"She is very bold," Pekins said.

"Winners usually are," Skite answered.

"You hid me away here, Rat, and you took everything from me. Literally took it. Are you going to do the same thing to her?"

"I saved your life," Skite said, sounding like they'd been over this before. "You are just as free to walk out that door as she is."

"I am nothing," Pekins said, his voice a growl through his teeth.

"You are whatever you choose to be, Pekins," Skite said. "And you've proven to be quite good at whatever that is. I'm not standing in your way. I'm simply charging you for my services. Do you think that thirty percent is too high?"

"She's going to make a killing, unless she's planning on just giving it all away." He stopped himself up short, looking at Stasia again. "You aren't, are you?" he asked.

"I will charge what the market will bear," she said. "It's the only way to make sure that the people who need it get what they need."

He licked his lips.

"Not many people know that," he said, and she shrugged.

"My father is an honest man."

He considered that.

Drew breath like he was going against his better instincts.

"I have a network of couriers and cartmen," he said. "I have connections with various market merchants through the city who either wholesale or sell directly to the public, depending on their situation. But you don't need me. You need to go straight to the millers."

"I'm having carts built as quickly as I can," Stasia said. "I'm buying them from merchants who have given up selling with prices where they are..."

Pekins scoffed.

"Fools, the lot of them."

Stasia shrugged an agreement.

"... but that's just not been enough. I really don't want to repurpose my entire fleet, either, if I don't have to, because they're doing important routes and because I don't want to draw any more attention than I'm already going to."

"How much canvas do you have?" Pekins asked.

"Not enough," Stasia growled. She'd overlooked it. That was how you kept the back of a cart private. She didn't know why she hadn't thought of that.

She'd used hay, instead.

"It's not easy to get," Pekins warned. "But my carts

all have an adequate supply."

"I have weavers in the artisan district who owe me some favors," Stasia said. "I'll make it happen."

He nodded.

"Good to be owed favors."

"Good to be handing them out," Stasia answered.

Skite smiled.

"She has the cards, Pekins. Make her an offer she's going to take."

Pekins worked his mustache again.

"Ten percent," he said. "Up to twenty carts a day, with fifteen percent for anything above that."

"I use a system of receipts," Stasia said.

Pekins blinked at her.

"What does that mean?"

The heat from the goldbrew was spreading, making it out to her hands now. She was having a hard time staying intently focused.

"It means that my cartmen don't handle money," she said. "The customer signs off on the quantity of goods delivered and the agreed price, and I collect the money later, with a different man."

"I don't like going twice," Pekins said. "But I suppose that's your problem, and not mine."

"You would need to give me the receipts for all deliveries, and I would pay based on that," Stasia said.

He looked at Skite, then sighed.

"I suppose you'll be wanting me to watch over the goods once they're unloaded, then, too?" he asked.

"Oh, I'll be charging her for security separately," Skite said. "You're just transit."

Pekins looked at Stasia again.

"You'd be better off just burning the ships at harbor," he said. "You know that. You're inviting all manner of problems, doing this."

"Verida runs on bread," Stasia answered. "I'm working on bringing in beef, but not in any quantities that are going to change anything. The best way to save a system is through the way it's always worked before. This is how we keep everyone from starving to death, and I'm very willing do what it takes to at least try."

Pekins looked at Skite, now.

"Even you and your precious Rats may not be able to hold up under the storm this is going to unleash."

"Rats thrive when everyone else suffers," Skite said. "When the city falls, we will be the last ones standing. Do you have an agreement?"

Pekins considered Stasia for a moment, then nodded.

"I suppose we do," he said.

"Yes," Stasia said.

Skite picked up the shot glass and tipped it back, waiting while Stasia and Pekins did the same, then he took Pekins' glass, tipping it onto the ground and then tucking it away somewhere.

"And thus I am dismissed," Pekins said, standing. "You know where to find me when the ships come in."

"I do," Skite said. Those words were frightening.

Pekins grunted and left.

Skite turned to Stasia with amusement.

"Have you done wrong by him?" Stasia asked.

"Took his fortune and killed him," Skite said. "Dumped his body in the river. Dead men are especially useful."

Stasia tipped her head at this, but he moved on without further comment.

"How did things go with the captains?"

"Ella had me all ready to fight with them, but all four of them took the orders and just immediately set sail. I think most of them actually guessed what I wanted them to do, even with the sealed orders."

Skite nodded.

"My father did know how to pick them. Every venture across the sea has elevated risk, but I can't imagine any of those four ships being set upon by pirates or finding rocks. How did it feel, watching your treasure sail away like that?"

Stasia dipped her head.

"I've never felt like that before," she said, and he grinned.

"Wait until you see them come in," he said. "It's just a shame you won't get to see them dock at the port. You may not even be able to see them, from the docks here."

She nodded.

"He's probably right about the wheat causing problems," she said, and Skite nodded.

"Ella and I discussed it," he said. "And you're probably right. Did she invite you up to the estate?"

Stasia nodded.

"She mentioned it."

"Pekins is a safe mind, and Crescent... wherever he ended up... is hard of hearing in the best possible way. I think you are still probably safe until the first loads hit the shore here. But you need a plan for after that."

Stasia nodded.

"We should at least shake hands on what you're going to do and what I'm going to pay you for it," Stasia said.

He nodded, filling both shots once more. Stasia wrinkled her nose.

"Is a handshake really not good enough for you?" she asked. "You have to incapacitate me with alcohol in order to be sure I mean it?"

He grinned, setting the bottle back down.

"Doesn't pay to be a lightweight in business, in the Black Docks," he said, sitting back in his chair. "But my terms, at least, are simple. I will guarantee the safety of your product so long as it is in the Black Docks, understanding that that will likely take additional resources on my part, compared to what a normal shipment would require. I will unship it and deliver it to this location. You will be allowed to come and go as you please, but you or Pekins will be required to be here, personally, to sign off on any product that leaves the premises. This may be a burden to you, but it is the only way to ensure that my men do not allow unwarranted removal of product. In exchange, you will turn over to me a tenth of your landed product, to be stored elsewhere and dealt with separately."

He'd told Melody that he normally charged three.

It was a lot.

To get the grain off the ships and into the warehouse, then have men sit around and make sure nothing happened to it.

At the same time, it was what the service was worth. She couldn't possibly handle the volume of grain that was going to come off the ships. Skite would have the manpower and the resources to deal with it, and it was something she couldn't buy.

"Done," she said.

He lifted the shot to his lips and downed it.

Stasia sighed and took the third shot.

He took her glass and flicked it out as well, then disappeared both glasses and put the bottle down on the floor next to his foot.

"Are you ready for this?" he asked.

She shrugged.

"How can you know until you've done it?" she asked.

He looked at her with concern.

"You are catapulting yourself into a new echelon of prestige and notoriety," he said. "Even if everything goes perfectly, people are going to come to you, now, proposing business or expecting your help. I can head off some of it with my reputation, but women still come to me, begging me to intervene on behalf of their children or their husbands in some dispute or another. People with power - and that includes all people with money - are the last resort of people without."

Stasia chewed on her lip for a moment.

"Do you do it?" she finally asked.

"I am a hard man," he said. "I do not spill my power casually or profitlessly. But where a man has served me, or where he might yet have purpose, I will sometimes intervene in situations."

"I don't have to let anyone know that I am as rich as I'm likely to be, after this," she said.

He gave her a simple smile.

"You don't have to act like you have money, it's true," he said. "I certainly don't live like it, when I'm here. And perhaps no one will find out. I would never accuse you of needing the trappings of wealth. I've seen your apartment. But what will you do, instead? Remove all of that money from the economy and simply sit on it? Give it away? I can hardly see you doing either, and anything else will eventually expose your name."

"What would you advise I do?" Stasia asked after another moment.

He shrugged.

"I ran away from my wealth until it finally caught up with me. But neither of us are able to just neglect it. I expect you'll find the way of advertising your status and putting your money to work that serves you best. Buying lots in ships is a relatively passive way to do it, and they tend to come to you, once they know you're doing it."

She nodded.

"Is that what you do?"

He laughed.

"No, I just follow the trails my father laid down," he said. "He had habits, and while I'm certain he would have jumped at any number of opportunities I simply haven't been there to see... he would have launched those ships on schedule, because the arrival out of the dark side of Dernat is a good quarter of his yearly trade. But I just do what he always did and let it be. Ella manages the estate, better than he did, I might add, because it is so nearly her only consideration, and I am left free to do as I will, here. But you do not have an Ella. Your gentleman is not going to leave his own calling anytime soon. So you have to find a solution for yourself."

Stasia nodded, looking around the warehouse.

It was going to be stocked to the rafters with wheat in two or three weeks.

From there, it was up to her to figure out how to get it to the mills and to get flour pouring back into the bakeries.

That was all she'd been thinking about.

She laughed.

"You think like I've already been successful at this part," she said, and he nodded, serious.

"That's how you win," he said. "First, you assume you're going to, and second you plan for what comes next."

It was something her father might have said.

She swallowed, feeling the chair tip underneath her.

"You will sleep here tonight," Skite said, standing and helping her to her feet. "I have a place for you that will be safe. In the morning, you will go back about your business as normal, and in twelve days, you will return here and we will all three of us wait together for word from the ships."

Stasia let him steady her, then they walked to the door.

"Is Ella here tonight?" Stasia asked, and he nodded.

"She is," he said.

Stasia wasn't sure why she'd asked, but it made her

feel better.

Maybe it was that her left knee kept giving out and Skite was holding her up with his hand under her armpit.

She would be fine in a bit.

It was just too much, too fast.

Over four hours, it would have been fine.

He walked her through the door and along the road. The apartment that he took her to was above a dark shop of some description, and it had a bed.

It was plenty.

She hired away a butcherboy. She started carting beef for Lord Marley. She procured lumber for four more carts. She bought eight more horses. The new carts would be pair-haul carts, particularly with a full load of grain in them. She hired an accountant - the queen's accountant won out - and she hired Babe's friend to carry money.

She met with Ella's and Melody's students at the bar. By her guess, a quarter of them were already broke; a few had been taken, a few had purchased raw goods with the intent of turning them into finished goods themselves, which was a business, but it wasn't going to move fast enough to compete with the rest of the class, and she suspected that a few had figured out how to launder the seed money to show it was lost, and had split the villing out to just keep it. These came and asked for another coin, and Stasia found herself sad at how much profit they were losing out on, given how much some of the other students were making.

The ones who were going to be competitive to win, Stasia could identify immediately, at least from among the ones who turned up to talk. A table of them formed even by the second week, and they sat and swapped strategies and stories, welcoming Stasia in as a kind of wise peer and peppering her with often very-specific questions.

Ten days after the ships left, she went to two of the mills, negotiating a price for wheat. The millers were desperate, and they wanted firm commitments from her, but she wouldn't give any to them. Both of them had a very small limit to what they could take, right now, and Stasia suspected it was because they were all but out of money. It was probably better for both of them, since Stasia would be taking a risk on them deciding not to honor their signature on a receipt and just taking the grain, and she would prefer to get bit over the smallest amount of wheat possible before she figured out which of the millers were going to honor their debts.

At the eleventh day, she spent the day with Babe.

He knew that she was going to disappear for a little while, and he had offered to ask for a leave from the guard to come down to the Black Docks with her and watch her back or help haul, whichever one she needed.

"The queen is in as much danger as she has been since the night you killed all the warlocks," Stasia said. "Once rumor goes out that there's a lot of grain coming in, if this is about trying to make her do something specific, it may trigger a panic and they may come after her in an unplanned way."

"Might be true," Babe had said. "But you're the one paintin' a target on your own back."

"I'll be down at the Black Docks," Stasia said. "You know that I'm safer there than anywhere else in the city. And I'm planning on just disappearing until I'm more sure that I'm safe to come back."

"Jasper says the castle ain't safe enough, right now, and that he talked to Ben about lettin' you stay at the guard house. You can do that if you need."

"Really?" Stasia asked.

"Really," Babe said. "We've got eight warehouses

we're lookin' into, might be keepin' stores of grain, but everybody's full of bristle. We're not gettin' anywhere close on our own, because these are the kinda fellas that'll risk killin' a man, even in uniform, to see if they can buy a day to hide again."

"So I can stay at the guard house because of that?" Stasia asked.

"Because you're in it with us," he said. "And because of what happened last time. Ben sees it that you're doin' the King's business, and he's willin' to give quarter for a bit. That's all."

"And this had nothing to do with you?" Stasia asked.

He grinned.

"Not a bit," he said. "Jasper came to me, asked if I was seein' you tonight."

"I don't know the last time I saw Matthias," Stasia said. "I miss you guys."

"They ask about you often," Babe said. "Mostly to tease me, but they mean it, too."

"Do you think it will ever be normal again?" Stasia asked.

Babe settled onto his elbows on the table, frowning with thought for several moments before he answered.

"Jasper'd say Verida has a bill comin' due, and it's gonna cost us somethin' to pay it. I don't necessarily disagree with that. He sees things I don't. But I'm just not so sure there's ever been anything I'd point to as what normal was. You came to Verida at a time, and because we were happy you took it to mean that's how things always was, but it ain't the truth. Things go where they're gonna go, and nothin' ever stops 'em. Normal is a moving target that folk make up to tell themselves that everything's okay. This is just as normal as the next day."

Stasia nibbled at the remains of her dinner.

"No," she said. "I hear you, and I hear where you're

coming from, but this isn't normal. Everyone being afraid and being angry and being hungry isn't normal. You're right that the routine changing is unavoidable, and romanticizing what was, before, doesn't help appreciate what is now. But I'm not going to let you take away what was really amazing about this city, before Constance died. I just won't let you."

Babe smiled and nodded.

"And right you shouldn't," he said. "When are you goin' to ground?"

"After this," Stasia said. "I'm walking from here, and I've got everything I think I need for two weeks in the Black Docks packed, there." She indicated her knapsack, the same one she had taken up into the mountains. It had brought her home once. "And then... we'll just see how things go."

He nodded, reaching across to cover her hand with his.

"Nothin' in the world matters to me like you do," he said. "You come home safe, and if you need us to show up, don't you let your pride keep you from callin'. You know we will. Not as King's Guards, but as your friends. Because every one of us loves you, and you know it a fact."

"I do know," Stasia said. "And I miss you guys because of it. I miss my friends. But this is not normal, and I won't let it be normal, and after, I'll be able to spend more time with you because I won't be fighting off things that are so... dark."

Babe shrugged, then nodded.

"We'll both hope so," he said. "But Jasper ain't wrong about a bill comin' due, and it's the likes of you and me who are gonna end up payin' it, because we can."

Stasia nodded.

"Then let's be ready," she said, then grinned. "I'm going to go make a whole bunch of money, now, if you'll excuse me."

He stood and took her satchel, putting it over his

shoulder and then offering her a hand up to stand.

A year ago, she didn't think she would have let him do that.

But this wasn't a year ago.

They went downstairs through the more crowded, noisy part of the bar, and outside into the deep dim of late sunset. The sky overhead was in colors, but the streets were in shadow already.

He handed her her satchel, then pulled her around the corner of the building, pulling her face to his.

She put her arms around his neck and kissed him back.

At first, it had felt like a goodbye, one that he wasn't willing to say out loud because it would have admitted how worried he was about her, but it changed quickly, and he put his arm around her back, holding her tight there.

This.

This was what she'd imagined at a thousand corners around the city.

And it was better than her imagination.

His breath was hard against her, and she bit at his lips because it made him kiss her harder. His hand felt for a seam at the back of her dragonskins, but there wasn't one.

He broke away, looking over her shoulder and down her back.

"It really is good armor," he muttered, and Stasia put her forehead against his shoulder and laughed. She might have cried, otherwise.

"I'll be back soon," she said, and he put his cheek against hers and nodded.

"I'll hold you to it," he said.

She kissed his cheekbone and went to retrieve her knapsack from the ground. She waved once as she set off, and he stood there, leaned against the wall, and raised a hand in farewell in return.

Day twelve.

She knew that it would probably take more than a day to load the ships fully with grain and get them on their way again. It might take an entire day to strike a contract, and then start loading the ships.

Twelve days was irrational.

And yet, she sat at the dock bar with Sly, watching the horizon all day.

He drank casually, speaking sometimes, but he seemed to have no problem spending the entire day just watching in quiet.

She liked him.

She had no idea what he saw in her, but she liked him.

Day thirteen, Skite joined them.

He had men coming up to him all day with questions or reports, and he took them quietly there at the bar or walked a little ways off when he wanted privacy, and then he returned.

Like Sly, he was comfortable with the quiet.

Day fourteen, Ella was there.

She and Skite talked all day in happy, conversational tones about anything and everything. The weather, the weight of Veridan coins, the number of coins that must have been on the bottom of the river and how to find them, the eye colors of sheep.

Ella swore that they came in more than just brown.

Skite said that she'd had a vivid dream that had confused her reality.

The port was busy. Busier than Stasia might have expected, given that it was supposed to just be a small, local port with a smaller amount of local fishing activity.

Men came and went in little boats, leaving them tied to the piers and paying the dockmaster their coins. Few of the ships had more than a single triangular sail on a short mast and more were rowed with no consideration for wind. Short-distance boats. A minority were of a reasonable size, with below-deck holds and rails along the sides, but again, most of them were just a wooden leaf shape toodling around on the water. The waves came in low, when they came in at all, so at least the harbor was well protected from the waves that hit Verida elsewhere.

A crew boat came in and the harbormaster came to collect their coins, then pointed at the bar.

Skite stood.

"You'll want to be the one to greet them," he said, looking back at Stasia. Sly clapped her on the shoulder and she set off to follow Skite down the length of the pier. The two men who had disembarked from the crewboat spotted her quickly.

"Miss Fielding-Horne," one of them said.

"Purple," the other one said. "I wouldn't've believed it."

"Aye, but you know me," Skite answered. "Speak your business. We've been waitin' here for it all day."

The better-dressed of the sailors - and it wasn't saying a lot, but his equipment and weapons were sturdier and cleaner - spoke.

"All is well, lady," he said. "The ship is laden full and ready for unloading, and there are two more ships in our wake. Captain Torte invites you aboard."

"Only two?" Stasia asked.

"Unusual to have them all come in at once," Skite teased. "They may have gotten caught up in Boton, trying to fill orders. Don't jump to conclusions. I will not go with you, but you should see to your goods."

He indicated and Stasia nodded, following the sailors

back to the rowing boat and letting them situate her where they wanted, then they set off again. The men were strong and almost bored with the work, and very soon she started to make out the sails of the first ship over the waves.

It wasn't much longer before she was reaching up to a net and having more soldiers pull her up onto the ship's deck, where Captain Torte stood.

"Miss Fielding-Horne," he said. "Well met."

"Well met, indeed," Stasia said. "How was the market?"

"Rolling in grain, as you expected," Torte said. "Greer and I went in together to buy one of the largest lots of wheat, split between the two ships, and I have cashbox left over. Even once I feared for the safety of the ship's return."

It was riding lower in the water. Her eyes had picked it out immediately.

Stasia swallowed.

"Skite will be organizing a set of boats to ferry all of the bags ashore," she said. "After that, they are no longer your concern. I will take my papers and my cashbox, paying the crew's portion here and now, with the utmost gratitude."

Torte crossed his arms and lifted his chin to look at her.

"Tis a risky thing you're doing here," he said. "You know that."

"Worse to stand by and watch the city starve," Stasia said. "Will you or your crew be endangered by having participated?"

He laughed.

"The port is a sacred place," he said. "Sailors of all stripes would die to defend the sacred independence of each and every ship's crew, regardless of who owns the boards. Empty of your cargo, we will sail back to Port Verida and return to our boredom. Perhaps you will discover that you need our services again in the future, since the Westhauser heir seems to have no vision for them."

"I'm afraid Westhauser is too upstanding to unload at the Black Docks," Stasia said playfully. "Perhaps he'll come up with some other worthy cargo for you to carry, instead. It's a shame to waste such beautiful ships as these. But, tell me, your man said that there were only two ships in your wake."

Torte held up a hand.

"The fourth was unable to secure a full cargo at the first," he said. "We left without him, because a ship such as his may transverse the Pirate Islands freely as he likes, and to stay behind would have insulted him. I would look for him tomorrow."

Stasia nodded.

"Good. It is all good news. Are your crew boats suited for taking grain back to the docks, or will they capsize?"

Torte snorted.

"You know very little of sailing, don't you? Just enough words to be convincing?"

"You've spotted it," Stasia said, and he looked around at the crew.

"Well, you heard the boss," he shouted. "To the longboats, every man not serving before the mast. Those staying aboard, load 'em up and get 'em on their way. We unload this ship!"

Stasia smiled, watching the men spring to action.

"You ought stay," Torte said. "I'll run up a signal flag to Greer, and he'll send a boat across for you once he makes anchor."

She nodded.

"As you say," she said. A man in a vivid blue shirt came to escort her up to the helm, leaving her there next to the wheel, where a man with scars and a bandanna was standing lazily.

"Easiest transit I've done in ten years," he muttered. "Whole world is going soft."

The men loaded the boats in just minutes and set off toward the shore again. They'd covered the bags of grain with heavy canvas tarps, and they looked like just any other cargo ships, heading into the Black Docks.

The man with the blue shirt returned, followed by a scruffy man carrying Stasia's strongbox.

The blue shirted man handed her a roll of papers inside a large piece of leather, and Stasia took them, reviewing them easily. Purchase orders from Boton and an accounting of how the money had been spent. She could have counted what was left in the strongbox, but it would have shamed everyone.

"First Mate Evans," the blue shirted man said. "If you need anything, please ask for me."

She nodded, and the scruffy man put down the box, both of them going back to join the ongoing frenzy of activity as they set up the deck crane to start pulling palettes of grain up out of the hold.

That was hers.

She had bought it.

She had arranged for it to be here.

And she was going to sell it.

About fifteen minutes later, as a fleet of boats were visible on their way to shore, Evans appeared again, pointing behind her.

"Greer is sending across his crewboat," he said. "I'd like to get you ready to disembark. It will be on this side of the boat, if you please."

She picked up the strongbox under her arm - it was plenty light now for her to do it - and she rolled the purchase orders up in the leather, then followed Evans to the side of the ship and waited.

Once more, she was afloat, heading to the second

ship, where she had a nearly identical reception, other than that Greer was salty that Torte had beat him here and would get unloaded first. It might cost him a week, he thought, that thirty minute gap.

The third ship had found it harder to make a purchase, and the orders were more complicated and more expensive. She got help from the sailors, getting all three strongboxes back into the crewboat, and they rowed her in to shore again, where they carried the strongboxes for her to the bar, where Sly and Ella yet sat.

Stasia threw herself onto a stool, unrolling the purchase orders onto the counter and setting about doing the accounting.

Ella counted out the stacks of villings like they were nothing, giving her the total from each box. Two of the boxes matched to the copper - Botonese copper, but close enough for accounting - and the third was off by a jagger.

Stasia totaled up the grain from the three ships in her head, then rolled the scrolls closed and put them away.

Sly hadn't shown the first iota of curiosity about what was going on.

He really was fabulous.

"Where did Skite go?" Stasia asked.

"I think he'll be at the warehouse for the first bit," Ella said. "They're good at this part. They do it half a dozen times a year, though this is probably going to be the longest stretch of work a lot of these men do all year." She giggled. "There's going to be a lot of beer, at the end of it. Regardless, they can get goods onto a cart and get the cart going, and the boats can't keep up with the carts, so it just takes Veil watching over them to make sure everything actually goes on to a cart."

"And when does Skite take his cut?" Stasia asked.

"Usually at the end," Ella said. "Though he didn't tell me anything about it. Whatever the two of you agreed to, it's a secret, as far as he's concerned."

Stasia nodded.

She hadn't thought there was anything the couple kept from each other.

"Was he fair to you?" Ella asked. "Sometimes he goes a bit Skite on things and forgets that he's not..."

"A murky black monster from the depths?" Sly offered.

Ella sighed.

"That."

"I think so," Stasia said. "He could have asked anything he wanted, at that point, and frankly I wouldn't have had much choice. So I don't think he took advantage."

Ella sighed.

"So. How do you feel?"

"I don't think I've actually realized it's happening, yet," Stasia said. "It's all completely surreal."

"I've never done an honest day's work in my life, so I'm no help, there," Sly said, and Stasia grinned despite herself.

"It isn't over," Ella warned. "But this is... it's remarkable, Stasia. I know exactly how many men trade through this port in this kind of volume, and you are in a very select group."

"Now it just remains to be seen whether I can make good on it," Stasia answered. "But at least it's here."

They watched for hours as the grain poured in across the black boards of the docks and disappeared onto carts.

Stasia followed one of them from the port to the warehouse, finding more young men working to unload the carts as fast as they came in and piling up the grain in neat, cross-hatched stacks that were still against the back wall of the warehouse.

She was going to fill the entire place.

It really was just starting.

Skite saw her and waved her over to the table where they'd sat, that first night.

"So?" he asked. "How did you do?"

"Greer and Torte managed to get under my estimate by about six percent," she said, unrolling the orders and showing him. He put his fingers down the row of figures.

"Patience paid eight over," he said.

He was as quick with figures as she was, and she was impressed.

"I knew that it was a target and not a realistic goal across all four ships," she said. "It's well within my expected range."

He nodded, finding the total weight on each of the three orders, and glancing over at the next cartload of grain as it came in.

"Still, they went for it, with loading up the ships. I've never gotten cargo weights like these out of these ships."

"I told them to fill up unused bunk rooms," Stasia said. "They didn't have a massive journey back to budget supplies for. And, you've got to admit, it packs in pretty well."

Skite grinned.

"It does at that. Well, Miss Fielding-Horne, I would say that your adventure has been a success, even if your fourth ship doesn't come in."

"Don't say that," Stasia said. "There's a crew on that ship, and if it doesn't come in, it means they've all died. I don't know if I could live with myself."

He took a moment, then nodded.

"Yes," he said. "Then you aren't cut out for this end of the business, in the long term. Sailors know the odds. Even to Boton and back, accidents happen and ships get lost. You can't expect to make their decisions for them. You avoid pushing the captains beyond what they're willing to do, hire captains with a very good history of bringing home the fleet, and you let the men do their jobs. Would you say the same of a squadron of men up in the mountains?"

"Yes," Stasia said without hesitation. "I could never send them to their deaths, either."

He gave her a tight smile.

"Then we are all glad that you aren't the queen," he said. "Though we are also all glad that you are such a clever, capable merchant. We agree on my ten percent?" he asked, giving her a figure.

She nodded.

"Good," he said. "We will keep a tally of what actually comes off the boats, in round numbers, and make sure that we are within a normal loss rate for the transit in to the docks, and then I will take my ten percent when we are something approaching eighty-percent complete. As I said, I will store them elsewhere, and they are not of any further concern to you."

Stasia nodded.

"When the fourth ship gets here, we'll adjust the totals, but if you want to take eighty to ninety from each ship, it might make the calculations easier."

Skite nodded.

"Just so. I will stay here to oversee the unloading and the counting, and you should remain at the docks until they are done for the night. I have given you my word that this will be done correctly, and I have every confidence that it will, but normal loss rates are something that you can influence if you frown hard enough at certain parties."

Stasia tried not to grin.

It was just... easy.

Her ships were here.

She was talking about hundreds of pounds of wheat going missing because someone walked off with a bag, or because one of the ferry boats tipped over or got hit by a rough wave and soaked the grain.

Even losing a full ton, it wouldn't change anything about this from an absolutely unqualified success.

"Go on," Skite said, rolling up the orders and giving them back to her. "We need to do this as quickly as possible. Word is going to spread, no matter what we do, and the longer we take, the more ears it's going to hit."

She nodded, feeling a bit queasy again on top of the giddiness, but took the orders and went back to the docks.

"What do you want to do with these?" Ella asked of the strongboxes as the evening wore on.

What she wanted to do was turn them back into paper so that she didn't have to worry about them, but that wasn't really an option.

Seeing her struggle for a moment, Ella spoke again.

"I have the carriage here, and I'm going back to the estate tonight," she said. "If you want to consolidate them, filling and locking one of them, I would be happy to hold it for you at the manor until you get an opportunity to retrieve it."

"Ella, you're amazing," Stasia said. "Thank you."

Ella smiled.

"You get used to it," she said confidentially. "But it takes a while."

Stasia shook her head.

"I'm not sure I ever will."

Ella winked, and they went back to watching.

Finally, the sun sank low enough that it wasn't safe to send boats back and forth any longer, and the laborers quit. The docks emptied out but for the late-night fishermen, and Sly stood.

"Well, unless you are going to go roof running again with me tonight, which I gather you're likely exhausted with excitement already, I'm going to carry this box for Lady Westhauser to her fancy carriage, because apparently that's what I'm good for today."

"It's heavy," Stasia warned, and Sly coughed dramatically, lifting it, but went on. Ella hugged Stasia.

"Be safe," she said.

"I'm armed," Stasia answered.

Ella left, and a few minutes later, Skite arrived.

"Are you ready for your bed for the night?" he asked.

"I'm more exhausted than I could have ever guessed," Stasia said. "And all I did was sit."

"It gets easier as you go along," he answered, offering her his elbow.

She took it, looking around at the completely changed docks.

"This is the only way I've ever seen them," she said. "Quiet, like this."

He looked around.

"Most days aren't like this one," he said. "But I do think that this is one of the best ways to see the Black Docks. Just... shadows. Quiet."

They walked for quite some time before he unlocked a door and handed her the key.

"I'm not leaving anyone to watch over this place," he said. "But I will do a walk around it to make sure that no one is watching it. Alone and unwatched is the safest you can be right now. I entrust you to your own devices."

She nodded.

"Thank you," she said.

He looked at her for a moment like there might be something else he was going to say, but he shook his head.

"Rest as well as you can. It only gets harder from here."

He wasn't wrong.

The fourth ship turned up just as Torte had guessed,

late in the day, the next day, and she spent a full day at the dockside bar, watching grain go past.

And the next day.

And the next.

It was, most of the time, overwhelmingly boring, but at the same time, as she watched the quantity of grain she had procured come in, she realized just how daunting a task it was going to be to get it all back out.

The fifth day, she went and absconded with the olive cart again, taking a full cartload of grain up to the first mill and walking away with a receipt and an empty cart.

She could have asked for her cash on the spot, but she wondered if the miller even had it, or if he was counting on getting flour out to bakeries and getting paid in order to pay her.

So she didn't call it.

The sixth day, she worked at the warehouse with Skite, making sure that all of the grain was going to have a place to go and how it would be organized. She needed to move a few dozen cartloads before the last of it came in, and she had about a week and a half to do it, at the rate that the ships were unloading.

The warehouse was going to be stuffed to the gills, and Skite was concerned about how easy it would be to set fire to the whole thing. He added another Rat to the guard list and had the men put heavy leather tarps over each of the towers of wheat as it was completed, in hopes of keeping the flames off of them if a fire did hit. He told her that he'd seen it done right a few times, where an entire building went up, leaving the goods inside cooked but otherwise untouched.

She had to move so fast.

She went back to the apartment that night, unlocking the door and locking it behind her, and then going up the stairs to the small room where she'd been staying.

There was a tiny stove and cupboard where she was

keeping coffee and tea for her mornings, but the room smelled of coffee as she walked in, and she found a man sitting at the single chair at the table.

"We need to talk," Lord Palora said.

Stasia considered running.

If he knew she was here, the dangerous men he doubtlessly employed also knew she was here.

And if he was here, there was every chance that they were here, too. Simply not... here.

So... she was safest in this room until she wasn't.

Which meant that he was here to offer her information. He didn't have to plan on that being what he was going to do for it to be what he was going to do.

And she would take it.

Even if it was terrifying.

She would take it.

"Why are you here?" Stasia asked, going to the window and opening it.

"I said," he answered. "We need to talk."

"I'm not sure I have anything to say to you," Stasia said.

"You're making a big mistake," Palora said. "And I'm here as a token of friendship and because I hate to see a young person like yourself get so far down the wrong road without someone at least trying to tell you that you've made a profound mistake."

She went to sit on the bed.

"All right," she said. "I'm listening."

"You have decent taste in coffee," he said, indicating the mug on the table. "I haven't had that before. Where did you get it?"

"You should spend more time in the Black Docks," Stasia said. "There are all kinds of things here that you can't get anywhere else."

He licked his lips and nodded, nudging the mug with

a finger for a moment, then stirring himself and nodding.

"Yes, you don't know what you've done, young lady. I'm a bit... disappointed that your father didn't warn you, but, alas, here I am, cleaning up another man's mess."

Stasia stood.

She wasn't going to sit while he spoke to her like that.

Trying to figure out what to do that didn't look agitated or angry, she went to lean against the wall.

It worked for Jasper and Skite. It would work for her.

"I'm not in the mood for a lecture," Stasia said. "I'm very tired and very busy."

He gave her a thin smile, clasping his hands together and tapping his index fingers against his lips.

"You see," he said. "You've made a grave mistake. You think that you're being clever, but you should know that the things that you don't understand often have explanations you haven't begun to grasp, which is why things like trade should be left to better men."

"Oh," Stasia said.

"Yes," he said, giving her a warm, fake smile. "You see, we all know that the Veridan grain crop was destroyed by stone elves. It's a shame, that loss, and it has hurt the city considerably, but when we turned our eyes abroad to save us, what we found was incredibly inept Botonese treatment of their wheat. They're selling it at fire-sale prices because they mishandled it and it's all contaminated with mold. If you sell it to a miller who sells it to a baker, you will cause hundreds or thousands of Veridan deaths."

"If the Botonese wheat was contaminated, I would have heard of deaths in Boton," Stasia said, and he shook his head.

"They're covering it up," he said. "Trying to sell the contaminated product here, instead."

"Then why haven't I heard about Verida putting an embargo on it?" Stasia asked. "If you know."

"Well," he said, giving her another fake smile. "As you know, my influence with the king is presently insufficient. Finwalk doesn't want to alarm people with rumors of contaminated grain, and I have taken it upon myself to simply ensure that none of it reaches Veridan shores."

Those two things were different.

Weren't they?

What did influence have to do with it?

He kept talking.

"It's been... difficult to do, without an actual royal blessing, but merchants are a reasonable lot, and where they aren't reasonable, they're... susceptible. Some men are very hard to pressure, but merchants, they have this universal belief that they can fight and struggle their way to success. And if you threaten their success, they all... eventually break."

"So which is it?" Stasia asked. "Are you here to reason with me or threaten me?"

He shifted in his chair, sipping at his coffee and looking at his nails for a moment.

"That depends on you," he said. "Entirely. Now, I am willing to help you out, here. I will take possession of your contaminated grain, at a discount to what you paid for it, but you at least won't lose your entire investment. It must have been... near enough to breaking you, wasn't it, what you paid for that grain?"

How was he here? Had the millers sold her out?

They wouldn't have known where to find her.

He had been here before she'd gotten home. He'd been watching her for longer than just yesterday. Even if the millers were actively sending information to him, or if he had spies watching the mills, they couldn't have gotten Lord

Palora here, today, if they hadn't found out about the grain before last night.

Right?

She couldn't be sure.

How had he known?

"I'm fine," Stasia said.

He sighed.

"Regardless, your option is to let me compensate you as a token or accept that it is worthless and write it off entirely. There isn't a third option."

"I disagree," Stasia said. "There's almost always a third option. The men who make it in this business are the ones who find them most consistently."

He gave her a thin smile.

"Your father," he said. "One of the hopeless optimists. He... took pressure to convince. Perhaps that's why he didn't say anything to you. Perhaps he was ashamed, or didn't want you to know."

Oh, that bolt landed true.

What had he done to her father?

"You aren't powerful enough to keep my father from doing anything he wanted," Stasia said.

And if the contamination was real, her father wouldn't have taken pressure to change his mind. He would have gone along with it, even made it public knowledge.

"Why don't you just tell everyone that Botonese wheat is bad?" Stasia asked.

"It would cause an international incident," Palora said. "Finwalk is so fascinated with the Botonese. Fascinated with the products of their markets. Keeps giving them precedence over good Veridan products. Won't call an alarm and make those dirty-handed merchants angry."

"You can't keep a secret this big," Stasia said. "The merchants wouldn't keep their mouths shut. They gossip like seagulls."

"They do," Palora said, going to get the kettle and pouring more hot water through a cheesecloth of coffee grounds. He put the kettle back on the stove and wrapped the cheese cloth around the grounds and dipped them into the mug, squeezing them out several more times with his gloved fingers. "They do gossip like children. But when they know that the king is intent on not starting a panic among the peasants... you tell them that their bread might be suspect, and they begin blaming every illness, every accident, every death on the bad bread, and they get very upset."

"They get more upset when they starve," Stasia said.

He raised his shoulders.

"They should have planned better," he said. "It's just wheat."

And a dozen other products. Stasia bit her lips.

"Ah, I see," Palora said. "That's why Melody keeps you around. You share her soft-heartedness for the little people. They're very necessary, you see. They are. And I very much appreciate that my staff polishes my shoes and trims my hair and does all the things that they do. But there are simply... enough of them. If they cannot find the ways to keep themselves alive, perhaps we have found ourselves... with an abundance. Do you see? Men and women, and their children, who eat our bread and fill our schools and our streets, but without producing enough to merit their own daily bread? You of all people, schooled under your father's tutelage, ought to recognize that a man who does not produce enough to feed himself and his family is a net loss to society, and I, personally, have no interest in the prospects of his children. It's like the yearly flooding of the Wolfram. Sometimes we need to wash away those who aren't strong enough to withstand it."

Stasia felt a bit queasy.

He was actually saying this to her.

In the same speech where he was trying to tell her to

be reasonable, to throw away her grain to avoid killing people.

She swallowed.

Anger just about spat words at him.

That she wouldn't have allowed him on the castle grounds, if she were Melody.

That he was a monster.

That he was a liar and she could see through it.

He spread his fingers.

"It's a hard reality, and the truth is that a young woman like yourself might not be ready to confront it," he said. "So I am here to apply pressure, if needed, in order to ensure that the right thing happens, here. That grain will never go to market. If you do not sell it to me, tonight, accidents will befall the lovely Lady Westhauser, the girl called Alice who works at your father's estate, and, if I'm suitably annoyed, your sister Alyssia. They are all routinely unguarded, and their accidents will be... trivially easy to arrange. They have no relationship amongst themselves, and the police will find nothing worth investigating. The men that I am capable of employing are very talented at these things."

"And what will keep me from telling them?" Stasia asked.

"If you breathe a word of this conversation to anyone, I will find out, and I will ensure that you live long enough to hear the news of the three deaths, and no longer. You're so very fond of adventuring. I'll simply have someone steal away that lovely mare of yours, and everyone will assume that something terrible has befallen you..." He waved with the back of his hand. "... elsewhere."

That was a good one.

If for no other reason than that he was in effect threatening Schotzli, too.

"I'm not selling you that grain," she said. "It's mine."

He sighed.

"It's a shame," he said. "I had thought that you would have the ability to see the importance of this matter. Your greed startles me. Selling it to the mills would kill hundreds. The quantity of wheat you're bringing into the city, it might be enough to kill most of the city. Do you see it? I cannot permit that to happen."

She shook her head, and he stroked his goatee for a moment, then smiled.

"I'm just curious," he said. "Where did you get the list?"

"List?" she asked, still trying to figure out her next move.

"The one you gave the students," he said. "I'm going to need to punish someone for speaking out of turn, and it would save me so much time if you would just tell me."

"Why are you doing it?" Stasia asked.

He smiled.

"Because the queen made the wrong choice," he said. "She and I had spoken, and she understood that I was the best candidate, then she chose Finwalk instead, for whatever reason. Maybe I said something that she found offensive. Women like that, they tend to take things so personally. But she sacrificed the best interests of the city. And there are a lot of people who can see that. I'm simply finding them all and letting them know that there's still time to fix the problems that are cascading from that first mistake."

"The merchants wouldn't go along with it," Stasia said. "They wouldn't."

He shrugged.

"When you have the majority, you can convince the rest to do as you say, or you can... you know, convince them one way or another that the other things they might do aren't worth doing."

"The majority?" Stasia asked.

"A great number of strong men, men who understand the importance of Verida and Veridan commerce, they can see that we ought to favor Veridan products, foster Veridan industry. And another great number of men, strong men, men who understand the importance of Verida and Veridan commerce, recognize that they need to thin their ranks and their numbers to the men who actually believe these things, and one of the ways you do that is to remove yourself until the situation is as it needs to be."

He'd lost her.

The first part sounded like protectionism, which was the stupidest possible strategy for a city like Verida that thrived on imports and exports in almost every industry she could think of. The second part, though, sounded like he'd talked merchants into not doing their jobs in order to punish men they didn't like.

Which... Those two things weren't connected at all.

"Who told you?" Palora asked.

"I figured it out on my own," Stasia said, and he grinned, laughing for a moment, then stroking his goatee again.

He stood, drinking his coffee and putting the mug back into the cupboard. He went to get his absurd cape, swinging it up onto his shoulders.

"Come take her," he called. There were footsteps on the stairs.

Stasia darted to the window, finding the grip up above it where she'd found it the first night she'd stayed here.

Tonight she had her boots on.

She climbed.

At the roof, a hand reached down.

"Don't pull me off," Sly whispered.

She'd been about to.

It might have pulled her loose of the building, but she

wasn't about to get herself captured.

Not by that man.

"What are you doing here?" Stasia asked, letting him pull her up onto the rooftop because it was just easier.

"A flour mill exploded today," Sly said. "Skite heard about it and asked me to keep an eye on you tonight, in case it had anything to do with you."

She put her hand over her mouth, thinking of the poor, harried man with his desperate need to keep his mill running.

"Was anyone hurt?" she asked, and Sly shook his head.

"I don't know. Skite didn't say. We need to move. Fast. There are four guys down there and..."

There was shouting below them, and Sly set off at a run.

The sun hadn't quite finished setting, and the shadows we very, very long, but there was enough light to see by, up on the rooftop.

Stasia followed.

Sly was better than her.

In the golden light, she could actually see how nimble he was, how strong. And how clever. He saw paths from one place to another that she would have never considered.

She had so much to learn from him.

But this was how to learn it.

She followed.

They ran for about twenty minutes, long enough that Stasia was beginning to get winded, when he looked back. She hung her head over her knees, sucking air, and he slapped her back a couple of times cheerfully.

"Bet they didn't see that coming," he said. "Who would ever think it of a merchant's daughter?"

"Where are we?" she asked.

"Skite's building," Sly said. "Actually... all of this is his, but... you know, definitions. He lives on the first floor, below us."

"He threatened Hidalga," Stasia said.

"Who did?" Skite asked, stepping out of a particularly deep shadow.

"You climb, too?" Stasia asked. Sly grinned.

"Skite does a bit of everything," he said. "If that's it?"

Skite nodded.

"I don't want you tangled up in this," he said. "Get to ground and be at the bar tomorrow like normal."

Stasia watched after Sly.

"He didn't save my life," she said. "This time. But it was close."

"A thief's skills are notably useful in a great number of situations," Skite said. "Tell me of my wife. Who threatened her?"

"Lord Palora," Stasia said.

His face went very cold, then he nodded, licking his lips.

"You need to get out," he said. "Where are you safest, within the city?"

He didn't want her dragging this back to Ella again.

"The guard house," Stasia said.

His jaw worked and he nodded again.

"And..." He hesitated, his eyes severe and focused on the rooftop off to Stasia's right. "Is Lord Palora in the Black Docks?"

"In my apartment, half an hour ago," Stasia said.

"Did you have anything important there?" he asked.

She shook her head. Ella had all of her papers and her money at the Westhauser estate.

Skite sucked air through his teeth.

"Oh, what I wouldn't give to go put a blade through that man's flesh this night," he said. "What else did he tell you?"

Stasia gave him the short version, trying to avoid guessing, but it was hard, with as obtuse as Palora had been.

He nodded again, his face still frighteningly stern.

"Do you care for Alice?" he asked finally.

Stasia boggled at him.

"Yes," she finally said.

He looked sideways at her.

"I believe that she was likely a bluff, just adding a name to the list. But I will send Sam. You met him, yes? I will send him tonight with a letter of introduction from you. He will help keep watch over her tonight until we can react for tomorrow. As long as Alyssia is at home, I doubt anything will happen to her. The nobles like to feel safe in their own beds, and I don't think that Palora will open the door to assassinations on the estates. Gentlemen's agreement, you see. Which leaves Ella and you. You can understand that I need you to see to yourself."

Stasia nodded quickly.

"I can get to the guard house on my own if you can get me across the river," Stasia said.

"If I were the one doing it, I would have men watching the bridges, since they're the only way in and out," Skite said.

She nodded. Obviously that had occurred to her, as well.

"Thing is, it's not true," he said, breaking his stillness with a sharp motion toward the front edge of the roof.

She followed him down the face of the building, now completely in shadow and working by touch, then landed on the sidewalk next to him and set off.

"I'm sorry I keep bringing trouble on your house," Stasia said, and he looked over at her.

"You think that's what this is about?" he asked. "That... ah. No. I need you to be here," he said. "We are going to move that grain. I detest being told what I can and cannot do, and to have a man come into the Black Docks and attempt to do it? I would do it if there were no profit at all in it for me. But I need you to be in the city, if we're going to do it. You need to sign the orders, and you need to be... visible. Word is already spreading, and if you are going to break Palora and his embargo, you need everyone else to believe that you are fearless and free from consequences."

"But... that's a lie," Stasia said.

He slowed.

"It is misleading," he said. "But if you go to ground and hide yourself away among your well-known wealthy connections, the lesser men and women of Verida will conclude that only one such as yourself could survive such impertinence. His threats will continue to work. You can talk it through with Jasper if you want, but I would use your connections with Melody to find a way to subdue Palora through other venues, and open up the city to more rebellious trade by ignoring his threats."

"I'm not asking you to. I'm just asking. But why wouldn't you just go kill him?" Stasia asked.

"I would," he said. "But obviously you know that. It's that a man like that keeps contingencies. I don't go up against a man like Palora until I've worked through all of his options and made sure that I've cut him off from every single one of them. I leave a man like that swinging on a single strand of his own ambition and self-preservation, and then I clip it." He sounded almost breathless, even as their pace eased further. "But you will believe me. I will not forget this and I will not forgive it. One does not make threats against my wife and survive."

He looked over at her, and Stasia nodded.

"He's critical to the war," she said softly.

"I don't care," he said even more softly.

"May I warn Melody?" Stasia asked.

"You may inform her that Palora threatened Lady Westhauser, and news of it reached the Rat King's ears. She'll know the rest."

"Is that not... going to get you into trouble?" Stasia asked, and Skite eased his posture again, picking up his pace and putting his hands into his pockets.

"I'll admit that most of the work I did before I took on the Rats, most of the police wouldn't have had any idea who I was nor how to look for me. They would have never connected me to any of the marks, because I had no connection to them. Those were easy days, as I think back on them. Today, I wouldn't worry for a moment about it, and I wouldn't ask you to worry about it, because in order to charge me with anything, they have to prove it. And I assure you, if they can prove anything I've done, they deserve to catch me."

Stasia nodded.

"Okay."

He glanced at her.

"You're awfully calm, discussing the intentional death of a man. Where is your idealism?"

"I think I lost it this past summer," she said softly, "or when they hurt the queen in front of me."

"Hard to see the world simply, when you've seen it ugly," Skite observed.

They approached Buddy's, and he motioned.

"You stay over there in the dark. If you have to run, go up and meet me at the docks."

She nodded, finding a shadow that suited her and leaning against the wall, more listening than watching, but her eyes up anyway.

Skite ducked into Buddy's for just a minute or two, which felt much longer, then he was out again and he motioned her forward.

"Letter for Sam," he said, handing her a pen and a

small piece of paper.

She took it and he turned his shoulder for her to write.

Daddy,

This is my friend Sam. He's going to watch over you tonight. I've kicked a hornet's nest. I'm safe, but I want to know you are. Much love to Tesh, Alice, and Yasmine,

Anastasia

"Is that enough?" Skite asked, looking at it.
Stasia nodded.
"I wouldn't give the staff names if I were being forced to write it," she said. He nodded.
"Well done. I'll get this to Sam and send him on yet tonight. You go on without me. I'll meet you at the docks."
She nodded.
Lots of dark places to hide, there. The lamps were infrequent, even compared to the rest of the Black Docks.
He gave her a sharp nod and set off once more, leaving her.
She climbed, working her way from the bar to the warehouse and watching the Rats from across the street as they spoke to each other and walked up and down along the building.
If she knew what she knew, she wouldn't have tried to burn down the warehouse, yet. There was only one full ship's cargo in there, and she could find another place to keep everything if the warehouse burned down at this point.
Would Palora know that? Would he care?
She couldn't guess at either. She didn't know how he'd known, in the first place.
She left and made her way to the docks, staying up

on top of the roof of the bar until she saw Skite come and stand at one of the flimsy rails at the shore of the docks.

She climbed down and went to stand next to him.

"You knew about the mill," she said.

"I did."

"And you didn't say anything to me," she said.

"Fires and explosions happen at mills sometimes," he said. "It's not very often, but it's something to do with the way flour burns when it's up in the air. I didn't want to worry you, after you brought the wheat to them yesterday, until I confirmed things. Wasn't the way I wanted to confirm it, but that's why you involve competent people."

"Was Sam annoyed?" Stasia asked. Skite grinned.

"Sam's always annoyed," he said. "But he'll do it. I've gone out of my way for him enough times that he doesn't even ask questions about being somewhere that he might end up in a fight. He enjoys those."

Stasia could actually imagine it, thinking of the bit of time she'd spent with him.

"Everyone wants to trade favors with you," she said, and he nodded.

"It's because I have a very high-end capacity for the ones I can grant," he answered. "It's good to be friends with the Rat King."

"I guess I know that as well as anyone," Stasia said, and he laughed.

"Oh, you're not friends with the Rat King. You're friends with Ella Westhauser, which leaves me beholden to you in an entirely different way. I would do virtually anything to ensure my wife's happiness, and it means that I don't even keep tallies with you. I'll charge you what's fair, when we're looking forward with our eyes open, but in an emergency? You've got a captive audience in Lord Westhauser."

She gave him a half a smile.

"I'm not sure I feel right about the idea of taking you up on that," she said. "It feels like extortion."

"Not at all," he said. "It's how things work in the noble world. Women form friendships with the aim of securing favors for their husbands. You just happen to trade in your own interests instead. Or in those of the city, which I would be even more ashamed to turn aside."

"Would you?" Stasia asked, and he frowned.

"Do you yet doubt my authenticity as a Veridan?" he asked. "Perhaps someday. Are you ready to go across?"

She nodded.

She couldn't understand how it didn't occur to everyone that they could just take a boat across the river instead of a bridge.

"Someone evaded my watchers, some time ago, using a small boat and putting in at the Black Docks," he said conversationally, nudging a man who had been slumped over in a boat drinking out of a bottle. He flipped a coin to him as he helped Stasia into the boat. "I've since closed the gap he exploited, but what I realized was that there was absolutely nothing to prevent me from using it for my own benefit."

"You do this often?" Stasia asked.

"A trick used often fails to work when you need it most," Skite said. "But this is worth it."

The man took out a very rough set of oars and started to work at them. It was pitiful to watch, but Skite was unconcerned, and so Stasia settled in to wait, watching the swirls in the black water.

They reached the other shore and Skite got out, helping Stasia up onto the wet stones there. She remembered these stones, the size of a man's shoulders across and slick black in the weak moonlight. Alfred had struggled on them.

So did she.

Skite walked her into the line of buildings that

constituted the shoreward limit of Verida on this side of the river, then looked at her again.

"You're on your own from here," he said.

"I'm fine, from here," she answered. "Go see to Ella."

He nodded and left without any further conversation.

Stasia found a building and started climbing.

She ducked under the barricade almost an hour later.

She had thought about climbing the outside of the guard house walls and just showing up, but that felt inexcusably rude, so in the end she just picked a point along the riverside street that she thought she couldn't see anyone being suspicious and she ran for it.

The barricade was such a simple construct, a log perhaps six inches in diameter on a metal bracket that let it go up and down, with a counterweight on the other end that kept it from being oppressively heavy. And yet, getting to the other side of it, she felt safe.

Yes, someone could have grabbed her around the shoulders and dragged her back over it.

They could have ducked under it just as easily as she had done.

But she was in the guard house, now, and someone would notice.

Which they did.

"Who goes there?" a man yelled from one of the little watch stools against the front facade of the guard house.

There was the sound of swords drawn and Stasia put her hands up and went still. In the flickering lamplight, they couldn't see her clearly, and even if she knew them, they would still need to come look her directly in the face to identify her. With as many new recruits as there were, these days, there was a good chance she was going to have to beg to appeal to Jasper.

Hopefully he was in tonight.

"Stacy?" the man asked as he got around to where he could see her face. He put the sword away. He was one of the younger men, but he'd been with the guard since at least when Matthias had joined, and he knew her well.

"Heya, Pierce," she said. "Are the guys in?"

"Are you all right?" he asked.

She nodded.

"I'm in trouble."

"Stay there."

He went upstairs, leaving a younger guard to watch the barricade on his own - or with Stasia, depending on how you looked at it - and a few minutes later, Jasper and Babe came out of the bunk house and started down the stairs.

"Are you all right?" Jasper asked.

"I'm fine," Stasia said, taking a step back from both of them to keep them from trying to check her for injuries. "Completely healthy. But I just had a very unpleasant exchange with someone, and I need a safe place to stay for the night, until I figure out what to do next."

Jasper looked over his shoulder at Babe.

"Thank you, Pierce, that will be all," Jasper said, grabbing Stasia's shoulder and escorting her back to the weapons room at the back corner of the yard.

He closed the door and Babe leaned against it, crossing his arms.

No one was coming through that door.

They'd more easily go through the wall.

"Speak," Jasper said.

Stasia nodded, giving Babe and Jasper a more detailed version of the conversation with Lord Palora than she had given Skite, because she'd assumed Skite would be able to fill in more of the blanks on his own.

"Is the grain bad?" Babe asked. Stasia shook her head.

"I don't think so," she said. "Too much of what he said was internally inconsistent. It was like he wanted me to feel afraid, more than that he was trying to convince me of any one thing. I don't doubt, though, that it at least resembles the story that they're telling the other merchants at the port. Couple that with some strategic threats, to men who don't have the same caliber friends I do, and I could see merchants waving off their ships completely, pretending that the ship is basically a plague carrier. Leave the captains to figure out their own orders. I mean, if you asked me six months ago if such a thing was possible, I'd tell you that Veridan merchants are the hardest men in the world, and they'd fight tooth and nail to keep a ship in once it's made port, but..." She shook her head. "Watching them freeze up with a glut of marketable stuff because they're afraid they can't replace it? It's been... eye opening, how many merchants at Verida just coast on the fact that things have always worked pretty well. I don't know what my father and his trading partners are even doing at this point, and I intend to ask him quite pointedly, the next time I see him."

"I can send Sterling and Matthias to watch over your father and your sister," Jasper said, and Stasia shook her head.

"Skite sent someone I've met to watch over my father's household," she said. "And he said that Alyssia ought to be safe as long as she's at home, so we have the night."

Jasper nodded, accepting that as enough.

"Why are you still in the city?" Babe asked. "You're welcome here, like I told you, but if they're gonna come lookin' for you, wouldn't you be better off someplace harder to find and more comfortable?"

"Skite thought it was best for me to stay in town," Stasia said. "So that as people find out that I'm shipping grain successfully, they'll break ranks and go for it. I don't really like it, putting everyone unwittingly in danger like that, but he said to talk to Jasper and see if we didn't come to the same conclusion."

Babe scowled, but Jasper nodded.

"I can see the logic in it," he said. "We'll discuss it in the morning."

"If she's gonna get out of the city, the time to do it is now," Babe said.

"Should I remind you that you're encouraging her to go run and hide behind the man whose advice you so wholeheartedly reject?" Jasper asked.

"Useful and wrong can exist in the same man," Babe answered.

Stasia grinned.

"I'm tired," she said. "And I'd really like to be here tonight. Please. Just... please. We'll eat, we'll talk, and tomorrow we can make a plan. Right now I'm just... I'm tired and I want to be with my friends."

Jasper nodded.

"Of course," he said. Babe still didn't look happy, but Jasper was already past it.

"The miller," Stasia said. Jasper shook his head.

"He got out," he said. "Didn't see what started the fire, but heard the boom as the flour went up and got out. Mill can be rebuilt, but it's going to take a lot. I think he's probably done for."

"You went?" Stasia asked, and he nodded, giving her a grim smile.

"I had a guess it was related to you. I was there around the time they got the fire out, talked to everyone."

She sighed.

"I ruined his life," she said.

"Couldn't know that," Babe said. "Not reasonable to expect a man'd go to those lengths to keep wheat out of

Verida."

"Maybe I did," Stasia sighed. "And I just decided it was worth it because Verida needs wheat that badly."

Jasper shrugged.

"You are sure you're unharmed?" he asked.

"I'm fine," Stasia said. "Palora wasn't even armed, and I was wearing boots this time."

"All right," Jasper said. "I will go make arrangements for you upstairs. I'll give you a couple minutes."

Babe stood to let him out, then leaned against the door again.

There was no reproach in his eyes.

"Were you afraid?" he asked.

She shook her head.

She'd been... stressed, and she was still on the tail end of the jitters from the rush of anxiety when Palora had showed up, but she'd always thought that she would make it out the window, and that once she was out the window, she was going to be very difficult to catch unless they'd brought a climber to do it.

They would next time.

She needed to plan on that.

Skite could climb.

She hadn't really seen that coming.

She brought her focus back in.

"I was ready," she said. "And I don't think he was armed. There were armed men there. I know that. I... I was careful, but I was ready."

He nodded, considering it, then nodded with more conviction.

"Can't ask for more than that," he said, stepping away from the door and putting his arms out toward her.

She stepped into them with a relief she couldn't have anticipated.

He held her tight for several minutes, then kissed her

hair.

"You're safe here," he said. "As long as you want to stay. But have you thought about what you're plannin' on doin' next?"

She shook her head, burying her face in tighter against his chest.

Why had she left?

No one had forced her.

All of that exhilaration on the ships and at the warehouse... it was just... silly. Foolishness, even.

Here.

Here was where she wanted to be.

"Gotta be strong, now," Babe said. "If the grain is bad, then so what? We gotta help 'em find ways to bring in other food. If the grain ain't bad? That's breakfast for half the city, the kids are goin' hungry now, and everybody's sufferin'. We gotta find a way, and if I gotta stand guard at a wheat mill for the next month, I'll do it."

"I don't think it will come to that," Stasia said, running her knuckle under her eyes and stepping away, going to lean against a table.

"No?"

She shook her head.

"No. I've got an idea that... whatever it is that happens next, it's going to happen fast, and it's going to be... decisive. If Skite can keep them from burning down the warehouse, and he seems to think that he can, I've got enough wheat in there to change the shape of things in the city, and if I can drive prices down, Palora is going to start losing friends. He as much as told me that it's an embargo, and they're losing money if I'm making it. He can't... he can't let it happen. He has to stop me. And if he can't talk me out of it and he can't burn everything..." She shook her head again, her mind spinning. She was tired. "I don't know what he'll do. But Skite is right. I have to be here to force his hand to do it."

"You don't have to do nothin'," Babe said. "You can go up to the Westhauser estate, and we'll see to whatever comes next."

"Babe," Stasia said sharply. "I know that you don't like what's going on here, particularly because Skite is involved, but you are not going to be able to get along like that, if you speak to me like that. All right? You do not just take my problems and make them go away."

Babe ducked his head, a meek smile curling at the corners of his mouth.

"I'm sorry," he said. "I just keep thinkin' back to that night that the warlock took you and I didn't know where you were or if you were alive. Hurt me more'n I can say to go off and fight the rest of 'em and leave you to that man to save you or not. And I don't need you pointin' out, either, that I wouldn't have found you and he did. I know it every single day. He's a good friend to you. One maybe I'm even glad you've got. But... He lets you take risks you oughtn't. Maybe even nudges you into 'em. And I don't like not knowin' where you are and whether you're right, maybe more when he does know it."

Stasia licked her lips.

It had been a bad night, the one with the warlock.

One she hadn't really talked about with anyone, really, because she avoided thinking about it. Going back to her apartment and Babe washing her feet and then staying there, on the floor, where she felt so safe and protected, that part she could think on, but what had happened in the moments before Skite had gotten there, and the wild flight away from Tillith on the roof... No. She didn't think about those things at all.

She also didn't think about what had been going on with him, that night.

"The last time you'd gone up against a warlock, you

ended up with a dagger in your chest," she said, her voice tight. "There are things in the world that can kill you, and someday you're going to find yourself fighting one, and it doesn't even matter if I'm there or not. If it can kill you, if he can kill you, I can't stop it. You ask me to accept that about you, because you have a duty you've pledged to the King, and... mostly I can. It's who you are. And I... I love that about you. But you can't ask me not to do this just because you're afraid for me. I sat and watched you lay on a table with a dagger in your chest. We both have to just... go. We do what we do. Neither one of us plans on dying any time soon, but... we can't try to hold each other back just because there's risk out there."

He hesitated for a long moment, then worked his mouth, attempting to find words.

"Can't we?" he asked. "Don't there come a day, we can just say to each other, you and me, we's enough. And we'll go... be enough... just the two of us?"

Oh, that was gentle and true enough to break her heart.

"You said you wouldn't ever give up being a soldier," she said.

He licked his lips and he nodded.

"I talked to my mate, the one who retired, who you're payin' to tote around coins. And... he's bored, true enough. That part, I didn't get wrong. But I didn't see it, how happy he was. Spendin' his days with his wife, where before he didn't get but a few hours a week with her? I ain't seen that man smile before in my life, the way he did talkin' about his girl. And... I'm comin' around, maybe, to seein' it that life is long, and maybe duty ain't the only callin' a man has in it."

It was perhaps the strongest expression of love he could have ever spoken aloud.

She walked across the room and kissed him.

He wrapped her up tight, like there was no way

anyone was ever going to force him to let go of her again, and the fleeting thought that they were in a room full of weapons and needed to be careful was gone almost before she thought it.

She'd never touched him before when he wasn't wearing his leather armor. The softness and the size of his body were startling, because they were different, but they were also poignant, because without the leathers, he was still profoundly different from any man she'd ever known.

The men that she spent time around were strong. They were forged by the world to be strong, because if they weren't that strong, they would be dead. But Babe was something else. Babe was born strong, and forged into something that was simply bigger than it had been before. She could imagine the violence that his body was capable of - she'd seen it more than once - but the power that was within him was only interested in shaping itself to her, like an armor that she didn't wear, but existed all the same. She'd seen boys kiss, the mean ones who grabbed hair and took, and she'd imagined that perhaps all strong men were the same, and while there was a roughness to him that excited her, a wildness that made her breathless and that continued to make her wonder if he might not be around the next corner as she walked around the city, there was nothing mean about it. And there was nothing nothing nothing about it that took.

He was hers, and by the same token she was his.

Someone cleared his throat and Stasia sprang away from Babe with the same energy that he broke loose, his eyes low. Stasia felt her face flush hot and red as Colin stood in the doorway, his arm in a sling.

"What happened to you?" she asked.

"Got in a scrape with one of your warehouse friends," he said. "And purity and truth aren't much when you're four on one."

"Yeah, but you still beat them," Stasia said. "And I wish I could have heard what you said to them while you were fighting them off."

He grinned wider.

"We've all missed you, but I swear I've missed you most," he said, putting out an arm at face level like he was about to kiss her. Babe's arm caught him across the chest with an audible thump and Colin coughed dramatically as he stumbled away, laughing.

"Come on up," he said. "Most of the guys are asleep, and I'm no good making a bed like this, so Jasper sent me down to get you. You're slumming with us, tonight, huh?"

Stasia shrugged.

"It's just for a little bit," she said. "But this was the one place I knew to go."

He winked.

"Always and always," he said, going to stand with his back against the door. Babe took the torch from the arena back out into the arena and Colin closed the door behind them, then all three of them went up the stairs and past the door to the mess hall.

Stasia had never been allowed in the bunkroom before. It was something sacred, somehow. She knew the young recruits weren't allowed in here until they were claimed by a squad leader, so it was a trespass for her to be allowed in.

And yet, no one stopped her. Neither Babe nor Colin so much as paused as they went through the open doorway and into the dim room.

"Over here," Jasper called softly over snores. Stasia got close and Jasper indicated.

"I was guessing you hadn't slept in a bunk before, so I put you on the bottom. Babe is there, I'm over there, Matthias is up there, and Colin is down at the end, there. Sterling is home with his parents tonight."

Stasia nodded.

The bed was made. It was simple, a wool blanket over linen sheets with a pillow, but the tidiness of it was appealing and it was... hers.

"Rest well," Babe said. "Ain't nothin' comin' in this room without the lot of us knowin' it."

He kissed behind her ear and disappeared.

Stasia sat down on the bed, looking around just to familiarize herself with the space so that she would know it again if she woke in the darkness, then she slipped her boots off and put them against the wall, next to another King's Guard's boots, and tucked her feet up under the sheets to loosen them. She slid into the bed and put her head down on the pillow, her mind still working at everything that had happened that evening.

It felt like she would be awake for hours, trying to make an understanding of it, and yet, sleep came almost immediately.

She woke to the sounds of quiet conversation and of men and women getting up and getting ready for their day. Boots scraped the floor. Beds squeaked. Buckles jangled.

Stasia stretched and shifted, wondering what time it was.

It was barely dawn outside, by the look of things, and she would have preferred to sleep another few hours, but it was time.

It was always time.

She swung her legs out over the floor and reached for her boots.

Two beds down, Babe was laying with his fingers woven behind his head, looking up at the bed above him thoughtfully.

He caught her motion and looked over, smiling quietly, then turned his head back to look at the bed above.

It was a marvel he even fit in that bed, as she thought about it.

She stood, going to find Jasper and Colin at a washbasin by the door, talking.

"How did you rest?" Jasper asked.

"Better than in my own bed," Stasia admitted, moving aside so that Matthias could wash.

Jasper motioned her out onto the walkway, and she wondered if he'd changed his mind about letting her stay there, if she hadn't been regarded as invading by the rest of the guard when they woke up that morning.

"I've been thinking about what Skite said to you last night, about staying visible," he said, leaning on the rail and keeping his voice low. "I think that he's right. I think that you need to get grain moving into the mills, and that the mills need to run."

"But the fire," Stasia said, and he nodded.

"I'm going to go see the King today," he said. "I'm going to ask him to give the millers a loan from the castle treasury to allow them to hire guards to stand watch and to allow them to buy grain, should it become available."

"That's corruption," Stasia said. "You, my friend, going to the King and asking him to fund the purchase of my goods though a third party. It's the very definition of corruption."

Jasper considered for just a moment, then smiled.

"You forget that we have a King," he said. "And what he chooses is the very definition of not corruption."

"But if it comes out that that's how I did it, it's going to look like I was successful because I literally had the backing of the king," she said.

"And do you have a better idea?" Jasper asked.

"I need to talk to Ella," Stasia said. "But if the mills

need protection and the people need flour, it seems like there's a natural symbiosis there. I can sell wheat on consignment, if I must, in the short term. And if I can facilitate contracts between the millers and people like the Highrock family, such that that mill only produces wheat for the Highrock district for a specific period of time..."

"That's got its own raft of issues," Jasper said. "If you invite the Highrock family in, or any other gang in the city, you're inviting them to come manipulate your business and skim your profits indefinitely."

Stasia knew that. She knew that her father intentionally avoided working with illegal groups because there was no way to force them back out of your affairs.

"It's why I need to talk to Ella," Stasia said. "I need to find a way to start, and then... hopefully it won't be something that I have to replicate all across the city before it isn't worth it to Palora to fight me on it anymore."

"If you started someplace more... upstanding," Jasper said thoughtfully. "Recruited the blacksmiths who can't get ore or bars, right now... They might be willing to work on behalf of their neighborhoods and leave again once things change. I just wouldn't start, or even include, Highrock. Use the men who are already close to the mills, pay them an actual wage to stand guard, and then let the fact that they are honest men work for you."

"How's that?" Stasia asked. "I mean, which reason seems most obvious to you?"

"Honest men talk," Jasper said. "They don't keep secrets just because it might benefit them to have secret knowledge further along the line. It will become common knowledge that the mills are running and that the crafting district has bread, that the mills are under threat and that maybe you have to come stand guard in order to get your flour, but it's there. Let the millers arrange for who is going to cart it away at the end of the day and who is going to show up that evening to keep the watch again."

"Easy enough to slide in someone who is willing to burn the place down, for Palora," Stasia said, and Jasper shook his head.

"It is, but it isn't," he said. "Some men will do anything for the right coin, but men who have put blood and sweat into a business are the ones you want to trust first with the responsibility of choosing who will protect it."

"And we can't get the police to do it," Stasia said.

"Not if you don't want Palora getting involved again and trying to say that you're selling tainted wheat. Have you considered what might be keeping him from doing that, now?"

She hadn't.

"The truth?" she said.

"If you please," he said.

"No, the truth," she said. "He can suppress it if he keeps everyone afraid and from talking to each other, but as soon as a rumor like that hits the court, the queen is going to do something about it, and the truth is too hard to keep caged, when everyone is looking for it."

He smiled.

"That could be it," he said. "You're certainly not wrong. But I wonder if he isn't holding it back as a cudgel to go after the first person who defies him. Or if he doesn't have a worse accusation to make, like you didn't just import tainted wheat, but you knew it, and you didn't care that it was going to kill people. Turn it back on you and put you on the defensive while he comes through and righteously destroys the whole shipment."

"Half of it is still on the ships," Stasia said.

At least a good third.

"Then he can take Lord Westhauser down with you," Jasper said. "That could be a win for him. Eliminating an independent noble? They're all more or less independent, compared to the way the merchants work, but they're socially very interconnected, and no one trusts Westhauser because he has no alliances. They might even throw in with Palora just to see Westhauser tarnished."

Stasia turned her head to look at him.

"They would, wouldn't they?" she asked, and he nodded.

"Every last one of them."

She put her face into her hands.

"I can do the trade. I can do the math. I can make connections between supply and demand. But when they get politics involved... they can beat me just by saying that they win."

"Hey," he said.

She sighed.

"Hey," he said again.

She lifted her face to look at him once more, and he shook his head.

"The secret," he said. "The one that no one tells. Is that you are real and they are fake. If you win, even if they tell you that you lose, you won. It's just going to take time for reality to catch up with them. Do you see it?"

She blinked, considering that.

If she could sell the grain, if the grain could get itself turned into flour, if the flour made it to bakeries and people ate it, and if she got paid for the whole thing...

"It's all just words," she said, and he nodded.

"It's words and anger," he said. "And anger can be dangerous, and lies can live in dark corners for longer than you can imagine, so I'm not saying don't fight the political war. I'm just saying that it isn't real. What you're doing is real, and if you win, it doesn't matter what the politics say about it. You have won and you will come out having won."

She looked at her hands again, folding them to hang over the rail in front of her.

"Do you believe that?" she asked. "Every time?"

"Without fail," he said. "They can thrash and fight and throw up costs and demands and they can say so much, because words are free, but in the end, without needing to do anything else, the real wins."

She shook her head.

"I'm... shocked, I think, that I'm more pragmatic than you," she said. "But reputation matters, and the man who writes the history determines how the future works. If you go back three generations, what actually happened doesn't matter. What matters is what people believe, what they remember, and what got written down."

"That is interesting," he said. "And I see your point. But there's a different history, down there on the street below us, that has nothing to do with reputation or history books. And that's whether or not people think that tomorrow is coming, and whether or not they have any say in how it's going to look. And that's what shapes the real future, in my mind. If you can keep the King and the Queen out of the way, and keep Lord Palora and his ilk from taking what's there and claiming it as their own, giving a whole city hope is going to shape the next hundred years or more. You are standing at a moment, Stasia Fielding. Can you feel it?"

"And it doesn't matter whether people believe that I'm a corrupt, greedy merchant who pulled strings and cut corners to bring in a load of moldy wheat, when what actually happened is that a lot of people got to eat?" Stasia asked.

"And the men who see what you've done, the insightful ones who can see through Palora's smokescreen, they're going to follow your lead. Your little students running around and making nuisances of themselves at market - yes, I've been hearing about them and I can't stop smiling - they're going to step up and they're going to do the same thing. Have you considered that you ought to turn around those four big, beautiful ships and send them straight back to Boton again?"

Not for an instant.

Well.

Okay.

"I would need twelve of them to feed the entire city, at the delivery rate we got so far," Stasia said. "Though I'm not sure the market in Boton would hold up to that kind of demand."

"So send them further afield," Jasper said. "All up and down the shore, there are communities that would love to load up a huge ship with wheat at Botonese market prices."

"Why, Jasper, you're talking like a proper merchant," Stasia teased.

"I spend a lot of time around one who absolutely loves to talk," Jasper answered with a grin. "And I know you're trying to do this clean, prove that anyone can do it. But the second you decide that you're ready to stack the deck against Palora, you know we're there. I think that you're theoretically right, up to a limit, and I'm trusting you to know where that limit is."

"It was supposed to be such a big crop this year, too," Stasia said. "It's just a shame."

Jasper frowned.

"It was, wasn't it?" he asked. "Same as in Boton? I'd forgotten, but I'd heard that, and then the stone elves went on their burning spree."

"Yeah," Stasia said. "I was there when the Westhauser estate was trying to figure out how to get everything in."

"Isn't that odd?" Jasper asked. "That it would all get burned down, and then someone would try to run the rest of it out of the market?"

Stasia frowned.

"I don't think so. It's an opportunity to exploit. The wheat burned, so Palora went after it."

Jasper looked at her.

"What if it didn't go that way?" he asked. "What if it went the other way?"

"What do you mean?"

"What if Palora found a way to get the wheat burned because he had a plan to do this?" he asked.

"You think that he went after the other twenty markets I identified, the same way?" Stasia asked, a mix of sarcasm and skepticism, then her eyes went wide. "Could he? What if he did?"

"You tell me," Jasper said with amusement, watching her think.

The markets were diverse. They were difficult to control. She would have told you that there was no way to keep wheat out of Verida, if someone had asked her a year ago, and she still thought it today if she didn't let herself look too closely at what had actually happened. And the ones that she thought were being actively manipulated were... If she was going to try to break the city, they were good choices, but if she was trying to pragmatically break the city, she would have gone after much smaller pressure points, things that were hard to see, things that would have slowly trickled through the market.

Not wheat and iron nails.

She blinked quickly, trying to see it all in her mind's eye.

"But not Palora," she murmured.

"Not Palora what?" Jasper asked.

"If he was going to do it, he wouldn't want to do it slowly and cautiously, would he?" Stasia asked. "He would want to... show off how powerful he was, do it in a big way that everyone who knew could see that he was capable of something that no one else was... right?"

"You know the man," Jasper agreed. "What are you thinking?"

"I think that I picked the one that I saw most clearly, but it's possible that they're all the same. That these were just... What if they were just the ones that he could immediately see a way to crush them, when..." She caught herself, shaking her head. "No," she said. "What I'm suggesting is that he's in league with them. It's not possible. The stone elves burnt the wheat. Not Palora."

"Can you prove that?" Jasper asked.

Um.

No.

No, she couldn't.

She couldn't believe otherwise, but...

She looked over at him, feeling... panicky.

"What if he planned this before the stone elves even left?" she asked. "What if this has been the plan since..."

"Since Melody failed to name him king?" Jasper supplied, and Stasia put her fingers to her mouth.

"That's exactly when he would start planning, isn't it?" she asked, and he nodded.

"As I said, you know the man."

She rested her forehead on her fingers.

"I need to reevaluate all of those markets," she said. "I just threw a giant classroom full of students at them, and Palora as much as said that I'd gotten the list right, or enough right, anyway."

"You don't," Jasper said, and she frowned.

"I'm missing so many things," Stasia said.

"Of course you are," Jasper told her. "There are too many things, in the first place. You need to win this fight. With the wheat. I don't actually think that you'll even need to pick another one, because the rest of the city is going to sweep in and do the rest of the work for you, once you prove it can be done. But, yeah, maybe once you get a few more steps down the road toward selling bread, figuring out where the weak points are in the other markets might help the people who are ready to go exploit them. And maybe you even want to jump on that, too, who am I to say no? But you need to keep your eyes and your mind on this fight, until you see your path to winning it, or decide that you have to abandon it. Don't let divided attention lose you fights that you could win."

Stasia nodded slowly, still wanting to work on it.

The problem was that she needed to go out and see and talk to people and figure out where the gluts were.

It was always about finding the gluts and tapping them.

Always.

She tried to even her breathing as Babe came to lean on the railing at her other side.

"What's the plan for today, boss?" he asked.

"You're taking the day off," Jasper said. "Going to go sightseeing with Stasia for something to do. Might go down to the Black Docks and just wander a bit."

"Hear it's lovely this time of year," Stasia said, and Jasper laughed.

"Hear it's lovely this time of year."

Skite needed to know.

This was the right decision. She knew that. She understood it. She was behind it.

And yet, she couldn't focus for anything.

Babe kept talking to her and she kept finding that she'd missed at least the last two or three sentences when she realized that the noises were his, and she felt bad, because generally she found every word out of his mouth to be worth considering carefully.

"What's goin' on?" Babe asked.

"Jasper asked me a question I didn't know the answer to," she said. "And it's just a whole new set of possibilities to figure out, and... I don't know enough to figure it out."

"What is it?" Babe asked.

"Jasper asked me if maybe Palora wasn't involved in destroying the supply of wheat in Verida, even while the stone elves were still here. And... I asked why he did wheat and not everything else, and it was supposed to be a joke, and then I wondered, what if he did the same thing everywhere else, and I can't answer that, and maybe he did and I just never looked, and if he did... If I could prove it, I could actually get justice for at least some fraction of what's happened since the stone elves left."

"Or put it right," Babe said. "More'n it is now. What did Jasper say?"

"To focus on getting wheat to market, because that's hard enough, by itself."

He grinned.

"Good advice," he said. "But I ain't never seen you take it, when it means not tryin' somethin' that's teasin' at you for attention."

She looked sideways at him and he laughed.

"Do you?"

She rubbed her forehead.

"No," she said. "I'm trying to think, what have I seen, what have I heard, what have I noticed, that if I put them together in a new way, I could prove that Palora went through and destroyed supply chains in order to give himself an advantage politically and then economically, later. If he knew that the supply was going to crash, buying up everything produced downstream and hoarding it would be hugely profitable. And I know the goods that he probably did it on. That much I'm pretty sure of. But I thought that he was... seeing it happen, or picking markets that were sensitive and just... buying up the entire supply consistently, but... I said it at the beginning, that's a fool's errand, because the supply just grows when you try to buy it all out. So if you crush it before everyone knows what's happening... That's where he wins. But Verida doesn't have a lot of native supply of anything, so..."

How do you crush a supply that exists somewhere else?

She couldn't work it out.

They walked a bit longer and she nudged Babe.

"How has the hunt for the warlocks been going? You guys had found one of their suppliers for magic stuff?"

He nodded.

"We were close for a few days," he said, "but they figured it out, we think, and they changed the handoff, and then the whole thing went cold. It was a great opportunity, but we couldn't make good."

"And Colin got hurt, trying to figure out where they're keeping all of the grain?" Stasia asked.

Babe nodded.

"And when we got there, they'd emptied the place out."

"And no one saw anything happen?" Stasia asked.

He grunted.

"Not the kind of place where anybody sees anythin', anyway," he said. "But far enough away from most folk that the odds were against us, anyway. Probably picked for that reason."

"And now they know we're looking," Stasia said.

Babe sighed.

"I reckon they do," he said.

She shook her head.

"How do we get ahead of them? I just..."

"You win this fight," Babe said. "Same as Jasper told

you. You are ahead of 'em, and they're runnin' scared, if Palora himself came to talk to you in the Black Docks. Use that well, and it don't matter if you got any other shots at cuttin' 'em off. But that ain't to say you can't be lookin' at the same time." He paused. "That said, though, I still need to know what your plan is, while we're here. I want to keep us out of blind alleys and around people as much as we can. Ain't a place where a crowd is safer than on your own, but we'll try."

"I need to go to the docks," Stasia said. "I need to talk to Skite and make sure that everything is okay. I want to go talk to the warehouse and let them know that they need to be alert. And then... I need to go talk to another miller and set up a delivery. And I have to choose a strategy to keep the next mill from blowing up, when I do it."

"Not a bad day," Babe said. "You got a mind to go up and see to your sister, while we're out?" he asked.

She nodded.

"As you say it, I should. I don't want her coming into the city and getting in trouble, just because I assumed she was safe for a night."

"Hey," Babe said, nudging her. "You okay? Gettin' away is one thing. Wakin' up the next morning knowin' someone's after you is another."

"I woke up surrounded by the safest men in the whole city," Stasia said. "I'm walking with the scariest individual man I know. I haven't had the first thought about being unsafe all day."

"Someone comes at us, you gotta make a choice," Babe said. "You go up a wall, I ain't gotta worry about you unless they got a climber with 'em, and then I can't help you at all."

"Oh," Stasia said. "Yeah, I can see that. So I need to work it out in the first three seconds, if someone's going to chase me up a building, if I try to get away. I don't like running when you're in a fight."

"And I'd rather you not be there, if you got an option on bein' safe," he answered. "Lets me think on beatin' them rather than keepin' you outta reach."

Permission given, again.

She took it.

"Okay."

He nodded.

"If you run, go find Skite if you can. I doubt they'll go up against him, direct, because the Rats will come after anyone they see as a threat to any of them, and that's a war Palora don't want, just now. No guarantees, but that's my best bet."

Stasia couldn't imagine that he was happy, sending her to Skite for safety, but it was good counsel all the same.

"If they're warlocks, I'm headed for the guard house," Stasia said. "Skite beat the one, that one time, but I don't want to lean on his luck, like that."

Babe considered, then nodded.

"Only if you reckon you can keep away from 'em the whole way," he said. "Whole squad'd rather you stay alive, if it's all the same."

"I can get behind that," Stasia answered.

They walked a bit further before she spoke again.

"If there's more than one warlock..." she said.

"Yes?" Babe asked.

"Would you run, rather than try to fight them?" she asked.

"No."

"Why not?" Stasia asked.

"If I get a chance to swing a sword at those creatures, I'm gonna do it," Babe said. "No talkin' about it further than that."

But one, all by himself, had managed to stab him. No one knew what would kill him and what wouldn't, so Stasia had to continue to assume that the right hit would end his life.

And she couldn't look that thought in the eye.

"It's my job, Stasia," he said. "I can't just run away from it. No one else in this city has any chance against 'em. I gotta do it when I get my shot."

She looked over at him for a moment, considering arguing with him further, but instead she nodded.

She knew that.

And it was always going to be like that, for him.

Either she could live with it or she couldn't, though she had an instinct that she was going to have to make that decision an awful lot of times before it finally stuck.

"Okay," she said.

They made it to the warehouse, where she found Bluster leaning against the front door, picking his teeth with a knife.

She'd started to learn the characteristics of the individual leaders within the Rats, and she would have pegged that as more of a Tiddle thing to do, but Bluster looked like he was at least capable of doing it without slicing his teeth out of his mouth.

"You spoke to Skite today?" Stasia asked.

Bluster looked at her for a moment, then at Babe pointedly.

"Come on, mate," Babe said. "You know well as I do, wouldn't make skidge of difference I'm here, to Skite, what you're s'posed to tell her."

"Traitors are traitors," Bluster answered. "You always kick a traitor when you get a chance."

"This ain't your chance, mate," Babe said, his voice going slightly deeper, somewhere in between a threat and revealing a confidence.

Bluster grunted, then looked at Stasia again.

"Skite's screenin' the men at the docks with Veil," he

said. "Told me to pound anyone who didn't belong, sort it out later."

He looked at Babe again, trying to work a permission out of that, but Stasia shook her head.

"He's with me," she said. "Therefore he belongs. And he's on our side, right now, collectively."

"Don't try reasonin' with 'im," Babe said. "Too thick to know anythin' more complex than his own fists."

Bluster clenched his fists slightly, still deciding something, and Stasia sighed.

"You know better, Bluster," she said. "This isn't what you're here to do. We're going. Thank you for standing watch."

"Ain't doin' it for you," Bluster answered, and Stasia shrugged, pointing her feet toward the docks and making her way easily enough.

"You got to know the paths pretty clear," Babe said.

"You get a unique perspective, running around up on the rooftops," Stasia said. "But I've been walking from here to the docks for weeks, now. I know all three routes that don't double back. And a few that do."

Babe grinned.

"You don't know the half of the secret ways, 'round a place like this one," he said. "But I'm also not sayin' I'm happy with you knowin' your way around this place at all."

"You rather I get lost?" Stasia asked.

"I rather you not be here at all," he said.

"Option long off the table," she told him, walking faster to get to the docks. They passed a cart covered in a tarp, but Stasia wondered if there was really any purpose to it, at this point, that tarp. Everyone who mattered knew what was under it.

They found Skite talking to men as they got onto the little boats that rowed out to the ships.

Stasia waited until the next three boats left the

docks, then Skite came over to stand next to her.

"You make it okay?" he asked.

"I assume everything is well at home," she answered.

"Put my guards on alert," he said. "Sam sent word this morning that your fathers' guards are on alert, working two a shift, and are quite capable of holding the house against a trained military force of at least fifteen." He peeked around Stasia at Babe. "I understand that that was your design?"

"Noble houses all have the same weaknesses," Babe said. "Shorin' 'em up ain't all that special a skill, if you know what you're looking at."

"I'm taking more grain to the mills," Stasia said. "If they'll even buy it from me, at this point."

"I've been to Highrock, today, too," Skite said. "With a note from Ella for her brother. Marcus is going to send six men to protect the Peakwood mill this afternoon. Bring a full load of grain, and they'll escort the flour to Highrock, leaving men on guard through the night to meet your next cart in the morning."

"Why?" Stasia asked. "You're supposed to be a hard-nosed negotiator. Why are you using your connections to do this?"

"Let's go with that my wife still holds fondness for the people of Lesser Highrock, and the family can't eat all that bread, so at least some of it will go to the people in Lesser Highrock first, and then Greater Highrock next, and perhaps people she cares about won't die. I'm not using Rat connections for it, so it's different, anyway."

Stasia thought that using Ella's underworld family connections were awfully close to crossing between that Lord Westhauser side of himself and the King of the Rats that he was supposed to be down here at the docks, but she didn't push him.

"I will get grain up there today," Stasia said. "But I need to get to the rest of the city, if I can, too. We have a new theory that we're chasing."

"I'm interested," Skite said. "As long as we're just chatting."

Stasia nodded.

"I'm concerned that the destruction of all of the grain up on the estates was too convenient for Lord Palora's plan to completely eliminate the market in it," she said. "I need to see if anyone has taken intentional actions to destroy any of the other supplies of my key resources."

"The stone elves destroyed the grain," Skite said. "Not Palora."

"Are you sure?" Stasia asked, and he nodded, watching the men row across the black water.

"I am," he said. "Men in my employ shot arrows at them while they ran around with torches."

Stasia paused.

"Oh," she said. "Then maybe it did go the other way, and he just saw an opportunity in the destruction."

"You thought that Palora caused the grain to be destroyed," Skite said slowly. "What if... he still... did?"

"You're suggestin' a Veridan noble was able to command the stone elf armies?" Babe asked. "Highest treason I've ever heard of."

"The stone elves might have listened to things that the warlocks told them to do," Stasia said. "But there's no path from Palora to the stone elves. It's not possible."

Skite drew a slow breath, then nodded.

"What if it is?" he asked. "What if I can prove it?"

"I'd be right interested in puttin' you in front of the queen," Babe said. Skite shook his head.

"This is not testimony I will be repeating," he said. "You may do what you want with the information, but you will not attribute the theory to me."

He motioned, and they followed him away from the docks, through a quick maze of tiny streets and into a ramshackle apartment that the walls were so worn they let the daylight through.

Skite went to lean by the cloth window, watching outside for several moments, then he nodded and turned his attention to Babe and Stasia again.

"Some time ago," he said slowly. "Years, now. I had an interaction with... Qelador. I understand Jasper killed her with his own hand."

"And I seen the body," Babe affirmed. Skite nodded.

"I was told, at the time, that the magic she used on me was quite unique to the fact that she knew me, but to this day, I don't know if it's true. Leaving aside the details of it, what I was doing at the time and why, I came to discover that she was in the employ of... Lord Hightower. Quite completely acting as his agent, in her interactions with me. What if... as in days of old... the assassins that were taken and returned went to their old clients with their new skills, in order to access the copious resources that come from working in novel, niche ways for the noble class?"

"You're sayin' that... a Veridan noble is payin' a cadre of magic users with known ties to the stone elves, who'd actually be usin' those ties to sabotage the Veridan economy in order to... make himself richer and maybe get himself named king?" Babe asked. "Without worryin' that the high-power magic assassins he's been payin' are still mostly only interested in wipin' the whole city off the map?"

"Tell me, exactly, how much more of a stretch that is than the theory you walked in with, that the moment he heard that he wasn't going to be king, he started plotting to starve half the city?" Skite asked.

"Point taken," Babe answered.

Skite looked up and down the street once more, then put his back to the wall, crossing his arms.

"If my theory is accurate, though, Palora has got an idea that he's using the warlocks, and they've got an idea that they're using him, and either way, the one who wins that, we lose. On the other hand, knowing that our two enemies might be working together does simplify things."

"Do you think that the warlocks are using magic to make the city feel hopeless?" Stasia asked.

"No one can tell you the answer to that but the warlocks themselves, I think," Skite said. "I asked Tinman about it, and he refused to come out of his room for reasons that I won't trouble you by repeating. They are classically representative of the gap in understanding between those with magic and those without, crossed with a mind that did not learn Veridan as its first language."

"Would certainly make it easier, if takin' out Palora took out the warlocks," Babe said. "But I don't figure on that actually bein' the case."

Skite shook his head.

"They're assassins, underneath everything else that has happened to them," he said. "They are the first and foremost in the city at using those around them to achieve their ends, and when those ends are no longer advancing, they will disengage and move on." He held up a finger. "It's actually something I've been thinking on. When you first engaged them, they were in a semi-militarized formation, being run by a central point of authority. That's likely the only reason they stood and fought you, at any turn. Once they go back to working as individuals, I would be very surprised to find any of them interested in participating in an extended face-to-face fight. They will melt away as quickly as they can, because that's how an assassin wins. He comes to you when you don't see him, and he ends you before you ever know he was there."

Babe considered that, then scratched his chin.

"I'll put a word in Jasper's ear," he said. "It's good counsel."

Skite drew breath and looked out the window again.

"I don't like the idea that they're in the middle of this. Even knowing Qelador is gone, they are an unknown quantity, and I don't like going against those. I need... to observe them and figure out what it is they're capable of, what they want and what they're willing to risk to get it. Once you have the measure of a man, you can kill him, but until that, you are at risk of being the one who has been measured."

"Will they be on the Palora estate?" Stasia asked. "The warlocks? Is that why Jasper and the squad haven't been able to find them in the city?"

"Oh, I expect you can't find them in the city because they choose not to be found," Skite said. "But it's possible that they've taken up quarters at the Palora estate. It's strategically located, if you know how to get south from there. It lands you in the artisan quarter, which is a nice quiet quarter to ease your way through, if you're a man of the shadows."

Stasia had no idea where the Palora estate was, but it didn't surprise her that Skite knew.

In fact, it would have surprised her if he hadn't.

"We can pay a visit," Babe said. "Go up under the king's banner, get a sense for it."

"Would your stone elf be willing to go?" Stasia asked. "See if he can tell if they're there?"

Skite snorted.

"It's actually an ideal solution right up until you meet Tinman, which you won't. He won't go, and I'm certain enough of it that I won't ask him, because asking him something so obviously impossible will make him mistrust my judgment."

Stasia sighed and looked at Babe.

"I don't like you guys going into it blind and just... seeing if you can poke a badger in his lair."

"If they went up with a business proposition from the

king, they could accomplish several visits without tipping their hands that they're looking for information," Skite said. "Give Palora the impression that the king is crumbling and coming to him for help? Maybe even suggest that threatening you was what tipped the scales in his favor as the king and queen realized that they were so outplayed? You tell that man that you like his cape, he'll feed you dainties and brag to you all day without ever wondering what other reason you might have for being there. His ego is brighter than the sun, in his own eyes, and often blinding."

"So the Rat King knows Palora, too," Babe said.

"Oh, I know him better than the lot of you put together," Skite said. "I'm just awaiting my moment."

Babe frowned, opening his mouth to say something, and then thinking better of it and closing it again.

"So the squad goes up to Palora and pretends to negotiate for the king," Stasia said. "How do they turn up signs of the warlocks? Check for skites laying around?"

Skite laughed.

"If only it were that easy," he said. "I will leave that to the ever-clever Jasper to work out. I have no more insight than he has, given that I've only killed one of the beasts, and he's killed considerably more."

Stasia looked over at Babe.

"Well, that blows up the rest of my afternoon," she said. "You want to go take grain up to the mill and then... I think it's time for me to talk to the queen."

Babe nodded.

"I'd be glad to accompany you," he said.

She looked at Skite again, and he nodded.

"Your treasure is safe in my care," he said.

"Thank you," she said, and he smiled.

"Perhaps in the next day, we can discuss whether it's time for me to take my cut of the proceeds."

"Go ahead and do it," Stasia said. "Have Veil sign the

count, and I'll take it as given that you've done it accurately."

Skite cleared his throat.

"You do me a disservice, trusting me like that," he said, trying to control a smile. "What will happen if words goes around?"

She grinned.

"People will start thinking that the Rat King is a desirable trading partner, if the richest independent woman in the city trusts him so implicitly," she said, then winked. "I'll be back tomorrow, if I can."

He nodded and gave Babe a little nod in salute and left. Stasia turned to face Babe.

"What do you think?" she asked. He rolled his jaw to the side, watching the door.

"I think that man has no right to be so useful as he is," he said. "And I'm gettin' annoyed at it bein' so reliable."

Stasia grinned.

"You're coming around," she said. "It does happen occasionally."

He grinned back.

"Let's go get ourselves a cart to load up."

The Highrock family was waiting for them at the agreed-upon mill.

Stasia hadn't spoken to this miller in her initial sweep, so she had to go through her normal way of doing business, even as the load of grain got unloaded and the mill began to turn. The man was a bit grim and a bit gruff, but Stasia could see why Skite had chosen him as the first miller to get a load of wheat after the explosion.

She took the ten percent earnest money on the load and left with Babe, walking back along the river toward the castle.

"Do you want to check in with Jasper, first, or do you want to go to the castle with me?" Stasia asked.

"You gonna show me how you're goin' about comin' and goin'?" he asked.

She shook her head.

"I can't."

He shrugged.

"S'pose I can get myself in," he said. "Where would I meet you?"

She considered.

"Can you get to the king's sitting room?" she asked.

She didn't like going there, because it was where everyone had gone when they were dying after the fights with the warlocks, because the table was still there that Babe had been lying on, but she also figured that he might have a harder time getting himself up to the queen's chambers instead.

He nodded.

"So long as he ain't usin' 'em, palace guard won't stop me."

"I'll leave word for Melody that we're waiting for her there, and then meet you," Stasia said, and he grinned.

"Ain't you somethin'?" he said, then laughed. "I'll be there."

She let him go on without her once they were in sight of the castle, not wanting to give away anything about where the door was that she was using, and then she walked the long way around the castle. She had never gone straight from the front gate to the side passageway, for fear that someone who was just as curious as Babe was might try to follow her without her noticing.

She slipped through the gate, nodding to the as-always stoic guard, then went through the back routes up to Melody's sitting room and left her a brief note, then went through more normal corridors to get to the King's sitting room. She found Babe there on his own and she went to sit with him in the formal chairs, trying to keep the table out of her range of vision.

"It's right, keepin' the queen up to date on what you're doin'," Babe said. "But we go much further than this, I'm gonna have to get both Jasper and the King involved, too."

"Get me involved in what?" Finwalk asked, coming through a doorway at the back of the room. Babe stood quickly, and Stasia looked around.

"Where's your guard?" she asked.

"He likes to give us the slip," Babe said wryly. "Thinks he needs to be alone to think clear thoughts."

"Don't know why everyone's so surprised by that," Finwalk said, going to a small desk and getting out a stack of papers, a pen, and an inkwell. "I assume that you're here for a reason. Hello, Anastasia."

"Good afternoon, your majesty," Stasia answered.

Most men addressing her by her first name would have been patronizing or intentionally rude, but Finwalk said it like a friend. It charmed her greatly.

"Yes, your majesty," Babe said. "I should not be the one bringing you this report; we had hoped to speak with the queen and then I would have reported to Jasper for him to brief you…"

"And here she is," Finwalk said as the door opened and Matthias stood in the doorway for Melody to walk through. "So I'll just sit in on the first conversation and save you a trip across the river."

Babe gave him a little nod that looked remarkably uncomfortable, to Stasia's eye, given that Babe was not wont to wear his thoughts on his face, and she thought that she saw a twinkle of satisfaction and humor in Finwalk's eye to be disrupting the normal paths of communication thus.

And then she liked him more.

Finwalk came to sit on the couches across from Stasia, and Melody went to sit down next to him. Matthias remained by the door, alert.

"Do you need to be there to... do your thing?" Stasia asked him.

He gave her a half a smile.

"Does it bother you that I'm formal when you never are?" he asked.

"I think you know the answer to that," Stasia said indignantly, and Matthias came to sit on a chair nearby, his head still up and listening and his mind clearly engaged in anything that might reveal itself to be a threat, but at least he wasn't standing there, drawn tight like he had been.

"All right, Stasia," Melody said. "What's this about?"

"We're entertaining a new theory," Stasia said. "And it's political enough that I wanted to let you know what we were thinking about, and that... it may need to directly involve the king's guard soon."

"All right," Melody said, as Finwalk raised an eyebrow.

"You're commanding my men around, now, are you?" he asked.

"No," Stasia said, too quickly. He'd been teasing her, but now she had to finish the sentence or she just sounded defensive. "We're going to go talk to Jasper after this, and he's going to make decisions. It's that Babe has a pretty good guess what he's going to want to do, at least categorically, and if he does..."

"It will involve direct and significant action," Melody said. "I understand you."

Stasia nodded.

"The goods that I identified bounties on in your class."

Melody nodded.

"Very unanticipated, but a good twist, I think. I'm

fascinated to see what happens."

"I think that that is a very good approximation of the list of goods that are being artificially manipulated by specific merchants and other players in the city."

"Someone's manipulating the marketplace?" Finwalk asked. "I would know about that."

Stasia twisted her mouth to the side.

"They're doing it specifically to get rid of you, I think," she said. "So they'd probably be willing to go a long way to keep you from being able to see it... I think."

"Get rid of me?" Finwalk asked. "How do they think they'll be able to do that?"

"Palora, dear," Melody said. "Keep up. He wants your crown."

"But it's mine," Finwalk said. "I like it, now."

Again, teasing. Stasia really did like him.

"How do you know this?" Melody asked.

"Well, Lord Palora showed up in the secret apartment I've been living in, in the Black Docks, last night and asked me who gave me that list," Stasia answered. "So that's a good start. Then he was going on about the good men here and the good men there, doing good men things and protecting Verida, and... I think he's blockading the city, invisibly, from a specific list of goods, and simultaneously getting the suppliers to either stop sending goods to market, cutting them off from their markets by getting their transit merchants to stay out of the market, or outright destroying the sources of the goods."

"He said that to you?" Finwalk asked.

"He uses a lot of words and never actually says anything," Stasia answered. "That's why I want more people to be thinking about this before we go with my best guess what he was even talking about."

Finwalk nodded.

"I hate the meetings that he shows up to. They

always run long."

"What would you expect Jasper to do?" Melody asked Babe, and Babe shook his head.

"With respect, she ain't done yet, mum," Babe said.

Stasia nodded as all of the heads - save Matthias' - swiveled back to her again.

"I have a tip that... I must leave in confidence at this time... but that I believe wholeheartedly that the warlocks have, in the past, worked with nobles in the city as... employees of sorts. Or using them as patrons, perhaps. And then there's the wheat."

"What about the wheat?" Finwalk asked. "I'd heard that you brought in a massive shipment. Why is it not going to market as fast as possible?"

"You heard about the explosion at the flour mill?" Stasia asked. "Palora specifically showed up to gloat about it. But that's not it, either. The stone elves burned all of the wheat at the estates. We thought that it was because it was ripe and dry and would burn easily, compared to everything else, but I started asking myself, what if Lord Palora staged the stone elf attacks and hired men to do it, himself, specifically because he was going to run up grain prices? And then Lord Westhauser told me that they had seen with their own eyes that it was the stone elves doing it. And when you combine the fact that Palora seems to be admitting that he's manipulating specific markets, including wheat, that nobles and warlocks have worked together before in much the same way that nobles and assassins work together, and that the wheat was all burned by the warlocks' allies..."

"You come to the conclusion that Lord Palora is hiding away the remaining warlocks and trying to bring the city to ruin... to convince Melody to name him king instead of me," Finwalk said.

"Potentially," Stasia agreed carefully. "I can't prove any of it, obviously, but I know that he's involved because he showed up and I believe he intended to kill me, or have me killed, at any rate. He threatened certain other individuals to try to convince me to sell him all of the wheat at a loss and put out a story that the wheat was contaminated with mold coming out of Boton and that it had to be destroyed. I think that that's how he's keeping the wheat out of Port Verida, too. Telling the merchants that they bought contaminated wheat and he's just saving them from the embarrassment and risks of selling it unwittingly. I don't think there's anything wrong with the wheat, but... he did seem to be trying to convince me that there was."

"Well, that's certainly an interesting play," Finwalk said. "I've been talking to people all over the city about why things are behaving the way they are, but I couldn't get a straight answer from most of them. And then you walk in here and tell me it's because one of the most important nobles in the city is intentionally disrupting everything. I've got to tell you, I find it hard to believe."

"Do you, or are you just trying to push her into proving it further?" Melody asked. "Because I am convinced. What action do you think is advisable?"

"You could send Jasper and the squad up to the estate," Stasia said. "Lord Palora's. And tell him that they're there to negotiate on behalf of the king."

"Oh, you're going to drag me into it, then," Finwalk said.

"Would you stop?" Melody asked. "She's too earnest for this game."

Finwalk grinned.

"You may tell Palora that I am interested in negotiating a... partial reduction in the taxes at Port Verida for a specific set of domestic merchants who are key to the finished-goods export business. He's been advocating for them for weeks, trying to get all export tariffs waived. You may also tell him that I am interested in discussing him taking a more active role on the economic committee, rather than just... wasting his talents on the military."

He stuck his tongue out like it tasted bad to say the words, and Melody shook her head.

"Speak with Jasper," she said. "He will have ideas as well. Ensure that any offers he makes to Palora have been approved by both myself and Finwalk before he goes, but we understand that in a real negotiation, there may have to be... extemporaneous considerations to be made. You will be looking for evidence of the warlocks being there? Will you be trying to find and engage them, while you are there?"

"It depends on what Jasper thinks," Stasia said. "I'm well out of my depth here. This is my part of the job, and now I'm out of it. You need to let the experts do theirs."

"We ain't gonna be lookin' for a fight, right off," Babe said. "I can as much as say that. And I ain't got a clear idea on how we're gonna be lookin' for 'em, either."

"You should speak to Meggin, my healer pixie," Melody said.

"What?" Stasia asked, and Melody nodded.

"They took her nephew, in order to gain her loyalty," Melody said. "I have spoken to her twice since then, and while she accepts that she is disgraced too far to ever come back to the role that she had, she is a pixie crossed."

"I don't know what that means," Stasia said.

"A pixie crossed is an enemy for life," Babe murmured. "Where do we find her?"

Melody gave them an address and vague directions, then Finwalk stood.

"Well, this has been fun," he said. "We should do it again soon. Make sure you check in with me at each stage, and tell Jasper the same. Keep Ben informed, as well. I don't want to run this, myself, when I've got a man who's actually good at it who could be doing it. I assume that you guys have got the ability to win, if you do get in a fight."

"They did, last time," Melody said calmly. "They will come through again. Here, they have my utmost faith."

Babe bowed over his knees, then stood.

"We'll get on, then," he said. "Go, find Jasper, track down Meggin, make ourselves a plan. Like you say."

"Good luck," Melody said, also standing. Matthias sprang out of his chair and went to open the door for her as Finwalk drifted back to his papers again. Stasia and Babe went out into the hallway after Matthias left, and Babe looked at her.

"You goin' out your way again?" he asked, and she shook her head.

"No, today, I think I'm going to go out the front gate," she said. "Just to be unpredictable."

He smiled and offered her his arm.

"Well, here's to unpredictable, then," he said. She put her arm through his and they went on.

Jasper sent Colin to get Meggin as soon as he heard what was going on, then he left word at the guard house as to where they'd gone, and they went up to the bar up the street as it opened, taking their table by the front window.

"All right," Jasper said. "Tell it to me again, but make sure you don't leave out any details. We didn't have time to go through it all last night, and I want to be sure there isn't anything you're missing telling me that would change the right answer."

Once more, Stasia told the story, including the part that she'd told him the night before and what Skite had said in the little apartment that day. Jasper watched her speak with intensity, only pausing her to ask questions once or twice before she got to the end.

"All right," he said. "I wish I'd have known that

months ago, but at least I know it now. We had assumed that the warlocks would be without allies within the city. I should have at least considered that they have marketable skills and experience finding buyers for those skills. We'll wait for Meggin, to see if she can give us any more information... another thing I should have considered before now... but today may just be the day of things coming together."

"I'm surprised the queen trusts her," Stasia said. "I mean, after everything? I don't know if I could ever speak to her again."

"You're accustomed to a very different political environment," Jasper said. "It's not surprising that you expect your confidantes to be loyal to you or to just excise them. Melody, and the rest of the court, live in a world where you work with people on one thing and against them on another, and often it is a matter of life and death, getting it right. You allow your alliances to be fluid in order to be effective. She's more willing to see the hard compromises other people make."

"Did they ever find Meggin's nephew?" Stasia asked, and Jasper looked over at Babe.

"We told 'em all no," Babe said, his voice very low.

Oh.

Oh.

"I want them all dead," Stasia said softly.

Babe looked at her with a sort of quiet reckoning, not quite surprise, but... evaluating.

"You actually mean it," he said, and Stasia nodded.

She did.

"They're hurting people on purpose, because they can, and they don't care. Everything that you think Skite is? They really are. And no one can stop them but us, which means that we can't just throw them in a cell and walk away. No one can hold them, that we know of. There's no way to keep them from doing it again but... for them to be dead."

Babe nodded.

"You're right," he said.

"Usually people don't have to think about it like that, though," Jasper said. "That's our job. They just want it to go away. So when they say that they want someone dead, they mean something much darker."

"I might mean that, too," Stasia said. "They deserve it."

"They deserve worse," Sterling said.

"They do," Babe said.

"How are you going to find them?" Stasia asked. "I just... The city is so big, and hiding is so easy."

"You think it is until you try to do it," Jasper said. "And then you realize that those of us who have hunted people for a living for many years are quite adept at using unexpected information to give us clues, and that you're leaving a scent trail behind you just as sure as if I were a hunting animal coming for you."

It was grim, but it was powerful, too.

Sterling got out a deck of cards and started shuffling, dealing cards for a mindless luck-based game that they played until Colin got back with Meggin.

The pixie woman looked stiff and unhappy, sitting down at the table directly across from Jasper as Colin took the chair next to Babe.

"I understand that Queen Melody has asked that I assist you in some way," Meggin said.

"The men who took your nephew," Jasper said.

Meggin's wings twitched audibly.

"What about them?" she asked. "They haven't contacted me since I left the queen's service."

"We killed most of them, which likely includes the ones who interacted with you directly," Jasper said. "It's our best guess that three remain. It could be more and it could be less. But we are hunting them and we are looking for help in tracking them down and... killing them."

Her wings twitched again.

"You will?" she asked. "You won't try to bring them in or try them for crimes?"

"On the one hand," Jasper said, "I consider them to be war combatants, which means that I am right to attempt to kill them right up until they surrender as prisoners of war, and on the same hand, I have no expectation that justice against them will be possible, and so we must settle for death."

Her neck was still so rigid.

"If you have any survivors, you will hand them over to me for pixie justice," she said.

"I cannot in good faith do that," Jasper said. "I don't believe that you would survive them."

Her eyes said that she had every intention of surviving those men, and that she defied them to survive her.

"Then you had better ensure that they are all dead at the end of your encounter," she answered. "Because the law of Verida is on my side, and they will come to us next to answer for kidnapping and killing my nephew."

"You have my word that they will never fall into pixie justice," Jasper said, and she nodded once.

"What is it you need of me?" she asked.

"You were the queen's healer," Jasper said. "And you probably had more direct interaction with these men than anyone else I know, save perhaps Stacy and Melody herself. How many of them did you meet?"

"One," Meggin said. "He would come to my room at the castle with a piece of my nephew's wing each time, to prove that they still had him and that he was still alive, and they would tell me what they wanted me to do and they would ask me questions about what Melody and the rest of the court were talking about."

"Did you know that he was coming, on the nights

that he came?" Colin asked.

Meggin looked sharply at him.

"Of course not," she said.

Jasper looked over at Colin, as Colin sat up slightly.

"You're lying," he said. "You did know."

Her wings shifted again.

"What are you?" she asked.

"A new man," Colin said. "You knew that they were coming. How?"

"They didn't tell me," she said, and Colin shook his head.

"No, I'm not accusing you of that, though it would hardly be worse than what you've already done, anyway. How did you know?"

She stood quickly. If she'd been the size and bulk of a normal human, her chair might have tipped back behind her.

"You're like them," she said. She glanced at Babe, but thought better of it and went around him to grab Colin's chin and jerk it up to look at her. Colin went along with it without protest as she looked him in the eyes from much too close a range. "I didn't see it before. It's growing, you know."

"We know," Colin said.

"You aren't like them at all," Meggin said. "But you're exactly the same."

"We're nothing like them," Jasper said. "In any way relevant. But that is as much as I will say about it."

"That's why you were able to beat them," Meggin said. "And survive..." She motioned at Babe without looking at him.

Stasia felt... vindicated, finding that someone else was as haunted by that moment as she was.

"We are the only ones who can go against them and expect to live," Jasper said. Stasia thought of Skite, the quick spasm of activity leaving a dead body in the corner, and she turned her face away. Skite had gotten stabbed, saving her. He could have died. She needed to deal with that, some day, but she wasn't ready yet.

Not today.

"I don't know what entrance they came through," Meggin said, her eyes firmly on Jasper again. "I needed to know when they were coming so that I was never with the queen or any of her family when they found me. I feared that they might kill her daughters. So I put a cast on each of the doorways and the external windows that told me when someone with abnormal magic was there. It took me weeks, and I suspect that there are few inside of or outside the castle who could find each and every door and window the way that I did, but I always knew... when they were coming, with just enough time to retire myself to my rooms for when they found me."

"They were in the castle and we never knew it," Babe said.

"And they never laid a finger on the queen," Sterling said.

"We don't know that," Colin warned. Jasper kept his eyes steady on Meggin.

"Can you replicate that cast in such a way that I would know if someone with abnormal magic had used a doorway?" he asked.

She blinked at him for several moments, like doing calculations in her head, then she nodded.

"Perhaps. It would be impossible to tell if it had worked until it did work, but... yes, I believe I could transfer the cast to someone else."

"Could we cast it so that you knew?" Colin asked, and she shook her head.

"No. Only the one who lays the cast holds the lead," she said.

"And could they detect that the cast was there?"

Jasper asked.

"I knew that I took my nephew's life in my hands, laying those casts," Meggin said. "I was as careful as I could be. But I cannot tell you for a fact that they did not know it was there."

He glanced at Sterling, who nodded.

"Worth the risk of it," Sterling said. "I'd rather have hard knowledge than surprise."

Jasper nodded.

"Me, too," he said. "All right, how quickly can you put together such a cast?"

"Tomorrow morning," Meggin said. "Though, I'm confused why it didn't find you."

"I don't have magic," Jasper said. "None of us do."

She looked around the table, resting on Stasia.

"She's the only one here who doesn't," she said.

"You see magic on us," Jasper said. "But it is not ours."

"What happened to you?" Meggin asked.

"Those are our story," Jasper said. "And it isn't one for us to share, I'm afraid. You know that I have the confidence of the queen, and I expect that you will honor that, even as you have lost it."

"Oh, I still have her confidence," Meggin said, her wings rustling again. "Because I have all her secrets. The ones she thought she was hiding from me, and Constance before her. She just knows that I will not betray them, even as I allowed them to get close enough to her to nearly kill her. You will never know what all of this has cost me."

"I won't, it's true," Jasper said. "But this is your moment to set it right, or at least get some of it back."

"I will help you, if I can," Meggin said. "But you should find someone who can take care of you. All of you should. There is something strange about you, and you should have a pixie healer attending to you periodically to ensure that there aren't things that you need to be doing that you wouldn't think of with your mundane human minds."

"Tomorrow morning," Jasper said. "Bring it to the guard house. If you need to teach me how to use it, there is a weapons room there that is private and should work. We go hunting for warlocks tomorrow."

Meggin nodded firmly and stood.

"Yes," she said. "I will go get started on it now."

Jasper watched her leave, then looked over at Stasia.

"Where are you sleeping tonight?" he asked.

"I haven't been to see my sister yet," Stasia said. "I could probably stay there, tonight."

"Take Babe with you as an escort," Jasper said. "Or Sterling, if you think the Gormands would tolerate him better."

"Hey," Babe said.

Sterling grinned.

"I'm very charming."

"I need to go see the queen," Jasper said. "And king, apparently. Be back at the earliest you can. I'll figure out where I'm going to stash you for the day with Colin, so that they can't come track you down while we're up negotiating with Palora."

"Could just go out to sea, I suppose," Stasia said offhandedly, and Jasper turned to look at her from where he'd already begun to stand up.

"What did you say?" he asked. She shrugged.

"I mean, they get here by boat, so I'm guessing that they tolerate it okay, at least, but... they're supposed to hate the water, right? If it's actually about magic and not about, like, just what they were raised to believe about the water?"

"But you're hard to find, on a boat," Jasper said. "That's clever. I'll consider it."

He stood and put his hat on.

"Stay sharp," he said. "We've put pressure on them,

now, and they're going to either start putting existing plans into action or start making mistakes, and we need to be ready to react to either."

"Yes, sir," Sterling said.

"Yeah," Colin said. Babe looked over at Stasia.

"So who do you want goin' with you, to the merchant row?" he asked.

"Oh, come on," Stasia said. "Don't pout. It's you, of course."

He stood.

"Then let's get there while I've still got some light to go through the defenses to check them out," he said, offering her a hand.

"Are you getting any better?" Stasia asked Colin as they started for the door.

He wiggled his arm.

"Bad time to be out of commission," he said. "Not that making sure you're safe isn't worth it, but I hate letting these guys go up on their own."

She put her hand on his shoulder, then continued on with Babe.

"Could the pixies not help him?" Stasia asked.

"That's after they did," Babe said. "Bone broke in two places. That he'll get to use his arm again is because we had the pixie at the castle to look at it."

They went out onto the street, and Babe looked over toward the guard house.

"Long walk from here," he said. "Reckon Alfred'd like a trip out of town like that?"

Stasia's heart lurched at the idea.

"I've missed him so much," she said, and he nodded.

"He misses you," he said, turning toward the guard house and walking along easily.

"Are you not worried about what comes next?" Stasia asked.

"Your sister ain't half as bad as you make her out to be," Babe said.

"Not her," Stasia said. "We actually had... kind of a moment, after dinner the other night, and I've been meaning to go see her. Tomorrow. Going to fight."

He squeezed her hand and laughed gently.

"Tomorrow is what I look forward to," he said. "All the rest of this runnin' around and hopin' not to find ourselves in trouble we can't handle? I just want the fight. I'm ready for it and I'm expectin' it. It's what I'm good at. Knowin' you're gonna be in excellent hands, somewhere off where Jasper finds to stash you for the time bein'? All I got to think about is a sword in my hand and the man there in front of me, and I swear to you, Anastasia, I ain't gonna let another one of 'em get the best of me. I'm not the same as I was, that first fight. I can feel it, and I'm ready."

"You can't be sure of that," Stasia said. "You just can't."

He grinned.

"You know the mark of a good soldier?" he asked.

"Tell me," she answered.

"He knows that goin' against the enemy is his job and his callin' and he looks toward the field of battle as his home. You know the mark of a great soldier?" he asked.

She smiled.

"Tell me."

"He knows without a doubt that he's comin' home again after."

"Jasper said that you were going to die someday," Stasia said. "That all of you would."

"Likely," Babe said. "Wide view of things, inevitable. Got no idea what it's like to be in that man's head, seein' it comin' without him, like that. It ain't about not dyin'. It's about bein' sure. First fight with the warlocks, I didn't know what was gonna happen, but I knew I was gonna go face it with my brothers, back there, and that was what I was bred for. Good soldierin'. For this one I'm a great soldier. I know my way in and I know I'm gonna find my way home again."

"Do that," Stasia said. He squeezed her hand again, lifting the barrier to let her into the guard house. "You want to grab somethin' to eat for us while I tack up the horses?"

Her stomach gurgled, reminding her that she hadn't eaten anything since breakfast.

"Should I feel bad that the king's guard is feeding me?" she asked. "The whole city is hungry."

He shook his head.

"The woman working hardest to fix it gets to eat without feelin' bad," he said. "Go on. I'll be ready in about ten."

They arrived at the Gormand estate just before dark, Stasia taking the horses to the stable herself and making sure that they had size-appropriate lodgings before she went up to the manor house with Babe.

The ride with Alfred hadn't been long enough. She wanted to actually go out for a few hours and just take in the countryside, perhaps at the Westhauser estate sometime, to thank him for the safe trip home, but for tonight, that just wasn't going to happen.

Two men were holding the doors at the main entrance to the manor when Stasia and Babe came out of the barn, and Stasia led the way up the hill.

She went through the doors with a quick glance at one of the men, just to acknowledge he was there, and she found her sister standing in the grand entrance wearing an elaborate dressing gown.

"Anastasia," Alyssia said. "What are you doing here at this time of night?"

Stasia looked back out the doors.

"It's dusk," she said.

"Dinner was an hour and a half ago, and I had turned in for the night when they told me you were coming. It is entirely unseemly for you to just show up here unannounced like this. And with a man, no less. Anastasia, what in the world do you think you're doing?"

"You're in danger, Alyssia," Stasia said. "I came to warn you."

Alyssia's posture changed dramatically, and she took half a step back.

"How? Why? What's happened?"

"I did something bold and reckless, and the man who doesn't appreciate me doing it threatened to hurt you in response," Stasia said.

Alyssia put her fingers to her chest, then looked around wildly.

"We have men who act as guards," she said. "They're... here somewhere..."

"That's fine," Stasia said. "For tonight, we're going to stay here, and my best information says that you are most likely safe as long as you stay at the manor..."

"Most likely?" Alyssia demanded. "You come to me and tell me that my life is in danger and all you can tell me is 'most likely'? What am I supposed to do?"

"Lady Gormand," Babe said, taking a step forward. "With your blessin', I'd like to make a round of the manor, take in the security you have here, the systems they're usin', and see if I might not be able to give you some suggestions on improvin' 'em. Would that be okay with you?"

Alyssia flared her nostrils, looking from Babe to Stasia and back.

"I can't do this," she said. "I cannot."

And she turned and went back up the stairs.

"Miss Fielding-Horne," an older woman said,

coming around a corner. "I ought to have known. Here to make more trouble, are you?"

"Lindle," Stasia answered without looking. "I'm afraid I know how to make very little else."

"Who have you brought to us?" the head of household asked.

"This is Babe, of the King's Guard," Stasia answered. "He is here as my escort and because he wants to help see to the safety of the estate. With your blessing."

"With my blessing," Lindle said. "Now that Lady Gormand has failed to give hers?"

"Best if I do it while there's still light," Babe said, and Lindle lifted her nose to look at him.

"You may go," she said skeptically. "But only so long as you do not disrupt any of the men who are at their jobs, presently. There is much to be done on the grounds, and I cannot afford some man who thinks that he knows better than everyone around him to make trouble."

"Of course not, ma'am," Babe said. "Wouldn't dream of it."

Stasia watched after him, thinking hard about going with him, but knowing that she had a battle to win, in here, first.

Lindle could still kick her out. She had come unannounced and uninvited, and it was becoming more common knowledge that her father had disinherited her, which meant that her social standing within this house was tenuous at best, unless Alyssia claimed her.

Maybe Stasia had been hoping for something more like their last moments at her father's house, with Alyssia, but she was hardly surprised at the reception she'd gotten.

"And what am I to do with you?" Lindle asked.

"I wouldn't hate something to eat," Stasia said, and Lindle snorted. It had been the wrong answer, but Stasia had had a hard time not poking at the woman the entire time she had lived here.

"Stasia," a woman called from upstairs, coming sweeping down to hug her.

This was one of the maids from Boton who had crossed with them, who had known Stasia from her earliest childhood.

"Oh, Manda," Stasia said. "I've missed you."

"Why are you here?" Manda asked, looking back at Lindle. "It's so late."

"I couldn't get here earlier," Stasia said. "I need a place to stay for the night."

"I'll go set you up a room," Manda said.

"I have a member of the King's Guard with me," Stasia said. "He would need one, too."

Manda paused.

"Why?" she finally asked, as Lindle sniffed.

"I want to make sure that Alyssia is safe," Stasia said. "I've had someone threaten me, and threaten her as a threat to me."

Manda snorted.

"Then clearly they don't know you very well."

"Shut your mouth," Lindle said.

"Don't say that," Stasia said. "I don't want her to die. I just don't want to live with her if I can help it."

"She has no standing, here, to demand our hospitality," Lindle said. "I haven't agreed to her staying, yet."

"What's this I hear about Minstrel disinheriting you?" Manda asked, mostly ignoring Lindle. "Surely that's just a rumor."

"I asked him to," Stasia said. "It happened, and it's real, and I'm happy."

Manda frowned.

"Well, that does sound like you," she said. "So there hasn't been a falling out between you two?"

Stasia shook her head.

"No, not at all. I just wanted to lead my own life, and he was willing to let me."

"All I know is that you will not be a burden on this household after your father passes," Lindle said. "May that be many decades in the future. And that you are not permitted to be a burden on this household now, just because it is convenient for you to do so."

"She's the Lady's sister, disinherited or not," Manda said. "And I'm happy to prep a room for her and her guest. This is not an undue burden on the house, Lindle."

"It is an undue burden on the Lady," Lindle answered. "And I will not have this woman coming in here and upsetting her. I'm not even sure I believe that there's a threat. Clearly she lives to make trouble."

Manda looked over at Stasia as though she couldn't really argue that, and Stasia shrugged.

"As long as she stays here, we think she'll be okay," Stasia said. "And I'm here because I care about her. Whether or not you believe me about the threat."

Lindle sniffed.

"Why would anyone threaten Lady Gormand?" she asked. "That's just ridiculous."

Manda patted Stasia's shoulder.

"I'll go prepare a room for you and your guest. If you go back to the kitchen, Patricia is probably still back there, and she'll find something for you to eat."

The woman winked, then gave Lindle a dark look and started up the stairs.

Stasia looked at Lindle to see if she was going to go along with it, and the head of household sighed dramatically at her, shaking her head.

"Your impertinence knows no bounds," she said, putting an arm out. "Go find yourself a brief meal, then go up. The household has retired, and you are taxing everyone beyond their normal duties. I expect you to be in bed within the hour, and to take your breakfast and go."

"If Babe finds weaknesses in your security, your butler should consider them," Stasia said. "Is Gevalt going to be here at all, tomorrow, do you know?"

"He is in the city for the rest of the week," Lindle said. "And I will not disturb Quince with these inappropriate distractions."

Stasia paused, then squared up her shoulders to look at Lindle.

"Do you know that I work for the queen?" she asked. "That I am the first of the queen's guard, and that I do things on her orders, when she has need of me?"

Lindle drew her head back.

"I hadn't heard such a thing," she said. "I've never heard of a queen's guard, either."

Stasia nodded.

"I came here to ensure that my sister is safe," she said. "If you try to send me away without my having accomplished this goal, you will find that whatever nuisance I made of myself, before, I am much more capable of bending your life and your routine out of shape now. My sister matters to me, and I will not let you throw me out until I have seen to her safety. Is that clear?"

Lindle pursed her lips.

"Since when?" she asked.

That actually hurt. Stasia could understand it, but she had thought that people would have known the difference between the rivalry and feud and an outright disdain for her own sister's well-being.

"She's my sister," Stasia said. "And a dangerous man went out of his way to tell me that if I wasn't a good girl and did what he said, he would kill her. I think it suggests that I care about her a great deal."

"Is that true?" Lindle asked. "Or are you just here

causing mayhem?"

Stasia raised one eyebrow.

"How bored do you think I am?" she asked.

Lindle sighed.

"Very well. Find yourself something to eat and I will see about acceptable clothing for you to wear tomorrow. I assume I'm right in noting that you have brought nothing of use with you, this evening."

"I brought a sword and I brought Babe," Stasia said. "I assure you that they are both of great use."

"Babe," Lindle muttered. "That would be the guard with you?"

"Yes," Stasia said. "The one who is going to put his whole heart into trying to make this estate safer. If he has anything to say to you, I would listen very carefully, because it could save someone's life."

Lindle pursed her lips dryly, then nodded.

"I have other matters to attend to," she said. "I assume you can find your own way to the kitchen?"

It was backhanded. Stasia knew it. Only servants went to the kitchen, in the Gormand estate. But she chose to take it as an opportunity to show them that she had no problem with spending time in and around kitchens, here or anywhere else, so she went, finding another of her father's Boton staff there and sitting at the kitchen table talking to her until Babe found her.

Patricia made a heaping plate of food for Babe, who devoured it, and then they went upstairs.

"The men are that way," Stasia said, indicating. "I'll be over here."

"Really?" he asked. "The place is big enough that visitors are split up men and women?"

"Oh, there's a couples wing, as well," Stasia answered. Important that none of these people might accidentally see each other in the hallway in the morning. It would be scandalous.

Babe snorted.

"Was it that way at the Westhauser place, and I just missed it?" he asked.

Stasia pressed her lips and nodded.

"At the Westhauser estate, they're not separated by wings. They're separated by wings and floors," she said, then grinned. "Ella just doesn't care all that much."

Manda appeared from the women's wing, smiling at Stasia.

"Is this your companion?" she asked warmly, and Stasia nodded.

"Babe, this is Manda. She came across from Boton with us. Manda, this is Babe of the King's Guard. He's helping me keep an eye on everything, here, tonight."

"Security here ain't half bad," Babe said. "Gave a few notes to the butler man downstairs. Don't know if he'll want to do anything about it, but the man who set this place up knew what he was about."

"Is Alyssia really in danger?" Manda asked. "Everyone's whispering, and no one knows what to think."

Stasia nodded.

"I have a good source that says that she should be safe here, that they shouldn't be willing to come after her at the estate, but she shouldn't go out until it's done."

Manda shivered.

"The guards outside, they know?"

"They do," Babe said.

"And you're just going to go to bed?" Manda asked.

Babe nodded.

"I done what part I can, and I'll take sleep when it's there to take," he said. "If there were a real threat to her here at the house, you ought know, I'd be the first to sit watch."

Stasia nodded.

"That's true. If he's going to go sleep, it means that

everyone else should stay alert, but not worry. She just needs to stay here."

Manda nodded.

"She doesn't go out much, anyway, unless it's shopping. I think she's having a group of ladies to tea, tomorrow."

Stasia looked around the open space there at the top of the stairs, then nodded.

"Good. Only women, only people she knows, and always here and never somewhere else. That should be okay until I figure out how to make sure she's safe everywhere."

Manda gave her a quiet little laugh.

"Don't know why you're telling me," she said.

"Because I have to leave again in the morning," Stasia said. "And Lindle won't listen to me, and Alyssia won't even talk to me. You spread the word and find someone who can turn Lindle's ear, and then make sure that Alyssia hears her. I can't make a dent in this house. You know that."

Manda paused, then hugged Stasia fiercely.

"Such a big heart," she murmured into Stasia's ear. "I know a lot of them were always keen on overlooking it, but you've always had such a big heart."

She blinked tears as she stepped away, then motioned Stasia onward.

"I'll show you where you're sleeping," she said, then looked over at Babe. "One of the men should be by in a minute to escort you. If you're still here when I get back, I'll go clap my hands at them and make sure they get moving. We'll get you bedded in nicely, before long at all."

He tipped his hat to her and Manda put her arm around Stasia's waist.

"You okay?" Manda asked as they walked.

"Of course," Stasia answered.

"Are you sure?" Manda asked. "I didn't think I would ever see you turn up here voluntarily."

"I couldn't just ignore a man threatening my sister," Stasia said, then looked over her shoulder. "And I needed a place to sleep where no one would come looking for me."

"You're in trouble, aren't you?" Manda asked. "I knew it."

"Manda, I'm sorry," Stasia started, but Manda tightened her grip around Stasia's waist in a friendly way.

"It's not an accusation, child," she said. "I just know you, and I know that look of yours. You're worried, and it isn't just about Alyssia."

"I am worried about her," Stasia said. "But I'm involved in something very big and very important, and... there are some people I really care about who are going to take some very big risks tomorrow, and I can't even be there for it. I have to go hide somewhere else."

Manda looked over at her.

"You found someone who could talk you into hiding?" she asked. "And it wasn't someone intent on teaching you lessons you didn't want?"

Stasia laughed gently at the memory.

Under the piano in her father's study, back when she'd been brazen enough to go into it without an invitation.

"I did," she said. "And... I'm doing things that are big enough that... sometimes I need to go hide."

"Are you happy?" Manda asked.

Stasia nodded.

"Happier than I think I've ever been," she said, and Manda smiled at this.

"And what of the guard back there?" she asked. "Who is he?"

"A friend," Stasia said.

Yes, they'd told the rest of the guard, and her father, and actually Alyssia, too, but she couldn't say the words casually to Manda.

Didn't even know what the casual words were.

"Are you sure?" Manda asked.

"Why?" Stasia countered, and Manda squeezed her again.

"Because of the way your face lights up when you look at him," she said. "And the way his shoulders are always pointed at you, even when he's looking at something else."

Stasia put her head on Manda's shoulder.

"I think I love him," she said.

"And he loves you," Manda coached, and Stasia nodded.

Manda kissed the top of her head.

"Then my blessings on you both," she said. "I'm happy for you."

She let go of Stasia and went to open a door to a dim, lamplit room.

"This is you for the night. I'll make sure your young man is settled in nicely, too, before I turn in."

"Thank you, Manda," Stasia said. "I'm sorry I only came up here because I was in trouble."

"There are a lot of us who only ever wanted you to have a big, beautiful life, the way your mama wanted for you," Manda said. "I'm just happy I got to see that it's happening."

She blew a kiss and closed the door, leaving Stasia with a dressing gown on the bed and alone with her thoughts.

She should have come back here before, but it would have been - and still was - inappropriate to come to see the staff. In the Gormand household, the staff were seldom seen and never heard, for visitors.

It hurt her, the thought of leaving in the morning and not getting to say goodbye to Manda, or even see most of the others, but she could find no way of making it happen any other way, so she let it go.

She put on the dressing gown and brushed out her hair, then attended to her teeth and took the little pot of scented lotion and put that on her hands and her face. It had pixie magic in it, she realized as the cream cooled and warmed her skin at the same time, and she wondered what it did, specifically, but she didn't care all that much. It was temporary, and it was indulgent. Everything here was.

She went to get into the bed, arranging the pillows and the blankets to suit her, then lay down, looking at the wall in the deep dark, wondering what would happen tomorrow.

If Jasper didn't find the warlocks at Lord Palora's estate, he would just keep looking.

Stasia would keep bringing grain up to the mills and, little by little, things would fall apart.

She needed to move the grain faster, but that was a question of word getting out that it existed and finding more people willing to defend their own source of flour, the way the Highrock family was doing it.

It would be complicated and difficult, but it would work and it would happen, and for tonight, it was tomorrow's problem.

She rolled over and pulled the blankets up over her shoulders, just for the weight of them, and went to sleep.

The room was so quiet.

Monaga, Ella's head of household, was invested into discipline about having her girls be quiet as they moved about in the mornings, but Ella was not, and she talked and laughed and moved around like a normal person, when she got up in the morning, and so when Stasia slept at the Westhauser estate, she often woke to the sound of voices and footsteps.

At the Gormand estate, just as she remembered it, she woke up to the sound of perfect silence.

Sometimes the wind would blow firmly enough to get a slight whistle around the stone faces of the house, but the windows were kept such that they didn't hiss or blow, and the floors were thick and the walls were thicker, and the entire house was silent as a tomb until you got downstairs and found people who were allowed to speak to each other.

Stasia couldn't wait to be gone.

She got up and put on her dragonskins again, ignoring the dress that someone had hung from a hook on the wall since she'd gone to bed, and she put her hair back up and glanced at herself in the mirror, then went downstairs to find Babe at breakfast with a number of the guards in the kitchen.

They were laughing and swapping stories in the way of soldiers that Stasia now recognized, and they fell quiet as she came in, not so much a mark of respect as an awareness that an outsider had appeared.

Stasia knew that she didn't belong at that table, that she didn't want to belong at that table, but she still had a sense that she wished that she could go anywhere Babe did and be able to see what he was like, there.

She wanted to see all of his faces.

He smiled and put a hand out.

"This is the lady, gentlemen," he said. "Which means I ought to go get the horses ready. Gonna be as much a day today as it always is."

He stood and took his plate over to the sink, then came over to Stasia.

"You ready in about fifteen?" he asked, and she nodded.

"I could go now," she said.

"Eat somethin' good," he said. "So long as it's there."

He went past and Stasia went to the counter of staff-food, filling a plate and taking a seat at the rapidly-emptying table as the guards shuffled off to their posts for the day.

She ate and she went out, finding Babe talking to another of the guards as he stood next to Alfred and Peter by the barn doors.

"Stasia," a voice called, and Stasia turned around to find Alyssia standing in the doorway behind her.

She looked like she was afraid to come outside.

Stasia walked back to her.

"Good morning," she said.

"Am I really in danger?" Alyssia asked, and Stasia nodded.

"I'm sorry, but I think you are."

"And it's your fault?" Alyssia asked.

Stasia considered, then shrugged and nodded.

"I suppose it would be true to say that it is," she said.

"You've done something to make someone angry, haven't you?" Alyssia asked.

Stasia nodded with slightly less reservation.

"Yes."

"And you came here to warn me," Alyssia said.

"I did."

"And I'm safe at the house?" Alyssia asked.

"We think so."

"Who is we?" Alyssia asked.

"Someone I trust very much to know," Stasia said.

"And you'll tell me when it's safe to go out again?" Alyssia asked.

"I'll send word," Stasia said. "Written with my own hand."

"I wouldn't know your handwriting," Alyssia said.

"Yes you would," Stasia said. "You always said it was terrible."

Alyssia paused, then nodded.

"I do remember that. You haven't gotten any better since then?"

Stasia grinned.

"I certainly haven't cared any more," she said. "It will probably be delivered by one of the King's Guard, as well."

"How do you have the King's Guard running errands for you?" Alyssia asked.

"I run errands for them," Stasia told her. "Look, don't worry about it too much, okay? Just stay home. Have parties, do... whatever else it is you do, but just don't go out. I think that's the only real risk. It may all be over today. I don't know yet. But... stay in. Okay?"

"Okay," Alyssia said. "It's true that threatening me is... something someone would do to make you do something?"

"Or not do something," Stasia agreed. "Yeah."

"Huh," Alyssia said, then looked back and forth furtively and stepped outside to hug her. "Stay safe."

"Doing my best," Stasia said, finding her way around the awkward entanglement of arms to hug her sister back. "You feeling okay?" she asked.

Alyssia stepped quickly back inside and put her hand on her stomach.

"I feel awful," she said. "But the midwife says that's a good sign that I might be able to carry this one."

This wasn't the first one? Stasia felt bad for not knowing that.

"Well... don't worry, okay? We're taking care of it. It's going to be okay."

Stasia didn't think she had ever said those words before, it's going to be okay, but there they were, popping out of her mouth like it was nothing.

Alyssia smiled.

"Okay. I'll see you soon for lunch?"

Stasia nodded.

"Very soon. Yes. Definitely."

She turned and went back down to the stable, where

Alfred was staring off at the mountains and Babe was having a conversation with Peter that seemed to be quite intent.

"You remember up there, don't you?" Stasia said to Alfred, rubbing his nose. "Thinking about it? Do you miss it?"

It hadn't occurred to her that he might miss the mountains until that moment. She missed him, and the long days riding with Jasper, the way it had felt personal and private and like something that no one else would ever get. That connection to all of the lives out there with her, this tiny bubble of world that was only hers...

But Alfred had roots up there, one way or another. He'd been built for that world, and she wondered if he didn't hate life in the city, particularly after having been up there.

He rubbed his nose on her chest and she took the reins from Babe as he went to go mount up.

Stasia scratched Alfred's ears and went to go join Babe, heading down the driveway to the road and setting off at a quick trot across the cobbles.

It was nice not to have to worry about stone elves, up here, again.

The noise of the cobbles and of the merchant class slowly waking up into their work for the day rose around them as they went, then they started passing more and more carts and carriages. At the first, there hadn't been much need for conversation, and then as they got closer to the guard house, there wasn't opportunity.

As the building came in sight, Stasia realized that she'd missed her entire last chance to talk to Babe before this happened.

She looked over, feeling a jolt of fear and regret, and he seemed to know exactly what had happened. He shook his head, giving her a quiet smile.

"Ain't no need," he murmured as they waited at the gate for one of the young men to come open it for them.

"Things are just as they're s'posed to be, and bein' afraid just robs it out."

She nodded again, then dismounted as one of the recruits held Alfred's head for her.

As if she needed that.

She thanked the young man, anyway, then followed Babe up the stairs to the mess hall, where all five of the squad were now assembled.

"What is Matthias doing here?" Stasia asked.

"He's here for you," Jasper said. "Queen wants to see you before you go poof for the day. Colin is gonna meet you at the bar downriver from the castle. You remember the one?"

"I do," Stasia said. Colin looked particularly unhappy that his arm was still in a sling, and Matthias might have looked displeased that he was not going with Jasper, Sterling, and Babe, but these were the things that were already agreed upon.

"Did she come?" Stasia asked, and Jasper nodded, letting the corners of a small leather square fall open to reveal what looked like light pink beads.

"They break open when they touch certain things," Sterling said. "We have the list. They should work for us."

"And then you'll know?" Stasia asked. Jasper nodded.

"And then I'll know."

She sighed.

"I need to get more grain moving," she said. "Can I do that before we disappear today?"

"Don't move it yourself," Babe said. "Send your man a message that he's up. Let him take a share, and you disappear."

Jasper glanced over, then nodded.

"What he said."

Sterling was watching the room like a hawk

surveying a field.

"What do you see?" Stasia asked him and he frowned.

"Hmm?" he asked.

"What do you see?" Stasia asked.

He blinked, coming back to the conversation.

"What do you mean?" he asked.

She raised her eyebrows, turning around to face the room.

"You're looking at something," she said.

"Am I?" Sterling asked.

"You're looking at everything," Jasper said. "You gotta get that under control before we get to Palora's. See everything, but don't look at all of it."

"Yes," Sterling said. "They know there's something going on, but the number of them who can guess is... I would say that it's quite small, but the truth is that it's none of them. They're trying to figure out if Ben knows."

Stasia saw men eating breakfast.

"I don't like the number of things that we do without them all knowing," Matthias said. "Being in the King's Guard means secrets, but it isn't supposed to mean secrets from each other. These are our brothers, and we're off on our own, without them. The discordance of that isn't easy on anyone."

Jasper looked over at him.

"Yes," he said slowly. "I can see how that would be true. Which of them would you tell everything that you know, if you were to tell anyone?"

Matthias scanned the room once more, nodding at this one and that one who caught his eye and returned his attention, then he shook his head, sitting over the table to look at Jasper.

"None," he said.

"Then we take the situation as it is, and not as we

wish it to be," Jasper said. "And as it is, we have a special role and our own brotherhood. We cannot wish it otherwise."

"Except me," Colin said.

"Do you think that one of us would fail to keep watch over Stacy, today?" Jasper asked. "As we confront the man who threatened her life two days ago? No. One of us would. You won by lot of condition, but this is not a wasted role, nor a created one. Someone must keep her alive, because she is going to keep Verida alive. Hold your ground, man, and respect that it's important ground to hold."

Colin sat up slightly.

"Yes, sir," he said. Jasper gave him a sharp nod.

"Then unless anyone else has good reason to delay further, I propose we go, before Palora can cause more problems. We take the problems to him."

"Wrap 'em up in a bow and leave 'em on his doorstep," Babe muttered.

"I can only hope that this is the day that we find the rest of the miserable creatures and end them," Sterling said.

"And open the port back up," Stasia added.

Jasper shook his head.

"We need to not get ahead of ourselves," he said. "This is likely to be little more than a bluff and an exchange of early words. A fight wouldn't be against our interests, but it's unlikely to happen for precisely that reason. Palora wants to use his advantages in secret, and against a great many people, not in a face-to-face battle with the likes of us."

"Person most likely to see them today is Colin," Matthias said.

The whole table turned, and Matthias shrugged.

"Don't you think?" he asked.

"Should I stay, then?" Babe asked.

Jasper considered Matthias for a long time.

"He isn't wrong," he murmured thoughtfully, then he

stood. "But Colin it will be, because we are hiding her away where no one is like to find her, and I need you with me to discourage an ambush at Lord Palora's house, should we be underestimating them."

Babe blew air through his lips, standing as well, along with the rest of the table.

"We took on bigger odds'n this, last time," he said. "Don't reckon I care how many of 'em there are."

"I do," Stasia interjected. "You guys need to pick your battles and do it right. All it took was one of them to stab you when you weren't ready for it."

Babe gave her a look that suggested that it had been a bit insulting to bring that up, just now, but Jasper nodded.

"The direction is set. Everyone is as careful as they can be, today. Colin and Stasia make a call on where to sleep, tonight, as they see fit to do it. Be unpredictable, and be smart. Good luck to us all."

Matthias motioned to Stasia, and she gave Babe a quick wave of goodbye, then followed Matthias down the stairs and across the yard.

"Do you know what it's about?" Stasia asked.

"No," Matthias said. "She just insisted that I catch you before you disappear for the day."

Stasia frowned. She'd just spoken to the queen. What could have changed in the last day that was so urgent?

She crossed the river and went into the castle with Matthias through the front gate.

One of the queen's ladies approached quickly.

"Queen Melody is in the back gardens," she said. "She's expecting you. Both."

Matthias gave her a slight but formal bow, and they went around the side of the castle, walking a long way through the gardens before they found Melody sitting on a bench by herself.

She lifted her face as Matthias approached.

"I need you to keep a good watch, please, Matthias," she said. "Ensure that no one is in hearing range of our conversation, if you will."

"Yes, mum," Matthias answered, giving her a much deeper bow and striding away again.

Stasia watched after him.

"Does he ever get tired of it, do you think?" Stasia asked. "Following you around all the time and not being able to do all of the things he used to?"

"Of course he does," Melody said. "I tire of it, and it's my life I'm living. Unfortunately, he is preternaturally good at it, which means that he will continue to do it until the stakes have dropped substantially. But that is not what I brought you here to talk about."

"The stakes?" Stasia asked. "What else is there?"

Melody nodded.

"I have word from the docks," she said. "Or, rather, Finwalk does. There are three large ships coming into port, heavy-laden with wheat from Boton. It will happen today. And we need that wheat to come off, no matter what happens. It is absolutely critical."

Stasia considered.

"Who ordered them?" she asked.

"We did," a voice said.

Stasia jerked her head as a young man in an ill-fitting linen shirt walked down a path toward her. He was accompanied by the biggest woman Stasia had ever seen. Not fat. Nothing resembling fat. But where Melody was tall in the way that calling her 'tall' in Verida might have been seen as an insult because it implied her lineage was elvish - oh, the irony - this woman was so wide at the shoulders and the chest that it couldn't have possibly invoked the willowy figure of elves. She was just... scaled up in every way, and Stasia found herself very distracted by her for several moments.

"Casset," she finally said, standing. "What are you doing here?"

He grinned.

"Just passing through," he said. "But I bring news from Katrina. She says it's gonna cost you an arm and a leg and a pretty lily to boot, but she needs Verida strong, and that means fed. When she heard that no one was managing to get in or out of Port Verida with wheat, she took it personal, and decided to make a go of this honest merchant thing for herself. She took the Flying Phoenix and the Bad Cat and the Indomitable and she took 'em up to Boton, filled 'em to brimming, and she's on her way here, now."

Melody turned her head to look at Stasia.

Stasia was... at a loss for words for several moments.

"Matthias knew he was here," Stasia said.

Melody nodded.

"Yes."

"And he know why he was here?" Stasia asked.

"Melody nodded again.

"Yes."

"But he didn't say anything to Jasper."

Melody pressed her lips.

"I believe it was Babe he wanted to avoid informing," she said. "He thought that Babe would either demand that he accompany you or that he and Jasper would agree to postpone today's work while they help you negotiate what's going to happen at the port. And while it is absolutely critical that this grain make land, it is also very critical that Jasper's squad complete their mission as quickly as possible, as well. I made a decision and Matthias followed my orders."

Stasia watched her for a moment, feeling betrayed and confused.

"But he only follows the king's orders," she said. "And he's Matthias. It means he agreed with you, too."

"I would not put the burden of this decision on him,"

Melody said. "I did not ask his opinion."

"Babe isn't going to forgive him," Stasia said.

"I do not require that he does," Melody answered. "These two events happened at the same time, and they are both critical. If we can get a flow of wheat into the city, the paths of producing flour are too myriad for any man to shut them down. This isn't enough, yet, but it may be the moment that breaks the market open, as everyone races to be the next ship to hit the port."

Stasia could see it.

She really could.

And she couldn't fault the queen for wanting Jasper's best men at Palora's. Even with what Matthias had said, Stasia thought that it was more important for Babe to be there with Jasper than with her.

They were drawing Palora's attention.

"Who knows about the wheat?" Stasia asked. "They found out about it, when I did it."

Melody looked over at Casset, who grinned again.

"Three pirate ships sailed into Boton Bay," he said. "We bought wheat. We don't exactly hand over a manifest and a shipping destination, when we do that."

"You really think this is a secret?" Stasia asked.

"And I think that there aren't many people who are going to turn aside these crews," Melody said. "They'll unload, if you can find people who will buy from them and resell."

They couldn't wander around the city, looking for brave millers.

It was just enough that Stasia worried that it might actually collapse the market. It was so tenuous, as it was.

But Melody was right. They couldn't turn it away, either.

"I'll figure it out," Stasia said.

She'd had weeks to plan, for her own grain, and it

was sitting - or still unloading - at the Black Docks into a warehouse, not doing anyone any good.

Was she going to get pirate grain to market before her own?

"I need you to send a message to Skite," Stasia said.

"I anticipate Lady Westhauser for tea this afternoon," Melody said. Stasia nodded.

"Tell her to tell Lord Westhauser that Pekins should go for broke."

Melody nodded.

"I will do that. Should I anticipate that cutting our teatime short?"

Stasia nodded.

"I would."

Casset straightened from where he'd been leaning against a tree.

"So is that it? Captain's wheat'll get unloaded, she'll get paid?"

Stasia didn't have the cash to buy four more shiploads of wheat.

She was going to have to figure out something.

"I'll make it work," she said, and he grinned.

"Then we're off," he said, looking around. "This place is crazy. Never seen anything like it in my life."

"I'll pass on your regards, thank you," Melody said.

He grinned and set off, the large woman following along beside him. She and Stasia met eyes for a moment, both of them curious, then Casset rounded a corner of the path and they were gone.

"Do you really believe you can do it?" Melody asked.

"Used to be, you just take it to the wholesale auction houses on the port row, and it's as easy as that, but most of them have closed down, and the ones that are still open don't have the audience to sell this much grain. I'm going to have to find someone else who can take it on, if I can even get it off the ships."

"It's an opportunity we cannot afford to lose," Melody said.

"I see that," Stasia answered. "Babe and Jasper aren't going to be happy with you."

"He said that he was less than half a day in advance of the ships," Melody said. "There is little time. I can't afford either of you to be distracted, so I cannot afford to be concerned with their opinions of my decisions."

Stasia sighed, then nodded.

"I've got a lot of work to do."

Colin was at the bar where she had met with Jasper and the rest of the squad, the morning before the queen had been attacked on the street by the warlocks.

Colin was just sitting at the bar, now, waiting for her. The place was deserted.

He rose when he saw her.

"You ready?" he asked.

She shook her head, and he frowned.

"What's going on?" he asked.

She looked around.

"News," she said.

"All right," he answered, turning to head for the back stairs.

She followed him up into the room above, which was empty save for a table and four bench seats.

"Talk," Colin said.

"There are three ships coming in to Port Verida with grain," she said. "And I have to figure out how to get them unloaded and sold without anyone interfering."

Colin blinked at her.

"How are you supposed to do that?" he asked.

She had an answer, but she didn't like it.

He raised his eyebrows at her.

"All this time, if you had a way to do it, wouldn't you think you'd have already done it?"

Palora is running off the merchants who are bringing it in by threatening them, here," Stasia said. "These are pirates..." She hesitated, astonished she was even saying the words. "... bringing in three ships' worth of grain to sell at market. So he doesn't have any leverage on them. If I can get there and find a way to keep the port master from preventing them from doing it, or whoever else might be involved... The next step is to find people to buy it from them..."

She shook her head.

The details were dizzying.

"All right," Colin said slowly. "And who's going to do that? Where are they going to put it? Why does Melody think that everything is going to change, just because the ships are coming? Today?"

Stasia sighed.

"Because I know they're coming," she said. "And Palora doesn't. And he doesn't have anyone to threaten until the grain is about to sell."

Colin spread his hands.

"Are you going to buy it?" he asked.

"No," Stasia said, finally, admitting defeat. "I'm going to ask my father to."

"Absolutely not," Minstrel Fielding said as she stood in his office at the ports. He hadn't been at home, but she knew where he shared a small office space with a few of the other very notable merchants. She'd spotted one of his runners and waylaid the young man, getting him to send a message that Stasia was waiting for him there. She let herself in - the security was incredibly lax because the space was basically only used for meetings during the day - and she and Colin were waiting for him when he arrived an hour later.

"Absolutely not," he said again for emphasis. "The grain trade in this city is polluted beyond recognition, and I do not play in markets that I don't understand what's going on there."

"Daddy, the city is starving," Stasia said.

His face softened.

"I know that, darling," he said. "And I'm very sorry that it's happening. I wish I could help. But someone else, who knows the market better, is going to buy that grain and sell it to them. I will not be involved in it. There is too much dark water involved."

"Dark water?" Colin asked.

"Unknown players," Stasia said without looking back at him. "I know, Daddy. But the dark water is winning, right now. I think that there is a lot of bad faith going around, politics and worse, and the merchants who are involved in the trade are manipulating it to their advantage, punishing the city. And I don't think that's the only place it's happening. You know it's true. You've known it for months. There are strange things going on, and it's smart to stay out of markets where they're being manipulated like that, because they can turn against you unexpectedly, but today it's right to play against them, and that's what I'm doing. I just... I don't have the capital nor the distribution resources."

"I'm not a distributor, Stasia," Minstrel said.

"I know," Stasia said. "And that's part of why this is so hard. I don't know which distributors I can trust. I suspect that most of the ones I could have trusted are out of business, now, which was part of the point. There's a cartel forming, and all of the honest players are victims to it. They're forcing men to join. But they can't do that to you, Daddy. Because you're too big and too independent and too honest..."

Something on his face twitched, and she stumbled back a step.

"Daddy?" she asked.

"Stasia," he said.

She frowned. Hard.

"Daddy," she said darkly.

"They said that you live alone in an apartment without a proper lock on the door," he said. "That they know where to find you and that..." He made a sound like his throat had closed. "... that I would never see you again. That your body would just drift out to sea."

He had always been a tall, strong man, in his way. Slender, but lean rather than skinny. He'd been upright. Proud of who he was and what that meant.

As she watched, his shoulders sagged forward and his back bent, like an old man under too much weight.

"Daddy," she said, stricken. "When I sent Sam to warn you...?"

He shook his head.

"I have been avoiding specific markets for many weeks," Minstrel said. "I would have warned you, but I knew..."

"You knew that she would dive in headfirst," Colin said.

Minstrel nodded, going to find a chair.

He collapsed into it, and Stasia stared at him, forlorn.

"Daddy," she said. "Did you really? Did you do what he told you to, even when you knew..."

"I knew it was dangerous," he said. "And I knew that... You were safe in Birch. Even when you went riding into Boton, no one knew who you were well enough to make trouble for you, and no one knew when or where to predict you. But Birch was safe. No one dared send trouble to Birch. And then we came here, and you... you just involved yourself in all of it, like a fish finding water for the first time, and you were so happy, and I was..." He lifted his eyes from the floor. "I was so proud of you, Anastasia. So proud. And I thought that we had found our way, and our place. And then... these terrible things that came with the war down out of the mountains, and... the threats..."

"You didn't know, at dinner that night," Stasia said. "With Babe. Did you? I would have known."

"I didn't know," he said. "I was still trying to understand. But then he came..."

"Palora," Stasia said darkly.

"Palora? Lord Palora?" Minstrel asked. "No the harbormaster came to me and told me that there were certain commodities that were off-limits to me, that they were being claimed by native Veridan merchants, and that if I complained to the queen or king, or so much as spoke of it and it came back to the nativist collective, they would very calmly hire an assassin to have you killed. What has Palora got to do with it?"

Stasia glanced at Colin.

"He's at the heart of it," Colin shrugged, going to get another chair and sitting it down at an angle to Minstrel's, just next to him. "Your daughter, if you'll forgive me saying this, is already up to her neck in all of this. She ran from Palora two nights ago. They were prepared to kill her then. So at this point you've got nothing to lose, helping us. They're working on breaking the power that Palora has, backing him, but your wonderful, lovely daughter has been waging an economic war on this city for weeks now, and she needs reinforcements. Given, right now, we don't know who's on our side and who's against us, she came to the one man she was certain she could trust. This is your moment to come through, sir, and there's nothing to lose, doing it."

"And what happened to you, then?" Minstrel asked.

"I'm a member of the King's Guard," Colin answered.

"I assume you know better than to dishonor me by suggesting the fact that I was injured in the line of duty is evidence that this enterprise is too dangerous. Because my life exists to serve the King's interests."

Minstrel looked at Stasia.

"Will you run?" he asked. "I'll put you on a boat, now, today, for Boton, and with you gone and... I'll get word to Alyssia and get her out of here, too, and then maybe..."

Stasia shook her head.

"No, Daddy. The city is starving. You don't get to get your daughters out of harm's way. There are ships coming in today, now, and they need to be paid and unloaded."

"The harbor master won't let you do it," Minstrel warned. "He'll label them plague ships and send them away again. He warns them first to just leave, and if they don't, he marks them."

Stasia knew that getting an official plague mark from a harbor master was all but death to a crew. Only a few ports would let them dock.

She looked at Colin again.

"Can't help you there," he said. "Don't know anything about it."

Stasia put her hands on her hips, angry and frustrated. She didn't know what Katrina would do, if her ship was marked, or threatened. She couldn't let it get that far. She had to come up with something.

And then her fingers found the pocket above her belt, and she tipped her head.

"Daddy, if I could get the wheat off the ships, would you warehouse it and see to transporting it or auctioning it? Would you stand up and show the rest of the merchant community that this is happening, and if they want to be a part of it now, while the profits are just... unthinkable... that this is the moment to take the risk and go for it?"

"I don't know, Anastasia," he said. "I don't know if I can do that."

Stasia pursed her lips and stood straighter.

"Minstrel Fielding, you have the resources to do nearly anything you choose. Find me a place to store this grain, procure the coins necessary to pay it off, and make it happen. I'm going to start unloading it within fifteen minutes of it making port, and I expect you to be prepared."

He looked up at her, almost amused if he weren't so grief-stricken.

"And what of your sister?" he asked. "Will you leave her fate to these terrible men?"

"I have it from the mouth of an assassin that the nobles don't like to fear death in their own homes, so they have an agreement to not attack each other at home. A convention. I'm concerned for her, yes, very much, but I believe that she is as safe as she can be, so long as she remains at the Gormand estate, and I have told her as much. Once this falls apart, Daddy, we can go after the men who threatened us. Threatened you. But we have to strike now. The food is here. The people need it. You have to take your stand now."

"You really believe you can get the grain off the ships?" Minstrel asked.

Stasia nodded.

"That's my part," she said. "You do your part, I'll do mine. If I fall through, you haven't done anything wrong, have you?"

He shook his head.

"You play a dangerous game, Anastasia."

"But I win," Stasia answered. "I'll be back here fifteen minutes after the ships make port. Be ready."

"I will, my darling. Stay safe, or all of this will have been for nothing, to me."

He stood and she hugged him, then rushed for the

door with Colin following quickly after.

"What are you going to do?" he asked.

"I need paper," Stasia said. "And a really nice pen."

"A really nice... what? Why does your father keep calling you Anastasia?"

She looked over at him and he grinned.

"Come on," he said. "I've got a friend who lives near here. I bet he's got pens."

"Lead on."

Colin had fancy friends.

The young man had greeted them at the door of a townhouse within sight of the ships' sails at the harbor. He wore a fine black suit with a crisp white shirt under it, and there was a fresh flower in the button hole on his right lapel. Stasia did her best not to stare at the white gloves he was wearing.

"Abline," Colin said cheerfully. "How are you this morning?"

"Colin," Abline answered with matching cheer. "I thought you were unavailable for the foreseeable future. I would have called on you. Hello, who is this?"

The two men hugged and Colin stepped sideways to indicate Stasia.

"Abline, this is Stacy Fielding, also known as Stasia Fielding-Horne. Ha, you thought I didn't know. Stacy, this is Abline Marque, a dear friend and very important gentleman in certain sub-districts bordering the docks."

Abline laughed.

"Are we off on an adventure, or can you come in for a sit?"

"Stacy actually needs to write a letter, and I immediately thought of that astonishing writing desk you bought last year. I'm certain it gets plenty of use, but I thought that maybe you wouldn't mind her borrowing it for a quarter hour or so?"

"Of course not, of course not," Abline said jovially, stepping back and to the side to invite them in. Colin put his hand on the small of Stasia's back to escort her into the home, which was strange, but she went with it, finding herself in a tidy and well-apportioned townhome of exactly the quality she would have anticipated, for as expensive as she knew the real estate was here.

"This way, please," Abline said, leading them up a set of narrow stairs to a second floor where there was a street-facing sitting room, and a small office looking back over the rest of the city. He took out an ink pot and a fountain pen, then opened another drawer to pull out a stack of fine linen paper.

"Will this suit?" he asked.

Perfectly, thank you," Stasia said. "Do you happen to have wax?"

"Of course," he said, opening a top drawer and taking out a selection of colors and putting the candle up to the lamp to light it. He got out a melting spoon, which Stasia didn't strictly need, but she appreciated the quality of it anyway, then stepped back again.

"I have burgundy ink, if you want to do something different," he said, and she shook her head.

"I'm afraid that would not only be unnecessary, but unappreciated," she told him. "Thank you."

"Then I will leave you to your correspondence," he said, turning to Colin. "I have Altan pears just off the ship, if you would like one."

"Second season," Colin said. "Of course."

Stasia looked back at them, amused and perplexed that Colin knew the seasonality of Altan fruit crops, but she turned to her work, writing a selection of letters and sealing them. She blew out the candle and put the supplies back away, then went downstairs to the sound of laughter as Colin and Abline told each other stories.

Colin dropped his foot off of a chair as she appeared, sucking juice off the core of a pear and then tossing it into a waste bin. He put his fingers into a basin there along the wall to rinse them off, then flicked the water off and turned to shake hands with Abline.

"Can't thank you enough," Colin said. "Might be some men by asking about us, or might not. You can tell 'em the truth or you can pull rank, up to you."

"I don't think I'll be in, later," Abline answered gladly. "So I'm afraid they'll have to call again another time."

He turned his attention to Stasia.

He came over to her and put one hand behind his back and the other out toward her, asking for her fingers.

She gave him her hand and he put the backs of her fingers to his lips in a low, angular bow, then he stood straight again.

"I am very glad to have met you, Miss Fielding-Horne," he said. "I hope you should find another excuse to call some time that you aren't quite so otherwise occupied."

She smiled.

Some men, it would have been an invitation with overtones, but Abline was of a breed of dandy who was simply happy to see everyone and sad to see them go. He meant nothing by it but that he genuinely hoped to see her again.

"Perhaps Verida isn't such a big city as I thought," she answered, and he grinned.

"Very well said," he told her, turning to shake hands with Colin once more.

"Whatever this infernal business that you've got going on, I do hope you wrap it up quickly so that you can go out with us again soon."

"You no more than me," Colin answered. "Heather sends her love."

Abline gave him a little bow, then escorted them to the door again.

Stasia looked over her shoulder as he closed the door behind them, then looked at Colin.

"Do you have a surname, Colin?" she asked.

He hesitated, smiling off and away from her, then he nodded.

"Havenport."

Stasia knew of the Havenports.

"Why doesn't anyone use it?" she asked.

"Because it's distracting," he said. "Why do you let us call you Stacy?"

"Because you called me Stacy at the first and I kind of liked it, having a Verida name."

He nodded.

"I have a guard name. It's not a secret, and the guys all know, but the Havenports don't have anything to do with the job."

"But why didn't you tell me?" she asked.

He looked over.

"What name do you prefer?" he asked.

"What do you mean?"

"I call you Stacy. Babe calls you Stasia, anymore. Your father called you Anastasia. The queen calls you Fielding. Ella calls you Fielding-Horne. Which one of those is you?"

"They all are," Stasia said. "I don't mean to be confusing."

He nodded.

"Colin is who I am. Havenport is... who I was. A long, long time ago. I'm not ashamed of it, and I still have dinner with my folks as close to once a week as I can manage it. My brother and I play field ball up at the big court up north whenever we get time, and I go to the theater with my sister every time her favorite troupe puts on a new play. My sister's kids are... actually really clever, interesting individuals. But I'm just Colin. That's which one I am."

Stasia frowned at the road ahead of them.

"I barely know you at all," she said. "I barely know any of you."

He shoved her with his shoulder playfully.

"You think you know me less than Abline does?" he asked. "Or my sister? We are what we are, Stacy, and that's who we are with each other. Doesn't matter how we got here, and it doesn't matter what faces we put on with other people. You're part of the squad, and you're one of us. It means you know all of the pieces that matter."

She looked over at him.

"I want to meet Heather," she said, and he grinned.

"Any time." He paused. "Just don't tell her too many stories about before. She knows most of it, but there are some of them I'm still working up to."

She raised an eyebrow at him, and he ducked his head.

"Stuff is weird."

She nodded.

It was.

She looked in the direction of her father's office, feeling profoundly sad again.

"I can't believe he would do that," she said.

"Where are we headed?" Colin asked.

"Portside," she said. "I'm going to go watch the ships come in."

They took up seats portside, and Stasia remembered for the first time that she was supposed to be hiding.

Well, at least she didn't think that the warlocks were going to think to come look for her at a dockside bar, eating hot bread and drinking weak beer.

"What does a pirate ship look like, anyway?" Stasia asked. "Do they fly a specific flag? Or put skulls on the rails or something?"

Colin laughed.

"I suspect that the skulls would smell bad," he said. "I've never seen one, though, so you can never be sure."

They sat and ate and chatted for about an hour, watching as the smaller ships came and left. The port was quiet by any standard, and the sailors weren't walking past, laughing and talking like they usually did. The ships just sat there at the docks, kind of easing up and down, rolling with the waves where the Sorbine met the Wolfram, canvas rippling in the breeze just enough to make noise now and again.

"I remember my first day here," Stasia said after a while. "Boton Bay is bigger than this, but Port Verida was just so completely stuffed with activity. I didn't want to be here, but I admired how much they'd managed to cram into so little space, here, given that they had to dig out the entire port."

Colin looked out over the water and nodded.

"And now..."

He shook his head.

"And now we've scared all of that life off," she said. "It makes me so angry, to see something so healthy go dead like this. It's like... you can't just fix it at the end, you know? You can only hope that it grows back to what it was. It's so easy to kill something compared to trying to grow something."

Colin sighed, then nodded again, propping his temple up on his fist as he looked into his beer and set it back down on the counter.

"The problem with all of this is that the guard can't do anything, really, to grow something. We're, all of us, looking at you to fix it when it's all done. Aren't we?"

She blinked, still angry at how quiet the docks were, here in the middle of just an ordinary day, and comparing them to her first memories of almost getting knocked into the water because they couldn't get two carts past each other on the dock with Schotzli trying to get around them without letting them bump into her.

"What they're counting on is that when it grows back, they'll have been in charge the whole time, and they get to take all the profits," she said. "But I'm not going to let that happen. This place is too important to let some small group of men be in charge."

She heard Colin laugh quietly, then pick up his beer once more.

"And that's why none of us are worried about it all that much," he said. "It's in good hands."

She stood, watching the horizon.

"That's a ship," she said.

"A big one," Colin said without standing.

She'd mistaken the sails for clouds, at first, but as they came over the horizon, the shape of the mast became clear.

Fifteen minutes after that, another ship hit the horizon, and ten minutes after, a third. They were traveling together.

The first ship was getting close to the port, now, and Stasia waited to be certain which pier it would be docking alongside before she set off, Colin a step behind her as she went.

The frontmost ship was beautiful.

Stasia often admired the craftsmanship that went into the finishing details of ships and the technological elegance in their fundamental design, but the Flying Phoenix

- for that was without a doubt which ship this was, from the figurehead - was beautiful even beyond ships' standards. She had a sleek look to her, despite how much larger she was than all of the other ships, save the ones designed for going to the dark side of Dernat.

Stasia stood on the dock, waiting as the pirate sailors on the ship threw down mooring lines to the dock staff to tie off the ship.

The gangplank came over the side of the ship and a woman stood up at the top of it, looking down at Stasia.

The harbormaster was approaching quickly with a ledger in his arms, and Stasia looked over at him.

"He's coming to threaten you," Stasia called up to the woman without looking at her. "Just so you know."

"I'd like to see him do it while looking me in the eye," the woman answered.

Stasia smiled.

"Permission to come aboard?" Stasia called, looking up at her. "With my friend, Colin, of the King's Guard."

"Announce yourself," the woman said.

"I'm Anastasia Fielding-Horne," Stasia said. "Head of the Queen's Guard."

The woman looked down at her, taking measure of her, then nodded.

"I assume this conference needs to be quick, then," the woman said, and Stasia nodded.

"Come aboard," she said. "Teal, slow him down."

"Yes, Captain," a thick-bodied man said, coming into view and starting down the gang plank.

Stasia let him past, then went up with Colin behind her.

Katrina Swift was a tall woman. Not quite as tall as Queen Melody, Stasia thought, but with a great hat on that made her seem considerably taller, yet. She wore a long, bright red coat with brass buttons on it, and carried a long saber of a sword on her left hip.

"Anastasia," the woman said. "I would have pegged you as nobody of consequence."

Stasia blinked quickly, remembering, then grinned at the memory.

"One and the same, ma'am," she said. "I spoke to Casset this morning."

Katrina shook her head, looking out over the city.

"A city this size, and that man manages to find the same girl twice. Only my first mate. Please come with me."

She turned and led the way to a door under the raised deck of the forward-facing side of the ship, opening it and letting the two of them through.

Stasia found a very nice chair in front of a table, there, and Katrina walked past, hanging her hat on a peg and going to sit on a velvet bench that ran along the front edge of the room, under a wide window that had view of the figurehead. Stasia sat across from her. Colin went to stand by the door.

"I'm here because Verida is starving, and a starving city cannot buy the goods that I steal from their increasingly impoverished merchants," Katrina said.

"Oh," Stasia answered. "I'm... Look, I'm glad you're here, but I'm just here to set a price for your grain and tell you that the harbormaster is here to make threats about marking your ship as a plague ship if you attempt to unload any of it."

Katrina had been getting out a bottle of goldbrew, but she stopped.

"He's what?" she asked.

Stasia nodded.

"He wants you to turn back. I need to get to the other ships, too, before he sends them away."

"They won't leave without my orders," Katrina said. "Why are they sending away food?"

Stasia shrugged.

"Power."

The woman shifted, moving smoothly again to uncork the bottle and take three glasses out of a little cabinet behind her head.

"How interesting," she said. "I need you to tell me more about this."

Stasia shook her head.

"I'm sorry, I really don't have time. Do you want me to make an offer on the wheat, or do you want to tell me your opening price?"

Katrina went still again, looking at her curiously.

"Casset spoke of you little," she said finally, setting the glasses down in front of her and pouring three. Stasia felt bad. She was not drinking that. "But what he did say was that you were compelling and to the point. Compel me."

"If that man gets here and your... Teal doesn't keep him from trying to stop the ship from unloading by any means necessary, he is going to mark you as a plague ship, and I cannot get the grain off of here, after that. I can deal with him, but first I need an agreement from you that I am going to buy this wheat at a fixed price per weight. I will send someone to you later with coin to finish the deal, and he will provide the means to transport it at that time. I will do my best to be here when that happens, but as you might imagine, I have a lot of other places I need to be today. The man who hands you the coin is free to send the wheat wherever he likes it, as far as I am concerned. I just need a price."

Katrina picked up her glass and swirled it, glancing over at Colin.

"And who is he?"

"Today, he's keeping me alive," Stasia said.

"You have injured bodyguards as your best option?" Katrina asked.

"My injured man is going to kill a lot more people

than the average bodyguard," Stasia answered. "The uninjured options are off doing more important things than even this. Price, please, ma'am."

Katrina nodded and stated a price.

Any other month Stasia had been alive, it would have been extortion. Right now, it was going to give her father an easy fifty percent markup, even at the very end of the sale. Starting off, he might get four times that.

"And does that extend to the other ships, or am I negotiating with them individually?" Stasia asked.

"Their cargo belongs to me," Katrina asked. "I'm just... employing their services to transport it."

Stasia named another number, twenty percent lower - she just couldn't help herself - and Katrina considered it, then nodded.

"Very well. But I want it all in coin. None of this paper nonsense that you land folk deal with."

"Of course," Stasia said, taking out the contract and looking around. Katrina produced a pen and Stasia put in the sale price, noting with the pen the names of the three ships, that they would be weighed out at the port scales for final price with the estimated first half paid upfront. Standard contract terms. She calculated the estimated first half, then signed it and handed Katrina the pen. The pirate queen looked at her quizzically once more, then also signed. Stasia rolled the paper and put it away, standing.

"I am glad to have done business with you," Stasia said.

"I would say that I very much wish to speak with you after this is all over," Katrina said. "Because I do not understand what has just happened. But I suspect that I cannot command that audience, can I?"

Stasia looked at the glass of goldbrew.

"No," she said. "I am afraid I am otherwise engaged, this evening, and I can't imagine that a pirate such as yourself has any desire to remain at port for much longer than she absolutely needs, do, would she?"

Katrina smiled.

"No. No, indeed. Watch for my man, though. I may send you correspondence at some point through him. It isn't very often that people interest both Casset and myself."

Stasia gave her a little bow and turned for the door.

Colin sneaked over to the table and tipped back the third glass of goldbrew.

"Mmm," he said. "I knew it by the smell that that was a good pour. Thank you, Captain."

Katrina gave him a little nod, then Colin raced forward to get the door and open it for Stasia.

"You sure you've got this?" he murmured to her as they walked back across the deck. "I could pull rank as Guard."

"Only as a last resort," Stasia murmured back. "If I fail, I doubt you're going to have much luck."

They went quickly down the gang plank, finding the big man called Teal shouting at the harbormaster and his two assistants down on the dock.

"Sir," Stasia said as the red-faced harbormaster stuck his finger in Teal's chest. Stasia wouldn't have done that. Not for anything. Teal wasn't as big as Babe, but he didn't have Babe's placid nature, either. There was a moment that she was certain that Teal was about to take a swing at the harbormaster, and then a voice called from the deck.

"Teal," Katrina said, her voice low and even, but incredibly commanding. "Return to your station."

Teal gave the harbormaster a good, hard glare before going back up the gang plank and past Katrina.

"Very good," the harbormaster said. "Now, as to the matter of the goods on board..."

"Sir," Stasia said, again, louder this time.

He ignored her, heading for the gang plank.

Colin dodged in front of him, tipping his head to the side and indicating Stasia with his arm.

"She needs a moment of your time, if you don't mind," he said.

The harbormaster shuffled uncomfortably, but in the end he was unwilling to go against a direct request from a man in a brown leather uniform.

Colin flicked his eyebrows at Stasia with humor, and she attempted not to smile.

Point, Colin.

The harbormaster looked over his shoulder at Stasia.

"What is it?" he asked, sounding put-upon.

"I have orders," Stasia answered, taking out the second of the papers she'd written.

He drew a short sigh and came to take it.

He glanced at the wax seal as he took out a dull knife from his belt to break it open, then he looked at it again.

And again.

He turned it in the light, putting it within an inch of his eyes, then he looked at her.

"This is the queen's seal," he said.

"It is," Stasia answered. "Would you like to start over, perhaps?"

He used the knife to lift the wax seal off of the paper more carefully as Colin's eyes got wide, over the man's shoulders. He was staring hard at Stasia.

Stasia ignored him.

To whom it may concern,

The ships identified by the head of the Queen's Guard, Miss Anastasia Fielding-Horne, are of critical importance to the city and the crown and are not to be interfered with under any circumstances. Any other orders from any other member of Veridan society will be countermanded in this situation, or it will be considered a direct action against the Queen.

Please show utmost cooperation and respect to Miss Fielding-Horne as she goes about her business, and prevent any and all other parties from interfering with her.

Thank you and good day.

Stasia hadn't signed it. That had felt like counterfeiting something. But she had the seal and she had the title, and she wasn't lying in anything she'd written.

She waited.

Colin read over the harbormaster's shoulder, his eyes growing larger by the moment, and then a great grin spreading across his face.

The harbormaster looked at the seal once more.

"Is this a trick?" he asked.

"No," Colin answered. "That is the queen's seal."

"It's not forged?" the harbormaster asked.

Colin looked at Stasia, who shook her head. His eyes went wide again, and he grinned.

"No," Colin said. "It isn't."

The harbormaster looked from the letters to his assistants, then shook his head.

"Well," he said. "You've read it, same as me. Leroy, you stay here and make sure that no one interferes with the proper unloading of this ship. Vince, you stand at the head of the pier. If anyone who might have argument with this shows up, you direct him to me."

"I will be sending someone here with payment and directions for the destination of the unloading of this ship and two others," Stasia said, indicating the second ship as it presently moored nearby and the third one, visible in beautiful detail as it drew ever closer to Port Verida.

"Yes, miss," the harbormaster said. "I will get two of my other men to stand guard on these ships, as well. Yes, miss."

He looked at the letter again, then bustled away, leaving the young man Leroy to absurdly stand guard at a gangplank overseen by pirates.

Colin hustled Stasia away from the gangplank and out of earshot.

"Why do you have the queen's seal?" he asked quietly.

"She gave it to me," Stasia answered. "Beyond that, I don't think I have a reason you need to know."

He grinned.

"You could have told me," he said.

"Would you have been comfortable with me using it?" she asked.

He paused.

"It depends on why she gave it to you," he answered.

"And I won't tell you that," Stasia answered.

"Did you just use the queen's seal fraudulently?" Colin asked.

"I'll have to ask her and find out," Stasia said. She got out the copy of the letter and handed it to him. "You can verify that that is an identical copy to what I handed to the harbormaster."

He read it quickly and nodded.

"I can."

"Then you hold on to it and when and if it comes up, you can be my witness to what I just did."

He shook his head.

"It doesn't keep everything safe once it gets off the ships," he said.

"One step at a time," Stasia said. "I have a contract to go show to the other pirate captains, and then we have to go find my father and tell him the price I got."

Colin hesitated, looking back at Katrina as she stood, watching them from aboard the ship.

"I drank with a pirate," he said.

"You did," Stasia answered, setting off toward the second ship.

"Babe is gonna be furious," Colin said. "I drank with a pirate."

Stasia grinned.

"Let's hope we're all still in one piece to tell each other about it tonight."

He nodded and hopped to catch up with her.

"I drank with a pirate."

The other two captains were just as interesting as Katrina was. The captain on the Bad Cat, Skinny Andrew, was tall and lean and muscular, and looked at her the entire time like she was trying to get away with something. The captain on the Indomitable was quiet and calculating with little motions like a mouse counting coins. He didn't introduce himself and he didn't invite Stasia on board, but he did agree that he would start getting the grain ready for unloading and when a man came by with the signed agreement that the estimated payment had been made, he would allow that man to direct the rest of the unloading.

"This might actually work," Colin said as they went to go find Stasia's father at his office again.

"Just keep moving," Stasia told him. "There are still plenty of pieces to fall apart."

Minstrel Fielding was in his office with four of his most consistent trading partners, arguing over details that were just musical, in Stasia's ears. Which warehouses had space, which cartmen were still in business and could be rallied on no time at all, which auction houses would be willing to take large-lot grain sales this afternoon?

"Have you sent messengers to the local markets that you're doing the auctions?" Stasia asked at a lull.

The five men looked at her, and Minstrel put out a hand.

"My daughter, Stasia," he said. "She's the one who has procured this, and has been developing a rather deep awareness of the local market structures within Verida for delivery models."

"I can't afford to do local delivery models," one of the men said. "We're talking about bulk quantities that do not absorb, at that level."

"So break them up," Stasia said. "If you can't find people willing to do the transit work for you, tell the people who are desperate for the final product and let them figure it out."

Another of the men looked at her.

"They don't want grain," he said. "They want flour."

"Also their problem, once you sell it to them," Stasia said. "They can take it up to the mills, or they can hire someone who's willing to run one on ox-power locally for the time being. They aren't that hard to set up. They need product. They don't need you to figure out how to get all of the rest of the pieces to work."

The men looked at Minstrel, who shrugged.

"Any arguments?" he asked.

"I'll get foot messengers running," the third man said, one that Stasia knew from meals. He was one of Minstrel's closer friends.

"Now," Stasia said, stepping forward. "Everyone here knows that there have been threats pertaining to this particular cargo, is that correct?"

The men shifted uncomfortably and Stasia looked at Minstrel as she went on.

"I don't know which of you have been threatened,

but I'm going to assume that it's all of you. Because you are the kind of men who would see the way the market is behaving and you would respond by finding new supplies for all manner of things the city is hurting for right now. And you haven't. Which means that each of you is likely afraid of what's going to happen when we do this, and you may even be considering bailing out or betraying us to the men who are making these threats, in hopes of saving yourselves and your loved ones." She paused. "I see no dishonor in protecting your families. But if you want out, you should leave now and forget that these conversations ever happened, as we will forget that we ever saw you."

"Stasia," Minstrel said. "You are speaking to my friends as though they are children."

"And yet, we've been acting like scared children while your daughter has gone around the city making things happen that none of us could have conceived of," her father's dinner friend said. "Perhaps we deserve it."

"We will secure the shipments," the second one said. "We have already discussed this, and the conclusion must be that none of us anticipate living and working in a city that is better for the way the new men intend to run it, and if we are going to avoid that happening, we must be involved in the fight against them."

Minstrel nodded.

"This is our consensus," he said. "We are ready."

"Okay, then," Stasia said, getting out the contract copy and the one that established payment. She handed them to her father and he glanced through them quickly, nodding.

"I see," he said.

"Do you have it all in coins?" Stasia asked, and he glanced at her with a raised eyebrow.

"Have I given you such cause to doubt me?" he answered. "I am taking up fifty percent of the shipment, and the others are taking a quarter apiece of the remainder. We are going to get everything unshipped as quickly as possible, but the professional concerns that do such things are largely defunct, so we are stringing together solutions as quickly as we can."

"We need to move," Stasia said. "Get everyone going that you can, add solutions as you find them."

Minstrel looked around the room.

"Are we prepared for the consequences of this action?" he asked.

There was a long silence.

"They don't like seawater," Colin finally said. "Put everyone you need to keep safe onto a ship and send them on a Pirate Island vacation. If that's what you've got to do. But go now. We don't have much time before this gets out and the consequence start happening hard and fast."

Stasia nodded.

"I'm going to go get a cart," she said. "Because if there's nothing else for me to be doing, I'm hauling grain. Have a destination ready for me when I get back."

The merchants nodded and Minstrel started for the door.

"It begins," he said.

"Are you sure about this?" Colin asked as they walked. "You did your part. This is the point where you were supposed to be off hidden somewhere. Jasper and Babe are not going to like it."

"I have carts," Stasia said. "The city is run on carts, but they aren't running like they used to. They still exist out there, somewhere, so when things get going again, they'll all come back, but when you're fighting a freeze, you need all the motion you can get. If I'd have known about this yesterday, I would have pulled every cart I own to come down here and help."

"It's only a matter of time before they find out that it's happening," Colin said.

"Wouldn't it be marvelous if we had the ships unloaded and the grain tucked away by then," Stasia answered.

"Everyone is going to know where the grain is," Colin said.

"So we'll protect it as fiercely as we can and sell it faster," Stasia answered. "The mills are going to run full time, and anyone with two big stones and an ox is going to be trying to figure out how to make flour out of them. It's not going to crater the price of wheat, because we still don't have an adequate supply out of the estates, but it's going to move things. And if we can get this moving, we can get other things moving... this is the thing that's going to trigger the slide. I can feel it. Can't you? That's why Palora is fighting it so hard. It's been too long and the city hasn't caved, and his men are feeling antsy, sitting on all those lucrative resources... If we start dropping the price of grain, they'll panic and sell and..." She looked over at him, feeling breathless. "We win."

"I get it," Colin said. "Well, no, actually I don't, but I get that you get it. But we should be hiding under the library at the university, right now."

"We... what?" Stasia asked.

He grinned.

"I used to hang out down there when I was at university," he said. "I remember thinking at the time that you could search the entire city twice and you'd never find someone, hiding out there. That was my plan for today. They've got beds down there in this room that someone put a bunch of book cases in front of, and you have to know it's there, but it's where students used to crash when they were studying, I guess, years and years ago, and now it's just..."

"Something only a few uncharacteristically curious people know about," Stasia said, and he nodded.

"It's a good idea," Stasia said. "I'm sorry I didn't get to use it. But this is... this is where I need to be."

He nodded.

"I'll go with you," he said. "I'll even be proud to have been a part of it. But when Babe and Jasper hear about it..."

"You want me to lie and say that I made you do it at knifepoint?" she asked.

He laughed.

"Would you?" He paused. "No, wait, actually get out your knife. I can't lie anymore."

She didn't like playing with blades just for the fun of it, but he was playfully in earnest, so she took out the blocking blade from Babe and pointed it at him.

"Cooperate," she said. "Or else."

Colin stepped into the dagger, to where it pressed against his leathers with real force, though the tempered leather was much too tough to give, yet.

"But it goes against everything I know my commanding officer would want me to do," he protested.

"Too bad," Stasia snarled, enjoying herself.

He grinned.

"That'll about do it," he said, and she put the dagger away.

They got to the livery stable and put the mare there into traces. Stasia had all of her dual-animal carts up north, ready to move the grain up there. Tomorrow, she was pulling all the stops. If Palora was going to stop her, he was going to have to stop her everywhere. For today, she'd have to rely on what Pekins could do on his own.

The mare had already done her route for the day, and Stasia felt a bit bad, taking her out again, but she'd get an extra measure of oats for her trouble, and she wasn't an old nor a broken animal. She was happy to see Stasia, and she went to work willingly, walking ahead of the empty cart.

Colin walked on the other side of the mare's head, back down to the port. As they got close, the conversation around them stirred, people whispering and talking, running and shouting, catching up to each other to whisper again.

The rumor mill was astir.

Before long, they started passing carts laden with bags of grain, boys running along yelling, and the rumor mill grew louder.

Stasia looked across at Colin, grinning.

It was happening.

Two ports bringing in grain, sending it everywhere. Like the river itself, there was no way you could stop it.

It would just burst out somewhere else.

She was going to win this.

She got to the port proper and found her father directing cart men. Everything was chaotic, but he seemed completely comfortable and in his element.

They would probably have whole carts' worth of grain go missing today, but they could afford it, and as far as Stasia was concerned, that was probably for the best. More rivulets of supply off where they were harder to stop.

He waved at her and pointed.

"Flying Phoenix," he called. He took a paper out of a stack in his hand and caught the attention of a boy running past, pointing at Stasia. The boy took the card and ran it over to Stasia, handing it to her with a little head-bob, then running off again.

She looked at the address there, smiling.

He had a system.

She had no idea what he was doing for accountability, beyond that, but she suspected there was an established port system in play, and that it simply didn't apply to her because she wasn't going to run off with the grain.

And if she did, he didn't care.

They walked out to the Flying Phoenix, where pirates were unloading grain from an on-ship crane system, getting the carts filled with grain one by one. She was in a line of six standing carts, and it took perhaps twenty minutes to get to the front of the line. The boardwalk here was wide enough to turn a cart around and come back the opposite direction. They loaded the cart and she turned, heading back to shore and then off toward the address her father had given her with a thinner but very present line of carts going along in the same direction.

It was happening.

They unloaded the grain at the warehouse, where men were already standing around outside with much smaller carts, their eyes alight with hope.

Dealers, millers, restaurant owners.

Word was spreading.

It was happening fast, and Stasia realized abruptly that if these men knew that the grain was here, anyone else in the city might know, too.

And the warlocks, of all people, were going to be paying attention to such things, if they really did work for Lord Palora.

She looked over at Colin as the men got to her cart and unloaded it.

"It occurs to me that this is spreading fast," she said.

"Library sounding like a good idea, yet?" he asked.

She looked at the cartmen, as they turned to go back to the port and pick up another load, another payment, and she shook her head.

"We just need to be ready," she said. "In case they come here ready to try to shut it down."

"If he was going to send special assets to take down warehouses full of grain, he would have done it before now," Colin said, intentionally ambiguous, and Stasia shook her head.

"I'm not so sure," she said. "Before, he was still just fighting with me. Today? This is a problem that's going to blow everything up immediately, if he doesn't get it under control."

"Look, I'm game," Colin said. "But you really shouldn't count on me for a lot. I can fight left-handed, but that's only worth something against someone who wasn't as good as me, to start with."

She looked over again, rubbing the mare's nose as she thought.

"What are we going to do, if they show up?" she asked.

Colin looked sideways at her.

"Unfortunately, we're about to find out."

He took hold of the mare's reins and turned the cart, walking down a wide-for-Verida alley and turning at the end of it into a narrower alley that was dark from the two lines of buildings that backed up to it. The mare began to struggle to get the cart wheels over the bits of trash, there in the alley, but Colin asked her to stop before Stasia was ready to give up on it.

He breathed gently, dropping his hand.

"They're here," he said. "You were right. Apparently this is where they make their stand."

A man stepped out of the deep shadows ahead of them, two long daggers in his hands and a leather pouch at his hip.

"Well, well," he said. "We've been waiting for the right time to meet you. Tillith had such an interest in you, we couldn't understand why, but now it appears we aren't going to be able to discuss things with you to our satisfaction before we kill you. It truly is a shame."

"He's talking to me, isn't he?" Stasia asked.

"I don't know anybody named Tillith," Colin

answered. "Was that the guy you embarrassed, getting away from him not once, but twice?"

Another shadow detached from the wall, a tall woman who was looking at her fingers as she worked them in the air.

Stasia looked at the wall.

She could go up.

Babe would tell her it was what she was supposed to do. Make it so that Colin didn't have worry about her.

The problem was that Skite could climb.

She had an instinct that that wasn't just a Skite thing, though it could have been, but more of an assassin thing. Because she could see how that would be useful, in general.

And if she got up too high on a wall and one of them followed her up, pulling someone down from over your head was trivially easy, and that was... well, all ways of dying seemed undesirable to her, but that was one she really didn't like the idea of.

So she stayed on her feet as the tall woman stepped into the weak light coming down from between the buildings overhead.

She blew through her fingertips, looking at Stasia with that odd, inhuman expression.

"I should have come to you in your sleep," she murmured as something looking like dust swirled within the curl of her hand. "Your breath goes in, your breath goes out, and then never again returns. Such a... quietness to it."

She blew through her hand once more, and the dust scattered toward them. Stasia tried to block with her arm, but there wasn't much value to that. The cloud expanded and washed over them, invisible but for an idea of it at this distance, and the mare sagged, falling to her knees and then hanging from the cart harness with her face sideways on the ground. She was completely motionless.

Stasia looked over at the animal, startled and grief-stricken, but Colin stepped forward, drawing his sword.

"I'm afraid you're going to find we're both stronger than that," he said.

"She didn't deserve that," Stasia said, turning her attention back to the warlocks.

"She served the wrong side," the woman said, reaching into a bag passively.

There was a third set of footsteps behind them and Stasia turned to watch as a man climbed the back tail of the cart, up and over, walking through the bed of it and watching Stasia. He had a sword.

Stasia drew her own.

Well.

Three against two, the three being the strongest, fastest, and most powerful manner of human creature Stasia had ever heard of, and the two being Stasia and an injured Colin.

Stasia glanced once more at the mare, wondering why that was the part of this that she regretted the most, then went to put her back to the wall. Colin glanced over at her, but didn't react.

"If you're interested in surrendering at this point, I'm willing to discuss it," Colin said. "But I've got to warn you that you shouldn't expect any offers, after this. The consensus is that the only safe warlock is a dead warlock, after the bad turn of events with the last guy Stacy over there adopted."

Stasia watched the man climb off the front of the cart, his feet finding the cobbles like he hadn't noticed the cart going by, sword out. The man with the daggers had stopped, about two body lengths away from Colin and Stasia, just waiting as the woman worked something new in her fingers.

Stasia turned her attention back to the man with the sword.

With anyone else, she would have expected some phantom of emotion on his face, pleasure at having her cornered and knowing she was an inferior opponent, grim focus at the business of taking life, curiosity at what she would do. There was none of that.

He swung the sword and she blocked.

One.

She'd blocked once.

She was pretty proud of that.

He attacked her side and she blocked again, the blocking dagger finding itself in her hand to form the cross to control where his blade ended up.

She had no space to retreat.

With three of them, it had been the right decision - the man with the daggers certainly didn't look like he would hesitate to stab her in the back if he got a chance at it - but it left her no allowance for mistakes or for him to overpower her.

She counter-attacked.

Why not?

He blocked easily, and she stepped to the side, hitting at him again.

He blocked again.

No curiosity, no pleasure, no nothing.

It was deeply unsettling.

There were noises, elsewhere, but Stasia was facing the man who was likely going to kill her, so she didn't worry all that much about what was going on in the rest of the alley.

She wished good things for Colin, but they'd invested themselves into an outcome - no point evaluating it, now - and now they were paying for the chances that they'd taken.

Did she wish she was under the library?

Hard to say.

If she was, the mare would be in her stall at the barn.

Funny, again, how that tipped things for her.

She blocked and stepped sideways a fraction again. The man took a big step to the side, cutting off the path along the cart toward the open alley, where she could have backed away from him.

There was another ghost of something going past, and Stasia blocked three fast attacks, then missed a fourth, which hit her in the arm hard enough that her hand went fuzzy, but the dragonskins held.

The blocking dagger fell to the ground as her grip failed her, and the sword hit her again in the side under her elbow, knocking the air out of her. Once more, the dragonskins held, but she was struggling to keep her sword between herself and the warlock as he raised his arm again to strike her.

He was going to beat her to death, or he was going to find exposed skin and...

Sounds.

His head twisted and Stasia bent double, trying to force her body to draw air again.

Was it magic?

Had the woman actually stolen her breath?

Could she even still breathe?

The stroke across her back never came.

There were more noises and she realized what she'd heard.

Not this time.

Nor the time before.

The time before that.

That had been hoofbeats.

Big ones.

She staggered against the wall lifting her face as the man Stasia had been fighting turned to face the men dismounting on the far side of the cart.

Babe and Sterling were already moving, Sterling

coming at the man with the sword with the sense of lightning skipping across the surface of the ocean.

Jasper was shouting directions, many of them aimed at Colin.

Was Colin alive?

Over there.

Still upright.

Stasia held her stomach, air finally sucking into her body with the sound of a sob that she hadn't intended.

"Get her," Jasper said, riding past the cart on Olivet, sword drawn, face set.

Babe was at her shoulder.

"How bad?" he asked.

She swallowed, finding tears streaming down her face. It wasn't pain or fear. It was just this strange physical reaction to the blow to her side.

She brushed them off, shaking her head.

"Kill them all."

He nodded, pushing her behind him and pointing.

"Stay with the horses," he said.

She went over to where Peter and Gladys stood, pressing her back against Peter's chest and hugging her arms.

The woman directed her attention to Jasper and Olivet, and Stasia braced, trying not to look at the sagging mare attached to the cart.

Even if Jasper survived, losing Olivet...

The woman put her arms out, shouting words at him, but Jasper and Olivet scarcely slowed. The man with the daggers realized, too late, what was about to happen, and moved to intervene, but Olivet went up on his hind legs, striking the casting woman in the chest twice and coming down on her.

Stasia was glad that it was too dim to see what happened after that, but Jasper and Olivet weren't done. They spun to face the man with the daggers, a flurry of activity happening between Sterling and the man with the sword that Stasia couldn't focus on as she watched Jasper and Olivet.

The man shouted at them, then stepped swiftly to the side and plunged one of the daggers into Olivet's chest as the gelding shoved him with the same motion.

The man fell and Jasper was on the cobbles in a sweeping motion, sword out.

Once more, Stasia was glad she couldn't see the result of what happened to the man with the daggers, but even as Jasper was attacking the man on the ground, Olivet spun toward the woman again.

Stasia had once watched a field mule - one of the really big working animals let out to pasture outside of Boton - go after a coyote that would have been a threat to the calves in the same field.

The coyote was ferocious and angry, but he had nothing on the mule. It had pinned its ears back and chased the coyote to the edge of the field, actually cutting it off and attacking it directly. If Stasia hadn't seen it with her own eyes, she wouldn't have believed the malice in the ordinary working animal. He'd caught the coyote with a front-footed blow to the face, and the predator had gone down. The mule had pounced, not giving an inch, and had pancaked it with a truly absurd show of grudge against the animal, long after it must have been dead.

So it was with Olivet.

The great gelding trod on the warlock woman while Jasper put an end to the man with the daggers and Sterling and Babe closed in on the swordsman and put him down two, three, four times. Each time he got up, he found Sterling and Babe waiting there to put him down again.

Finally, he didn't get up again.

Jasper straightened and put his sword away as Olivet made motions like he was scraping off his feet on the cobbles.

"He's hurt," Stasia called. "Olivet."

"I know," Jasper called back. "You get him?" he asked of the third warlock.

"Just like the other ones," Babe agreed. "Almost felt sorry for the odds, this time."

Jasper nodded, going over to Olivet and pulling the dagger out of the gelding's chest. He put his palm hard to the place where the blade had been, looking up at Olivet while the gelding kept his head up as though he were keeping watch.

Jasper nodded and dropped his hand, and Stasia widened her eyes.

There was no sign that Olivet had ever been injured. She ran around the cart, looking up at Olivet as she got close, but he showed none of his casual signs of playful malice. His nostrils were wide and his ears were forward. She went to touch his chest where the dark fur was damp with blood, but there was no hole, no pour of blood.

"Is that where you learned it?" Babe asked, looking over Stasia's shoulder.

"You two have more in common than you might think," Jasper said, turning his attention to Colin. "Report."

"I'm not left-handed," Colin answered.

"I'm aware," Jasper said. "Report."

Colin nodded.

"Probably off duty an extra two weeks, but in no urgent need of a healer," he said. Jasper turned his face to Stasia.

"Report."

"My arm hurts," she said.

"Broken rib," Babe said. "I recognize that anywhere."

She touched her side, gasping at the discovery of how much pain there was, there.

"Ouch," she breathed, and Jasper nodded.

"Gentle on that until it heals," he said. "Don't want it shifting around."

Stasia worked her jaw, trying to put the pain back wherever it had been before, but it was resistant.

"Pixie'll help," Babe told her gently.

"You two?" Jasper asked.

"Clean," Babe said.

"Perfect," Sterling answered.

Jasper nodded and Olivet threw his head up, removing his reins from Jasper's hand and going over to sniff at the mare.

Stasia looked away.

"Hey," Jasper said. It was directed at Stasia, but she didn't know what he intended to say to her.

Was it terrible that she felt worse about the dead mare than the three humans laying on the ground?

No. She wasn't going to agree that it was.

The mare hadn't done anything to deserve this.

Olivet put his nose down to where the mare's muzzle hung, snorting at her with the universal mistrust of dead things.

But he didn't jerk away.

He snorted at her again, and the mare answered with a deep guttural noise, shifting.

He snorted once more, and the mare shifted, lifting one shoulder to try to get her foot under her.

"Unharness her," Jasper said, and Babe and Sterling moved quickly around Olivet to get the harness traces. They struggled to unbuckle them under her weight, but she found her feet once she was loose, then lifted her head slowly, looking around with the whites of her eyes showing. Olivet stepped across Sterling, putting his neck over the mare's back and snorting again. A moment later, Peter and Gladys came and joined him, forming a thick layer around the mare.

Stasia looked over at Jasper.

"What just happened?" she whispered. He shook his head.

"I told you there was more to him than we knew," he said.

"Was she dead?" Stasia asked. "Or did he just wake her up?"

"If you don't know the answer to it, neither do I," he said. "I'd trust him to let you know when she's ready to go, but, unless you're prepared to just leave the cart here, she's the only one who can pull it out."

Stasia glanced at the body-shaped masses on the ground without actually looking at them.

"It's not done, though, is it?" she asked.

"Our part is," Sterling said.

Colin was leaning against the wall as though he was more injured than he'd let on, but now he stood.

"We're with you," he said. "But this is as far as the King's Guard goes. After this, it's just friends looking out for friends."

Jasper shook his head.

"True for the lot of you," he said. "But not me. You guys keep her safe, go get the rest of the grain unloaded, stand guard, whatever you need to do. Babe, you make sure she gets home safe tonight. If that's at the guard house one more time, so be it."

"You think there are more threats out there?" Babe asked.

"Verida is full of assassins even after the faeries took their pick of them," Jasper answered. "And where there aren't assassins, there are bruisers willing to make problems for coin. Palora is in our hands, but he isn't going to like it. Even if he's likely to lose, he's still dangerous. Go finish the fight, but keep her safe. I'm going to go end the rest of it."

Stasia didn't know what that meant, but Jasper didn't

seem inclined to explain any further. He went to get Olivet, who came along easily now, and Stasia did a not-look at the dead men again.

"What do we do with them?" Stasia asked.

"Inform the police," Jasper said. "Tell them that we killed them in a legal fight, and they'll send the body-men to take care of it. Finwalk will pay for it."

He mounted up as Olivet took off, and Stasia watched after him.

"Anyone else wondering what happened while he was up fighting the stone elves?" she asked, and Sterling laughed.

"Every single day."

She looked at Colin.

"There's a seat up there," she said.

He wrinkled his nose, then nodded.

"I might just take you up on that. You've got a busted rib, though, don't forget."

Until that second, she'd managed to do just that. She grunted, and Babe looked at Sterling.

"Port ought have a pixie healer around here somewhere, don't it?" he asked. Sterling nodded.

"I believe there is one."

Colin gave him an address from memory - that was interesting - then Babe motioned.

"You go get him and meet us at the port. I want to go get the size of this thing."

"It's big," Colin said, and Babe went to hitch the mare again, leaving Gladys and Peter to walk to either side of her.

"Of course it is," Babe muttered. "Anastasia Fielding-Horne is involved."

"So..." Stasia said as they walked. Sterling was

running ahead to fetch the pixie, and Colin was up at the front seat, so Stasia and Babe were on their own with the three horses behind them. Stasia didn't think they were going to fit through the next alley like this, but she would try to talk the hill chargers out of flanking the mare once that actually became a requirement. "You showed up."

"'Course we did," Babe said.

"How?"

"He got your arm, too, didn't he?" Babe asked.

"My dagger," Stasia said, remembering.

He took it out of his belt and offered it to her.

She would have been devastated to lose that one.

It had been a gift from Babe.

She put it away gingerly, the muscles involved in gripping quite tender from the blow to her upper arm. She wouldn't be able to lift anything for a few days, and climb for a few days beyond that. Babe gave her a concerned look.

"The rib is broken. You're right about that. My arm is fine."

"I ain't gonna like the look of it, when I see it, am I?" he asked. She gave him a saucy look.

"Who says you're ever gonna see it?" she asked, and he grinned.

"Unnatural, runnin' around Verida in full sleeves," he said. "Nobody does that."

She looked pointedly at his armor, then turned forward again, trying to plan for the turn off of the alley. It didn't go on forever.

"How?" she asked.

"Jasper did a job of it, playin' at the king foldin' up and givin' in to Palora, tryin' to keep his crown and get Palora to play nice at the same time. By the end, I was convinced we were done for, and Palora was struttin' around like a prize cock. Sold him hard. And then a messenger came in and whispered to him, Sterling caught that it was about wheat at the port, and Palora just went off. The threats that came out of that man's mouth..." He shook his head. "Noblemen think different. All I can say about it. But we got ourselves dismissed and came back to the guard house, Matthias comin' clean that he'd been there to send you to the port for grain. We didn't know how to find you, so we were just takin' the walk down to check in. And then Jasper got the... sign? from the magic that three warlocks had gone in at Palora's, and then left again, and we put it together. Started at the port, gettin' from your pa where you'd gone, then we were just searchin' the route, lookin' for you and got there... when we did."

"They beat you," Stasia said, and he nodded.

"Don't know how," he admitted, "but I ain't surprised, neither. They had knowledge where to look for you, where we had to start at Port Verida. You held your ground, though. Saw it, myself. Held on long enough, and that's always the only job you got, something like this."

It hurt to take a deep breath.

And she was starting to get twinges when she took shallower breaths, too.

"The pirates," she said.

He glanced at her.

"Pirates?" he asked, and she nodded.

"Casset, the one who came last time, he was at the castle to warn Melody that the pirates were bringing three loads of wheat to Verida today, and she told me to come make sure that the grain got unloaded."

He found her hand.

"And you did it," he said.

"I forged a letter from the queen," Stasia said, and he jerked.

"You did what?" he asked, and she nodded.

"Colin saw it," she said.

"How?" Babe asked. "You'd need her seal, for

anyone to believe you."

Stasia took it out of her pocket and showed it to him, then tucked it away again.

He stared for several moments longer.

They got to the corner and Stasia coaxed Gladys out of the way, handing her reins up to Babe and then swinging the cart wide to try to make it around the corner in one go.

It didn't work - the alleys were just too narrow - but Babe went to the back end of the cart and lifted it to shift it sideways a foot and a half to get around the corner of the building, and then again to get it lined up in the next alley, then he came to walk with her again as Gladys took her position once more by the mare.

"You gonna tell me why you have that?" Babe murmured, and Stasia shook her head.

"Nope."

He sighed.

"All right. What happens next, with the port?"

"If I'm fit, I'll take three or four more loads of wheat before dark," she said. "We want to get the ships completely unloaded, if we can. Then we start looking for how do we sell it again."

"You bought it?" he asked.

"Nope," she said. "My father bought half, and four of his associates split out the rest. The warlocks... they aren't the end of it."

"Then why are you the one lookin' to sell?" Babe asked.

"Because it's in the queen's interest," Stasia said. He grunted, then nodded.

"I can see my way to the end of that."

They made it back out to the main road, passing carts of grain with boys running alongside and people talking and laughing, and Stasia smiled at Babe.

"It's going to change things," she said. "Not all at

once, and not all of them by itself, but it's going to change things."

He nodded.

"I can feel it, too," he said. "Just gotta get to the other end with all our people alive."

Jasper stood with his chin up, waiting for Finwalk to arrive.

Ben was sitting on one of the couches in Finwalk's shared sitting room, the same one that they had come to after Melody had been injured by the warlocks. Petrault was here, too, arms crossed and prepared to argue, even though he had little to no idea what was going on.

Ben didn't know about the warlocks, and Petrault had little idea beyond that there was a known and passionate group of very capable men looking at the possibility of assassinating the queen, and that he needed to be ready.

Jasper had arguments with how the palace guards did their jobs. He always would. But he had to give it to Petrault that he and his men had stepped up. If the warlocks had ended up here, Petrault's men were going to give them a fair shot at resistance, until Jasper's squad turned up.

Jasper waited.

Somewhere out back in the gardens, Olivet was running loose, a nod to his contributions to taking out the warlocks quickly, with two young stable boys tasked with keeping him out of the flowerbeds and away from the orchards. There wouldn't be much on the trees, this season, and the grounds crew kept the fallen fruit picked up to maintain spotless grounds, but Jasper still didn't want to risk a colicky horse after everything else today.

Finally, the door behind him opened and he heard Matthias' footsteps coming into the room, with Melody behind him.

Jasper had heard a rumor that Melody opened her own doors, now, but he also knew that that was going to be a challenge that Matthias would take personally.

Melody went to sit down at the gilded table, finding a glass of honeyed wine there waiting for her.

"Is Finwalk in conference?" she asked.

"Just finishing up, mum," Ben said.

Melody looked at Jasper.

"Have you spoken to Miss Fielding today?" she asked.

He nodded.

"Yes, mum. I just left her. She had a few upsets this morning, but she is in good hands, now, and appears to be twice as determined as she was before."

Ben looked over at him, seeming a bit tired.

"You're speaking in code," he said. "At some point, I am going to pull rank on you, Jasper, and force you to tell me what's been going on at my guard house."

"I'm afraid you don't have rank to pull, Ben," Finwalk said, coming in. "I'm finally up to date, myself, save a few secrets that came from before my tenure on the throne, and I'm prepared to discuss what happens next. Jasper will keep his tongue and not spill crown secrets, because that is what he is so excellent at doing, and if you need information, Ben and Petrault, both of you, you will get it from me."

He sat down at the table and smelled the second glass of wine.

"Mmm, honey," he said, smiling, then looked over at Jasper again. "Tell me how this morning went, first. Groveling?"

"Groveling?" Ben asked, and both he and Petrault looked pointedly back at Jasper.

"On the King's behalf, of course," Jasper said. "Palora was very convinced, I believe, by my diplomatic attempt to negotiate additional power for Lord Palora in exchange for not going directly against King Finwalk in open court. He gave me a list of demands, which you will forgive me for having forgotten at this moment. The display was... repulsive, and repeating it here would be inappropriate."

"I expect you to remember those demands, later," Finwalk said, and Jasper gave him a little bow.

"Of course, your highness."

Finwalk nodded.

"Go on."

"I marked the doors with magic from Meggin, the pixie healer, to track when and if foreign magic came through, but while we were there, someone interrupted our meeting to inform Lord Palora of something quite important happening pertaining to wheat at the port. Matthias signaled to me that it was something of interest to us, so I allowed him to show us out at that time, and we rode back to the guard house, where Matthias informed me that Miss Fielding-Horne met with the queen and an unknown man and woman early this morning, and that Miss Fielding-Horne had left with the intention of going to the port. Knowing Miss Fielding-Horne as we do, we assumed that Lord Palora and she were at cross purposes again, and we set off to the port to support her as we could, leaving Matthias at the castle to resume his guard of the queen."

"Does the young woman often required your assistance with her personal affairs?" Petrault asked.

"I want to know the answer to that, too," Ben said.

"She went on my behalf," Melody said evenly. "At my direct request, in point of fact. Do not underestimate the significance of that."

"Yes, mum," Ben said.

"Yes, mum," Petrault echoed.

"Miss Fielding has personal relationships with those within my squad," Jasper said. "And no one has or will ask an accounting of what those entail. In this instance, though, we know that Lord Palora is plotting against the crown, and also that whatever she was involved with was likely working against Palora's interests. I used my professional judgment to deduce that it was likely that supporting her in her efforts would be working in the interests of the crown, and the rest of the afternoon's events supported that inference."

"Go on," Melody said.

"As we were on our way to the port, the magic that we got from Meggin indicated to me that three individuals had gone into the Palora estate who were possessed of an unidentified magic, and that they shortly thereafter left again. At this time, I became concerned for Miss Fielding-Horne's safety, and we went to the port as quickly as possible, where we found three ships unloading carts of grain, Botonese wheat, in a scene of chaos that would have been familiar, last year, but that this year has been completely absent from Port Verida. I located Minstrel Fielding and spoke with him, hoping and finding that he did know where his daughter had gone, and we traced her steps to the warehouse where she and Colin, from my squad, had delivered a cartload of wheat, but no one had any knowledge of where she had ended up, after that.

"We did a search, looking for where Colin might have gone to have a fight with the men that Lord Palora sent out, and eventually stumbled on to the location that Colin had chosen for his stand. Both Colin and Miss Fielding-Horne were on the losing ends of their fights, but holding their ground with distinction and courage, and we were able to step in and turn the tide of the fight against the men, killing all three of them."

"Are you sure they're dead?" Melody asked.

"After last time, we are being very careful to be certain," Jasper said. "There is not a one of them that I am at all concerned that they will rise again, mum."

She nodded.

"So Lord Palora lost his scary men today," Finwalk said. "Because Melody and Miss Fielding did something unexpected and forced his hand."

"That is my read of the situation as well, sir," Jasper said. Finwalk nodded.

"Good. Go on."

"I left my men with Miss Fielding-Horne to go continue doing what it is she is interested in doing, whether that be getting to safety or continuing to assist in the transit of wheat, because I trust her judgment and because I believe that her person continues to be critical to the conflict with Palora."

"I agree," Melody said.

"Begging your pardon, mum, but you would," Petrault said.

Ben shook his head.

"And what of Palora, now?" Finwalk asked.

"If our read of the situation is correct, sir, he continues to sit at the head of at least one and likely two cartels of traders, attempting to push the Veridan economy into enough pain and crisis that it will force Melody to name a new king. The strategy from Melody and Miss Fielding-Horne has been and continues to be one of economic counter-measure, wherein Miss Fielding-Horne turns back the economic pressure on the members of the cartel, selling goods at inflated prices, but preventing the crisis that would precipitate political action and meanwhile exposing the participating traders to great losses. It is her opinion, I believe, and it is mine as well that the Botonese wheat could very well be the tipping point necessary to crack the will of the merchant cartel and force them into the markets to control their losses. It is also my expectation that, if it were to become known that Lord Palora's attack dogs have been subdued by the crown, at least some traders would enter the market freely, as they have been held from trading by threats against themselves and those around them."

"And what of Palora himself?" Finwalk asked. "I can't exactly ignore that all of this has happened. He remains a threat to myself and the interests of the crown."

"I'm afraid that that is well above my political involvement," Jasper said. "The noble class considers themselves to be indispensable for reasons a man like myself cannot quite fathom."

Finwalk nodded, the corner of his mouth coming up.

"Well said," he said. "I cannot remove him from power, because he is too important at court. The war would go against us dramatically, if he were not there to ensure the correct dispensation of supplies."

"Are you certain that's true, sir?" Jasper asked.

Finwalk frowned.

"Who would you recommend to replace him?" the king asked.

"If I may speak freely," Jasper said. "I've never understood why supplying the resources to the military and actually routing those resources up to the mountains are under the same command. Certainly General Red would be able to, himself or through delegation, handle the oversight of necessary resources up to the conflict zones. He ought to also be able to identify what supplies he needs, in order of priority. As far as procuring those supplies goes, that is a trivial endeavor that could be assigned to someone no more elevated than the head of the kitchen staff here at the castle."

"But General Red is not a noble," Finwalk said, not arguing with him.

"No, sir, he isn't," Jasper said.

Finwalk looked at Melody.

"Is there any reason I couldn't have a commoner on my councils, where the man is truly the expert in a domain?" he asked.

"Nothing in the law, your highness," Melody answered lightly.

Finwalk nodded thoughtfully.

"Palora will be stripped of his power," he said. "But not of his title nor his land. It is unlikely that this story will be commonly accepted nor passed around the nobles, and if I take his land, they will feel as though I am threatening all of them. It will destabilize the court. But everyone knows that he is angling for more power, and it is entirely within my rights to stop him, for whatever reason I find appropriate. I will give thought to the idea of bringing in General Red to council, and assigning him to oversee supplies, as you say. We cannot afford another onslaught at the edge of the city as we have just survived, so we must do this delicately, but I will not have a man who is so willing to bring Verida to the edge of destruction in the name of his own power running around and continuing to make problems into the future. I will accept the costs, but we must attempt to minimize them."

He looked from Ben to Petrault.

"Are there any further questions from the two of you?" he asked.

"I want to know why the queen has a young woman running around the castle unescorted and without any proper standing to be here," Petrault said.

"She is the head of my guard," Melody answered simply. "And you will respect her as peer, within the castle walls."

There was a very, very long silence. Jasper knew better than to break it, though he didn't know who else would, either. It was a massive reorganization of power, within the castle, and Stasia would never understand exactly how profound that was, nor how to cope with it. She just didn't have the acculturation to grasp it. Though Jasper could see how that would be the point.

Finally, Finwalk spoke again.

"Very good," he said. "We have a plan, and it appears that the original plan, the one from Miss Fielding, is working quite well. Are we sure that there are no more of these magic creatures running around our city?"

"I cannot prove it," Jasper said. "But now I can tell you if they are coming and going from the Palora estate."

"Good," Finwalk said. "In the meantime, we will put out rumors that the enforcers are dead or deserted, and we will continue to support the efforts to break the embargo at Port Verida. I think that your young friend is right, for what it's worth. I wonder if we aren't just days away from the first defectors pouring into market and triggering the rest of them to rush in after."

Jasper nodded.

"I trust her judgment, sir," he said.

"Good," Finwalk said. "You are dismissed to go do whatever it is you would be doing instead of talking to me. Thank you, gentlemen."

He finished his wine and stood, leaving through one of the back doors. Ben and Petrault waited a moment longer, then also left. Jasper looked at Melody.

"I'm curious," he said. "The warlocks attacked Miss Fielding-Horne, it appears. Killed the horse that was drawing her cart at the time, but the attack had no impact on Miss Fielding-Horne at all. Would you know anything about that?"

Melody shifted to look at Matthias, then smiled and sighed.

"I don't have any idea what he manages to glean," she said. "At this point, I assume it's most everything. I've been taking tea with her almost once a week for months. It's amazing what you can manage, when you have that much time to work with, compared to, say, a few hours up in the mountains?"

Jasper nodded.

He'd thought it would be something like that.

"I'm grateful," he said.

"I didn't do it for you," Melody answered warmly, and he nodded. Jasper turned to make eye contact with Matthias.

"Are we going to win?" Jasper asked, and Matthias nodded.

"It's a matter of days, not weeks."

Jasper smiled.

Matthias was getting very good at this.

Stasia met Babe for the Water Lily Festival.

The school session was over at the University, and Stasia had handed out her bounties on the key markets. The results that Ella and Queen Melody had gotten out of the class were quite remarkable, from a trade and economics perspective, though Stasia knew that Queen Melody was actually just very happy to have been able to hand-select a number of women to come and see her at the castle, act as low-level members of the court, and go involve themselves with situations inside and outside of the castle.

Ella was thrilled with the community of traders that had sprung up in the weekly sessions at Felligan's, with promises that they were going to continue to meet into the future. Of the top ten percent of the class, fully half of them had dropped out of the university to become merchants.

The market was wild, dangerous even, but Stasia had six big warehouses around the city, including the one at the Black Docks, stocking up goods where prices dropped unreasonably low, and she would resell everything as the market got back to normal.

She spotted Ella in the crowd and waved, grabbing

Babe's hand and working her way over to where Lord and Lady Westhauser were standing.

Skite looked over at her appraisingly.

"You haven't been around as much, the last three weeks," he said.

"Did you need help selling your grain?" Stasia answered, and his face changed into a slight smile.

"I assure you, I did not, but you would have been the first person I consulted with."

Stasia dug into her bag - she was actually carrying one, today - and took out the purple-bound book that he had gifted her out of his library.

"I wanted to show you this," Stasia said.

He opened it, frowning and taking a step to get better light on the pages from the street lamp overhead, then turned page after page after page.

"You need another one," he said, and she nodded.

"This one will always be the most important one," she said, as he looked at the last page of figures more carefully.

"All of this in the last few months," he remarked.

"Half of it is filled up with transactions that my father would have lost to rounding error," Stasia said. "Once I really got going... Well, I'm looking forward to reducing complexity a lot, as things get back to normal. I just kept finding stuff that I could make a profit at, and for a while, if I could make a profit, I went for it, every time."

He closed the book and handed it back to her.

"It is a masterpiece," he said, and she smiled.

"Thank you."

"What you did," he said quietly, watching as the queen came into view up on at the railing above the river, "it was nothing short of heroic. People are going to talk about your father and his friends, bringing in grain to the city, and they're not going to know. The city isn't going to know that it was you who made all of it happen. And even then, they aren't going to see the plan that broke the freeze in the markets, and they aren't going to see the mind that saw the cause of that freeze. You will never be appreciated for what you've done, outside of some very small circles."

Stasia smiled.

"Good thing that those are the only circles whose opinions of myself I care about," she answered.

Ella turned, grinning over her bag of fried dough balls, then turned to look up at the queen again.

"I don't care that I sit with her for tea twice a week," Ella said. "It's still the most magical thing I know."

Stasia lifted her eyes as the queen turned to take an armload of water lilies out of a basket behind her. Melody turned to face to the river and tossed the lilies out onto the water.

"The river flower blooms again," Skite murmured, stepping forward to stand next to Ella and put his arm around her.

Babe stepped over next to Stasia and she looked over at him happily.

"To another year of possibility," he said, and she nodded.

The queen stepped back out of sight and Stasia looked at Babe.

"Do you want to get something to drink?" Skite asked.

"Can we meet you?" Stasia asked. "I've got a stop to make."

"Felligan's," Ella said. "We'll get a table. It's going to be packed."

Stasia glanced over and nodded.

"We'll be there."

Skite and Ella started to shift their way through the crowd and Stasia took Babe's hand and set off the other direction.

"What's goin' on?" Babe asked as the crowd finally began to thin out enough for them to talk.

"I want to show you something," Stasia said.

He frowned, but put his arm around her waist and went along without further question.

They went past the castle market going along the main Wolfram, then turned at the first branch and went to cross on the bridge into the next section of Verida. Stasia turned out along the river branch. This was the branch north of the Sapphire, and she knew very little about it, but the street lamps were close enough that everything was going to be well-lit, even after the sun finished setting, and the cobbles were clear of debris in a way that you only got in the nicer sections of town where the traffic wasn't so bad.

This was the route that the meat markets would take to get to the rest of the city, and the rest of Fisharbor emptied this way, as well, but they were far enough off that the scent didn't make it here, and the traffic was pretty devoted to those specific industries, which meant that it was a bit thinner than many of the other trade corridors within the city.

Stasia turned off of the river a little way along, the cool air heavy with humidity that would layer everything thick with dew by morning, just the way things worked this time of year. Stasia was getting the hang of how it worked, and she could appreciate this season for the potential it had.

"Where are we goin', again?" Babe asked.

"It's just a little further," Stasia answered.

Through most of the city, the roads ran in long, curving lines where buildings pressed up against them in uninterrupted rows. Even in the wealthier neighborhoods, the homes faced cobbled streets in long rows with infrequent cross streets.

Here, though, the roads felt more like branching

streams, hitting fork after fork as they trended generally uphill, everything feeding down toward the river.

Stasia liked it.

She liked it a lot.

Three forks up, left, left, right, she turned to go through a pair of stonework pillars with open wrought-iron gates between them.

"Stasia," Babe said. "What is this?"

"It's mine," Stasia said quietly.

She looked over at him as he stopped dead.

"What?" he asked, and she nodded.

"I'm going to be scaling back everything that I'm doing as quickly as I can," Stasia said. "I had a bunch of cash that I don't really want to reinvest, because... it's just too much, and because as the markets get back to running normally..." She shook her head, looking at the house again. "Everything just happened so fast," she said. "I heard that one of the port merchants was selling his house. I think that he'd gotten himself underwater, leveraging purchases to keep them out of the market, but... anyway..."

"This is yours?" Babe asked. She nodded.

"It is," she said quietly. "Do you want to... come see, inside?"

He nodded, looking dumbstruck.

"Okay."

She turned motioning to the gates.

"I know that you'll want to talk about having guards, so when I saw the guard house, there..."

She was... It was overwhelming. Babe wasn't the only one who couldn't believe this was happening.

"I saw it," Babe said, reaching over to take her hand.

She got to the front door of the great stone-and-brick house and pulled the bell chain, taking a step back.

"You gotta ring at your own house?" he asked.

"I don't plan on carrying a key," she admitted. "I do

too much silly stuff to risk losing it."

The door opened and Tesh smiled.

"I wasn't sure if you'd make it after the festival," she said, turning her attention to Babe. "Good evening."

"What?" Babe asked.

"I spoke to my father, and he agreed it was time to bring the Boton staff down to the house on the Sapphire," Stasia said. "It's an easy enough house to keep, and I was... in need of a head of household and staff, so..."

Alice put her head through a doorway off of the entrance.

"You're here," she called cheerfully. "Yasmine says the kitchen is much better than the house on the Sapphire. She's ordering in all of the equipment she's going to need and filling the pantry."

Stasia smiled.

"We'll have a housewarming party as soon as she says she's ready," Stasia told her, and Alice beamed, then disappeared.

"You'll have to bring in a lot of extra staff for a party," Tesh warned, and Stasia nodded.

"I won't do it often, so don't get used to it," she told her new head of household. "But I trust your judgment, getting through it the once."

Tesh gave her a little nod and Stasia drew a breath, looking around.

The inside of the house was lovely. Most of the furniture had been included in the contract, including the wall decor, so she had to do very little of that type of thing.

"You really made this much money, just... doin' what you did?" Babe asked.

"I went all in when the markets were irrational and I won," Stasia said helplessly. "I'm as surprised as you are."

Tesh snorted.

"Your father isn't," she said. "If you'll excuse me, the

work of opening a house back up is immense. I would like your permission to hire laborers to get it moving to something resembling a schedule."

"You ought have a man here you trust, watchin' over outside workers," Babe said.

Stasia nodded.

"I'm in the market for a butler. My sister says she has a younger man up at the Gormand estate who might be ready to step up into managing a simple household, like that. I'm going to be speaking to him tomorrow at lunch." She paused. "I would be... grateful, if you would come with me, actually."

He frowned, but nodded.

"If you like."

"Once he's here, you may hire as many men as you and he agree to, for the work," Stasia said. "I anticipate a gardener, as well as a stable man."

"You ought to get a carriage," Tesh said gently.

"I'll hire one," Stasia said. "If I need one. I don't anticipate using one often enough to keep a carriage man employed."

Tesh lifted her chin, but when they'd talked about her trading out with the Botonese staff in order to come here, they had agreed that Stasia would expect a less formal existence than her father, and Tesh needed to be prepared to adapt to that.

"All right," Tesh said finally. "I'm going back to work, and then we'll be retiring. If you go out again, I would appreciate you taking your key."

"Of course," Stasia said. "Of course."

Tesh gave her a little nod, then turned and left.

Stasia hauled a nervous breath and looked at Babe once more.

"What do you think?" she asked.

"I don't know what to say," he said.

The ideas were all there, but she still couldn't put

words to them, and when they came out, it was going to be in an uncontrolled rush. She could feel it, and she knew she was going to embarrass herself, so she held them back once more.

"Let me show you around," she said.

They walked through the sitting room and the dining room. Stasia took him into the kitchen, where Yasmine was singing to herself as she worked, and then back through into the study and the library.

As they started for the stairs to go up, they heard a clacking noise and Babe stopped, watching with his mouth open.

"What in the queen's name...?" he said.

"That's Marvin," Stasia said, kneeling to greet the tiny donkey as he rubbed on her face. "He lives here, now, and I need you to be okay with that."

"That woman agreed to... that?" he asked, and Stasia nodded.

"I'm going to get a boy to tend him and clean up after him," Stasia said. "And he has a room at the back of the house that opens up to a paddock, so I expect he'll be outside more than he's in, but..." She put her forehead against his, then stood. "He means a lot to me."

"Schotzli live here, too?" Babe asked. Stasia grinned.

"She's out back at the barn. Has a whole paddock to herself, for now, though I'm going to bring in some of the working animals I've been keeping at livery and keep them here, instead."

Babe shook his head, and she took his hand, going upstairs as Marvin trotted off on his own adventure.

There was a large sitting room upstairs and rooms for guests that she walked him through, though the failing light didn't do them justice.

Finally she got to the main suite, the double doors facing a formal, wooden hallway with chairs and a clock. She paused here, wanting him to understand before she opened the door.

He waited, and she turned, leaning her waist against the doorknobs.

"I told you... I don't even remember what I said," she said. "But what I meant was that... I didn't want to talk about marriage until I figured out who I was on my own. And... I think I've done that? But I didn't figure out anything I didn't already know."

She looked around and he took just a fraction of a step back, giving her time to sort through it, even as she couldn't look him in the face. She had no idea how deep the flush was on her cheeks, but she knew it had to be there.

"And I wasn't intending to end up in a place like this. I mean, it's silly, right? I've spent my entire life doing all this stuff that was... let's be honest and call it what it was. I was trying to prove to everyone that the nobility and the money didn't own me. I was my own person and I wasn't what I was supposed to be, just because... because my father had money and everyone expected me to act a certain way. So I kind of did the opposite every time I got a chance, and then for me to end up here... No one is going to understand why this is okay, when everything else made me so angry all the time..."

"It's a nice house, Stasia," Babe said.

She looked up at him, then nodded and looked at the floor again.

"I was supposed to go through this journey and try a bunch of stuff and grow through all of it and then end up here, because I went through everything else, the way my father did, but then... houses like this aren't for sale very often, and it's beautiful and I can keep Schotzli and Marvin and... there are trees. There are actual trees on the property, and it's shady during the day and there's a little pond, back at the corner, and... it's got fish in it and frogs, you can hear the frogs at night, and..."

"It's a nice house, Stasia," Babe said. "Ain't gotta apologize to me for none of it."

She swallowed.

"I'm trying to explain," she said.

"Are you tryin' to tell me that you were plannin' on this bein' the house where we live together?" he asked.

He said it so easily.

"I needed to do it on my own," she said quietly. "That it was mine... before... that I did it on my own..."

She'd angsted over this the entire time, but she'd also known that this was the only way she was going to do it. She just hoped that Babe would understand.

He took another half-step back, looking up and down the hallway, then craning his neck at more the idea of seeing the rest of the house from here.

"What you're tellin' me is that I am now seein' one of the wealthier ladies in Verida, lowly soldier that I am, and she has taken on a new property that I am one of the first she chose to show it to, because my opinion and my reaction matters quite a lot to her." He paused. "And that she's hopin' I'm gonna take to it, because she'd like me to share the place with her, maybe, someday."

She nodded, just a tiny tick up and down with her nose.

"Yeah."

He held her eye, not giving anything away.

"Well, then, I'd best see the rest of it, oughtn't I?"

She smiled, still nervous, and pressed the door handles to open the two doors behind her. She pushed them aside and turned, revealing the main suite.

He walked through the sitting room and past the doors to the washroom and the closets, the small study and the open-air patio, going to stand at a window that faced the front of the property.

Stasia followed him quietly, stopping a few strides

behind him to wait.

"It suits you," he said. "Tells me that you ain't givin' up the game, buyin' and sellin', but there ain't nothin' wrong with that, neither. Close enough to the guard house and the castle for walkin' at night and in the mornin'. I can see why you thought that this was an opportunity you needed to jump at. Families in this part of town, a lot of 'em have lived here for generations, you know?"

"I do know," Stasia said.

He turned to look at her, leaning against the sill.

She hadn't asked him.

She hadn't told him until it was done.

He smiled.

"Still the most beautiful woman I think I ever laid eyes on," he said, then he laughed. "You do go big, though, don't you?"

"What do you mean?" Stasia asked, and he laughed again, looking around the room and taking it in for the first time.

"You gotta prove to yourself you've got an idea how independent you are, you do it all at once in one great wallop, goin' from a one-room apartment to one of the priciest neighborhoods in the city in the space of half a year. I gotta say, I'm grateful."

"Grateful?" Stasia asked, and he grinned wider, pushing himself off the window sill to come stand in front of her, looking down at her from an indecent distance. Stasia looked him in the face, finding his cheer contagious. She wasn't nervous anymore.

"Most folk, it would have taken 'em a good five or ten years to get here," he said. "With a lot of luck and determination and focus. And even then..." He shrugged, shaking his head. "Wouldn't have made it here. You just get it all out of the way. Point made. And then you bring me in here like you're afraid I won't like it, means you've got a mind that I'm gonna live here with you, and maybe that idea ain't so far off, for you, either."

"Is it, for you?" she asked, and he grinned again.

"Gotta be honest, I'd never considered living here with you until just tonight, but I'm sort of likin' the idea."

She sighed, all of the tension just gone.

He kissed her forehead.

"Happy Water Lily Festival," he said quietly into her hair. "The river flower blooms again."

"Happy Water Lily Festival," Stasia answered, closing her eyes. "Welcome home."

What Skite, one-time assassin and current King of the Rats, needs least in his life is more to do. Newly wed and trying to negotiate the sticky, political waters of the Black Docks - Rat territory - and their relationships throughout the rest of the city of Verida, he's still unable to resist addressing insult to Black Docks commerce when a nobleman refuses to pay for goods ordered and threatens to drive the flourishing local smithing industry out of business.

And so the heist is on.

He's assembling a crew that isn't much pleased with his decisions, the last year or so, and his new wife isn't about to be left out of the action as Skite flexes his conspiratorial muscles to go after one of the most powerful men in Verida. But Verida isn't a simple place to do business in the best of times, and Skite knows better than anyone that a plan is like as not to blow up somewhere around halfway through and leave everyone scrambling.

Verida is a land of elves and pixies and magic, but every Rat knows that that doesn't make it pretty. It's a good thing that Skite's good at winning ugly, because that's where this one is going.

MORE VERIDAN TALES

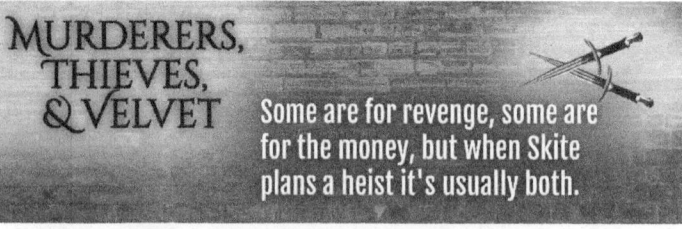

VERIDA
A City of Magic

A Four Book Series

A Four Book Series

2023

MURDERERS, THIEVES, & VELVET

Some are for revenge, some are for the money, but when Skite plans a heist it's usually both.

Nobody likes a pirate... unless they can make money off him.

EVER IN A PIRATE'S EYE

URBAN FANTASY BY CHLOE

School of Magic Survival

Sam and Sam

A twelve book series of angels and demons, magic and swords. Some of Chloe's first work, it's early, unpolished, and a favorite of her biggest fans.

Tell, the Detective

SCIENCE FICTION

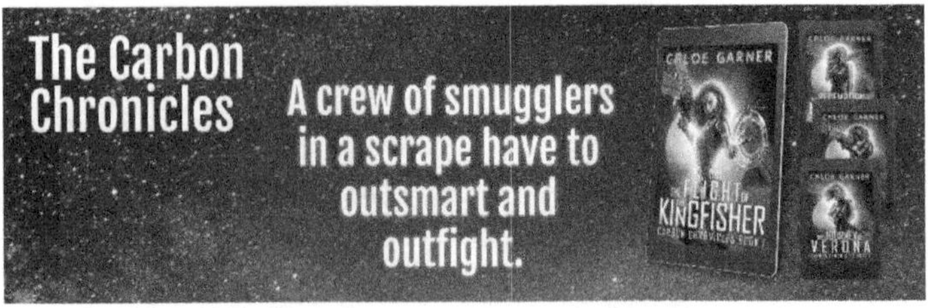

The Carbon Chronicles

A crew of smugglers in a scrape have to outsmart and outfight.

Portal Jumpers

What if our military had a portal between worlds?

Sarah Todd

A three book western series, but on a colonized planet. Why not?

ABOUT THE AUTHOR

Chloe Garner is a wanderer with a host of identities in her head fighting each other to get out. Chloe writes about the things that go bump in the night, the future, and all things fantastical. Find her on Twitter as BlenderFiction, on Goodreads and Facebook as Chloe Garner.

Check out her website, chloegarner.com, to see what she says about her books, a few freebies, and occasional thoughts. While there you can subscribe to her mailing list for release notices and all the latest news.

Made in the USA
Las Vegas, NV
04 February 2025